OUTPOST

ANN AGUIRRE

FEIWEL AND FRIENDS
NEW YORK

A Feiwel and Friends Book
An Imprint of Macmillan

Library of Congress Cataloging-in-Publication Data Available

ISBN: 978-0-312-65009-4

Book design by Susan Walsh

Feiwel and Friends logo designed by Filomena Tuosto

First Edition: 2012

10 9 8 7 6 5 4 3 2 1

macteenbooks.com

For Jenn of the eerily similar brain,
and Karen of the Twitter taunting

Nightjar

I woke to the cold kiss of steel on my throat.

Though I'd grown accustomed to sleeping safely since our arrival in Salvation two months ago, I'd lost none of my edge. Before my attacker realized I was awake, I knocked the knife away and tumbled him over my head. While Stalker recovered, I rolled to my feet and scowled. Momma Oaks would skin us both if she caught him in my room. People took reputations seriously, and mine was already bruised, due to my insistence on being myself.

"Good work, dove." Stalker's grin flashed in the moonlight.

"What are you doing here?" It was the middle of the night, but he loved his little tests.

"We've got incoming. I heard the second bell."

My ire cooled. He wasn't just checking my reflexes in spite of our precarious situation. Belonging to no one, we had to make sure we didn't wear out our welcome or anger the townsfolk by flouting their rules. Most seemed designed to discourage unauthorized breeding, and they didn't like it when I went off to spar with Stalker. It hadn't taken me long to figure that I wasn't a normal girl—at least by Salvation standards. So we trained in secret these days, no daylight matches.

"Let's have a look. Turn around."

With minimal fuss, I dressed in Huntress attire and strapped on my weapons, which I hadn't permitted anyone to take, despite complaints of how "inappropriate" it was for me to carry them. Most of those came from women who dropped by the Oakses' house to whisper their disapproval of my heathen ways. Savages raised me in a cave, to hear them tell it, but as I'd informed Momma Oaks, I earned my scars and blades. They could pry the latter from my cold, dead hands. Respecting the teacher's sensibilities, I did wear long-sleeve blouses to school to hide my Huntress status.

Stalker slid out the open window, the same one he'd climbed in a few moments before. If I didn't look forward to our nighttime matches so much, I'd latch it, but only those fights made me feel like a Huntress these days. Following him, I leapt to the branch of the tree and then swung down into the quiet yard.

It was a warm night, bright moon patterning the ground with silver. Each blade of grass felt heavenly beneath my feet. Once, I'd walked on broken stones and hard cement, deep in the belly of the earth. It had been a noisy place, full of echoes, soft moans, and whimpers in the night. But that world was gone.

Now I lived in Salvation, where the buildings were sound, white-washed, and clean, where men had their work and women did different tasks. I struggled with that reality. Down below, my sex hadn't mattered much. Most of our titles there were neutral with the exception of Huntress, and we retained that one because in the early days—before we realized females could fight as fiercely—only male Hunters protected the enclave. When the first Huntress changed everything, she wanted an acknowledgment of her achievement . . . and so the distinction remained, unlike the Builders and Breeders who had always been both genders.

They treated their young differently in Salvation as well. Regardless of the threat, brats weren't allowed to fight . . . but I'd spent too long defending the enclave to feel comfortable about lying abed while others battled on my behalf. They had built the town like a wooden fortress with strong fortifications and a sturdy gate; a protective wall with walkway and sentry towers kept the Freaks out, safeguarding the populace, but I wasn't sure it would hold forever. Both Stalker and I had asked to assess the numbers Salvation faced, and how well the guards drove them off. It seemed like a reasonable request, but the folks in charge— elders who were actually *old*—preferred that young people spent their time puzzling how to read and cipher numbers. There were also history lessons and endless tests on information that nobody in his right mind would ever be required to know.

I found it insulting. If someone already knew how to weave cloth, why would anyone waste time making him learn how to bake bread? It was a waste of effort, but they had rules for everything in Salvation. Breaking them had consequences, which was why I had to be careful.

Along with Stalker, I stole through the darkened town, avoiding dogs that would set up a racket. I found it curious that people kept animals for companionship and not food. When I'd asked Momma Oaks when she planned to cook the fat creature that slept in a basket in the kitchen, her eyes almost popped out of her head. Since then, she'd kept her pet away from me, like she suspected I meant to turn it into stew. Clearly, I had a lot to learn.

"I smell them," Stalker whispered then.

Lifting my head, I sniffed the night wind and nodded. Anyone who had encountered Freaks—or Muties as they called them Topside—wouldn't forget the stench: rotting meat and oozing sores. Once, a long time ago, they had human ancestors . . . or so the stories said. But something bad happened, and people got sick. A lot of them died . . . and some of them changed. The dead ones were lucky, Edmund claimed, but Momma Oaks always shushed her husband when he talked like that. She had some idea that we needed to be sheltered. Her protective instincts made me laugh, considering I'd fought more than most town guards. I paused, listening.

Weapons weren't quiet in Salvation, so if the fight had started, I'd hear the boom of their guns. That gave me time to scramble up to the southernmost sentry tower, where Longshot stood watch. He wouldn't run me off with angry words about how I ought to be in bed. Over the past weeks, he'd showed great patience with my questions. Other men said it was none of my business and reported me for unfeminine, improper behavior; more than once I'd found myself in trouble with Momma Oaks over my nocturnal jaunts.

As usual, Longshot didn't protest when we slid up the ladder and joined him. From this vantage I saw by flickering lamplight the land unfolding before me. If I pushed past, I could gain access to the walls, but then his fellow guards would yell at me for getting in the way. I didn't have a gun, so I couldn't shoot Freaks anyway. Plus, Momma Oaks would hear about my misdeeds again, which led to extra chores and a lecture about how I wasn't trying to fit in.

"You never miss a fight," Longshot said, cocking Old Girl.

"Not if we can help it," Stalker answered.

"It doesn't feel right . . . I'm used to helping. How many are there tonight?"

"I counted ten, but they're hanging back, just out of range."

That information sent a cold chill through me. "Trying to draw you out?"

"It won't work," he assured me. "They can prowl outside all they want, but if they get hungry enough, they'll charge, and we'll put 'em down."

I wished I shared his confidence in the power of walls for keeping bad things out. Down below, we had barricades, of course, but we hadn't relied on them exclusively. Patrols went out to keep our territory clear, and it made me uneasy to think of Freaks gathering. Who knew how many were out there? I remembered Nassau's fate; that was the closest settlement to where I'd lived down below. When Silk—the commander of the Hunters—sent Fade and me to investigate, the reality was worse than anything I'd imagined, Freaks feasting on the dead after they annihilated the living. It scared me to imagine such a fate here, where citizens weren't as tough. They had more guards, of course, and not all of them hunted, as we did down below. More citizens lived in Salvation, so they could spread the work out.

From the other side of the wall came the distant bark of someone's gun, and then the bell rang. Just once, which meant a kill. Two bells indicated incoming. I'd never heard more than two bells, so I didn't know if there were other warnings.

"How many signals are there?" I asked Longshot.

"Twelve or so," he answered, raising his weapon. "It's based on some kind of old military language, dots and dashes."

That didn't clarify anything, but before I could ask, movement in the perimeter caught my eye. As two Freaks ran toward the wall, Longshot sighted with Old Girl and dropped the first. It didn't seem sporting when the creatures had no ranged weapons, but most of the citizens here weren't trained to fight, either. A breach in security would be disastrous.

As I watched, the surviving Freak knelt beside its fallen friend and then shrieked as if we were the monsters. The sound echoed in the trees, full of grief and loathing. I glanced at Longshot, who was holding fire. The thing didn't run, although it could have. Its eyes glittered in the lamplight, showing madness and hunger, certainly, but tonight I saw something more. Or thought I did.

It's a shadow, playing tricks.

"Sometimes they sound like they have minds in their rotten heads," he said, as if to himself.

Then he took the second shot, so the other died beside the first. Afterward, Longshot rang the bell once, paused, and then once again, reporting his kills. The townsfolk had learned to sleep through the racket. This information was for the guards, so they could track how many bodies surrounded the town. In the morning, they would send an armed crew to drag away the corpses, far enough that if they attracted other Freaks, they could feed without the good folks of Salvation having to watch. I approved of the practice; fortunately, the people here didn't have to be lectured on the importance of proper hygiene.

That was the only thing Salvation had in common with College, the enclave where I had been raised. Up here on the safety of the wall, my knives couldn't do any damage, and I hated being useless. Stalker took no better to being cut out of the action. He had a valid point when he'd said, months ago:

You, you're like me.

I'd replied, *You mean a Hunter?*

Yes. You're strong.

It was true . . . but here, physical strength didn't matter. Neither did training. They wanted us to learn new roles and forget that we'd once led different lives. I found it tough, as I'd loved being a Huntress. Yet Salvation offered no similar role for girls; I couldn't even wear my own clothes.

For some time, we listened to the gunfire, until the bell stopped tolling death. Gradually the night noises resumed—and that was another way you could tell Freaks had retreated. When all the animals went still and silent, an attack had to be imminent. Now the hush filled with the peculiar churring of a bird whose name I didn't know.

"What is that?" I asked Longshot.

He always had the utmost patience for my questions, and this was no different. "Nightjar. They come for the summer before heading south again."

Not for the first time, I envied the birds' freedom. "Thanks. We'll get out of your way before someone catches us here."

"Appreciate it." Longshot kept his eyes fixed on the trees.

Stalker glided down the ladder with the grace that made him such a phenomenal fighter at close range. We took every opportunity to keep our skills sharp because, deep down, I couldn't believe the guns would last forever. Life down below had taught me to believe in nothing as much as my own abilities; Stalker's upbringing in the Topside gangs had given him a similar philosophy.

They'd placed Stalker in a different foster home, where he could do valuable work—therefore, they apprenticed him to the blacksmith—and Stalker said he didn't mind learning how to make weapons and ammunition. Tegan stayed with Doc Tuttle and his wife; it was a long month while she fought infection. I stayed with her as much as I could, though after the first few days, they made me go to school. Three weeks ago, she joined us in the schoolhouse. In the afternoons, she assisted Doc with patients, cleaned his instruments, and generally made herself useful. As for Fade, he went to live with Mr. Jensen, the man who ran the stables, and he cared for creatures like the ones that towed Longshot's wagon.

Of us all, only I remained with Edmund and Momma Oaks. She kept me busy sewing, though I had little aptitude, and it annoyed me to be saddled with Builder work. They were wasting my potential. I didn't see any of my old friends as much as I once had, and I hated that too. Sometimes I missed the house by the river, where nobody told us what to do.

These musings carried me through our silent progress away from the wall. By tacit agreement, Stalker and I didn't head to our respective beds. Instead, we had a secret place within Salvation, as we were forbidden to go into the countryside, a half-finished house near the north side of town. They'd gotten the roof on, but the interior hadn't been smoothed out, nor had the second story progressed past beams and slats.

Some young couple had planned to live here once they married, but the girl took a fever and died, leaving the boy wild with grief. Momma Oaks told me he went out into the wilderness without so much as a weapon. *It was like he was asking them to kill him,* she'd said, shaking her head in disbelief. *But I reckon love can do strange things to a body.* Love sounded terrible if it made you so weak, you couldn't survive without it. Regardless, their misfortune left Stalker and me with the perfect place to hide and talk—and spar.

"We don't belong here," he said, once we settled in the shadows.

I didn't think so either, not in the roles they intended us to play. They couldn't accept that we weren't stupid brats who had to be supervised. We'd seen and survived things these folks couldn't imagine. Though I hated to judge people kind enough to take us in, they weren't very worldly in some respects.

"I know." When I finally answered, I kept my voice soft.

People already said this place was haunted; that was why nobody had continued the construction. I hadn't even know what that meant until Longshot explained it to me. The idea of a ghost was foreign; that part of a person could live on outside his body made no sense on the surface, but sometimes I wondered if I had Silk's spirit in my head. I'd asked Longshot if people could be haunted like places, but he'd said, *I'm not even sure places can be, Deuce. You're asking the wrong man if you want esoteric knowledge.* Since I didn't know what *esoteric* meant either, I let the matter drop. Topside had lots of foreign words and concepts; I was digesting them as fast as I could . . . but so much strangeness made me feel small and stupid.

I hid those moments as best I could.

"We could leave," Stalker said.

In the dark, I studied my fingers as if I could see the tiny marks from the needle I wasn't accustomed to plying. "And go where?"

We'd almost died traveling from the ruins, and there had been four of us. Tegan wouldn't leave Salvation, and I wasn't sure about Fade. For all I knew, he was happy working with the animals. I hadn't talked to him to say more than a handful of words in weeks—and that was another reason for my quiet unhappiness. Sometimes I tried to bridge the distance, but Fade avoided me at school, and his foster father was a brusque, impatient man who shooed me away from the stables on the occasions I had visited. *Go on,* Mr. Jensen would say. *The boy doesn't have time to wag his jaw.*

"There are other settlements."

He'd passed through the same wreckage as I had while we pushed north. Most towns and cities had been overrun. In all these months, Longshot was the only human we'd seen in the wilderness. Even if we didn't like our lot, it made sense to stick it out until we were old enough to have some say in town decisions. Unfortunately, that could be a long time. That was incredibly frustrating because I wasn't a brat anymore; I'd passed my trials and become an adult. The things I had survived had moved me beyond childhood, and I had wisdom to offer, no matter how many years I had.

"Enough of this." He pushed to his feet and fell into a fighting crouch.

And *that* was why I met him in secret. He understood. Stalker wouldn't let me forget who I was. Momma Oaks had suggested I disregard my old life and try to become a "regular" girl. My first week in her home, she explained how females were expected to behave in Salvation. She made me long-sleeve blouses to hide my scars, and put my hair in neat braids. I hated the clothes, but the hairstyle was practical for fighting, at least.

He lunged; I blocked. Even in the dark, I could tell he was smiling as my fist slammed into his torso. Sometimes he let me land a few hits early on, but he would never admit it. We circled and sparred until I had no more breath, and several new bruises. Good thing my foster mother insisted on modesty, or I wouldn't be able to hide this night's work.

"You all right, dove?"

I wasn't; I longed for Fade and I hated lessons and I missed being valued for my skill. As if in consolation, Stalker tipped my chin up and tried to kiss me. I sprang away with an aggravated sigh. Though I wasn't interested in more than training, he had great determination that he'd change my mind someday. I couldn't see it happening. If he thought I'd ever breed with him, he'd better be ready for an argument that ended with my knives in his gut.

"I'll see you at school," I muttered.

After confirming the path was clear, I left the little house and headed for the Oakses' place. Climbing back into my room was more challenging than getting out. First, I had to shimmy up the tree, inch along the branch, and then leap over to my window. It wasn't too great a distance, but if I landed wrong, I'd fall, which would prove impossible to explain. This time I managed without waking the household. Once on my return, I had Momma Oaks in my room demanding to know what I meant by that racket. I'd pleaded a bad dream, which led to her *poor lamb*ing me, and hugging me to her ample breast for intended comfort. This always left me feeling awkward and unsure.

That night, I lay awake a long time, remembering times long gone, and people I would never see again. Stone and Thimble, my two brat-mates . . . they'd acted like they believed the charges against me—that I was capable of hoarding—and that still hurt. I missed so many people: Silk; Twist, the elder's right-hand man; plus the little brat 26, who looked up to me. In a fever dream, Silk told me that the enclave was no more; I wondered if I could believe that knowledge, but I didn't see a way to confirm it. I'd lost nearly everyone I cared about when I left home. Now it felt as if I'd lost Fade too. Up on the wall, when Longshot had killed its companion, the surviving Freak cried out, and that protest made me wonder if the monsters felt, like we did, if they could miss the ones taken from them. Wrestling with that uncomfortable possibility, I fell at last into an uneasy doze.

The nightmare began.

My flesh crawled with the smell as we made the last turn. I'd long since gotten used to the darkness and the chill, but the stink was new. It smelled like the time when the Freaks had surrounded us in the car, only a hundred times worse. Fade stilled me with a hand on my arm. I read from his gestures that he wanted us to stay close to the wall and move very slowly on the approach. He got no argument from me.

We came upon the busted barricade first. There was no guard posted. Inside the settlement, Freaks shambled about their business. They were fat in comparison with the ones we'd encountered on the way. Horror surged through me. For a moment I couldn't take it all in; the silence of corpses drowned every thought.

There was no one here to save, and our elders had killed the sole surviving Nassau citizen. That meant our nearest trade outpost lay four days in the opposite direction. Fade put his hand on my arm and cocked his head the way we'd come. Yes, it was time to go. We could do nothing here but die.

Though I was tired, terror gave my muscles strength. As soon as we gained enough distance through stealth, I broke into a headlong run. My feet pounded over the ground. I'd run until I buried the horror. Nassau hadn't been prepared; they hadn't believed the Freaks could be a large-scale threat. I tried not to imagine the fear of their brats or the way their Breeders must have screamed. Their Hunters had failed.

We wouldn't. We couldn't. We had to get home and warn the elders.

My feet moved, but I went nowhere. Running, as the earth opened, trapping me. Openmouthed, I tried to scream, but no sound emerged. Then blackness swirled in, carrying me away. Everything shifted.

The enclave sprawled before me, filled with a hateful crowd, their faces twisted with condemnation. They spat on me as I passed through the warren toward the barricades. I lifted my chin and pretended not to see them. Fade met me there. We stood mute while they rifled through our things. A Huntress flung my bag at my head, and I caught it. I hardly dared breathe when she stepped close.

"You disgust me," she said, low.

I said nothing. Like so many times before, Fade and I climbed across and left the enclave behind. But this time, we weren't heading on patrol. No safety awaited us. Without thinking, without seeking a direction, I broke into a run.

I ran until the pain in my side matched the one in my heart. At length he grabbed me from behind and gave me a shake. "We're not going to make it if you keep this up."

The scene changed. Pain and shame melted into terror. I had no choice but to leave my home. The unknown would swallow me up.

Soon the shadows devoured us and I could only see the vague Fade-shape nearby. "I'll go up first."

I didn't argue, but I didn't let him get far ahead of me either. As soon as he started to climb, I did too. The metal was slick beneath my palms; several times I nearly lost my balance and fell. Grimly, I continued up.

"Anything?"

"Almost there." I heard him feeling around, and then the scrape of metal on stone. He pulled himself out of what looked

like a small hole. Diffuse light spilled down, a tint different from any I'd ever seen. It was sweetly silver and cool, like a drink of water. With Fade's help, I scrambled up the rest of the way and saw the world above for the first time.

It stole my breath. I spun in a slow circle, trembling at the size of it. I tilted my head back and saw overhead a vast field of black, spattered with brightness. I wanted to crouch down and cover my head. It was too much space, and horror overwhelmed me.

"Easy," Fade said. "Look down. Trust me."

Morning came after a night of devastating dreams, most of them true, and with it a dull, throbbing headache. Still shaking, I sat up and rubbed my eyes. Everything had a price, and this was mine. During my waking hours, I could be calm and in control, but at night, my fears crept in on quiet feet, haunting my sleep. Sometimes my past felt like a heavy chain about my neck, but a Huntress wouldn't let it prevent her from moving forward and taking action.

Exhausted, I crawled out of bed, washed up in cold water, and got ready for school. As I trudged down the stairs, I shook my head at the waste. What did I need to learn that I didn't know already? But there was no convincing anyone of that. Apparently, it was a rule that I had to attend until I was sixteen—at which point I could remove myself. If Momma Oaks had anything to say about it, I would work with her full time, making clothes.

Sometimes I'd rather go back down below.

School

The school was the size of a large house, the interior space divided up by age groups. Colorful charts and pictures decorated most of the walls, except for the one where the blackboard hung. It was smooth, but hard like a rock, and Mrs. James, the teacher, used white sticks to write on it. Sometimes the brats scrawled stupid messages on it, often about Stalker or me.

Mrs. James moved among us, supervising our work. I hated this because I sat with brats younger than myself. I held my pencil awkwardly; writing didn't come as easy as using my knives. The brats laughed at me behind their hands, eyes amused and innocent. I couldn't even bring myself to dislike them for their careless prejudice.

They knew only safety and comfort. These brats were smug and self-assured, confident of their place in the world. In some respects I envied them. They didn't have nightmares, or if they did, they weren't about real things. Most had never seen a monster, let alone killed one. They'd never seen a Freak feeding on someone who died in the enclave, and then was cast out like garbage. They didn't know how ruined the world was beyond the walls; they'd never felt claws tearing through their flesh. Small wonder I had nothing in common with these Salvation young.

As for the teacher, Mrs. James thought Stalker was a savage. Fade she liked a little better, because his scars could be hidden, and he knew how to show a polite, distant face. He had been doing it for years, after all, well before we went Topside. Nobody saw anything he didn't intend to reveal. Mrs. James liked Tegan, much as all adults did, whereas she sighed at me, calling me an "unfortunate case of blighted potential," whatever that meant.

Today, she was running on about some terrible tragedy, determined we'd learn from our forebearers' mistakes. "And so, that's why it's imperative to pay attention to the past. We don't want to repeat such errors, do we?"

While Mrs. James lectured, my mind wandered. Things that happened in the enclave—that I hadn't questioned at the time—troubled me now. I wondered how bad a person I was for not realizing there were problems sooner. Sometimes worry and regret balled up in my stomach like a sickness.

I killed my first man when I was twelve years old.

It was my final trial, the last test I would undergo before being accepted as a Huntress. Though I had been training for it, this deed determined whether I had a fierce heart. I could still see his face, even three and a half years later; he had been weak and injured. The elders told me he was a Nassau spy, caught skulking inside our borders outside the safety of a trading party. I remember how he begged for mercy, his voice hoarse with despair. I'd steeled myself. It was the first time I'd held a knife, as brats owned no weapons. In hindsight, I should have smelled the stench of the elders' dishonesty, but I hadn't paid close enough attention.

"They brought me here," he'd moaned. "*They* brought me."

I'd believed he meant when they captured him in the tunnels, and I considered his plea a contemptible effort to avoid his fate. A failed spy could at least die with dignity. Though my stomach had churned, I cut his throat, and his cries went silent forever. For my first kill, I didn't know enough to offer him a cleaner death, piercing a vital organ instead. The elders had been pleased with me. Silk took me to the kitchen thereafter and Copper gave me a special treat. Most likely, the stranger had been captured for our ritual. They had done such things in the enclave and left us scuttling in the dark.

Though I had been in the light for months, the shadows still troubled me.

Sounding irritated, Mrs. James rapped her desk with brisk knuckles. "Will you do the honors, Deuce?"

My head came up, cheeks hot with humiliation. The teacher knew I hadn't been paying attention, and in this, she was like Silk. She believed making a public example of people motivated them to do better in the future. I thought it just taught them to be ashamed. I met her gaze squarely; I wasn't a brat she could intimidate, though I felt as she intended.

"I didn't hear what you want me to do."

"Read page forty-one, please."

Ah. So the class had moved from history to reading. The others settled in to be entertained as I sounded the words out. My pronunciation was slow and laborious, interspersed with constant correction from Mrs. James. I liked stories, but I didn't enjoy puzzling them out on my own. To my mind, books offered both entertainment and reward, but the recitation was best left to those who excelled at it.

Like Fade.

He watched me, dark eyes revealing nothing of his thoughts. At last, I struggled to the end of the passage and sat back, silently hating Mrs. James for putting me in this position. In six months, I could stop pretending. In six months, I became an adult. That chafed since I'd passed my majority already, according to the laws down below. It wasn't right that I could make my own way and choose my own course, until I reached the safety we'd dreamed of—and then it could be taken away from me.

That was enormously unfair. I'd once said as much to Longshot, who shook his head and laughed. *That's life, kid.*

The boys were old enough not to attend classes, if they chose otherwise, but they came anyway. Maybe they thought listening to Mrs. James was better than working all day. This way, they only did chores after school. For Stalker, I suspected it was also a matter of pride; he couldn't stand that Fade was so much better at reading, so he was working to catch up. Not that the teacher gave him any credit. For various reasons, she didn't like either of us very much.

Later, as the others filed out to eat their lunches in the sun, Mrs. James called my name. "I'd like to speak with you a moment."

I went up to the front, ignoring the looks and nudges. "Yes, sir?"

"It's ma'am," she corrected. "You call men sir."

Down below, we'd called everyone the same—with the exception of the Huntress title—regardless of what private parts they had. I wondered whether that made us more open-minded or less attentive to detail. Knowing she didn't like what she termed sass, I seamed my lips and waited for the admonishment that would follow.

"Why don't you take a seat?"

I was hungry; I didn't want to spend my break sitting in here, but I supposed that was what I got for daydreaming. "Yes, ma'am."

To appease her, I arranged myself in the chair next to her desk, reserved for pupils who misbehaved. I sat in it more often than I'd like, not through mischief, but obvious disinterest. She knew I was counting the days until I could cut free.

"You could have a bright future," she said then. "You're a smart girl. I know you think this is waste of your time, but it pains me to see someone who won't even try to better herself."

My lip curled. "Do *you* know how to kill a Freak with your bare hands? Can you skin and cook a rabbit? Do you know what wild plants you can eat? Would you be able to get yourself from the ruins where I was born all the way up north?" I shook my head, knowing the answer already. "In my world, lady, I'm already as good as I need to be, and I don't like your tone."

Knowing I'd pay for it, I strode out of the schoolroom and into the sunlight. Even now, it still felt unnaturally hot against my skin, but I'd come to enjoy the feeling. The sky was blue overhead, high clouds adding contrast, but not offering any chance of rain. It had taken me a while to learn the weather signs, what meant fire in the sky, and what meant falling water.

Shading my eyes, I glimpsed Fade with Tegan, who had made friends with some local girls. They were sweet, I supposed. I was grateful to Doc Tuttle for saving my friend, but I felt as though I'd lost her anyway to the changes that separated and fixed us with different foster families. Tegan wasn't the first, of course. Stone and Thimble went before, when I left College, my home down below. I missed them. You didn't forget a brat-mate bond, no matter how much distance came thereafter.

I knew all the rules in the enclave. Nothing here made sense. Everything I thought was right, people told me I shouldn't even consider. Day after day, they told me I was wrong—that I couldn't be *me* and still be a proper girl. I studied Tegan and Fade, considered joining them for a moment, but Fade didn't meet my eyes and while Tegan waved, it didn't look like an invitation.

Heart heavy, I went over to where Stalker sat, eating alone. With a faint sigh, I flung myself down. Girls weren't supposed to sit like I did, sprawling on the grass. Momma Oaks would complain about the stains on my skirt, but I didn't care; I loathed these feminine trappings. I wanted my old clothes back, designed for freedom of movement, and tailored so I could strap my knives within easy reach. I didn't understand why only men fought in Salvation when women could be just as strong, just as fierce about protecting their homes. It was a ridiculous waste of resources, and after growing up down below, where we made use of everything—sometimes four times over—that attitude struck me as completely nonsensical.

I peered at Stalker's lunch. The blacksmith didn't have a wife, which meant he always had simple fare, bread and meat, mostly, sometimes a crock of beans. He watched in envy when I opened my bag and found cold meat, sliced carrot, and a sweet round cake. It was a good meal; nobody could say Momma Oaks did wrong by her stubborn, unwomanly foster daughter.

"Want some?" I broke the pastry in neat halves without waiting for his answer.

It was spring, and the school year was almost over—just a month left. I'd heard they tended fields during the summer, growing food to last the winter. Living down below, I'd never imagined food that sprang up from the ground instead of being hunted or found, but it appeared some of the stories Fade's sire had told him were true. The mushrooms grew, but it wasn't the same thing; that felt less magical.

For that season, they needed Hunters to watch over the plants and those who tended them. It was the only time they permitted patrols, a decision I questioned. With me in charge, things would run differently, and we'd sweep the area, killing enough Freaks to make them wary. I couldn't survive three months inside these walls with nothing to do but pull a needle through cloth.

"Thought any more about what I said last night?" he asked.

"About leaving? Not until we know where we're going. It makes no sense to run off without a plan."

It wasn't just the need for caution, not that I'd admit it to Stalker. In truth, I couldn't leave Tegan and Fade, even if they were settling in better. There was a bond between the four of us, and we shouldn't split up, even if Salvation seemed to be doing its best to sever that connection altogether.

"Agreed."

"You still dealing well enough with Mr. Smith?"

It was a common name, so I understood, but it also referred to the man's trade. His father before him had worked the same forge, making metal goods for the town. Salvation had been here, in its current form, for fifty years—or so they claimed. Mrs. James reported this was a historic site, dating back to the Aroostook War. I had no idea what that was, but it sounded like a made-up thing. I tended not to listen when she rambled about Salvation's history. If I decided to stay, then I'd soak it in.

"He doesn't talk much." Stalker paused to eat the pastry, and then went on, "He's teaching me to turn scrap metal into knife blades."

"Sounds like it could be useful."

"It's the only part of this town that I can stand. Well, work . . . and you." The trapped feeling reflected in his wintry eyes.

"I wish you wouldn't talk like that," I muttered.

It made me remember an awkward conversation I'd had with Momma Oaks, who disapproved of how I'd traveled with Stalker and Fade. That first night, she'd trod from the stairs, looking pleased. "There, now. Your rooms are ready. I have a spare, and a cozy cupboard off the kitchen, room enough for a pallet, I think."

"I'll take the small one," I'd said. "It's what I'm used to."

"I didn't intend to make you share with those roughneck boys." In her tone, I heard what she didn't say; *make you share* meant *that'll never happen under my roof.*

I'd figured I knew what she was worried about, so I assured her: "We've been bunking together for ages. It wouldn't be a problem. I'm not interested in breeding."

"In . . . *what?*" Her face went pink.

Hm, I thought. *If she had children—and Longshot had mentioned them—then she knew more about the business than I did.* I decided she was messing with me, so I'd show her I could be a good sport.

"In all enclaves, there are those who sire brats to keep the population stable, the best-looking, brightest, and strongest." She knew that, of course. "But everybody can't do so or folks would starve. I'm trained for fighting and protecting, so I'd never do anything that could make me unfit for duty."

"Oh, child." Her eyes went liquid with sympathy.

I had no idea why, staring at her, puzzled. Surely they didn't permit just anybody to mix their blood. That couldn't end well. People would wind up stupid and squinty.

"I'm sure that's how it was where you lived," she said at last. "But it's different here. People fall in love and get married. They start a family if they're so inclined."

So when Stalker started going on about how I was the only

thing he liked about Salvation, it made me twitchy. The rules were different here, and I didn't want him to get any ideas about us finishing up that sad, empty house and filling it with our brats. The notion made me clammy with dread; I'd rather kill Freaks any day.

"Friday, we'll talk to Longshot about the patrols," I said, changing the subject.

"You think he'll take us on?"

"I hope so."

Momma Oaks had told me that Longshot always captained one of the squads that ensured the safety of the fields. I wanted him to choose me for his team so bad I could taste it. He knew we were capable fighters; he'd seen our bloody weapons when he picked us up in the wild. And he understood that we weren't tame, Salvation-bred brats. In fact, he was the only elder in the whole town who acted like he had more than a grain of sense. I suspected it was because of the supply runs. They'd taught him more about the world than the others could learn living within the safety of these walls. While they kept danger out, they also locked the ignorance in.

"They act like Freaks can't change," Stalker said quietly. "Like these walls are magic, not wood, and nothing bad could ever get in."

"*We* got in."

"But we *look* human."

I caught the faint stress on the word "look" and I frowned at him. "We're still human. We're just not like the rest of them."

According to Mrs. James, we were both bad as a barrel of rotten apples. She'd used that exact phrase in describing Stalker. Once, for falling asleep in class, she'd tried to whip him with a green switch, but he disarmed her so fast, she never saw it coming. Her face paled as he stood, slapping the rod lightly against his palm.

"I wouldn't try that again," he'd whispered in her ear.

Now she hated him, laced with fear, because he'd made her look foolish. A few of the Salvation boys studied Stalker from a distance, trying to copy his walk. Girls watched him too, when they thought he wasn't looking, but he noticed everything. Mostly, he thought they were weak and useless, just a bunch of Breeders.

I pushed to my feet, packed up the remnants of my meal, and strode away. In the time remaining, I ran laps around the schoolhouse, which made people stare at me. But I'd get weak sitting all day; work kept the body strong.

On my fourth circuit, two boys stood watching me, wearing identical mocking looks. They elbowed each other, bolstering each other's nerves, and then ran after me. They chased me around the side of the building, and I stopped, willing to confront them. At school, they picked on people who were different; girls through cruel whispers and mocking laughter, boys through more direct means.

I faced them. "Do you need something?"

"That depends. Did Mrs. James find a cure for stupid?"

The first pushed the second toward me. "Careful, it might be contagious."

"I heard you go to the bathroom standing up," the bigger boy said.

An odd sound escaped his friend—a combination of a snort and a chortle—like he'd said something both wicked and hilarious. Their cheeks went pink too. I guess I was supposed to be shocked by the allegation. I stared at them until they started to shift on the balls of their feet.

"Why do you keep running around the school?" the small one demanded. "Are you simple?"

"She thinks something's chasing her."

I was tired of this, weary of ignorant brats judging me like I was the strange one. These two deserved a lesson in manners, but if I taught it to them, I'd be the one in trouble. Somehow I curbed my temper as someone came up behind me.

"That's enough," Fade said softly.

You won't speak to me, but you'll rescue me.

It made me angrier that his presence could drive them away whereas I had to prove myself with my fists. Again. I'd been sent to Momma Oaks twice for fighting with the admonition if I did it again, I'd be whipped. Yet I never bothered any of these brats. They were the ones who wouldn't leave me alone . . . but try telling that to Mrs. James. She'd made up her mind that I was an instigator.

"Thanks." I brushed past Fade, unable to look at his face without a wave of unwelcome confusion and yearning.

Before he could reply, if he meant to, Mrs. James came out to chivy us inside. Fortunately, the school year was almost over. I had no doubt the teacher would use that time to torment me in ways that would make Silk proud. It didn't matter. I knew my own worth. A Huntress didn't rely on a bunch of brats for her sense of self, but on that last day, as class let out, I ran my fingers over the scars beneath my sleeves, reassuring myself I hadn't dreamed it. Salvation had saved me, but its protection came with restrictions. Its rules didn't permit me to be myself. Yet I'd been part of a community that needed me once. Maybe I would be again.

Someday. Somehow.

Confidences

After school, I checked in with Momma Oaks, who was cooking when I arrived. The kitchen had lots of gleaming wood, pretty curtains with touches of lace, hooks that held her spoons and pots, and cupboards full of food. There was also a table with a couple of chairs, where she and I sat to talk about my day. At first I found that odd, but she was determined to be a good foster mother. Since I'd never had a mother at all, I didn't know what to do with her attention. I suspected the truth would make her unhappy—that brats of all ages messed with me and that I hated school—so I always said:

"It was fine."

"Just 'fine'?" she repeated.

I had no idea what she expected from me. Did she truly want me to complain? That would earn me a slap down below. This felt like a test I kept failing, so I tried, "Mrs. James gets on me a lot."

"Are you cutting up in class?"

What does that mean?

"I just don't always pay attention, especially during history."

Her brow creased. "It must seem boring after your adventures in Gotham."

I nodded, addressing the bread and cheese she'd set out for me. Eating several times a day was my favorite thing about Salvation. I had breakfast, lunch, a snack, and then supper as well, and not just a few strings of meat or a mushroom cap, either. No wonder everyone looked so fit; it was a land of unimaginable plenty, and at mealtimes, I minded the rules much less.

"Well, not everyone's meant to be a scholar," she went on.

"Were you?" I asked.

Her answer surprised me. "I left at sixteen and married Edmund. I'm an excellent needlewoman and a fair cook, but I was never much for books."

"Me either," I muttered, pushing away from the worktable. "Do you mind if I visit Tegan?"

She smiled, apparently pleased that I wasn't going to sit and stare with a surly face at a pile of mending. "Of course not, Deuce. Be back by supper, mind."

At first, she'd questioned calling me Deuce, because it was nothing she'd heard for a girl before, but when I showed her the bloodstained card and explained its meaning, she stopped hinting I should pick something else. I toyed with the fragile card in my skirt pocket, a relic of the enclave and the naming ceremony where I got my scars.

"I will. Thank you."

I went out the door at a run, heading for the doctor's office. Tegan was in the surgery cleaning instruments when I arrived; she smiled but didn't stop her work. Without speaking, I commenced washing up beside her. It wasn't hard, but cleanliness was important, particularly in her foster father's work. Once we finished, she turned to me.

"What brings you here?"

With a shrug, I answered, "I just wanted to talk."

"About what?"

"How you're doing." I might've put that more tactfully, but I felt responsible for her, since I'd rescued her and dragged her out of the ruins. I'd also put a weapon in her hand and she had been injured—almost died—because I hadn't taken the time to train her properly. Swinging a club didn't make her a Huntress.

"So you're checking on me." Her eyes crinkled in amusement. "That's sweet."

"Are the Tuttles looking out for you?"

"They're great," she said. "Helping Doc, I feel important, like I'm doing something that matters."

"You are." That wasn't even a question in my mind.

"Rest easy. We found a good place. I'll always be grateful to you for getting me away from the Wolves and out of the ruins."

One thing I'd always wondered but there was never a chance to ask, so I said, "Tegan, did the Wolves mistreat all their females?"

It was possible, of course, that they had been stupid and savage and that they didn't realize harming the mother could damage unborn offspring. Just because my people understood something, it didn't mean the gangs knew it as well.

Her breath caught; and her face dimmed with remembered pain. "The girls who were born into the Wolves didn't question their roles. They didn't try to run. So they weren't punished."

I nodded. "It wouldn't occur to a female Breeder in the enclave to protest her situation, either."

"They haunt me," she said softly. "The two cubs I lost. I was only thinking about getting away so I could protect my little one like my mom did me. But instead, they beat me until—" Her voice broke and she curled her hands into fists. "I know why they did it—to break me so I wouldn't fight them anymore."

"They shouldn't have hurt you," I told her. "There were ways to hold you that wouldn't harm the unborn brats."

Tegan swiped away a tear. "So your people wouldn't have beaten me for trying to escape?"

She wanted reassurance that I came from better folk than Stalker. When I first met her, I'd thought that the enclave would punish anyone who treated a girl that way. But that was reflex, wanting to think the best of them. With the benefit of time and distance, I realized something; safety only applied to those who were born among us and who followed the rules blindly. Just witness how they treated Fade and a Builder named Banner. At first, I'd envied her apparent closeness with Fade, but then the elders killed the girl over her quiet discontent with their leadership; they made an example of her and framed it as a suicide.

Terrible things happened down below too.

So I couldn't lie to her. "If we found a female in the tunnels who was good only for breeding . . . if she fought that role, the Hunters would've cut her throat and left her for the Freaks. The enclave wouldn't have wasted resources training her. So, no, we wouldn't have beaten you, Tegan. *My* people would've killed you."

Her breath caught. "Then it's a good thing I didn't end up down below."

"It is, actually." Because it was unlikely she'd have survived the tunnels long enough to run into one of our patrols. It still amazed me that Fade had done so.

I could see her struggling with the revelation, hands clenched on the edge of the counter where we'd stacked the doctor's clean implements. "But . . . you're not like the rest of the Hunters, then. You protected me."

"That was after I left the enclave."

"So you're saying you'd have killed me. *You*, Deuce." Tegan met my gaze, her brown eyes begging for a denial.

I was about to destroy all her illusions. "If Silk ordered me to. I'd have felt bad about it, but I would have obeyed. Back then, I thought they knew more than me. Until a certain point, you know only what you're taught."

With a pained wrench, I remembered the blind brat who had come from Nassau begging for help. Fade and I carried him back with us to College, but once the elders heard his message, they had no further use for him. I hadn't wielded the blade that slit his throat, but I gave the boy to the Hunter who did. His death could be attributed to my silence—and so I couldn't let her idealize me. Though I'd learned better since I came Topside, it didn't mean I was a good person or instinctively kind. In fact, I had spent years battling the idea that I was too soft to make it as a Huntress. In many cases, I saw compassion as weakness.

"Is that why you like Stalker?" Her expression twisted as though the words left a sour taste in her mouth.

I lifted my shoulders in a shrug. "I understand him. We share common goals."

"He's like you," she said then.

"More than you are," I admitted. "Stalker and I came up with other ideas of right and wrong, different from what I see in Salvation. And, yes, the enclave did a lot of things that I'd fix if I could. At the time, I didn't know any better . . . but I'm teachable. I think Stalker is too."

"You'll forgive me if I'm not in a hurry to befriend him," she muttered.

"I don't expect you to. You two have history . . . bad history. He reminds you of the worst time in your life."

"So do you," she said softly.

Oh. That hurt, more because it was an unexpected blow. "I'm sorry. I didn't realize. Is that why—"

"It's easier to be around the other girls. They didn't see me at my weakest. They don't know everything that's happened to me, and I'd like to keep it that way. I hope you won't tell them either."

"Of course I won't. And I won't visit again, if it bothers you." I kept my face still and calm, my Huntress expression, and it didn't reveal any of my pain.

In Salvation, it seemed like I had nobody but Stalker and Longshot. Fade didn't talk to me unless I needed saving. The brats at school thought I was crazy and they treated me accordingly . . . and now this from Tegan. *At least you're safe,* I thought. *At least you have enough to eat.*

"I need some time. I do appreciate everything you've done for me. I just—"

"Want to settle in?" I suggested, not showing how I felt. "Make new friends?"

She nodded, visibly relieved. "I'm glad you understand."

"I do. I'll be going, then." And I wouldn't come back until she came looking for me. Not out of injured pride, either. A true friend would rank Tegan's welfare above her own loneliness.

She didn't stop me from leaving. Outside the Tuttle place, the weather had turned as the sun fell toward the horizon. Light streaked the sky in colors whose names I'd only recently learned. Today it glowed gold and orange with slivers of pink, like a speckled autumn apple. As we'd traveled, we had found a few growing wild, a bit withered, but still edible. A cool wind blew over me, lifting tendrils of my hair from the braids. It would be suppertime soon, and I hadn't started my schoolwork for the next day.

I ran through town, ignoring the whispers. A few women pointed at how I lifted my skirts. "Does that girl ever walk like a normal person? I can't imagine what they were thinking when they took her in."

I ignored them as I always did, though it hurt, each word like a stone hurled at my back. When I opened the front door, Momma Oaks murmured about me catching cold. Then she asked me to lay the table, and I did so without complaint. I found it fascinating how many different tools people used to eat a meal Topside. Food was scarce enough down below that we raked it off our plates as fast as we got it, and nobody carried extra weight, as people sometimes did in Salvation. That seemed marvelous, that people could pack on enough flesh to withstand a hard winter.

Edmund joined us and Momma Oaks took my hand, as she did each night. "Creator, bless and keep us. Guide us to live according to your laws and to appreciate your blessings."

The first time she did that, I wondered aloud who she was talking to, and she explained that she was addressing a being who lived up in the sky and watched over us. Though I didn't like to insult her, I thought her god had done a terrible job keeping his people safe. Given the current state of the world, it seemed far more likely the Freaks were his favored creatures.

My foster mother served us all. As I ate, I made polite conversation over roast meat, fresh bread, and vegetables. "How come your son never comes to see you?"

Edmund and Momma Oaks froze. Their expressions said my idea of courteous didn't match theirs. Pain flashed across her features, echoed in a spark in her eyes, and then she dropped her gaze to her plate, apparently unable to respond.

But I didn't understand why it was wrong for me to be

curious. I'd been living in their home for over a month; it seemed unkind that he hadn't come to check on his sire and dam. For all he knew, I was a dangerous maniac who might murder them in their sleep.

Then Edmund cleared his throat. "Rex has his own affairs to tend. He's busy."

"Oh." That sounded like an excuse. It was more likely they'd argued, but as I wasn't part of the family, I didn't push for the truth.

Silence reigned for a while. I had made them sad without meaning to, and so I feared asking another painful question. Eventually, once I cleared my plate, there was a sweet, which tasted as good as the canned cherries Fade had shared with me in the ruins. The dessert jolted my memory.

"What is it?"

"Taste it." Fade dipped his finger into the tin and offered it to me.

I couldn't resist, though I knew better than to let him feed me like a brat. Sweetness exploded on my tongue, contrasting with the warmth of his skin. Shocked and pleased, I pulled back and dipped two of my fingers into the tin in a little scoop. This time I caught more than the sauce. A round little red thing sat in the curve of my fingertips. I ate it without hesitation, two, three more scoops until I was sure I had red all around my mouth, and I didn't care. He watched me with amusement.

"How did you know it would be so good?" I asked.

His smile slipped. "I had some with my dad, once."

These days, Fade wasn't around enough to share anything with me; an ache curled through me like a metal hook. There had to be some way to fix things between us. A question from Momma Oaks drew me before I could decide what to do about Fade. After dinner, I cleaned up while my foster parents talked quietly in the other room. Fractured words reached me in fits and starts.

"—maybe we should tell her. She feels left out," Momma Oaks whispered.

". . . no point. It doesn't pertain to her."

With determination, I closed my ears and stacked the clean dishes in the cupboard, then strode into the doorway. "May I take a light upstairs?"

"Do you have homework?" Edmund asked.

"Yes, sir."

"Then by all means." Momma Oaks got the lamp from the far table and offered it to me. "Careful. Don't knock it over and don't burn yourself."

"We had torches," I told her, in case she thought fire was new to me. If they protected their young like this all over in Salvation, it was a wonder the brats could find the schoolhouse on their own. "I'll be fine."

Edmund nodded. "Good night, Deuce."

I ran up the stairs, the lamp casting crazy shadows along the walls. In my room, I buckled down and copied the passage that Mrs. James had assigned. Then I was supposed to write a page about what I'd just read. That took far longer, so I skipped to sums, which I found easier than reading. This was a useful skill, since it could be applied to inventorying supplies. That finished, I went back to my stupid essay and rambled about what the words meant. The teacher wouldn't like it, and she'd probably read my paper aloud to point out all the mistakes.

I'd survived worse. The brats could mock me. Women could

whisper. There would be bad memories, more nightmares, and the threat of Freaks outside the walls. I'd endure, no matter what.

Once I felt sure my foster parents were asleep, I dressed in dark clothes and slipped out the window. No bells tonight, but I needed to talk to Longshot. He'd be guarding the wall in his usual spot. I clung to the shadows, pausing twice to avoid detection, and then I clambered up the ladder. The moon shone on his white hair, so I recognized him straightaway. He cradled Old Girl in his arms; on my arrival, he didn't shift from his study of the darkness.

"Don't you ever sleep, girl?" His gruff tone concealed gentle humor.

"Sometimes," I said.

"Aren't you bored of plaguing me yet?" He leaned down to rub his knee in an absent way, as if he'd long since gotten used to the ache.

"I have some questions."

"No end to 'em, apparently."

"Don't you have anybody at home to miss you?" That wasn't what I meant to ask. It just slipped out. But he was always, *always*, on this wall, guarding Salvation.

"Not anymore," he said quietly. "What is it you want, Deuce?"

I squared my shoulders. "I want to be included in the summer patrols. I'll fight to prove myself in front of the other guards, but I wouldn't embarrass you by bringing it up with no warning. If you're dead set against it, I won't—"

Longshot held up a hand to silence me. "It's good of you to consider my pride, but if you win their respect, I'll take you on. But you better put on a good show, girl."

"I will," I promised. "When should I make my request official?"

"We'll be planting in a couple of weeks. Come then."

"Thank you."

"Don't thank me. This will ruffle feathers something fierce."

"If you came up someplace where men cooked the food, and then you went somewhere else, and they wouldn't let you fix supper, even though it was all you were good at, would you give up your skillet?"

He smiled at me and touched two fingers to his brow. "I reckon I would not."

For a while we stood watch together in silence. This was my favorite part of the evening because, to Longshot, I wasn't wrong or strange or in the way. With him it was all right to be a girl who didn't fit.

"When do you usually go on the trade runs?" I asked eventually.

"In the fall, after the harvest comes in. I'm back 'fore the snow sets."

I remembered how capable he seemed when he rescued us, loading everyone into his wagon along with the supplies. He'd never doubted, never hesitated. And he'd saved us all. If the opportunity arose, I'd pay him back someday.

"Do you need help?" I asked.

"Why, you interested in being my apprentice?"

"I might be." A hot flush washed my cheeks as I waited for him to tell me why I wasn't old enough or strong enough to do the job. Or worse, he'd say it was impossible because I was female.

But he surprised me. "It can be lonely, dangerous work, Deuce. Hang in there, get your education, and I'll see what I can do when the time comes."

I sighed. "It's hard. You're the only one who listens to what I have to say."

Longshot dropped a gentle, comforting arm around my shoulders. "Then speak louder, girl. Don't let them put out your spark."

For a long time, I stood in the circle of his arm and counted the stars. I ran out of numbers before brightness, and that felt like a promise of better days to come.

Challenge

The next two weeks passed in a trickle of sameness. Mrs. James complained about my poor work at school; other brats found fresh meanness to inflict during lunch. Fade and Tegan continued their quest to make new friends. Some nights Stalker crept in my window, and we visited Longshot, then sparred in the secret house afterward. Other nights I went to the older man alone, and we talked about all kinds of things, including why he'd volunteered for the trade runs when they were so dangerous.

"At first," Longshot had told me, "I went because Salvation needed me to be brave. Eventually, I continued because I enjoyed seeing the world . . . and finally, I kept at it because I didn't have anybody to miss me if something went wrong."

"I'd miss you," I replied, and he ruffled my hair.

That was last night.

This afternoon, I was nervous.

There was no reason to be. Longshot had said I needed to prove myself, but that wasn't the basis for my anxiety. I shuffled my feet outside the livery and listened to the animal noises within. I hadn't visited Fade in weeks, not since the last time Mr. Jensen sent me away . . . but Fade hadn't come to see me, either.

And he knew where I lived. His intervention at school was the last time I'd been near him—and I missed our old closeness. Bringing Tegan and Stalker into the fold had enhanced our chances of survival, but it also changed everything.

But I couldn't join the summer patrol without inviting him. Whether we talked or not, whether he spent all his time with Tegan, he was still my partner. At first, down below, that meant watching each other's back and trusting he'd fight to save me. When we came Topside, the bond acquired more emotional depth, an attachment that made me crave his touch and his company. So I gathered my courage and went into the stables.

After school, Fade helped with the animals, and I found him running a brush along a creature's back. It was bigger than the ones that Longshot used to pull his wagon, built along more graceful lines. The animal turned its head as I came in and whickered softly. It had pretty, long-lashed eyes and a shiny coat, probably due to Fade's attention.

"Deuce," he said.

The cool formality in his voice made something inside me curl up and whimper. If I had a title, like the teacher did, he'd be using it. And I didn't understand why. I barely remembered coming into town, but he hadn't been like this with me. No, the chill settled in later. There had been some occasional reserve on his part, of course, but not ice. Not permanent silence.

Unfortunately, I liked looking at him every bit as much as I ever had, which wasn't fitting for a Huntress. Such instincts came from my Breeder side, weakness passed through my dam—which had caused me trouble with other Hunters down below. It was dreadful suffering such impulses when I needed to be brave and tough. I didn't want to think about how nice it was when he put his arm around me, or how I'd fallen into his kisses with the same delight I took in a hot bath. At first, I was reluctant, but with care and patience, Fade taught me that not all contact had to be martial, and now I missed his mouth on mine.

"What are you doing?" That wasn't the question I intended to ask.

"Currying this beauty."

I gathered that meant using the brush, but I'd never heard Momma Oaks talk about currying anything, so it must apply only to animals. Sometimes I felt I'd never learn the things other people took for granted. Even Stalker, who fit here no better than I did, understood things instinctively about Topside.

"We're going to talk to Longshot about summer patrols," I said bluntly.

Fade arched a brow. "Who's we?"

"Stalker and me. You too, if you're interested."

"Haven't you seen enough fighting?" His tone made it seem like there was something wrong with me, like I should be glad to do nothing but attend school and sew with Momma Oaks.

"It's what I was raised to do. It's what I'm good at." I squared my shoulders, determined not to let him make me feel bad, even if my behavior disappointed him.

His next words filled me with hope. "You're still my partner. I won't let you go out there without someone you trust."

And I did trust him, no matter the problems between us. Some of my inner ice melted. "Come on then."

"Just let me tell Mr. Jensen where I'm going." Fade strode away through the stable, and a low argument rumbled between them. It didn't last long.

"Do you like him?" I asked a few minutes later as he fell into step.

He shrugged, a moody twist to his beautiful mouth. "Not really. But he doesn't try to be my dad."

Quite unlike Momma Oaks, who's determined to be my mother.

Fade didn't protest when we stopped at the smithy for Stalker. Neither boy suggested we invite Tegan. She wasn't a fighter when we made the trip, and it was ridiculous to imagine she'd want to get involved in the summer patrols. But I missed her. While *she* preferred the company of normal girls—she wanted to forget what she'd been through—there were no females that I considered friends in the same way. Yet sometimes being a friend meant letting people do things that hurt, like putting distance between you, just because it made them happy.

The town was laid out neatly within the protective walls. This site had been rebuilt three times, I remembered, one of the few history lessons that stuck with me. A real war had been fought nearby, and then the fort fell into ruins. They uncovered the site, some two hundred years ago, and rebuilt it as it was before. I didn't understand the reasoning but Mrs. James claimed it had to do with respecting "our" cultural heritage. Since I was descended from those the world hadn't cared to save, I suspected her pride didn't apply to me.

We passed through the town in silence, lifting a hand now and then in greeting to those who recognized us. The women fell silent when they saw me coming, eyes avid for some new offense to report later. White-washed buildings showed neat and tidy in comparison with the ruins we'd traversed to find this place. I still didn't understand the trade principles that governed Salvation, however. They used wood tokens to symbolize the value of goods and services. The boys and I had none, which meant we depended on our foster parents for every little thing. I hated it.

Single men who didn't have homes of their own stayed in the barracks on the west side, near enough to the walls that they could post more guards if necessary. Since I'd been in Salvation, it hadn't been; standard numbers had been sufficient to discourage Freak incursions. I should have felt better about that. Maybe I was just one of those people who couldn't rest easy unless things went catastrophically wrong.

Whatever the reason, I couldn't rid myself of this foreboding. The problems we'd seen from the changed Freaks would reach Salvation in time. It was only a matter of whether it was sooner or later.

Not surprisingly, Stalker and Fade didn't speak; they shared a core of deep-seated animosity, but they both seemed determined to fight at my side this summer. Deep down, I understood I could only have one partner. Part of me didn't wholly understand that. Why couldn't I be friends with both? They each brought something different to the table, and their combat styles weren't the same.

This isn't about fighting, a little voice said. But, unfortunately, it went away as fast as it came, and left me feeling foolish.

We found Longshot playing cards in the barracks; he had his sleeves rolled up, exposing weathered forearms. Even now I found his age marvelous and astonishing. With good food and fresh air, I might live that long too, provided the Freaks didn't get me. Which made my forthcoming request even less comprehensible when you got right down to it, but I had been reared to protect others. I felt less than whole if I wasn't living up to my own inner expectations. You could take the Huntress out of the enclave, but it didn't lessen her need to fight.

"Kids," he said with an inclination of his head.

That was what they called brats in Salvation. It was also the name for the offspring of the animals they kept for milk. That seemed more offensive to me than the word "brat," but evidently not according to Topside sensibilities. They also didn't like it when I called people Breeders, even when they had young.

I picked up Longshot's cue. "I heard you need a team."

Two bushy white brows went up; he played his role well, as if I hadn't forewarned him two weeks ago. "Is that right?"

"They'll be planting soon," Stalker said. "And you'll need people to protect the growers."

"And then later, the fields," I added.

Longshot tilted his head. "I'm aware of that."

"We want to be on your team," Fade clarified.

"All three of you?" The older man feigned skepticism as his gaze brushed over me in my long, full skirt. "Can you shoot?"

I shook my head. "But there are no walls out in the fields anyway. You'd have an advantage if you chose people experienced in hand-to-hand."

"And that's you?" His tone grew quietly amused.

That might've bothered me if I hadn't grasped his intent. Longshot couldn't afford to seem too willing at first, and I knew how I looked in this dress and Momma Oaks's braids, my Huntress scars hidden from the world. My gaze swept the barracks, where a number of guards watched us with equal measures of hilarity and impatience. Talk would only take things so far.

At random, I pointed at a young man who looked capable. "I'll prove it to you. Let's step outside. If I can't bring him down, I'll forget this whole idea."

There was a reason I was fighting for the honor of our group. The guards saw me as the weak link. While they'd consider letting

Stalker and Fade join the summer patrol, I had to establish my skill before they'd take me seriously.

The guard I'd singled out gave an incredulous laugh. "I don't wrestle girls."

"That's not what I heard, Frank!" someone cracked.

A hot flush flared in his cheeks. "Shut *up*, Dooley."

Longshot shoved back from the card table. "I don't see what it'd hurt, as long as you promise to abide by the terms."

There was no way this guard had trained as I had or earned the same combat experience. Down below, Hunters blindfolded us and taught us to fight according to what we could sense with our ears and noses. Eventually I got good enough to detect an incoming strike by the movements around me. So I could beat him easily.

Keen to show them what I could do, I turned my back to Stalker, who knew what I wanted. He unfastened the top two buttons on my dress, which I hauled over my head. The men in the barracks gasped, except for Stalker and Fade, who both realized I was always ready to fight beneath the feminine paraphernalia that Momma Oaks foisted on me. With knives strapped to my thighs, I was fully clothed in pants and the tunic I'd carried from down below.

"Do all girls—" a guard whispered, and another shushed him before he could finish the question.

"Outside then," Longshot said. "No bloodshed, fair play, and the first fall heralds the winner."

Those terms were acceptable. I felt sorry for the young man I was about to humiliate, but from his expression, he thought this was a big joke. Other guards snickered, whispering about my chances, and he raised both arms in anticipation of his easy victory, spinning in a cocky circle. So maybe he had it coming.

He grinned, showing a gap in his teeth. "I'll try not to hurt you."

Behind me, Stalker laughed softly, but I didn't glance at him to share a conspiratorial look. Instead, I focused on the one I had to beat to convince the others I deserved a place on Longshot's team. The guard advanced in no particular style, expecting I'd prove easy to defeat. His grab was clumsy, and I ducked and swung around behind him. When I planted my foot on his backside, the other guards hooted, and he spun, embarrassment blossoming on his face in scarlet patches.

"Don't play with him, Deuce." The reminder came from Fade.

In my head, Silk berated me. *Don't waste energy. Take him down.*

Even if the man had laughed at me, he didn't deserve to be mocked. So the next time he came at me, I swept his legs and pounced on top of him, my hands on his throat. If I'd been carrying my daggers, he would already be dead.

Silence fell, broken only by his quick, shocked breathing. And then the young man under me gasped, "I will be damned."

They had little close-combat training from what I could tell by that match. Or maybe he just hadn't thought me worthy of his best effort. Either way, I glanced up at Longshot to make sure he accepted the outcome. The older man nodded, so I sprang away, spinning in a slow circle to see if the guard had any angry friends ready to defend his honor. But the others seemed shocked more than offended.

To show I harbored no hard feelings, I offered my hand. Frank accepted it after a moment's hesitation and I pulled him up. He shook his head, eyeing me with a mixture of admiration and disbelief.

"It won't be a popular decision," Longshot said then, "but it would be criminal foolishness to waste talents such as those. If your friends fight half as well, I'd be honored to have all of you on my team."

Pride blazed in me. This was the first time I'd felt I could be happy in Salvation, like they might permit me to use my true skills. "How many members?"

"Eight. One patrol leader, which would be me, one recon specialist, and the rest for defense."

"I'm good at recon," Stalker said.

It was no joke. He'd trailed us through the ruins, and despite my sharp senses and Fade's intuition, we hadn't noticed a thing. I nodded my endorsement.

Longshot addressed all of us. "You'll receive a small stipend in exchange for your work this summer."

I guessed he meant we'd be earning our own tokens, which could be spent at stores in town. That would be nice, as I hated being completely dependent on my foster parents for anything I wanted. They were generous enough, but that wasn't the point; I needed to be independent. Only a brat took constant handouts without protest.

"I'd count it a favor if you'd recruit me too," the man beside me said.

Longshot studied him. "Why's that, Frank? I won't have you messing with this girl and making her life miserable. She took you fair and square."

"It's not that, sir." He paused, then lowered his voice. "I think I might be able to learn from her."

"I wouldn't be surprised. I guess I just need to find three more souls—" He hadn't even finished the sentence when three more guards stepped forward, volunteering to join the team. They all seemed driven by appreciation too, not judgment or anger.

Maybe it was all right to be different, at least among the guards. Perhaps my prowess mattered more than my sex. If they didn't gossip like the women, I'd like Salvation a whole lot better.

"When do we start?" I asked.

"Planting is a week from tomorrow," Longshot answered. "We go out then."

To protect the growers. That wasn't so dissimilar from the way things had worked down below. Part of me couldn't believe it. After all this time, I had a proper place in the world and important work to do. In time they might even teach me to shoot and give me a shift on the walls, like the other guards. Like Longshot, that could keep me occupied between trade runs.

If you're ever lucky enough to be chosen as his apprentice. You have to finish school first. That reminder cast a shadow over my excitement.

Nonetheless, I said, "Thank you, sir. I'll be ready."

The older man nodded. "Meet at the barracks next Saturday, before dawn. If Momma Oaks gives you any trouble, tell her to talk with me."

Warmth crackled through me. I wanted to hug him, though he wouldn't care for that any more than Silk would. So I contented myself with a sharp nod, and then I hurried into the barracks to retrieve my stupid dress. Muttering, I pulled it back over my head, and Fade did up my buttons. I could tell it was him by the warmth that prickled over my back. Down below, he touched me first for comfort, and then, like he drew solace back from my skin. Topside, he went from an arm around my shoulders to tasting sweetness on my lips. I was attuned to Fade's hands as I never had been with anyone else.

"I have to get back to the smithy." Stalker brushed my cheek with his fingertips in passing as he went, but I couldn't take my eyes off Fade.

His mouth tightened at that touch, and his jaw clenched. The two events connected in my head; maybe his distance had nothing to do with how he felt about Tegan, and everything to do with Stalker and me. The separation had started well before our arrival here. The more Stalker showed preference for my company, the more Fade withdrew.

I'd thought Fade was still mad at me because the Freaks killed his old friend Pearl—and we couldn't save her. Stalker had been the enemy in the ruins . . . and after we escaped from his gang with Tegan, he hunted us, using Pearl as bait. The Freaks attacked before we fought a second time, however, and turned Stalker into an unlikely ally. Fade blamed Stalker for Pearl's death, and I'd suspected he didn't like me training with the other boy for that same reason. Now I wondered if his aloofness might be more personal.

I'd never know if I didn't ask.

"Do you have to go right back?" It was the first time in weeks that I'd tried to breach his reserve, and anxiety sunk a fist into my innards, as I wondered if he'd reject me—and how much it would hurt if he did.

He weighed the question, and then murmured with a pained twist of his lips, "My work will keep for a while."

Reunion

Pleasure streamed through me. I hadn't expected that response, so I had no follow-up. "What would you like to do?"

Fade lifted his shoulders in a graceful shrug. The rules here were different from the enclave's. We slept apart, but during daylight hours, boys and girls fraternized without censure; there was no insistence on chaperones, for instance. Down below, I couldn't spend time with Stone unless Thimble kept us company, and I was never allowed to bring a boy into my living space without someone else present. Walking was more than we'd done together lately, so I resolved to enjoy it.

"Momma Oaks has a swing out back," he suggested, surprising me.

I knew the one he meant. It was sedate, a long wood seat on a platform, not so much for children as for those who had to watch over them. I'd never used it, myself, but it might make a comfortable place to talk on a sunny afternoon.

"Let's go." I didn't know what we'd say, once we settled, but I was in no hurry to disturb the tentative peace.

Yet we had to clear the air. Even if he could keep this up, I didn't want to.

Fade followed quietly as I wove through town, back toward the Oakses' place. To my relief, my foster mother wasn't outside hanging wash or puttering in the yard. That left us a clear path around the side of the house. The swing rested beneath the same spreading tree that permitted me to sneak out in the middle of the night. With a fond glance at that liberating branch, I took a seat, and Fade did the same. He sat closer than I expected, his thigh a whisper away from mine. It reminded me of how we'd huddled together down below after we learned what became of Nassau, and it took all my self-control not to curl into him as I had then. He was all that remained of my old world.

Fade hunched his shoulders, staring down at the ground between his knees. The grass was patchy, showing green and brown. Not that long ago, it had been covered with snow.

"I get the feeling you want to talk about something," he prompted.

Yes. But I was no good at it. Action served me better than words, and I didn't know how to express my dissatisfaction. I'd stumble and embarrass myself, but even so, that had to be better than endless distance. So I took a deep breath and shifted, angling my knees toward him. The movement set the swing to rocking gently. It was soothing in a way I couldn't put my finger on, reducing my fear about how difficult this might prove.

"Are you still upset with me?"

"Why would I be?" He parried the question without answering it, and I couldn't let that stand.

"You tell me."

Fade gave a quiet sigh. "I just can't be around you all the time. It's too hard."

"What is?" That made no sense.

"Seeing you with him."

No question he meant Stalker, but I was only around him because Fade wasn't talking to me. I'd seen a dog in town chasing its tail—and that was how I felt too.

"I don't understand."

Nothing much had changed since we arrived in Salvation, but Fade made excuses to avoid me. He chose to be with Tegan or strangers instead of me. I'd be lying if I claimed that didn't hurt. After the past couple of months, I had a collection of inner scars to match the ones I'd earned on naming day, and then later, proving myself in battle. Each time he turned away from me at school, it cut a little deeper.

"You were mine before," he said softly. "But somewhere along the way, I lost you. And now you're his."

That raised my ire, as precious little could have. "I wasn't yours, and I'm not his, either. I'm a *Huntress*, Fade, not an old knife that can be traded."

He had some crazy notions; that was for sure. But his expression lightened a little, an almost-smile playing at the corners of a mouth that I enjoyed looking at too much for my own peace of mind. The time in the sun had been good for him, bronzing his skin until it glowed, but he didn't need to be more attractive. In fact, I resented him for it because his fierce beauty compelled my eyes in ways I didn't like and couldn't control.

"I know your title," he said then. "You've made it clear that you live to fight."

"Then what's the problem?"

"I don't like sharing."

On some level, I understood that. Down below, resources had been limited, and when you earned your name, and they assigned you personal space, it felt like a miracle, having three feet that nobody else had any control over. Topside, we had more room, but conversely, I had less power. I owned nothing up here but my knives and my free will, since I'd given the club Stone made me to Tegan. That gave me a pang, as I doubted she valued it anymore, and it was my last piece of the big, sweet Breeder.

But I still felt Fade and I weren't connecting on the right level. His meaning remained opaque, like a shape I could make out at the bottom of a murky river, only I didn't know it was a monster until it lunged up at me. I had that same kind of uneasiness right then; I hated feeling stupid.

"Sharing . . . what?"

I remembered Stalker saying he thought I wanted him to touch me—and that was why he'd spent so much time training with me. I'd put that to rest, hadn't I? Did Fade think I wanted Stalker's hands on me too? If so, I couldn't imagine how the opposite gender managed to get out of bed in the morning. They might be lovely to look at, but clear thinking wasn't their strong point. Once more, I'd strive to make it clear only Fade had that kind of magic.

He frowned, like he suspected me of being difficult on purpose. "You."

"He's not my partner." This time, I used the word Fade had once before, meaning something different and deeper than just the person who guarded your back in a fight. It had an emotional context too, something I couldn't spell out, but knew deep within my bones instead.

"You're . . . not with him?" His hesitation irritated me, as I'd never once lied to him. When we were stranded in the wilderness and I was dreaming of Silk, who told me to keep the fire burning, I didn't tell Fade why because he'd have thought I was crazy, but I never lied.

"We're friends."

"He doesn't kiss you?"

Just one time in the woods when he caught me by surprise. Since then, I'd gotten better at heading Stalker off, forcing him to train with me and nothing else. His kiss hadn't melted me like Fade's did, either. Part of me wished they'd both stop with the Breeder nonsense and focus on more important business, but the rest of me wanted to be close to Fade. His arm felt good around my shoulders, as I recalled.

Before I could answer, he cupped my cheek in his palm, dark eyes searching mine. Apparently satisfied by what he saw, he leaned his brow against my head. My heart gave a treacherous thump at his nearness. It was late afternoon, sunny and bright, which meant anyone could happen on us. Though the rules weren't strict here, I might get in trouble for sitting so close and letting him touch me, but I didn't care.

"I missed you." I didn't mean to tell him so, even if it was true. Admitting need felt like weakness; it demonstrated dependence and vulnerability.

But when he lifted his head, his dark eyes shone brighter than I'd ever seen, like he held stars inside. "It's been awful without you, but I thought you chose him. I was determined to respect your decision."

"He's a friend," I said again. "But he's not you."

"Here, it's not like it was down below," he murmured. "There's no shame."

"In what?"

"This."

His kiss didn't surprise me. My response did. Delight surged from the moment his lips touched mine, and I pressed close, wanting to crawl out of my skin and into his. Fade wrapped his arms around me as if he felt the same, his whole body trembling.

Such strong feelings terrified and elated me simultaneously. These sensations were the reason for the noises I'd heard down in the enclave, Breeders huffing and moaning as they made a new life. Before, I always imagined it was an unpleasant chore, like patrolling the back ways, and you put up with the process in order to achieve the desired result. Now, I wasn't so sure.

When I pulled free, my heart beat furiously in my ears and I couldn't catch my breath. Wonderingly, I touched my fingers to my lips.

I breathed, "That's *dangerous*. How long have you known?"

"Known what?"

"That it could be so . . . so . . ." Words failed me.

"Good?" he suggested, but it was a pale description. Yet I lacked a better one, so I just nodded, and he replied, "Since the first time I kissed you."

I remembered the occasion vividly; I'd towed him out of the throng after he won the festival challenge—to keep him from losing control and attacking the congratulatory crowd. Afterward, he caught his breath while I watched over him.

"I never had a partner pay this much attention to me before."

That made me feel I'd overstepped. He'd had two before me, so he knew better than I did what constituted normal behavior. Maybe I watched him too closely. It was unsuitable, and Silk would demote me to Breeder if she ever found out.

"I should get back," I muttered.

"Not yet." In an unspeakable liberty, he snatched the tie from my hair, so it spilled around my face.

"Why did you do that?" My breath caught when he brushed

the strands around my face just so. Touching me. We were on shaky ground here. If someone saw us—

"I wanted to see what you'd look like."

Back off, *I told myself.* Walk away now. *Instead I froze, gazing up into his impossibly dark eyes.*

He bent his head and brushed my lips with his. His hair spilled against my forehead, sleek and startling. Shock held me immobile, shock—and something else. Part of me wanted to lean into him. I shouldn't want that. A Huntress wouldn't. Shame, confusion, and longing warred for dominance. Against my better judgment, I let my brow graze his jaw, just a whisper of heat, wrapped around me like a pair of arms. And then I drew back.

Even then, he had opened forbidden doors in my head, making me want things no Huntress could ever have. But Fade intrigued me with the reply, and I had to ask, "So you felt . . . glowy about me, even then?"

"'Glowy.'" He repeated the word with an amusement that I should have found embarrassing. "That works. And yes. I have for the longest time."

His surety summoned such warmth, as if I'd kindled a campfire in my belly, bright enough to banish the long weeks of doubt and confusion. He laced his fingers through mine and settled our joined hands on his knee, but he didn't attempt anything more. Just as well. I wasn't ready; but no wonder Momma Oaks was concerned. If all the girls Topside knew this about kissing, they probably had to worry about new brats popping up all over the place.

"It's normal to enjoy being close," I said, trying the idea out.

"I think so. Not that I'm an expert. I don't feel this way about everyone."

My brows went down. "I should hope not."

This, I thought. *He was afraid I had this with Stalker.* I was just figuring out this was what the other boy wanted from me, only of my own free will. Not as a nasty chore forced on me. I had no doubt he'd bred to keep the Wolf population up, but it couldn't have felt like this.

"I don't want this to be a secret thing," he said then. "People should know."

"What?"

"That you're mine."

I bristled a little at hearing it phrased that way. "Fade. This doesn't change anything. I still belong to myself, and while I choose to share this with you, it doesn't mean you own me."

"I'm not saying I do." His voice rang with frustration, like there was some crucial, hidden component between us I couldn't grasp.

"What are you saying, then?" I bet the girls at school with ribbons in their hair didn't struggle with such confusion.

"That I have the right to kiss you . . . and nobody else does."

Finally. I could agree to that. It would mean making my new status clear to Stalker, which might not go well. In hindsight, I felt pretty sure he wanted those rights himself. I'd feared Fade preferred Tegan, but maybe he'd sought her company because she was a familiar face, much the way I'd gone with Stalker. Everything seemed much more complicated now.

It also brought to mind a question. "When you asked if I would still choose you as my partner, is this what you wanted? Exclusive kissing rights?"

He ducked his head, a touch of color on his cheeks. "Yes."

"Then why didn't you just say so?"

"I was afraid you'd say no."

That, I understood. Hadn't I been terrified of seeking him out? He had a unique ability to climb inside and twist my heart. Maybe I had that power over him too. Stunning thought.

"I would never hurt you on purpose," I said. And relief flickered in his face, so I knew I was right. I went on, "If you don't tell me what's on your mind, I can't guess. Remember . . . I'm not smart about this kind of thing. Fighting—or training—is all I've ever known."

He touched my cheek. "We'll figure it out together."

My heart lightened. This Topside exile might be bearable after all, if I could fight during the day and enjoy Fade's kisses when we weren't working. I was glad I'd chosen to invite him into our patrol. It would have hurt him if he'd discovered I was out with Stalker, and I hadn't talked to him about it. He'd have seen it as another instance of me choosing the other boy over him, instead of the truth, which was that Stalker made himself more available—and he came looking for me.

But now I understood why. I had to be more careful. Welcoming him into my room—and talking about running away together—had probably given Stalker ideas about my intentions . . . and my feelings for him. I sighed faintly. The conversation where I explained the mistake didn't seem likely to go well.

"What's wrong?"

This was one burden I couldn't share. I had made the mess through my lack of understanding about how males and females related to one another, so I'd clean it up. But, really, where would I have learned? Certainly not down below, where I was a Huntress. Silk would have stabbed me if she'd caught me wondering about my *feelings*. Such weakness was limited to Breeders and rightly so.

I sighed. "I'm just sorry we spent two months apart."

"Well, I was done chasing you," he muttered. "I made it clear how I felt the night Longshot found us."

If he had, I didn't recall. I'd been feverish and terrified Tegan would die. Everything besides that vivid dream of Silk telling me to keep the fire burning was a blur. I did recollect lying in his arms, I thought, with our friend stretched across our laps, but I didn't know that meant anything special.

"I don't know what you said that night," I admitted. "But you're the most important person in my life. You're all I have left."

That was the wrong thing to say. His long fingers unfurled from mine. "So this is because I remind you of a life you liked better?"

"*No.*" I made the denial instinctively, but I had to be honest. "I do miss my life, Fade, but isn't that normal? I lived there for fifteen years. They were my friends and family, my whole world. I'm still trying to figure out how I fit in Topside . . . and the summer patrol will help."

"I don't know if you can understand, but I haven't had anybody who cared about me, just because I'm me, since my dad died. Everybody else wanted something from me, but it wasn't personal. I *need* it to be personal with you."

"It is," I promised.

Fade put his arms around me then and held me with desperate strength. My heart raced. *He needs you*, I thought. *Don't let him down.*

I couldn't remember ever being so happy . . . or so scared.

Patrol

The following week passed quickly.

When I wasn't working for my foster mother, I took shooting lessons. I didn't have a rifle of my own, but if a teammate fell, I should know what to do with his weapon. Though I lacked experience, natural aptitude with armaments stood me in good stead. Practice would make me better yet.

Not surprisingly, at first, Momma Oaks was unhappy with my inclusion in Longshot's squad. She tried to talk me out of it, lecturing, "There are certain rules to be respected here, Deuce, man's work and woman's work. Salvation has functioned successfully on these principles for a hundred years."

"I'm not from Salvation," I told her.

But she was just getting warmed up. "You're a citizen, though, and that means learning our ways. Women tend crops, spin cloth, sew clothing, prepare food—"

"But I'm not good at any of that," I interrupted. "You say there's a divine being in charge of the world, right?"

Her look grew uneasy. "Yes, but—"

"Then why did he let me learn to fight and get good at it, if that goes against his rules?"

"Mercy," she said on a sigh. "Don't let anyone else hear you say that. That's perilously close to heresy." I didn't know what that was, so I kept quiet. Momma Oaks went on, "If you do this, there may be consequences. People might be . . . unpleasant over it."

"Will they give you and Edmund a hard time?"

She squared her shoulders. "They might. But don't worry about us. We've suffered worse. Do what pleases you best, even if it sets tongues to wagging."

As I hadn't expected even that much support, I gave her a real smile. "Thanks, Momma Oaks."

My foster father didn't share her point of view. So supper was a subdued meal, and I heard Momma Oaks quarreling with Edmund after I went to bed. He seemed inclined to forbid my participation in the summer patrol, and she argued, saying such a course would drive me away, as it had Rex.

I knew there was a reason the son didn't visit. But that still wasn't my affair.

Sleep came quickly—and if I had the nightmare, I didn't remember when I woke. I rose early the next morning, dressed in fighting clothes—trousers and tunic—then ate bread and jam while Edmund snored. After breakfast, I washed up and braided my hair. A few minutes later, I slipped out of the house without waking either of my foster parents and hurried through Salvation.

Before dawn, I met the rest of the team at the barracks, as Longshot had requested. Fade and Stalker were already there, waiting with poorly concealed impatience, whether for me, or to see some action, I couldn't be sure. I had chosen to lock my window this past week, and Stalker must be wondering why, but I'd opted not to deal with that situation before we started our new job. It seemed best not to meddle with the balance—or maybe I was just being a coward. I had to balance the weight carefully so I didn't crack.

Fade didn't try to touch me, despite our new understanding, and I was grateful. I didn't want the other guards to think of me like that. To that end, I'd left off the woman's attire; instead, choosing what I'd worn for patrols down below. The men nudged one another, and I swallowed a sigh. The ridiculous restrictions on being female threatened to choke me.

Fortunately, our leader had no interest in my pants. Longshot was already giving orders in his laconic style. "We'll meet the planters at the front gate and serve as escort out to the fields. Once there, we break into squads of four. One will remain with the workers at all times. The others will patrol."

"Will we switch off?" one of the guards asked.

It was a smart-enough question that I forgave him for being amazed to see a girl in trousers.

Longshot nodded. "We'll rotate, so nobody gets bored and comfortable."

A wise precaution, I thought. If a team watched the planters poking seeds in the ground for too long, it could lead to complacency. And this was an important task. Without a successful growing season, there would be little food for the winter. Slaughtering domesticated beasts could only take the town so far—and I was more aware of the need for proper nutrition than most. It had been one of the immutable laws down below; we ate a certain amount of this or that, or we paid the price with weak, sickly bodies, sooner than the wasting required.

I wondered now if the elders down below had known as much about diet as they claimed . . . and if the wasting that took our people young had come about through their willful ignorance, making up answers when they had no clear understanding. At some point, one Wordkeeper must have decided it was better to invent rules arbitrarily than to reveal his own lack of knowledge. There were reasons for everything, no doubt, but I would never know them. That way of life was lost to me.

With a determined air, I focused my attention on Longshot, who was giving a few last-minute instructions. Then the others fell in, two by two. It was a more formal procession than I was accustomed to, but I learned the value of the order soon enough. In contrast, the planters were in utter disarray when we arrived. They were men and women both, chosen for their gifts in tending green and growing things. Unfortunately, most of them were not suited to life in the wilderness, and they found even the prospect of the short journey to the fields trying.

"We've mislaid a whole bag of seed," a small man whined, twisting his hands together. "It was put back in storage at the last harvest, and now it's simply gone."

With a dark look, Longshot left us while he went to sort the situation. As the man in charge of trade runs, he also took responsibility for the town resources. He looked older than usual this morning and mightily tired, as if herding these growers was more of a burden than he wanted. But he'd been doing this work for better than twenty years, a fact that never ceased astonishing me—and so he did it well, with the expertise born of long experience. In the enclave, elders only lived to be twenty-five or so, withered through some combination of factors I didn't understand.

I found the chaos fascinating, as people had seldom argued with the elders down below. Here, there were two women haranguing Longshot about the misplaced provisions, something about rodents and dry goods. I was trying not to laugh when Stalker came up beside me. His presence killed my humor quick because guilt sank its fangs into my gut and wouldn't shake loose. Possibly, I had given him reason to think I felt strongly about him . . . in ways that led to kissing. Sneaking out to meet him, where we'd talked about our mutual misery and contemplated the idea of running away together—how I wished I had never done it. I should have stuck to sparring. Those nights felt like promises broken now.

"These past few nights, your window has been latched," he said softly. "What am I to take from that, dove?"

I didn't fear his anger, but I would regret losing his friendship if it came to that, because he had proven to be fierce, loyal, and steadfast. Nonetheless, it was time to stop avoiding this talk. "I can't meet you at night anymore."

"Why not?"

Surely he knew, but he wanted to make me say it. "I—"

"Stop sniffing around." Fade set his hand on my shoulder. "She's with me."

I stole a glance at the other guards, but they were too busy watching Longshot's argument to pay attention. Thankfully so. I'd die if I forfeited their respect over such a ridiculous issue, over jealous boys and feelings.

"That true?" Stalker's face seemed oddly frozen under the scars, yet beneath the ice, he gave the unmistakable impression of pain.

I hated this, but I nodded. He squared his shoulders and wheeled away, heading to join the guards. Laughter followed, so he must have made some joke. If there was one thing Stalker was good at, it was adapting to new situations. He had to feel like he'd lost his only ally in this town but he wouldn't show it.

"You enjoyed that."

"I remember what he did to us," Fade said. "And what

happened to Pearl because he dragged her out, hunting for us. I set it aside because we needed his blades on the journey, but he'll never be my friend."

I saw things in less immutable terms. Raised in the gangs, I'd be a submissive Breeder. Considering where he came from, Stalker wasn't as bad as he could be—and he showed willingness to learn—but Fade would never share my point of view; and it seemed like a bad idea to provoke him when we'd only just gotten close again. So I let Fade revel in this moment without chiding him.

To my relief, Longshot tracked down the missing seeds in short order and at last the final wagon was ready to go. The distance wasn't far, but since most food had to be grown outside the walls, it seemed like a monumental undertaking to those who spent their lives within the safe confines of Salvation. They had marveled that four young people could survive in a wilderness filled with Freaks, wild animals, and heaven knew what else. Heaven was a new concept to me, like that of a soul, the place where people supposedly went after they died. Sometimes I wondered if I'd see those I'd lost or if the blind brat I'd failed to save would be waiting for me with a swift kick. It didn't seem like the sort of thing I could rightly ask my foster mother. But I wouldn't be going there anyway because only people who followed all the rules got into heaven.

The gates opened with a tormented squeak, doors gaping to let the convoy out—thirty-two guards, plus nearly as many growers. Such a to-do for the annual planting, but as far as I could tell, this was customary. The surrounding land was bleak as it had been the first time we passed through, but the promise of spring had kindled greenery on the trees. Likewise, the brown grass was coming back to life, but nothing on the horizon gave me hope that there were other settlements nearby. In its way, Salvation was every bit as remote as the enclave had been down below.

Since the mules couldn't set a fast pace, we walked alongside the wagons, alert to trouble. Twin plaits struck my back gently as I moved. There had been Freak presence in the area for some weeks, since well before our arrival, and this would be their first opportunity to strike at settlers outside the walls. If the Freaks were smarter, they'd figure out a way to get inside or to attack the town fortifications; it was as well for us that they weren't clever enough to strategize.

I smelled the monsters long before I saw them. In daylight, my vision was never the best, but it was impossible to mistake the stench carried on the spring wind. It reeked of dead and rotten things, of hopes irreparably lost, and the torment of endless hunger. In Mrs. James's history lessons, she said mankind held the responsibility for the creation of these monsters, something to do with hubris and meddling with matters better left to God. It was the first time I had heard the word "hubris." Ordinarily I didn't speak up in class, but that day, I raised my hand.

"What's hubris?" I'd asked.

The class tittered.

Mrs. James didn't quiet them, and her smile took a sly turn. "Excessive pride or self-confidence. Arrogance, if you will."

I could tell she thought the word applied to me, after our conversation where I said I didn't need to learn anything she could teach. I'd hunched my shoulders and wondered what humanity had done to fashion the Freaks. When I got time, I intended to ask Longshot or Edmund about the origin story.

"They're near," Fade said then, loud enough for the rest of the guards to hear. He already had his knives in his hands, and it gave me a thrill of pleasure to see his lean body tense, ready to fight.

Our fellows cocked their weapons, a clicking noise that prompted the growers to terrified whimpers, and one of them whispered, "Perhaps we should turn back. The planting doesn't have to be done today."

"And what day will be perfectly safe?" Longshot asked in disgust.

I could understand his impatience . . . and why he chose to go off on the long, lonely trade runs. The townsfolk he protected were as timid as mice, hiding in their walls. I much preferred having the enemy within reach of my blades, where I could see an end to the battle before the next one began.

Longshot didn't wait for a response. "Keep those mules moving. We're almost to the first field."

They could not have expected trouble in the degree we encountered it, a few straggling Freaks, perhaps, survivors of the last run at the walls. But a veritable host of them swept out of the trees, loping toward us with their monstrous gait. Inhumanly fast they came, misshapen skulls, yellowed skin, and bloody lesions. Their eyes swam in their heads as they ran, taking in the feast we represented.

Shots rang out atop the panicked growers' screams. They huddled in the wagons, covering the seeds with their bodies, as if that was what the Freaks had come to steal. But these creatures were eaters of meat; they did not forage for food from forest plants. They ate game when they could find nothing bigger or better, and they seemed to view humanity as their natural enemy.

There are too many, I thought, even as they fell, holes blown in skulls and torsos. The weapons were fearsome at a distance, but too many of them had charged, and soon they would be upon us. I hoped the other guards could fight at close range as well as they could shoot.

As for Fade and me, we fell in back-to-back, as we had ever done, and something sweeter than fear sang in my veins. I had my blades in my hand, and my partner at my back; therefore, I feared nothing, not even death.

They hit us like a wave from that great water I had seen, falling away from the rocky land. I wheeled into the fight with a laugh that made the other guards shiver a little. Strike, parry, thrust. This was the reason I had been born—to fight these predators and drive them away from my people. I wasn't a child. I was a Huntress.

Their blood spattered as I slew them, stinking of rot. It was a mushroomy smell, one that stayed on skin and clothes through several scrubbings. I had almost forgotten that over those months behind the wall. Beside me, Fade spiked his knife into a Freak's throat, and before it had fallen, another was on him, snapping with its bloody teeth. Gobbets of meat hung from its mouth, a taste granted from a guard who had not been so skilled with a blade as he was his rifle. I wouldn't think about that, not now. Longshot used Old Girl like a club, swinging free enough to cave in the skull of any Freak that drew too near the wagons. Stalker needed this fight, I thought. His rage manifested in every slash of his blades, and the Freaks went down before him in great piles.

But I couldn't watch anyone else for long. It required all my concentration to keep myself from being overrun—and by the time the last Freak fell, my arms burned from the unaccustomed motion. Despite my best efforts, Salvation had made me soft—and that, in turn, filled me with outrage. I had to train more. Fight more.

Breathing hard, I took a moment to survey the scene. So

many corpses. Two growers had panicked and tried to flee; they lay dead some distance from the wagons, ripped to shreds. Four guards had been lost. From the grave, heavy expressions of those around me, this was *not* typical of the start of planting season.

"Leave them," Longshot said quietly. "If we don't get these seeds in the ground, then they died for naught."

It was a grim procession that continued on toward the fields, and I wondered what greater woe the season had in store. If I had known then, perhaps I would have chosen my course differently.

Or not.

I was, after all, born to be a Huntress.

Unnatural

The surviving growers rallied enough to go about their business, at least, but they did it with a mournful air. It seemed to me that seeds planted with bloody fingers should yield a bitter fruit, but I didn't express my reservations. It was probably nonsense that would make everyone laugh.

But they hadn't chuckled at my fighting.

A few guards asked about my training as we watched over the field. Frank, the one I'd beaten to earn my place, seemed particularly interested. "Is it hard to learn to use knives like that?"

"It takes time," I answered.

"Is it dangerous?"

"You don't train with live blades when you're starting out."

"Would you mind showing me some moves sometime?"

"Not if you don't mind learning from a girl." Other men laughed at this.

But Frank shrugged.

He fell quiet then, and I waited for instructions. Ordinarily, the force split, and they planted more than one field at a time, but Longshot felt uneasy with that practice. He thought, given the numbers we'd faced earlier, that it was safest to plant them individually and not dilute our strength. After the battle that morning, I agreed.

I went over to Longshot after he settled against the wagon, Old Girl propped across one arm. "What's the planting usually like?"

"Not like this." His tone was grim. "Not in years anyway. Those numbers were downright . . . unnatural."

That couldn't be good news. All the way here, we'd seen evidence of heavy Freak infestation, but since I was newly arrived Topside, I didn't know what was normal. Fade had said they didn't live aboveground when he was a brat, but it was impossible to say when they'd first found their way out. I only knew they hadn't spread into Stalker's part of the runs, as he'd never seen them before hunting us.

As I considered, I decided Freaks couldn't have been born underground, as I had been, or they wouldn't be so widespread. The whole world seemed swollen with them, like a rotten corpse. Where they had first come from, I didn't know, but there must be a center, the deepest part of an infected wound.

"So there were more than usual?" Stalker asked, joining us. Some of his rage seemed to have burned down during the fight, but he still wouldn't look me in the eye.

"That was more than we'd ordinarily see in a year," the older man answered, brow furrowed.

"You don't usually guard the fields?" Fade asked.

Longshot shook his head. "No need. They don't organize. They rove."

"I told you, the ones we ran into have gotten smarter." I'd warned him on our arrival, but I didn't know how seriously he'd taken me.

Now he sighed. "Just what we need, as if life out here isn't tough enough."

The rest of the day passed without mishap. If there were other Freaks in the area, they decided to go after easier prey. But the attack left me with a strong sense of apprehension. They had lain in wait, and apparently they'd known the route that the convoy would take. They also must have been aware there would be more trips back and forth to the fields, not for a while, granted. But once the plants sprouted, the growers would return, and so the patrols would resume.

It made sense to me that they would try again.

My instincts were also telling me that if these Freaks were bright enough to plan a rudimentary ambush, there was no telling what else they might think up. These were definitely the smartest I'd ever seen, and it was downright terrifying. Stalker didn't have enough experience with the creatures to judge; I fell into step with Fade on the way back, wondering if he felt the same.

"What do you think?" I said, low.

"The monsters are different." He confirmed my opinion in a soft voice.

"Do you have any idea what's changing them?"

Fade shook his head. "If I did, maybe I could help somehow."

Yes, that was the crux of the matter. I cherished the small bit of respect I'd garnered in the fight today, and I didn't want to lose it by circulating wild theories with no solutions. Maybe my time down below had made me reluctant to offer my thoughts to the elders, but at this juncture I couldn't be faulted for caution. It was a precarious situation, and one that left my stomach tied in knots as we approached the front gates. We'd borne so much; the threat of losing my safe haven scared me—and if I wasn't fighting, fear preyed on me just as much as the next person. I was just better at hiding it than most.

"What happened?" the guard called.

"Muties," Longshot replied. "Six lost. Now open the gates 'fore it's dark!"

A rumble went through the men on the walls, and soon the word rushed through town. From out here, I heard the hue and cry of people carrying word. The men on the wall tonight had to be glad they weren't on summer patrol. Only a crazy person like me would feel like such a risky job made her life worth something.

They let us in without ceremony, and there were wives and husbands waiting to see if they'd lost somebody. To my surprise, I found Momma Oaks searching for me, Edmund in tow. The fact that he'd come out in the dark to meet us made me feel a little lighter. I'd wondered if he saw me as a nuisance who slept in his house and ate his food . . . but apparently not.

"You're covered in blood," she said on a little sob. Her eyes teared up, and Edmund patted her ineffectually.

"I'm not hurt." I didn't understand what was happening here.

"Hug her," Longshot advised me kindly. "She's lost children before, and now that she's adopted you—"

"Adopted." That was a new word. I didn't know what it meant, but I thought it had something to do with the way her hands fluttered toward me, and then back, like she didn't know what to do with them. Feeling awkward, I stepped in and added my consoling touch to Edmund's. *Women are emotional,* his gaze said. For the first time, I shared a moment with him of complete understanding. If this was how women reacted to things in Salvation, I didn't think I'd ever be one, no matter how many dresses Momma Oaks sewed for me.

"She'll be all right in a minute," Edmund told me.

"I'm fine now," she snapped through her tears. "We should get you home and washed. Those clothes may never come clean."

That, I understood. Down below, sometimes people would fuss about things, when it was really something else bothering them. That was a common human trait, it appeared. So, without protest, I went with my foster parents, while casting a bemused look over my shoulder at Fade. It seemed wrong that I should have both of them waiting when he had nobody. Mr. Jensen had *not* come to see if his assistant made it back alive.

"Wait," I said, refusing to be towed farther.

Edmund frowned, as this delayed his evening meal. "What's wrong?"

"Could we invite Fade for supper?"

Momma Oaks radiated surprise, but not because I wanted him there. "Of course. You can have your friends over whenever you like. Our home is yours, now."

Until tonight, I had thought of her only as someone giving me a place to stay out of obligation, out of charity. I hadn't known she cared. Why would she? I wasn't a proper girl, nobody she'd have chosen for her kin. And yet her regard was unmistakable; she had been *worried* about me. I didn't think anybody ever had been before. I was a Huntress, so if I went out and died, then I had done my job.

Warmth began in the pit of my stomach and it radiated outward until my fingertips tingled. On impulse, I gave her a quick hug as I had seen other girls do. Momma Oaks stared at me in wonder, as if I had done something special. She wasn't my dam, but I doubted the girl who had borne me down below would have given a moment's thought to my safety. The enclave had its rules and it didn't permit bonds to form between offspring and parents. For the first time, I almost understood what a loss Fade had suffered, because he could remember both of his.

I turned and ran back to the gate, where Fade still stood, watching us go. "Come eat with us."

He glanced down at his stained, bloody clothes and shook his head. "I can't."

"Wash, change, and then come. Please."

It was the last word that won him. I saw the yielding in his face, because it was something he wanted too, but for some reason, he was afraid. Stalker watched us, and that gave me an unpleasant twinge. But I couldn't change what I'd done to encourage him, only what I did going forward. And for me, it had to be Fade. My choice would *always* be Fade.

"All right," he said. "Mr. Jensen won't mind."

In his words, I heard a lot more. The man who had taken him in didn't care about him. He wanted the free help. And I was the lucky one, this time. But maybe I could share what I had, what I hadn't even wanted, with Fade, who was hungry for what he'd lost. Maybe I could make it better for him somehow.

I surprised him when I reached up and kissed his cheek. There were people all around who might judge me for having such impulses. They might think all sorts of things, but I didn't mind. He touched his face with a kind of wonder, much as Momma Oaks had when I hugged her. Until then, I hadn't realized I was so much like my own knives, sharp edged, cold, and perfect for keeping people at a distance.

That done, I ran back the way I'd come, to my foster family, and then together, we returned to the house that had become a home to me, quite unexpectedly. I had a cozy room all to myself, a finer bed than I'd ever known. This unexpected welcome made me determined to protect this town better than I had my own enclave. When it came down to it, they had thrown me away, down below. Taken my devotion and decided it was worth nothing in comparison with the need to keep everyone cowed by fear. Today, Salvation made me feel like I was worth something again, and so the unpleasant parts—like school, mocking brats, and Mrs. James—mattered less.

"He's coming," I said, breathless.

Momma Oaks smiled. "He seems like a fine young man."

"Was it bad out there?" Edmund asked.

It didn't seem strange that a man of his age would ask me for an update about the wider world. I had trained my whole life to protect people. He had another job in town; the shoes I had on, he'd made with his own hands. I didn't know how to do that, and it felt right to me that we each did the work to which we were best suited. I didn't need to know how to make shoes, so long as Edmund did. And he didn't need to fight, as long as I was here.

"I've only seen the Freaks gather like that in the ruins," I answered.

"Gotham," Momma Oaks breathed.

I nodded. "They were swarming when we left." That had been one of the primary reasons we went looking for a safer place.

"I think they're drawn to people," Edmund said, elaborating on his theory as we went. "Not just because they're hungry, but because they hate us. Blame us. For what they are. It's not just survival with them. I think it's war."

His words raised a cold chill on my arms, as they reminded me of Mrs. James's story about hubris and how the Freaks came to be. Momma Oaks made an unhappy sound but she didn't contradict him. Since Edmund had unintentionally reinforced the teacher's version of the story, I thought about the idea all the way back to the house.

As we went inside, I asked Edmund, "Do you believe Mrs. James's history?"

In the lamplight, he had a tired face and lines around his eyes from squinting at the leather he sewed all day. His hands were scarred too. He trudged to his chair in the sitting room and sank into it with a relieved sigh. Then he contemplated the question, one hand rubbing his chin.

"About how the Muties were born?" he asked.

"Yes, sir." That pleased him. He sat up straighter in his chair. I guessed people didn't often use an honorific for a man who made shoes. But to me, it seemed like an important job. Without Edmund, we'd all be barefoot and freezing in winter.

Seeming glad that we were talking, if not about the conversation topic, Momma Oaks went into the kitchen, leaving us to finish the discussion. She rattled pots and pans and the smell of dinner prompted a growl from my stomach. I had gotten accustomed to three meals a day, plus random snacks, in the quantity I desired.

Edmund nodded at thoughts he hadn't yet shared and then said, "It's true, so far as we know. The records are spotty, you understand, and in the early days, Salvation founders did away with knowledge they didn't approve of. They made a conscious choice to return to older, simpler ways in hopes of pleasing heaven better than what man had done before."

I studied him, puzzled. "So they had artifacts from the old world but they discarded them?"

"That's my understanding."

"But why?"

He pushed out a weary breath. "It's hard to explain, Deuce,

but I'll try. If you had a weapon you didn't fully understand, and you used it to hurt a lot of people, wouldn't it be better to destroy it so nobody else could make that same mistake?"

That, I understood. "Thank you. You've given me something to think about," I added, heading for the stairs.

I needed to change, so Fade wasn't left to make awkward conversation with Edmund. My nerves skittered as I ran up the steps. I couldn't say why this was different, as I'd eaten with Fade countless times as we traveled. But some part of me recognized there had never been an occasion like this one before.

In a great hurry I washed up and took my hair down from the plaits I'd adopted for fighting. The brown strands fell around my shoulders in unruly waves. I had a small mirror in my room, but as ever, I felt no connection to the girl who stood, playing with her reflection. I knew I wasn't as pretty as some girls at school, but that seemed irrelevant. I was strong and I could fight; surely that mattered more.

I scrambled into a green dress that I didn't hate, as it was simple. Wearing it instead of my own clothes would please Momma Oaks; she had sewn it for me without frills. Turning this way and that, I decided I was clean and presentable, so I went down the stairs at a run. Edmund was just answering the door, ushering Fade inside, and my heart thumped with silly pleasure. I'd spent all day with him, more or less, even if work hadn't permitted time for talking.

He looked different to me, somehow, since I'd accepted that our partnership had personal meaning. I'd always been fascinated by his face, but now I paid too much attention to his mouth when he spoke. I felt awkward, as if I had five thumbs on my hand, until he laced his fingers quietly through mine. Then I settled like a bird on just the right limb.

"We should see if she needs help," I said, tilting my head toward the kitchen.

Fade agreed with an alacrity that made me glad I'd suggested it. Had he once helped his mother in the kitchen? Clearly he knew what he was doing better than I did, so I took a seat at the table and watched them. *He should be here with the Oakses*, I thought. *Not me*. After the life I'd led, it wouldn't bother me to be used for my labor. It was, in fact, precisely what I was used to.

But Fade? I wanted him to be happy, more than anything.

Bittersweetness

Over a fine meal of fried meat and potatoes, my foster family made an effort to get to know Fade. They asked him what it was like down below, and then about life with his parents in the ruins. At first, I didn't think he felt comfortable talking, but the more Momma Oaks plied him with food, the less reticent he became.

Down below—and as we traveled—we'd survived on much less. So much to eat, freely given—and this was a basic meal by Salvation standards because it was left from last year's growing season. This seemed to me like a land of plenty. Part of me still couldn't believe Fade's dad had been right.

"So you lived in Gotham with your parents?" Momma Oaks asked. "I don't mean to touch on a painful subject, but how old were you when—"

"When they died?" Fade finished.

The older woman nodded. "Yes."

I was fascinated because I'd never asked him much about his life Topside, mostly because I had no faith he'd answer me. I had failed to believe him when he wanted to talk, and that left him faintly angry on the whole subject. So I looked forward to his answers.

"I was around six when my mom passed, eight or nine when my dad did."

Edmund and Momma Oaks shared a significant glance, though what about, I had no idea. "Were they . . . sick, son?"

Fade nodded, but from his expression, I sensed he didn't want to talk further. His face tightened; his eyes dropped to his plate. Discussing the illness would bring all those memories to life again; there was no call to salt a good meal with old sorrow.

So I said, "This roast is delicious. I've never had anything like it."

"It's pheasant," Momma Oaks explained. "Hunters went out yesterday and we bought one of the birds."

That gave me a pang. I would've liked to be included in a party that brought back meat for the settlement. It was what I ought to be doing, according to my training, not sitting in a schoolhouse. But we'd had that argument before when I first came to stay; and I had done well enough getting included in the summer patrols. *One step at a time,* I told myself. I couldn't expect to circumvent all their rules right away. It was enough that here, unlike down below, some citizens like Longshot and Momma Oaks were willing to hear about other ways of doing things.

I could live with the consequences. After all, the women of Salvation couldn't make life more complicated than they already did. Their whispers had followed me since my first day in town. Maybe they judged Tegan in the same fashion, and that was why she was trying so hard to fit in, making friends with their daughters. Whereas I chose to fight alongside their men.

After we ate, I did the cleanup while they chatted in the sitting room. The warm, soapy water felt soothing; it was a mindless task—scrub and rinse. Along with the sewing, this was one of my chores, and I was happy to do it in exchange for regular food in my belly. But I was starting to realize that even if I refused to help at all, Momma Oaks would still make sure I got fed. She was that kind of person.

It was full dark, so Edmund lit candles and lamps to brighten the gloom, a prettier glow than the torches down below, and they smelled better too. The air was all around fresher and cleaner here, even with Freaks stinking up the wasteland beyond. This was a cozy room, made more so by the warm yellow curtains on the window and the polished beams that framed the upstairs.

Momma Oaks settled in a chair next to her husband's, which left the small sofa for Fade and me. He didn't seem to mind, and he sat close enough to hold my hand. Since I'd kissed his cheek of my own free will before the whole town, guards and all, it seemed wrong to quail at this. My foster parents exchanged an indulgent look, amused at our affection, I suppose.

"We should have a story," the older woman said.

Edmund appeared amenable. "Which one, Mother?"

It struck me strange that he used that as an endearment for her, as she clearly wasn't his dam. But she didn't argue it, so I didn't either.

"You should tell the one about the founding of Salvation."

Inwardly, I groaned. Mrs. James had relayed this tale before, and I invariably wandered away mentally, before the long, boring recitation concluded. But I didn't want to hurt Edmund's feelings when I'd only just realized that in his way, he cared what became of me. He wasn't demonstrative like his wife, but he'd come out to the gate to make sure of my safety. So I squeezed Fade's hand, telling him silently to be polite, and he returned the pressure with a half-smile so lovely that it made me forget my unvoiced objections to an extra history lesson.

"In the old days," Edmund began, "humankind had horseless wagons that moved at incredible speeds and carriages that flew through the air. You could cross the whole country in just three hours if you took the flying carriage into the sky."

I shook my head in disbelief. We'd seen the remnants of the horseless wagons, rusted and useless, in the ruins they called Gotham. But I had never seen anything that made me think there had been flying carriages; I couldn't even imagine what they might look like. Birds, maybe? That sounded like the nonsense the Wordkeeper made up about the Topside world to keep us under control. Regardless, if Edmund had an imagination this powerful, his version might be more interesting than Mrs. James's, especially if it became more fairy story than history lesson.

"They had machines to do their work for them: solve problems, cipher numbers, and print writing. People grew lazy. They knew too many blessings, and so they lost the ability to appreciate what they had. They always wanted more, more, more, and that road," he intoned, "led down into darkness."

"What happened?" Fade asked, sitting forward, wide-eyed at the idea of machines that could do arithmetic.

Surely he didn't believe this. For a machine to count, it would need a head, wouldn't it? And fingers? That would make the thing like a mechanical person. I shook my head with a faint smile. Such fancies might be improbable, but they made for an interesting tale.

"There came endless wars of escalation. The dragon fought the eagle, and the hydra wrestled the great bear. They sent fiery death unto each other, but even that was not sufficient for the demon humankind had become. They created new weapons, time and again, dust and powder and gas—"

I was drawn, despite myself. "What's gas?"

"Like a mist," Momma Oaks answered. "Only instead of rising up out of the ground, it came from men, and it was filled with poison that seared the lungs."

Maybe that was why the Wordkeeper fixed on the idea that rain would scour our flesh from our bones. Stories had been passed down until they took a wrong turn, so poison gas became burning water. My tribe had been down below a long time, by any reckoning, and our reality lost touch with the actual state of the world.

"Some say it did worse than that." Suitably somber, Edmund went on with his tale. "The world fell to chaos, and the pride plagues came."

Momma Oaks answered the question before either of us could ask. I'm sure she read curiosity in our rapt expressions. "It was a disease that struck down great and small alike."

Fade and I shared a significant glance. Both his parents had died from something he thought had to do with the water they drank. It sounded as if a lot of people had. I wasn't positive pride had anything to do with it, but I didn't like to interrupt.

Edmund gained enthusiasm for his story. "People fled the ruins in droves, taking only what they could carry. Some of our brightest visionaries pushed north, where it was reputed to be safe and clean."

Like Fade's dad told him.

"They left behind the devices and idols that had brought destruction raining down upon them. In time, they were led to this site by the prophet Matthew, who predicted they would find a safe haven that had been built twice before, and in building here that sacred third time, for three is the trinity and the holiest of numbers, we would find sanctuary from the world's travails, so long as we cleave to the old ways and do not cast our eyes to habits that anger heaven."

I had no idea what that meant, nor any notion why heaven would care what went on so far below. But I'd managed to stay focused on the story this time, which I counted as a good thing. For once, I'd learned about history without passing out from boredom. That was a credit to Edmund's ability to spin a good yarn, and I said so.

"Thank you. That was way more interesting than Mrs. James." But I had a question. "I've heard the pride plagues gave rise to the . . . Muties." In my head, I still called them Freaks. "Is that true?"

"It's one belief," Edmund answered, nodding. "I can't say whether it's right."

"Now, we should go up," Momma Oaks said, casting a speaking glance at her husband, who rose immediately.

My foster father inclined his head. "We'll leave you two to talk a bit. Mind you don't stay up too late." With that, the older couple retired.

The ceiling creaked overhead, as they readied for bed. It was a homey sound, one that reminded me I wasn't alone. However unlikely, I had family in Salvation. Down below, only Stone and Thimble would have noticed my absence . . . and they wouldn't have mourned me long. Death was too much an accepted part of our world for it to be a shocking event.

"I like them," Fade said softly. Then he shifted closer, drawing me against his side as he had done to comfort me in the past. This time, it had other meanings, and I curled into him, accepting those new terms. His warmth felt delicious, sinking into my skin and making me indolent.

"They've been good to me." I paused, thinking about the story Edmund told. "Do you think there's any truth to it?"

"What part?"

"The world being like it is as some kind of punishment?"

He shook his head. "My dad never mentioned it. And he was right about a lot of other things. So it seems like it's just something that happened."

"Then why do you think they tell the story that way?"

Leaning his head against mine, he contemplated the question. He rubbed his cheek against my hair, and I was glad I had taken it down, so he could feel its softness, even if it wasn't bright burnished like some. At last he answered, "People try to make sense of things, and if they don't know the answers, they make them up, because for some, a wrong answer is better than none."

That rang true, as it echoed what I had been thinking about the Wordkeeper earlier. "I guess. But I'd rather have the truth, even if it was uncertain."

"That's because you're a brave and honest soul."

"Aren't you?" I asked.

"I try to be."

Which wasn't the reply I expected, necessarily, but he distracted me by cupping my cheek in his hand and kissing me. His mouth tasted sweet from the cider he'd had at supper, and it was hot on mine, delicate and delicious. One kiss turned into several; he ran his hands over my back, pressing me close. I touched his jaw, feeling his movements as he kissed me. Then I slid my hands into his hair, silky and cool, sliding through my fingers. The heat escalated until I couldn't sit still, and I fought the urge to climb on top of him. By the time he pulled free, he was shivering as if he had a fever. Worried, I touched his brow, and he gave a shaky laugh.

"I'm not sick, Deuce. You don't know your own charm."

My charm? I hadn't been aware I had any. *It must be the dress*, I thought.

"Hm."

I felt shaky, fluttery in ways that embarrassed me, like I could never get close enough to him, no matter how hard I tried. The warmth of his palms on my back made me want to arch like a sleepy cat. So I drew away, partly in self-defense, and left only my hand in his. From his expression, he understood the tactical retreat, but his fingers stroked mine as if to keep those sensations alive. Tingles spread from my fingertips up my arms to sharp little sparks in my elbows.

"Do you like it here?" he asked.

"In Salvation or with the Oakses?"

"Both. Either."

I nodded. "It's different, and some of their beliefs don't make sense, but overall, I do, very much."

"Then you're not sorry."

In his dark eyes, I saw another question, so I shook my head. "Not anymore. I wouldn't go back if I had the option. I have more freedom here."

A sigh escaped him, as if he had been worried that I wished I'd never left the enclave. I hadn't done that for him, though. I'd sacrificed myself so that my friend Stone wouldn't be sent on the long walk. The only regret I had was that I hadn't been able to explain to my brat-mate that I'd made a false confession to save him.

Fade took my hand between both of his and bowed his head over it, so a lock of night-black hair tumbled over his brow, hiding his eyes. "Can you explain why you spent so much time with Stalker if you weren't—if you don't—"

"If I didn't give him exclusive kissing rights?" I suspected he was asking a different question, but I couldn't identify its nature.

He glanced up with a relieved nod. "That. Can you?"

"He made it easy," I said, wondering if that was clear enough. "He was always around, and I got tired of my own company."

His brow went up. "So that's all I have to do? Show up?"

"It's a start," I muttered.

For a moment I thought he might get mad, but he laughed. "Well, I wasn't doing that. I gave up too easy, I guess."

"I didn't even know . . ." I trailed off, struggling to put my confusion into words. "I didn't realize you believed something about us that wasn't true."

A frown lingered on his face, a trace of doubt. It was like he had some picture in his head, and he couldn't put it aside. I had made things clear, though. There were no secrets standing between us. Then his expression cleared, as if he'd made some decision. Hopefully it was to stop being jealous for no reason.

"That was my mistake," Fade said, kissing me lightly. "I forgot that if you had something to tell me you'd say it straight out."

"I would."

He raised my hand to his mouth. "You don't recall, but as we came into Salvation, I told you how I felt. When you didn't reply in kind, I thought . . . well. Never mind."

"What did you say?" I asked, fascinated.

Fade laughed and shook his head. "I don't think so. You'll have to work to hear it again."

Whatever he'd said, I had a feeling it would be worth the wait. For the first time, I noticed that Fade had been sitting on the edge of the sofa the whole night. I thought back to when Edmund had been telling his story, and sure enough, he had been perched just like this. I wondered if that meant he was nervous, but before I could inquire, he changed the subject.

"Are you happier now that we're part of the summer patrols?"

I answered, "Of course. I need a purpose."

"I think everyone does."

Fade wrapped his arm about my shoulders, drawing me to his side, and I rested my head on his shoulder. "It felt good to fight beside you again."

His smile warmed me to the tips of my toes. "It did. I don't think anybody will question your ability to hold your own now."

He was right; I'd earned my place. Despite the day's losses and my quiet worry, I felt good about that part. "Do you remember when we go out next?"

"Two weeks, Longshot said. The seeds need time to take root. After that, we'll patrol regularly so the growers can tend the fields."

"Remove plants that don't belong," I guessed, "And make sure birds aren't eating the green shoots."

"That's what he said."

If today had been any indication, this task would keep us busy all season. We could expect more Freak attacks, and they might shock us with their capacity for planning. I wished I knew what form that animal cunning might take.

He pushed to his feet, then. "I should go. The Oakses trusted us to have some privacy, and I don't want to give them a reason not to invite me over again."

"Good night, Fade." I stretched up to kiss him.

The farewell lasted longer than I intended. With some effort, he pulled back, breathless, his hands curling into fists so he didn't reach for me again. "I *really* have to go now. Before I forget all the reasons why."

I went up to bed after he left . . . but guilt over the way I'd treated Stalker wouldn't let me sleep. I expected a tap on my window tonight, and I unlatched it because he deserved an explanation. I couldn't continue being a coward. Half an hour later, he slid inside and landed lightly. My room was candlelit, throwing long shadows. At once I saw that his anger had died into quiet confusion.

He stayed near the window, not approaching me. "I only came because I want to understand. You were lonely? You were using me?"

"No. We're friends . . . and sparring partners. That's what we always have been . . . and still are."

"You didn't make it feel like that," he snapped. "Or at least, you gave me the impression it might be more someday."

"I'm sorry."

"This hurts," he said wonderingly, as if he couldn't have imagined the feeling before I inflicted it on him.

"I didn't mean to."

He laughed, a bitter sound. "That's all right, then." Stalker climbed halfway through the window, just about done with the conversation—and me. But he turned for a final, parting shot. "He won't make you happy, dove. He's soft in ways you and I aren't. Ultimately, you're going to break him."

As I lay in bed, unable to sleep, those words echoed in my ears and I feared to my core that Stalker was right.

Bigwater

egan came to visit me a week later, and I felt glad of the break, as I was mending with Momma Oaks.

Of us all, my friend had changed the most in Salvation. She hadn't been as pale as Fade and I had to start with and her skin was naturally darker than Stalker's. Months after our arrival, her complexion took on a coppery cast, which complemented her dark curls prettily. She wore them piled on her head in an intricate style I couldn't hope to replicate, and she had on a new yellow dress that Mrs. Tuttle had commissioned from Momma Oaks.

I wondered if Tegan felt ready to resume our friendship. I'd missed her. Since Fade and Stalker wanted to kiss me, I couldn't talk to them about certain things. With my foster mother's blessing, the two of us fetched drinks and snacks, then went out to the swing. For several moments, only the squeak of the chain filled the silence.

In the distance, I heard men arguing, though not angrily, followed by the peal of children's laughter. Salvation had a different atmosphere from College's. Down below, it was tighter run—and there was less time for casual conversation. With our limited resources, however, it had to be that way. Here, people talked to each other more for the sake of it, exchanged news and tidbits of gossip without fear of censure.

"I'm sorry if I hurt your feelings when . . ." She trailed off, knowing I'd understand what she meant. "I just had so much to think about. First, it was my leg, and once I got better, there was school. I felt like I had to focus on fitting in, and—"

"I don't." Apart from my fellow guards, people had made that clear.

"You make your own rules. I respect that, but I'm not you. I want folks to like me. I love it here."

"I don't expect you to walk my path," I said.

She smiled. Over the past months, she'd put on some weight, so she no longer looked fragile. Clearly her foster parents had been feeding her properly, but despite their care, Tegan limped more than Thimble—and the thought of my old friend sent pain shooting through my chest. I didn't know what had happened to her or Stone, and maybe I never would. However, Tegan would get better as her leg healed; it wasn't a permanent disability. She was already stronger than she had been.

Ruthlessly, I put the past where it belonged and asked, "Are you still working with Doc?"

She nodded. "I've learned a lot. He says I have a real knack and I might be able to take over doctoring someday."

"You don't mind dealing with sick and injured people?" That required a fortitude I didn't possess.

"No. It makes me feel good, actually. With Doc's help, I'm learning how to make a difference."

At the school back in the ruins, I remembered Stalker yelling how she had no useful skills. He couldn't say that anymore.

"How does Mrs. Tuttle feel about it?"

A faint sigh escaped her. "At first, she wasn't wild about the idea. She said certain parties wouldn't approve, but Doc thinks it won't do any harm."

It sounded to me like Salvation could use some shaking up. New blood with fresh ideas might be just what the town needed. "I'm sure you'll make a fine healer."

She went on, "Anyway, I just didn't want you to think I'd forgotten what we talked about. Or the fact that I wouldn't even be here, if it wasn't for you."

"Fade too." If he hadn't carried her most of the way through the wilderness, Tegan wouldn't have survived. Stalker had taken a turn too, but I doubted she cared to be reminded that she owed him even a small portion of her gratitude. On the scales between them, it was inadequate for what she'd endured with the Wolves. Disquiet shivered through me.

In Tegan's place, I would've fought until I died. Nobody would've touched me while I still drew breath, so there wouldn't have been any unborn brats to lose . . . yet I would've died. Her path of quieter resistance led to survival through suffering. Tegan wasn't a Huntress, so according to enclave rules, she would've likely been a Breeder if we'd found her, because as Stalker had judged, she had no skills and no visible defects. Yet in the enclave, Breeders didn't fight their roles.

Tegan had. That meant her mother had taught her that she didn't have to bear young for the benefit of the group. Such freedom seemed foreign . . . and irresponsible. Down below, no one ever hinted that my own desires could be more important than the good of the whole. But that didn't make Tegan mistaken; it meant the Wolves punished her. And that, I did believe, was wrong. So far as I could tell, nobody had invented the perfect system, and it was awful to hurt people who disagreed with you.

That enclave had done it too. The Wolves should have turned Tegan loose when they realized she wouldn't conform.

"You're quiet," she said, breaking my thoughts.

"Just thinking."

Her eyes widened. "Sounds serious."

"Nothing I want to talk about," I answered, figuring she didn't either.

Maybe she read the truth in my face because she accepted it without question; Tegan broached another subject instead. "I know you think the other girls are dumb, but you might like them if you gave them a chance."

I couldn't imagine that being the case, but I agreed because it would please her. "I'm sure they're fine."

Unfortunately, that concession opened the door to something else. Tegan's brown eyes brightened and sparkled. "Justine is having a birthday party today, and I asked if I could invite you."

I recollected that Justine was a girl who loved making sport of me when I read during class—and she often sent boys to harass me at school—so this was the last thing I wanted to do, but Tegan seemed set on the idea. She'd trusted me enough to follow me out into the wilderness, though, so I could attend this party for her.

"What's a birthday?" I asked.

Tegan blinked at me. "The day you were born. You celebrate and people give you gifts. When my mom was alive, she threw a little party for me."

That idea seemed outlandish. "Why would people give you presents for something that was none of your doing?"

It wasn't like earning a name. I'd gotten gifts on my naming day because I survived for fifteen years, long enough to deserve them. That, I understood. This tradition made no sense at all.

"Because they care about you," Tegan said, seeming to realize I wasn't joking.

"But every single year?"

"Of course." She fought a smile.

I tried to wrap my head around it. "Maybe it's for surviving that long?" That seemed almost logical.

"That's . . . one way of looking at it."

"I'll be expected to bring something?" Comprehension of a custom wasn't necessary for participation. Since this would make Tegan happy, it was a small thing.

Tegan nodded. "That would be polite."

"All right. When?"

"This afternoon, I'll come by for you. It'll be *so* much fun. I didn't think life could be this good again." She was so happy, glowing, from the prospect of this party.

I wished I could ask for my club back, as she'd never use it again, but that went against all the rules of generosity. Maybe I could make another one. There was enough wood up here, for sure.

Shortly thereafter, Tegan left, and I went in search of Momma Oaks. She would know what a girl like Justine wanted. As it turned out, she did; and she went with me to the shop to help me make a good purchase. In the end, I took away some ribbons for Justine's hair. It was nothing I'd want, but my foster mother seemed convinced the girl would like them.

"It does me good to see you making friends and settling in," she said.

This was Tegan's doing, not mine, but I let the mistaken impression stand. "This is all pretty new."

"You're doing fine. And I'm proud of your place on the summer patrol." As we walked, I noticed sidelong glances and women whispering. "But not everyone feels the same. I want you to be careful."

I took a second look at the ladies paying me too much attention, and I agreed; those weren't approving stares. This wasn't news, since their judgment had been present from the first, but the awareness seemed angrier now. Frowns followed us along the main street, leaving me with the fear that doing what pleased me best might cause trouble for people who had been kind to me. Maybe if I tried to fit in and made the daughters like me, their mothers would care less that I held a position traditionally occupied by men.

It almost killed me to ask, "Do you want me to quit?"

"No," Momma Oaks said sharply. "I don't believe that superstitious nonsense, even if it's part of the town charter."

She'd lost me. "What do you mean?"

"About how the pride plagues were drawn down. That women must stay to women's work, or heaven will smite us again."

"Really?" I didn't know what I found harder to credit—that such nonsense had been written down or that people in Salvation believed it.

With the increased Freak activity, which Longshot had said was unnatural, it wouldn't take much for these people to start blaming me for their misfortune. Whether there was any truth to it or not, I accepted that flaw in human nature. Topside or down below, they always needed someone to blame. We walked home in silence, her distracted, me contemplative, and as we came in the door, Momma Oaks suggested a few improvements to my appearance.

To please my foster mother, I let her twist my hair. She used a bowl of water and strips of rag; and left them in for several hours, during which time I wrestled with the mending. In comparison to needlework, the outing sounded better all the time.

"Are you excited about going to Justine's house?" she asked as we worked.

"Not really." Lying went against my natural grain.

"Why not?"

"I just don't fit in with them. They giggle when I'm reading at school because I'm so old but I do worse than girls half my age."

Yet for Tegan, I'd go. I'd try to make people like me, using an ability other than stabbing monsters with my knives. If that wasn't a mark of true friendship, I couldn't imagine what one might be.

Momma Oaks leveled a steady look on me. "Well, her dad's an important man, practically runs the whole town. So it'll help if Justine likes you." She set aside the skirt with the ripped hem. "It's time for me to finish your hair."

"Fantastic," I muttered.

Against my better judgment, she pinned a knot of curls on top of my head, letting the rest spill down my back. I felt ridiculous . . . and if there was trouble, I assuredly couldn't fight. This time, I left off the trousers and knives off beneath my skirt, though I felt naked with the fabric swishing against my bare legs.

Tegan returned that afternoon, and she clapped her hands when she saw me. "You look perfect!"

After a short farewell, I took the small birthday parcel and followed Tegan out into town. I had no idea where we were going, but it didn't matter. She chattered about how much I was going to like everyone, once they had a chance to get to know me. I wasn't so sure, but I was willing to put forth the effort if acquiring a slew of female friends could offset the possible trouble from my place in the summer patrols.

"Justine," Tegan called. "You remember Deuce from school?"

Justine Bigwater was a pretty girl with a round face, wide blue eyes, and a crop of sunny curls. When she smiled, as she was doing now, she developed dimples in each cheek. She looked sweet, but the expression in her eyes made me want to take a step back, mostly because it reminded me of Silk's, just before she set down some awful punishment. But then the look vanished in the wake of simple delight, so maybe I was just nervous. I handed over her package with a mumbled wish for happiness on her birthday, and she took my present to set it with the others.

The Bigwater family was important—or so Momma Oaks had given me to understand. If I'd interpreted her words right, her father was Whitewall's equivalent; he had been the chief elder down below. So if I wanted to stay in Bigwater's good graces, I couldn't afford to offend Justine.

Justine's yard had been transformed for the gathering, set with tables and chairs and bright colored streamers. A man I knew by sight but not name played a lively tune on his pipe while girls chattered in knots of two and three. Feeling wholly out of place, I stuck close to Tegan, knowing it didn't matter at all here how good I was with my knives. Here, only talking mattered, and I'd never been the best at that. She led me to a group of our classmates, all strangers. Small of me, maybe, but I hadn't bothered getting to know people who chortled while I read.

Fortunately—and I suspected by design—Tegan greeted them one by one, using their names, and I made a note of who they were. The tall one, Hannah, smiled at me. "I see you eating all the time with that scarred boy. Is he sparking you?"

Uncertainty welled up. I didn't know that word. If Fade was here, I'd look to him for clarification, but I preferred not to reveal my ignorance to girls I hardly knew.

Tegan answered for me, her voice sharp. "Deuce has better taste than that."

Which made me bristle on Stalker's behalf. I felt pulled in three directions, and as if I would wind up being disloyal, no matter whose side I chose. I understood why she hated him, but it was hard for me to blame him when he hadn't been taught otherwise. The things I'd done on the elders' orders filled me with hot shame now. I had killed an innocent man as a test of loyalty, and I'd let them murder a brat in cold blood. My own hands weren't clean. Maybe Tegan's were; and she'd never hurt anyone who didn't deserve it. I couldn't help what I'd done before I learned it was wrong. I could only do better in the future. And the same held true for Stalker, whether anybody else believed it or not. Whether he could rise above the person he'd been in the gangs, well, that rested squarely in his own hands.

Tegan had asked me not to tell anyone what she went through. These shallow girls would think she was damaged, unclean, and that was their mistake. What she had survived made her stronger, far tougher than they could imagine. But I understood why she wanted to fit in and keep her secrets. I'd guard them with my life.

"He looks scary," Merry said then. She was shorter than me with straight red hair and a mess of freckles.

I nodded. "He can be."

"I heard you gave my brother, Frank, a whipping." That came from a girl who had just walked up. I recognized her because she looked like Frank, dark haired and slim, but we'd never spoken before. She giggled. "I wish I could have been there to see it. I'm sure he had it coming."

I smiled back, relief feeling warm as sunshine. "It wasn't personal. I just wanted to show Longshot what I could do."

"Tegan says you've killed a million Muties," Merry put in.

"I doubt that," I mumbled, blushing.

"But you have fought them," Hannah pressed.

I nodded. "It was my job."

Frank's sister shivered, rubbing her hands along her bare arms. "I can't believe you crossed the wilderness by yourself."

"There were four of us," I pointed out.

"That's right," Hannah said. "Tegan told us how terrifying it was. I don't think I would have survived."

Nadia, a thin, quiet girl who reminded me of Thimble with the intensity of her expression, murmured, "Did you really live in a hole?"

"Not exactly. It was more of a series of tunnels."

A couple girls laughed, thinking I was joking, but I suspected this wasn't how the party should go. I was supposed to be making friends, not reminding them how different I was. But before I could change the subject, Justine came up, unhappiness percolating in her eyes. The blue fire there said she blamed me for the fact that everyone wasn't clustered around her.

"What are we talking about?" she asked with false cheer.

"How dangerous it was for Tegan and Deuce getting to Salvation," Merry supplied, not seeing the danger.

"Oh," Justine breathed. "Yes, I expect normal girls wouldn't have stood a chance out there. And it wasn't prudent traveling with boys like they did, either." Her superior manner rubbed me the wrong way, but it was her party, and I was her guest. I had manners enough to know I shouldn't whip her arm behind her back and grind her face in the dirt.

Even though I kind of wanted to.

"Sometimes we don't get a choice," I murmured. "We do what we have to."

Hannah nodded. "I think so every time I do my chores."

From there, the girls then started talking about what kind of party they wanted for their birthdays, relieving me of the necessity of paying attention. As long as I nodded and smiled and looked interested, that was all they seemed to require from me. We ate a little, played some silly games, and then had cake, after which point Justine opened all of her presents—and there were a pile, bigger than anything I'd ever seen. And most of the gifts were brand-new, not scrounged. There were ribbons and hairbrushes, hand-carved combs, shiny bottles, a pretty new blouse with a curly collar, and a few things that I couldn't even name. Such plenty gave me a little pang. Down below, I'd seldom owned anything that hadn't belonged to someone else first, just my knives and club.

I wondered if Justine knew how lucky she was to have such good friends, and to have a family who would go to such trouble for her. Even here, I was on the outside, looking in, and trying to make sense of customs that seemed strange to me. *This,* I realized, watching her disinterest as she pushed small parcels aside to get to bigger ones. *This is what Edmund was talking about when he said the people had too many blessings.* The thought unnerved me because, from here, it was only half a step to people blaming Justine for the Freak attack that afternoon. Whatever reason the monsters had for hating humanity, I was sure it had nothing to do with a girl's party, or how many presents she received.

But others might not see that.

Sleepover

Walking home with Tegan after the party, I listened to her chatter with half an ear. It wasn't until she tapped me on the shoulder that I realized she'd asked me a question. "So did you like everyone? Merry said she's going to ask your foster mom if you can spend the night sometime this summer."

"They were nice," I said, wondering why I'd want to sleep at Merry's house when I had a bed of my own.

"Nicer than you expected?"

I nodded.

She bounced a little as we walked. "I just knew it would work out if you put in some effort and stopped skulking around with Stalker."

"He's not as bad as you think," I said quietly. "And he's completely alone."

"I never understood why you spent a minute with him when you had Fade staring at you all the time."

I stopped, incredulous. "For the last two months, he hardly said a word to me. He was always with you."

"Not *with* me. You didn't think—"

"I don't anymore."

"Deuce," she said seriously, moving again. "I may never get close to a boy. I'm not saying that to make you feel sorry for me. I'm happier than I've been since my mom died. I like the Tuttles and I feel safe with them. But Fade and me?" She shook her head. "Even if he felt that way about me, I couldn't. I need time to heal . . . and to accept that not all boys are like the ones in the gangs."

"They do seem more civilized," I offered, as we neared my house.

She nodded. "Here, they bring posies from their mother's gardens to girls they like. They ask your father's permission to walk out with you."

I hadn't known that. I wondered if Fade did . . . and what it meant, exactly. "Has anybody talked to Doc Tuttle about you?"

Tegan shook her head. "I haven't given anyone the necessary encouragement. Anyway," she continued, "it was always you. Fade talks about you with me sometimes, you know?"

A burst of warmth flared in the pit of my stomach. "I had no idea. What . . . what does he say?"

"How you ran through the tunnels together, hiding from Freaks, and watching each other's backs. Fade told me you saved him down there."

"He saved me too." So many times, and in ways I couldn't describe, as if I had been dying of a wound I didn't know I'd taken.

"He also said it was the first time he felt safe since he joined your enclave."

Our walk ended in front of the Oakses' house. I noticed anew how cozy and nicely kept it was, not fancy like the Bigwater place, but it suited me fine. Taking my cue from Tegan and what she'd said about spending the night with Merry like that was a *good* thing, I murmured, "I can ask Momma Oaks if you can stay over, if you like. My bed's big enough."

"That would be fun."

I ran inside and found my foster mother in the sitting room with a blanket spread across her lap. It was a particular kind of cover pieced together from scraps of fabric and it was astonishingly lovely. I'd be afraid to use it; that's how fine it was.

"I asked Tegan to stay the night. Is that all right?"

"It's a little late if it isn't," she grumbled, "since you already extended the invitation." But I could tell by the twinkle in her eyes that she didn't mind. "Of course, she's a nice girl. Did you check with the Tuttles?"

"We'll go do that now."

I lifted my skirt and darted out, ignoring her admonition not to run. Momma Oaks's quiet laughter followed me. "And to think I always wanted a daughter."

Tegan raised both brows. "Well?"

"It's fine. Do you want me to come with you?"

She shook her head. "I'll be back in half an hour or so. If I *don't* return, you'll know Doc found more important work for me to do."

"I hope not." As that would mean someone was sick or injured.

"Me too. I could use a night off."

I went back in the house to find my foster mother in the kitchen. A sweet and spicy scent filled the air already. If I was having a guest over, then she needed to make the evening meal special, no matter that we'd eaten cake at the party.

It was pointless, but I tried to talk her out of it. "You don't have to go to any trouble. I just want the company."

"You don't understand mothers at all," she said gently.

"I guess not. I never had one."

Momma Oaks touched my cheek. "I know, Deuce. Just accept

that I do for you because I want to. If I didn't, I wouldn't. It's just that simple."

For some reason, a lump swelled in my throat. "Thank you," I said thickly.

After asking her if she needed my help—and she declined—I went upstairs to tidy my room. It wasn't bad, usually, but the hair curling before the party resulted in damp rags all over, and my clothing wasn't as ordered as I preferred. By the time Tegan arrived, I had everything back in place.

I ran lightly down the stairs to greet her. "What do you want to do?"

Tegan stepped into the kitchen doorway, rapping her knuckles to draw my foster mother's attention. "Do you have a game cupboard?"

"I most certainly do. Let me show you."

I tilted my head, curious. She'd never mentioned it to me, but I hadn't known to ask for it, either. Inside the bureau in the sitting room, there was a cabinet full of interesting odds and ends. Tegan drew out four wooden boxes and we took them to the sofa to see what they contained. She unpacked the contents one by one, her expression brightening.

"Do you know what these are?" I asked.

"Most of them." She touched each one and named them for my benefit. "Connect Four. Tangram. Cribbage. Holey Moley. Checkers. This looks like a chess set, but that's a pretty complicated game. I'm not a very good player."

"I am," Edmund said as he came into the room.

On impulse, I pushed to my feet and greeted him with a kiss on the cheek. He was smiling when I sat down next to Tegan again.

"Could you teach us?" She tilted her head in a pleading look.

Edmund nodded. "Let me get washed up and change my clothes. If you girls still want to learn when I get back, I'll go over some basic strategies with you."

"Strategy." I turned the word over in my head. It sounded as if this game might prove valuable in other regards, if it sharpened my ability to plan. I might be able to apply what I learned about chess in a martial fashion.

When I said as much to Tegan, she shook her head and laughed. "You never think about anything but fighting, do you? Let's play this while we wait. It's not hard." She took the lattice and set it up, explaining that I fit my pieces into a slot and my goal was try to get four of them in a row before she did.

By the time Edmund joined us, I'd lost my first game of Connect Four, but I thought I had the hang of it. But it was time for our first lesson then; he proved an effective teacher, and soon Tegan and I knew enough about chess to try a match on our own. I was pondering my next move when Momma Oaks called us to dinner. It smelled delicious; she had cooked a dish where meat and vegetables were covered in cream sauce and encased in flaky pastry.

"This is *amazing*," Tegan said, after taking the first bite.

"It's my favorite. Thank you, Momma Oaks."

My foster mother lifted her fork with a satisfied smile. "It's enough that I'm cooking for people who appreciate me."

"*I* appreciate you," Edmund protested.

"Yes, dear, but you've been eating my food for years. You're not surprised by it anymore."

"That's true," he allowed. "I'd only be startled if it wasn't wonderful."

The older woman smiled. "You see, that's why I married him. He's such a smooth talker."

Tegan and I both laughed softly at their silliness, but it cast a warm glow over the meal that didn't fade even through the washing up. Once we finished eating, I picked up the games we'd left in the sitting room, and then I took a lamp, pausing to glance back at my foster parents. It was moments like these that made everything else worthwhile. Bad dreams and worse memories couldn't touch me now. I felt safe, but it was frightening too, because I had something lovely to lose. A nervous shiver rolled through me.

"We'll go up now, if you don't mind," I murmured.

"Of course not," Momma Oaks said. "You girls have a good gossip."

Tegan's tread behind me sounded uneven on the stairs. I led the way into my bedroom, set the lamp on my dresser, and closed the door. Then I made sure my window was latched and pulled the curtain. Since I didn't intend on going out again, I put on my nightgown and Tegan did the same. The two of us curled up on my bed, facing each other, legs crossed.

I spoke first. "How's your leg?"

She pulled up her nightdress and showed me the scar, cutting livid purple across her thigh. There were three dark dots beneath it; I studied those with curiosity.

"It looks better, right?" she asked.

"What happened there?" I indicated the marks beneath the initial wound.

"I don't remember Doc doing that, but I was out of my head with fever. Apparently he had to drain the wound, and since it was cauterized, he had to make three small incisions to let out the purulent fluid."

"Purulent?" I repeated.

"Infected."

"Did it hurt a lot?"

Tegan shrugged. "Probably. I don't remember much of the first week, though I know you stayed with me as much as they let you."

"How did he cure your fever?"

"He used a tea made of peppermint, yarrow, feverfew, and lemon balm. Nasty-tasting stuff."

I guessed those were the names of plants. "But it worked."

She grinned. "So it did. Doc was really relieved when I got well enough to complain about drinking it."

"What do you call your foster parents?" I wondered aloud.

"Don't laugh. But in private I call them Ma Jane and Papa Doc."

Tegan wouldn't wish to talk about her time with the Wolves, but I was curious about her. "What was your life before?"

"Before . . . the gang took me?" she asked carefully.

I nodded. "I remember my dam, but I don't know who my sire was. I just wondered what it was like for you."

She leaned back against the wall, her expression pensive. "When I was small, there were twenty of us. Four or five families."

"Where did you live? In the ruins?"

Tegan rubbed her eyes, as if they itched with tears, but when she took her hand away, they were dry. "In the university science lab. It was a good place to scavenge, central, and the building had lots of useful stuff. We grew our own plants for a while, just outside, on the lawn. There were all kinds of seeds."

"The gangs didn't bother you?"

"Not when there were more of us. I was pretty happy," she added softly. "I had my mom and dad, other kids to play with."

"What was life like?"

"We grew food. Prepared it. I helped in the gardens, mostly."

"You were a grower, then." It explained why the gangs found no use for her apart from breeding. They didn't plant things in the ground and wait for them to sprout; they scavenged and hunted to survive. "Why don't you volunteer for the summer harvest? I bet they could use you in the fields."

Tegan tilted her head in consideration. "I might, if it's slow for Doc. There's generally less sickness during warm weather."

I already knew how her happy life came to an end. People in their small colony got sick and died off, one by one. She lost her dad first, and eventually, it was just Tegan and her mom, running from the gangs instead of living safe and happy in the university science building. There was no need to make her relive that.

Yet I had other questions. "Do you ever wonder why some people take ill and die and others get well?"

"Yes," she replied fiercely. "And why some people never get sick at all. It seems there must be a system to it, but I don't know what that is. Neither does Doc."

"Frustrating."

"That's part of why I love working with him. I want to understand why the world works like it does."

"I hope you can figure it out," I told her.

"Me too."

That seemed to be my cue to turn down the covers. I dimmed the lamp, but not all the way, and then I got in bed. Tegan climbed in after me. As I'd told her, the bed was big enough that we shouldn't bother each other. It seemed miraculous that we didn't have to hunt our breakfast; someone would cook it for us when we woke up.

"You know the Oakses have a son who never comes to see them?" I spoke into the dark, rolling on my side to face her.

"Why not?"

I shook my head. "I'm not sure. They had a falling-out, but I don't know what it was about."

"That's too bad," Tegan said softly. "I'd give anything to see my parents again. I miss them so much."

"I know."

I hugged her in the dark but she didn't weep. This was a loss grown old and dull, like a knife left out in the rain. But Tegan returned the hug with full strength, and it made me feel important, worthy of her friendship even if I didn't come from perfect people. I'd bet none of her new friends received such confidences.

"Do you miss anyone from the enclave?" she asked eventually.

"My brat-mates, Thimble and Stone."

Tegan propped herself on one elbow, curious. "What's a brat-mate?"

"Someone who's raised up in the dorm, the same time as you. Brats often bond into packs of three or four and stay close, even after the oldest ones are grown and earn their names."

"Your brat-mates were older than you?" she guessed.

I nodded. "They left me behind . . . and it was awful. Lonely." I realized then that I'd never told her the whole story. So much of our time and energy while we traveled had been devoted to survival.

"Then you had to leave them for good."

In a rush I explained things to her fully—the rules about hoarding, the blind brat, how the elders treated Fade, Banner's alleged suicide, and how the headman routinely sent people on the long walk to put fear into the enclave's heart, which led to Stone being accused of a crime he didn't commit. By the time I finished, I had a knot in my chest, and Tegan's hand rested on my hair, not petting, just making contact, like she knew it was all about to overwhelm me. I hadn't grasped that it still hurt so much, but the ache lessened as I fell quiet. Sharing helped.

"So that's why you left. That sounds pretty horrible, Deuce."

"It was," I said softly. "I just didn't realize that while it was going on."

She sighed. "Because you weren't raised to know better."

A verbal reply was beyond me. So I nodded.

"In the ruins when you told me to give Stalker a clean slate, I hated you for it. But I think . . . I finally understand. Maybe he didn't see that he was doing wrong, until later. Maybe he knows now. I'll . . . try to judge him according to his actions."

"I don't care if you ever forgive Stalker," I said quietly. "That's between the two of you."

"Thank you for that. Thanks for being my friend." It was good knowing I had the power to comfort her too.

I hugged her words close to my heart as I fell asleep.

Disaster

A week after the party, I convened at the barracks before dawn along with the rest of the summer patrol. The days were warming up, and the light lasted longer; but for now, Longshot hoped to convey the planters safely to the fields under the cover of darkness. There had been a few runs at the walls over the past two weeks, but nothing like the numbers when we'd stepped outside. These recent strikes felt more like the Freaks were testing our resolve than really trying to get inside the town.

Or maybe they hoped we'd run out of ammo. But Salvation had been making its own gunpowder for ages, and the smith who worked with Stalker knew how to make bullets for the rifles, so it wasn't likely that would ever happen.

Unless they got smart enough to attack the trade caravans that left for the other settlements in the fall. I forced that thought aside. Even if they were no longer creatures of pure instinct, as they had been, Freaks couldn't be that crafty.

Longshot held the opinion that we'd decimated their population, and the rest of the season should pass uneventfully. I had seen too many shifts in Freak behavior to put my faith in that rationale, but I didn't contradict our leader. He had more years of experience in this particular war, so I contented myself with following orders. That had been my lot down below too, and at least Longshot appeared to have a good head on his shoulders.

That wouldn't stop me from keeping my weapons ready, however.

Fade greeted me by quietly taking my hand. Though I wasn't comfortable with open affection, I didn't pull back, and my forbearance paid off when he smiled in delight. I'd never get enough of his smiles, as I hadn't seen many of them. Down below, he was known for his intense personal reserve and brooding air.

Stalker strode past us without a glance in greeting, joining the older guards, who seemed to like him well enough. I managed not to follow him with my eyes, but I heard his words in my head. *He won't make you happy, dove. He's soft in ways you and I aren't. Ultimately, you're going to break him.*

I won't, I told myself. I, too, was softer than a Huntress ought to be. I'd proven it time and again, so that made me a perfect match for Fade. Didn't it?

Pushing those doubts aside, I fell into formation as the party moved toward the gate. There were no wagons this time, just the planters walking inside our line for protection; they carried the tools of their trade: shovels, spades, hoes, and buckets for ferrying water from the lake that lay beyond the fields. In the past weeks, it hadn't rained as much as the seedlings required, so in addition to weeding, we'd also be irrigating the fields to make sure there was food for the winter. Those were new words to me—"weeding" and "irrigation"—but I gleaned their meanings from the context.

The group shared a tense and sober mood . . . and after what happened last time we left the walls, I understood why. I slid my knives free from their thigh sheaths, attracting a glance from

Fade. Then he nodded, acknowledging my instincts. With a shake of his head, he told me he disagreed with Longshot; the trouble wasn't over.

Instead, I had the dark and unsettling impression that it was just beginning.

We marched out to the first field without seeing a single Freak, but the reason became clear. They'd already destroyed everything. Fragile green plants had been torn from the ground, and they lay dying, tiny roots exposed to the air. They had raked the neat furrows repeatedly with their claws until it was impossible to tell this had once been a site of renewal and hope.

To make matters worse, the Freaks had left us a sign, an unmistakable offering. We had lost six on our last patrol, two growers and four guards. Now there were six heads, mounted on stakes—just reasonably straight branches, true, but it reflected a forethought that chilled me to my marrow. These poor folk had been half consumed, faces and all, and the putrid, ragged skin showed slices of bone. They'd removed the brains, to eat I assumed, and left gaping holes in the back of the skulls.

A cry went through the growers as they noticed, and a few fell to their knees, some vomiting up their breakfasts, and others weeping for the lost. The guards held themselves more stoic, so their revulsion revealed itself only in the way they cut their eyes to the sides, unable to look on the desecration for more than a few seconds at a time. As for me, I took a long look, for this was the new face of an old enemy.

As warnings went, this one was masterful. Not only did it instill terror and revulsion, it also told us there were more Freaks hidden nearby. Watching. Waiting. And we had no idea of their numbers. Longshot thought we got most of them, but some had clearly hung back, then crept out after we left and eaten our dead. Horror crawled up my spine like a many-legged insect, insidious and inexorable.

"They're trying to starve us out," I said softly to Fade.

He nodded. "That's not simple instinct. That's—"

"Strategy," Stalker finished. It was the first time he'd spoken to me since he came in my window, but apparently he judged this situation worth setting aside his personal grievances.

"I don't like this," I muttered.

"It's a caution," Stalker went on. "The gangs post similar messages, just not with heads." He didn't elaborate on the difference, and I was glad.

Genuine fright flared. Though there was plenty of food now, one bad growing season could destroy Salvation's prosperity. Momma Oaks had a small kitchen garden for us to augment the crops planted for the whole town—and of which each family received a share—but it wouldn't be enough to last the winter. Other families didn't have the space or inclination to plant anything at all.

"What do we do?" a grower asked Longshot. "Do we clean up and sow a second time?"

It was an excellent question. But now that the Freaks had worked out the importance of this site, they could easily return. More substantial measures were required, and by his expression, Longshot knew it. He conferred quietly with other patrol leaders—all seasoned men who spent their winters guarding the wall. Finally, after some argument, and with the rest of us watching the horizon and sniffing the air, they came to an accord.

"We'll put the problem to the council," Longshot said. "Something's shifted in the way the Muties act. No point in hangin' around here waitin' to be ambushed. Let's get back and call an emergency meeting."

As we returned to town, people discussed the problem in low tones.

"We could build a wall," one of the growers suggested.

Another laughed with quiet scorn. "It's all we can do to get out for planting and tending, idiot. How would the patrols protect builders *and* planters? And you know how much trouble it would be to fell and haul that much timber?"

I followed the man's gaze out to the dark forest that bordered Salvation. Plenty of wood, sure, but it was also the staging ground for the last Freak incursion.

A second guard shook his head. "You couldn't pay me enough to go in there, even to protect men sawing down trees for the good of the town."

His misgivings made sense. There had to be another way.

"We could put a permanent guard on the fields," someone else offered.

That sounded more doable to me, but it would be dangerous. There was no shelter, just the endless threat of a sudden, gruesome death. The isolation and uncertainty could crack a lesser soul.

It went without saying that I'd volunteer. I was distracted, trying to work out how I'd present this to Momma Oaks when the world exploded with tooth and claw.

The Freaks hit us at the gate this time; it was quite a process to get the wheels and pulleys moving so our party could pass through. They came in low, around the sides of the walls, instead of a direct assault. These monsters had learned a measure of cunning; they had camouflaged themselves—even their hideous smell—with natural earth and greenery, so when they came at us from the sides, they were already closer than anyone could have imagined. They must have hunkered down during shift change and waited for us to return.

Another two minutes' better timing, and they'd have breached the walls, I thought, fear spiking in my head.

My knives slid into my hands by instinct alone. Those of us who excelled at hand-to-hand, including Fade and Stalker, planted ourselves before the gates while the other guards fired. It was pure madness with the report of rifles, howling, growling Freaks, snarling their intentions through blood-frothed mouths.

"Lock it down!" Longshot shouted.

And the gates groaned as guards towed on the ropes, slowly hauling the heavy wood back toward them. In their haste, one of them pulled too hard, unbalancing the mechanism and a metal piece sheared with a horrid twang. Behind me, the gate stood open by two feet, and over my head, men cursed as they ran for replacement parts.

The planters ran, screaming, toward that small gap. They thought walls still represented safety, but there was none outside of your own strength. I'd believed it down below, and I still did as I received the first rush, Freaks maddened by the possibility of success—and a feast greater than they'd ever known.

This is sheer cunning, and they have such numbers.

I became a creature of reflex and training, born to slash with my daggers. I fought three at once, wheeling away from claws and fangs. I knew firsthand how they could rend fragile human flesh—and how prone such wounds were to infection. My left blade opened one's throat, and I wheeled to take another, my spin low so that I sank my right knife into the Freak's belly. It keened, both clawed hands going to cover the wound, and its fellows paused to watch the death for seconds that cost them in other ways. But it was a gesture of respect that said the Freak I'd killed mattered to them. These weren't like the ones we'd fought in the tunnel, at the ruin of the iron carriage, who cared for nothing but the meat.

Fear boiled in my veins. I fought it even as I lashed at the Freaks. If I let this feeling grow, it would overwhelm me. I'd break and run, and if I did, others would. The battle would be lost. The Freaks attacked; therefore, they would die, or I would. It could end no other way.

My hands steadied.

None shall pass, I told myself. It was a vow in the silence of my own head. I shut out the external distractions, inner dread, and focused on my enemies. They were stronger than those I'd fought in the ruins, better nourished. They ate well in the wilderness, plenty of big, meaty game, which made me think they had another reason for attacking us. Certainly, we were a food source, but their hate-filled cries told me they viewed us as real enemies. It was a horrifying thought.

To them, we are the evil ones. We are the threat that must be exterminated.

The idea shook me so much that a Freak pushed me back, unbalancing my stance. Its claw raked a runnel in my stomach. I lost sight of the terrain around me and stumbled over the corpse of its fallen brethren. I landed hard, and my right dagger bounced out of my hand.

For this, I thought, *I deserve to die.* I'd failed in my training. Permitted my thoughts to break my concentration. The shame would kill me if this Freak failed. Nonetheless, I aimed my left dagger at its hamstring and sliced, driving it away from the killing strike.

In that extra moment, Stalker and Fade came from either side, cleaving the Freak nearly in two. They'd cleared a path to me, the dead falling in great waves behind them. Morning sunlight limned them, darkness and light, and they both offered me a blood-slicked hand to pull me to my feet. In that, I accepted help from them both, and I sprang up, away from my humiliation; they did not chide me. Stalker handed me my fallen weapon.

We went together back into the fight, and I focused. I stabbed and blocked, kicked and struck without consideration, without mercy. By the time we defeated the last of the desperate rush, we had lost five more guards. This time, at least the growers had gotten to safety—and we'd prevented the Freaks from pushing past us into Salvation. For long, terrifying minutes, we stood out front, crimson smeared and weary, waiting for those inside to finish repairs.

I trembled with exhaustion. Fade touched my chin lightly, drawing my gaze up to meet his. "Are you all right?"

"Not my most shining moment. But thank you for saving me." I directed my words to both of them, Stalker standing to one side. He nodded, but didn't approach, and I ached that I'd driven him away by choosing Fade, that we apparently couldn't have *anything* without the kissing. Sometimes I didn't understand boys at all.

At last, the gatekeeper called, "Come in!"

With Fade's help, I dragged a guard's body inside the wall, and others followed suit. We would not leave these men to be desecrated as the others had been. It seemed odd to me that I would find that offensive. After all, down below, we had routinely put our dead out to feed the Freaks. But they had never returned any of our offerings in such a hideous fashion. They ate until they could hold no more and then they left the rest for the tunnel creatures. Perhaps, then, it was the obvious loathing those poor impaled heads represented. I had never thought

Freaks capable of strong emotion, other than hunger, but it had become obvious that these were.

Once the gates closed behind us, the guards dropped the reinforcing timber. In the time I'd been here, I had never seen the great doors sealed in this way. Which established how unprecedented these attacks were. We'd warned them that the Freaks were changing, but even *I* didn't expect these tactics.

My heart thumped wildly in my chest, both in reaction to the fight and the alarm at the unknown. It seemed that the Freaks got smarter all the time, but *why?* Then again, if I could answer that question, I could rule the world. I puffed out a shaky breath and rubbed my hands along my arms.

"Any thoughts?" I asked Fade.

He shook his head. "If we could somehow study the Freaks, catch one or two and observe them, that might help."

I choked out a shaky laugh. "I'm sure that would go over well with the good folk of Salvation."

Fade trailed a finger down my cheek, and it came away tacky with blood. "You'll notice I'm not in any hurry to propose the idea to anyone but you."

I began, "Please tell me you're not suggesting—"

"No. I think all creatures have the right to be free, even those trying to kill us."

"And they're getting better at it all the time," I muttered, shivering.

In silence, I studied the people of Salvation for a moment. Gazing on their tired, hopeless faces, I thought, *They're not equipped to fight a war. Even their guards don't like leaving the walls.* And that was probably why I'd been included in the summer patrols, considering their feelings on proper women's work. Longshot's support wouldn't have been sufficient, otherwise, but they simply didn't have enough fierce Hunter spirits to protect everyone else.

This is your mission. This is why you survived the ruins and came Topside. Silk's voice rang unmistakably in my head, so clear that I looked around for her. The order roused the Huntress in me, spurring my desire to defend and my need for a purpose. The misery of Salvation's citizens only reinforced the calling. Word was already spreading, and people came in small groups to claim their dead. Quiet sobs filled the air, along with whispered fears and recriminations.

Fade wrapped an arm around my shoulders and drew me away, toward the well near the barracks. I understood his intention and we washed up in silence, listening to the distant drama of lives cut short. The wound on my stomach throbbed; it wasn't deep, but it required a bandage. As we returned, damp but clean, Longshot strode away, presumably to find Elder Bigwater.

It was beyond time for that council meeting.

Assembly

There was no building big enough to hold the combined mass of the concerned citizenry, so Salvation assembled on the green. It was a chaotic scene with everyone yelling at once and demanding answers. I stood at the back with Fade, interested in the outcome. Longshot had cornered Elder Bigwater and drawn him out.

This was the first good look I had gotten at Salvation's leader, since I wasn't important enough to merit his personal attention. He was a tall, thin man with cavernous cheeks, flesh sunken around the bone, and he had eyes deep-set beneath a protuberant brow. I guessed Justine took after her mother—and a good thing too. I couldn't imagine a young girl here faring well with that face.

Momma Oaks slipped up beside me, my foster father trailing in her wake as he often did. She checked me out in a visual inspection and then relaxed visibly when she realized I was all in one piece. Edmund smiled in greeting but didn't speak because the meeting was about to begin. Fade took my hand, and I drew some comfort from his presence, even if our safe haven had just suffered a tremendous blow. But I wasn't as unsettled as some, who wept quietly nearby; I had long ago internalized the lesson that safety was an illusion. That was one gift they'd given me down below.

"Quiet!" came sonorous tones from Elder Bigwater. He waited until everyone had stopped talking, gimlet gaze boring into those who didn't comply fast enough. "I collect there has been some difficulty with the spring planting."

"Eleven dead so far," a grower cried. "And nothing to show for our efforts!"

Elder Bigwater frowned. "I did not give you leave to speak. I'll hear the formal report from Karl before opening the matter for discussion."

Longshot summarized the situation much as I would have, sticking to the facts without judgment or embellishment. And when he finished, Elder Bigwater wore a darker look than sat comfortably on his hawkish features. He put me in mind of birds we'd encountered in the wilderness, black ones that hovered over fallen creatures in hopes of picking the flesh from their bones.

"It is, indeed, a dire dilemma," he said at last. "However, I am not interested in hearing you bewail our changed circumstances. If you have a workable solution, raise your citizen's token, and I will grant you the floor."

Citizen's token? I didn't have one. I exchanged a glance with Fade, who shook his head. Maybe it was age related, and we needed more birthdays before we'd be granted the right to speak in a public assembly. That didn't seem right. Age had nothing to do with how well my brain worked. At first, it was dead quiet, and then growers proposed some of the same ideas they'd offered on the way back to town.

The elder rejected the idea of enclosing the fields in another wall. "Unguarded walls are useless . . . and worse, it would grant them the opportunity to study close up and figure out how to climb over or destroy them. You." He nodded next at a planter who had his token in the air.

"We can't leave the fields unattended, it's clear," he said. "Guards need to be posted at all times."

"And who would be so . . . fearless?" By his hesitation, Elder Bigwater made it clear he meant foolish—that he thought this notion was no good, either.

But I didn't notice him solving the problem himself. He struck me as the sort of man who preferred to "lead" while everyone around him did the actual work and he reaped the benefits. The silence built. It seemed nobody would volunteer to risk himself like that.

In that moment, I felt vaguely ashamed of every guard present. What was the good of having such a fine home if you weren't willing to fight for it? Though still damp from the well and disheveled from the fight, I let go of Fade's hand and pushed through the crowd. There was no way I'd make a good impression on Elder Bigwater, but I didn't care, either. This town didn't need another normal girl in a fancy dress with pretty curls. Whether they knew it or not, they needed me.

"I will," I said, once I felt sure I had his attention.

To his credit, the elder made a thorough visual inspection, taking in the knives on my thighs and the way I stood. "You're one of the new young people," he said thoughtfully. I could see him calculating the odds of making use of me against the possibility of garnering disapproval by going against the old ways.

Yet something had to change. For the Freaks, it already had.

"Me too." I hadn't been sure if Fade would follow, but there he was at my side, braver than guards twice his age.

I stood a little taller. And then Stalker came up on my left. I knew a moment of pride to surpass anything that had come before, even on my naming day. We were teaching these people what it meant to be steadfast—to do one's duty even in the face of possible extinction. Maybe a few of them would choose not to cower behind their walls after this; and if the growing season came to fruition, it would be because of us.

"I reckon these younguns need somebody who knows the lay of the land," Longshot said, as he stepped up beside us.

There weren't enough of us. For a permanent outpost, we needed at least twenty men, so that some of us could sleep while others patrolled. We'd had more volunteers for the summer patrol, but that was before, when they knew they got to come home at the end of the day and leave the wilderness for the town walls. Though the fields weren't far in distance, it was a world of difference in terms of safety.

"You men should be ashamed," Elder Bigwater snapped. "Since none of you are brave enough to step forward, we'll draw for it." He turned to his daughter, who stood close by, offering a pretty picture in a dark time. "Fetch pencil and paper, Justine, and then write down all the names."

Her bright smile said she enjoyed the hint of power. A restless dread pervaded the crowds, women clutching their men's arms for fear they would be chosen. I didn't know how they could wait, myself. Justine returned, cheeks glowing from her run, and then she circulated through the crowd, taking down the identities of all town guards. They received special considerations and did no other work apart from their stints on the wall, but I didn't think much of their Hunter spirits. I suspected most just didn't want to turn their hands to real labor.

Once she finished, Justine placed the slips in a fine polished bowl. It was handmade, I could tell, and nicer than anything I'd seen down below. Guards glared at the four of us, as if we'd volunteered just to make them look bad. I didn't care about their bruised feelings.

Elder Bigwater beckoned to Longshot and then whispered with him for a few moments. When Bigwater addressed the crowd again, it seemed that Longshot agreed with my silent assessment of how many men we needed out on permanent assignment, for the elder said, "We'll pull sixteen names now, and if any should fall this summer, we'll draw to replace him." A low murmur of protest ran through the crowd, but not enough to drown Bigwater's booming voice, more impressive a sound than a narrow chest like his should make. He went on, "Momma Oaks, will you do the honors?"

Since she did the sewing in town, she had no hope of receiving special treatment from the elder for her cooperation. People needed what they needed. At his choice, some citizens relaxed a bit, seeming to trust she would be impartial. Others whispered among themselves, and one woman glared at me pointedly.

"It's *her.* All our troubles started when she came to town with her unwomanly ways. She'll bring the pride plagues back, just you watch. We'd be better off staking her outside the walls for the Muties. See if their attacks don't abate once we appease heaven with proof of our piety."

"Caroline," her companion gasped, sounding honestly shocked.

I pretended I hadn't heard the hateful comment, but it kindled a hint of fear. All too well, I knew how fast the tide could turn. They needed to finish this awful lottery, and disperse these folks before things got ugly. Salvation needed internal strife like it needed a hole in the outer wall.

With half an ear, I listened to the names being read off: Frank Wilson, Nick Gantry, Ephraim Holder, Odell Ellis, Will

Sweeney, Ty Frampton, Earl Wallace, Desmond Woods, Sonny Benton, Elroy Smith, Darrell Tilman, Gary Miles, Harry Carter, Ross Massey, Matt Weber, and Jeremiah Hobbs. Only one was familiar to me—Frank Wilson—the brother of a girl I'd spoken to at Justine's party, whose name I couldn't remember. The rest belonged to guards who never left the walls.

Their families surrounded the chosen men, weeping as if they had been singled out for a gruesome form of human sacrifice, like they'd be shoved outside the walls naked and unarmed. I shook my head with a faint sigh. Stalker watched with equal measures of repugnance and fascination, then he shook his head.

"Makes me glad I don't have a family," he said, low.

Fade nodded. "They have a chance at making it back, so long as they don't do anything stupid."

"I guess that's the problem." I smothered a grin, ducking my head so I wouldn't attract attention on this somber occasion by laughing at their sorrow.

Momma Oaks joined us then, her expression creased. "I don't know whether I'm worried to pieces or so proud I could bust. You'll be the death of me, girl."

Her words sobered me up fast. "I'm sorry."

Edmund added, "I do wish you'd thought to talk this decision over with us. We have the responsibility for raising you."

That was the problem. According to the system down below, I was *grown*. I wasn't used to discussing my decisions with anyone. Those above me in the chain of command gave me orders. Otherwise I made up my own mind. I didn't much like this reduction in status, and so I kept trying to achieve new standing that made up for my lack of birthdays.

Trying to be tactful, I said, more gently than usual, "You're both very kind, and I regret giving you cause for concern, but—"

"You can't be other than who you are," Momma Oaks finished. "And that means doing what you think is right. I understand, child. Truly I do."

"I'll miss having you around the house," Edmund said gruffly, and I believed he meant it. "I'll make you some sturdy boots tonight, fit for fighting."

"Thank you."

Edmund regarded Stalker and Fade briefly and then said, "It seems to me your friends could use a pair too. I don't promise they'll be ready in the morning, but I'll send a runner to the fields with them."

I doubted he could find anybody willing, given the current dangers, but I didn't want to discourage his kindness. So I said nothing while he knelt and took measurements for the two boys. Stalker in particular seemed stunned by the gesture; I wondered if anyone had ever done anything for him because they wanted to. It made me regret our lack of closeness because I couldn't offer comfort without upsetting Fade. I wasn't altogether sure why that should be so, but they had territorial instincts like all young animals, I supposed.

"I have to go tell Smith I won't be around to help with the crafting for a while," Stalker said, once Edmund finished with his feet.

"I'd better let Mr. Jensen know too." Fade didn't look pleased with the task.

I addressed the question to my foster parents, trying belatedly to make them feel included in my planning. "If you don't mind, I'll accompany Fade?"

"Come home after," Momma Oaks said. "I'll make you a special supper. Heaven only knows how long it will be before you have a decent meal again."

Out there, food would be the least of our worries, but I recognized her need to contribute what she could. And who was to say that memory of a delicious dinner wouldn't hold me later, reminding me why I was fighting? Nobody would hear from me that the cooks and builders didn't matter. We all had our roles to play.

Fade linked our fingers as we moved toward the livery. His grasp felt warm and sure, a certainty in a world full of shifting ground. He was beautiful in a way that hurt me, but it was the sweetest pain I ever knew, better even than the scars I took on my naming day. This ache swelled my heart and made me want to pull his head down to mine, even with the whole town looking on.

"I haven't thanked you for stepping forward with me," I said.

"Don't thank me for doing what my heart asks, Deuce. I'll be with you as long as you let me."

Which seemed like an odd thing for him to say. I'd never once asked him to leave me alone, even when I thought he was crazy. But maybe it had to do with his frequent losses. In his heart, I suspected he thought nothing could last forever, not even us. And that one day, I'd go away like his sire and dam had done—or that he'd be sent from me, for some reason we couldn't yet fathom. I resolved, then, deep in my soul never to let him go. I'd be the one never to leave him. I'd prove to him that some things could be for always—that *we* could be.

As we approached the stable, an angry voice bawled out, "Where the devil you been, boy? This crap won't shovel itself."

"Devil" and "crap" were foreign terms, but from Fade's taut, angry expression, they weren't nice, and he'd heard them before. "On patrol. I'm heading out tomorrow on permanent assignment, so you'll need to find somebody else to work in my stead."

"The devil I will," Jensen said, stepping into view. He was an unprepossessing man, weedy in height and manner. A strong, unfamiliar scent clung to him, sharp and somewhat fermented. "Do I need to take the strap to you again?"

My vision went red at the idea he had been whipping Fade, who had never mentioned a word about it. Didn't he trust me?

"Elder Bigwater accepted him," I said quietly. "I don't figure you have a choice in the matter."

The liveryman pushed by us with even more foul words—or I guessed they were by Fade's clenched fist. I put my hand on his. "Get your things, and come with me. You're not spending another night here."

Reprieve

When I came through the front door, the Oakses' house smelled of home. It was funny I should think such a thing, now that I was leaving for the guard outpost we were establishing in the fields, but the scent of fresh baked bread had become ingrained in my head as synonymous with safety and comfort. Momma Oaks came out of the kitchen, drying her hands on her apron. Since I hadn't asked her if we could have guests—and Fade had all his things in hand—puzzlement flickered on her face.

"What's this?" she asked, inviting me to clarify.

Since Fade clearly didn't want to talk about it, I told my side. "He needs to spend the night here. Mr. Jensen threatened to take a strap to him for leaving, and I think it's not the first time."

She straightened her shoulders, mouth firming into a white line at the idea. "That he's threatened . . . or actually done it?"

I guessed that did matter. Sometimes people's bark was worse than their bite, but I didn't think that was the case. So I said, "Raise your shirt."

If I was wrong, there would be nothing to see. His dark eyes snapped at me with shamed ferocity, and the leaden feel of my stomach told me I was right. Fade didn't want to do this, but with Momma Oaks waiting with a worried look, he complied. His stomach was fine—and then he turned. There, across his lovely, muscled back lay the evidence of his months in Salvation. Welts lay atop welts, some cracked and scabbed over, others red striped, and beneath it all lay blue-green bruises that said it had been going on almost since he moved from the Oakses' house. I could see in her face that the woman wished she had kept him with her, despite the impropriety. Salvation hadn't been as good to him as it had me.

"Arlo Jensen won't get away with this," she said with a tight fury. "Edmund!"

Fade tried to hide his humiliation, but I could see this was just making him feel worse. And yet, if we did nothing, then the despicable worm who hurt him wouldn't pay for his crimes. When Edmund saw what his wife wanted him to, his whole face went red, and he clenched his fists.

"I'll attend to it," he growled, stomping out the door.

Momma Oaks took Fade's hand, gently, and led him to the kitchen. "Dinner's almost done, but I need to treat your back."

He flinched reflexively, recoiling from the idea of her tending him. She read the rejection, and the sorrow in her expression said she understood that he wouldn't trust easily. So she assembled the supplies and put her hand on my shoulder. "I'll go lay the table. It might be better if you take care of him."

"Do you mind?" I asked.

"I'd rather you did it." His tone said he wanted to pretend it never happened, but that wouldn't make the injuries go away.

"Then I will. Take your shirt off."

He complied, laying it on the table beside him. We seldom ate in the kitchen, but the worktable would serve this purpose. My hands trembled a little. This wasn't like rubbing salve on battle wounds. Those didn't bother me. These did, because a human—who didn't have the excuse of mutation, disease, or insanity, whatever ailed the Freaks—had inflicted them.

I washed my hands in the soapy water and then dampened a towel. More than anything, I feared hurting him, but he trusted me to do this. I just wished he had told me sooner, though since we hadn't talked much, I supposed I didn't blame him. Tegan could have helped him, or even Stalker. There was no reason for him to submit to such maltreatment. Trying to be gentle, I washed his back, pausing when I felt him flinch. His knuckles whitened on the edge of the table, his head bowed. I couldn't tell what he was thinking.

"Almost done," I whispered.

For the last step, I smoothed healing salve all over, as light as I could. He shuddered a little, but I had no idea if I was hurting him. With my fingertips, I traced each strap mark, each bruise, and by the time I finished, I wanted to find Arlo Jensen and cut him into Freak bait. The mere thought gave me immense satisfaction. The places where his skin had broken open didn't appear to be infected, so there was no need for a deeper treatment, and they had clean scabs, so I didn't apply bandages either.

"Finished?" Before I could answer, he pushed to his feet and shrugged back into his shirt. He wouldn't look at me, as if I had betrayed him.

"Fade? Are you mad?"

"Not at you."

But it seemed so. "If I hadn't told her—"

"It's fine," he snapped.

"It's *not*. What's in your head right now?"

"I probably had it coming," he bit out. "Tegan's fine. You're fine.

Even Stalker seems to get along with his foster dad. And I was smart-mouthed, angry, because—" He gestured between us.

Because of us. Because of me.

"So it probably had something to do with my attitude." He shrugged.

I was already shaking my head. "No matter what you said to him or how you said it, this wasn't right. It was his failure, not yours. It *wasn't* your fault."

He hid so much, this boy of mine. I took a step toward him and before I could move again, he did, and then he was in my arms. He couldn't stand for anyone but me to touch him. And so, I held him carefully, wondering if I'd ever hurt him with a casual caress. Not that he would've shown me. He had suffered unimaginable pain already, and these scars would add to the many he'd collected over the years. Fade dropped his head just enough, resting his chin on my shoulder, and we stood that way until I heard Momma Oaks moving about in the dining room.

Then the front door opened and closed. Edmund was back. Fade stepped away then, and I laced our fingers together, drawing him with me into the other room.

"It's settled," Edmund said with satisfaction.

Momma Oaks demanded to know: "What happened?"

"I took the matter to Elder Bigwater. You know he has strong feelings about the mistreatment of children. Jensen will receive ten lashes and a day in the stocks."

He turned to Fade. "Not that it matters, but Arlo's off the wagon. If we had known, we never would have entrusted him with your safety."

"Off the wagon?" I asked.

My foster mother explained, "He's been in the corn liquor.

He's a mean drunk. And I am *so* sorry. Of course you can spend the night here . . . and you're welcome when growing season's over too." She was determinedly cheerful, fixed on the certainty we were both coming back.

"He can have my room."

I left Fade to chat with Edmund while I went to deal with the claw wound on my stomach. The throb had dulled to a low heat, only sharpening when I twisted at the waist. Momma Oaks fussed while she treated me, shaking her head.

"I'll never understand why you do this," she muttered.

I cut her a sharp look. "So you wouldn't fight for your children?"

The woman huffed out a breath. "Never you mind. Just lay the table."

Dinner was a surprisingly agreeable meal. Since my foster parents didn't carp on his injuries, Fade relaxed and enjoyed the food. I did notice he sat very straight, his back not touching the chair. He'd done that on the swing and the sofa too, and I hadn't realized what it meant. *Stupid. You might have helped him sooner.*

After the meal, we played a card game Edmund had been teaching me. It had a lot of rules and was nothing like any of the ones I'd learned down below. It required keeping track of point values and discards. Tonight, we divided into teams, Momma Oaks and Fade, against Edmund and me. I was gratified when they won, which left Fade smiling, and Edmund slid me a wink as he pushed back from the table, making me think he'd tossed the match. I liked him better all the time.

"We'll play chess when you get back from the outpost," Edmund promised.

I smiled. "I'd like that."

As the hour grew late, Momma Oaks cleared the table, and I

helped her. We washed the dishes in companionable silence. It was only when I was drying the last dish that she turned to me, hands on hips.

"He's important to you." It wasn't a question.

"Yes, ma'am." *Mrs. James would be proud of me,* I thought, *for remembering to differentiate by gender.*

"Is he the reason you're so set on fighting?"

"No," I said slowly. "I think it's the other way around."

She laughed quietly. "I'm not surprised to hear that. We'll be retiring now. Don't spend so long sparking that you don't get any sleep."

That was the second time I'd heard that word, and I trusted Momma Oaks enough to expose my ignorance. "What does 'sparking' mean?"

Her face softened as if with pleasant memories. "It means your sap's flowing, and you're blooming, so you enjoy spending private time with your young man."

Ah. Her explanation permitted me to make the connection to kissing. Come to think of it, "sparking" was a good word. When he touched me, I did feel like I had bits of light flickering all over my body. My cheeks heated at the idea that Momma Oaks knew about that kind of thing. But if she had chosen Edmund as her partner and borne his children, it was an inescapable conclusion. That gave me the oddest sensation, imagining them young and eager.

She went on, "I won't caution you further. You're a brave girl to have come as far as you have, and I know you have your priorities straight."

I took that to mean she finally believed I wasn't interested in unauthorized breeding. At this point, I liked kissing a lot, but anything more had to wait until my combat reflexes slowed; I couldn't risk a brat breaking up my best fighting years. Once I got old and sluggish, say twenty-four or so, then I might consider settling down and breeding with Fade, but that was so far in the future, I could hardly picture it, and my present looked anything but certain.

"Thank you for everything," I said.

Momma Oaks hurried over to me and gave me the tightest hug I'd ever had. She smelled of good things baking, and my eyes stung a little. Almost at once, she stepped back and muttered that she probably wouldn't be up when I left, but that she'd keep me in her prayers. In Salvation, that was a good thing, as it meant talking to the divine being who ruled the world from heaven. I couldn't imagine he even listened, but my foster mother took comfort from it, and that was enough for me.

I took a moment to compose myself after she left the kitchen, and then I went into the sitting room, where I found Edmund putting on his shoes and hat. "Where are you going?" I asked.

"I promised you new boots to march in tomorrow," he said quietly.

"You don't have to—"

"Don't be silly." That apparently ended the discussion because my foster father went out then, closing the door softly behind him.

Fade observed the exchange from the small sofa. He wasn't leaning back, so I figured the salve had made his wounds tender. Instead, he propped his elbows on his knees and studied me as if I held all the answers to the mysteries of the universe. That look quickened my pulse.

"He cares for you a lot," he said.

I nodded. "I thought for the first few weeks that I was a bother to them both, but it seems not."

"I'm glad you ended up with folks who love you."

I didn't feel like discussing that when I was doing my best to worry those kind people. "Are you tired?" I asked, changing the subject.

He shook his head. "This is the last time I'll be alone with you for a while."

"Could be the whole summer before it happens again," I agreed.

We'd be together, but there wouldn't be many quiet moments like this one. It'd be impossible to think about sparking while establishing an outpost in the fields. Which made me wonder if I was crazy for volunteering; I could be safe within the walls, spending moments like this one with Fade. There could be moonlight walks and sparking in the swing, whispered secrets and infinite softness. I'd given all that up to live rough and to fight for my life.

But I couldn't deny the Huntress in me.

"Then we should make the most of tonight." Fade stood and offered his hand.

I studied him in the diffuse lamplight, seeing how it glazed his raven hair. It fell in shaggy waves around his lean, lovely face. At this point, I knew his features better than my own. A half-smile played at the corner of his mouth, giving him a playful air. But even at play, Fade still exuded that dangerous edge, as if he were a wild thing tamed only to my hand. I drew in a soft, shuddering breath, then went to him, and put my fingers in his. He drew me in slowly, whether because of his back, or so as to avoid spooking me, I couldn't say.

So close, I could see the dark fringe of his eyelashes. His eyes were so dark, they held no other hues, but as I gazed up, I noticed his irises had a faint violet ring. I'd never seen such a look, full of melting tenderness and absolute adoration. I think I could have stayed like that all night, if he hadn't kissed me.

His lips moved on mine, then toyed with my lower lip. His teeth grazed, then his tongue. Sparks crackled to life, lighting me from within. Fade pulled me close with his hand on my waist, but even lost in him, I remembered not to put my hands on his back. Instead I curled my fingers into the nape of his neck, alternately pressing and stroking. Fade slid his hands to my hips and drew me against him so our bodies were flush and hot. I felt as though his heartbeat echoed mine, pounding out a thunderous tune. He drank my gasps and sighs with hungry lips, and I responded with all of me. Eventually, his mouth moved away from mine; then he kissed my ear, my throat, and a little sound escaped me.

"I think we'd better stop," I said shakily.

Before I forget that breeding is a bad idea for a Huntress. A few more minutes and I wouldn't care at all about how a brat would change my life. He didn't protest when I withdrew, but his hands trembled, which meant sparking had the same effect on him. That reaction made me feel better about having such poor control over my softer instincts. I smiled to show I didn't mind.

"Don't go to bed yet," he whispered.

"I wasn't planning on it."

We had spent more nights together than apart, at this point. In fact, when we first arrived in Salvation, I found it difficult to sleep alone. I was used to Fade, Tegan, and Stalker camped out nearby. I wasn't accustomed to silence and privacy, and I'd found it lonely. Though I had acclimated to my own bed, my own space, I still wished some nights to find Fade within arm's reach, so I could watch him sleep, his lashes curled like dark fans on his cheeks.

"What now, then?" I could tell from his expression that he was having a hard time not reaching for me, and I wanted to be close to him, but it wasn't smart. If he started again with the kissing, I'd let it go further than it should. My common sense had already packed a bag, prepared to abandon me for the evening. Luckily, I had an alternative in mind.

"There's something I always wanted to do," I confessed.

Fascination flared in his night-sky eyes. "What?"

In answer, I sat on the sofa and beckoned him over. "Lay down and put your head in my lap."

It took him a moment to find a comfortable position, but he managed it on his side, facing me, his head resting on my thighs. I exhaled in contentment and sank my hands in his silky, shaggy hair. I had touched it before, of course, but not at length, or at my leisure. In long, soothing strokes, I feathered my fingers down his forehead, temples, cheeks, and back up again. I traced the arch of his brows and the bridge of his nose. Once, I would never have permitted myself so much contact; I believed tenderness was for Breeders only.

But Fade needed this as much as I did.

"You always wanted to pet me?" he asked, his tone a sleepy sweetness.

"Is that all right?"

"It's . . . perfect." He was smiling when he went to sleep, and I held him, thinking there was nothing I wouldn't do for this boy.

Pressure

The sky was dark when I woke. I had a crick in my neck from holding Fade all night, but he slept on, as deep in dreams as I'd ever seen him. In these quiet, covert moments, he was wholly mine. No defenses, no pretense. And so I brushed his hair back, then traced the elegant line of his brows. His eyelids fluttered, and if I could've kissed them without waking him, I would have. I restrained the impulse because I sensed it had been a long time since he rested this well.

From across the room, a pair of shiny new boots sat on the bottom stair, which meant Edmund worked until he finished them, came home to find us curled up like puppies, and didn't say a word about it. I imagined him watching us, his face soft, and then leaving the present where I'd see it. Tears simmered in my eyes. Silently, I slipped out from beneath Fade, trading a pillow for my lap, and went to get my gift.

Hugging the boots to my chest, I headed to the kitchen. I hated putting them down, even to fix a quiet meal. There was always fresh bread and butter, along with a red and gooey spread Momma Oaks called strawberry jam. I didn't light the stove because that would wake my foster parents, and Edmund must've gotten precious little sleep. This would be good, more than we'd had some mornings as we traveled. As I spread the butter and jam, I remembered days when we'd eaten nothing but a handful of charred rabbit.

Once I finished preparing breakfast, I carried two plates to the sitting room. I woke Fade with a hand on his shoulder, and to my pleasure, he didn't reach for his weapons. He only gazed up at me with a drowsy, questioning smile. I saw the moment he recognized me, and his eyes brightened.

"I could get used to this," he whispered.

Vaguely embarrassed by the melting warmth in my stomach, I shot him a look. "Don't."

His smile widened into a grin as he eased upright and took the food. I ate quickly and in silence, knowing we needed to wash up and collect our things. It wouldn't do for us to turn up late on the first day. That reminded me too much of our initial patrol down below. Squashing the ache that rose up at the thought of my lost friends, I took the dishes to the kitchen and pumped a basin of water. Fade took his turn first, bathing with a cloth in the kitchen. I did *not* stand in the sitting room, imagining the fabric tracing over his chest. When he came to the doorway, I took my turn. I dressed in a tunic and trousers, then drew on my new boots. *Gorgeous.* Afterward, we grabbed our belongings and headed for the barracks.

By this time, the sky was lightening along the edges, showing glimmers of copper and rose. The colors burst in layers, a skyward delicacy that never failed to steal my breath. Soon, the sun would sting my eyes, but this quiet prelude to day's full onslaught offered the most perfect beauty I had found Topside.

"Nervous?" Fade walked beside me, matching his strides to mine.

"A little," I admitted. "This will be worse than anything

we've faced in Salvation . . . and we've been living soft for a while."

I hadn't forgotten the hardship of the tunnels or scavenging in the ruins while hiding from the gangs. Nor had the privation of the long journey dimmed in my mind. But, perversely, I took pride in what we'd suffered because we'd come through with only our weapons and our teamwork.

He nodded. "No shelter, but the weather will be good. It's warmer each day."

"I'm more concerned about establishing the outpost on a defensible site."

Fade thought about that and then said, "Longshot seems like he knows what he's doing."

"That's the only bright spot." If they'd put someone else in charge of this project, I doubted it had any chance of success.

The town was quiet at this hour; we saw only guards stirring, some on the walls, and others on the way to the barracks. I nodded in greeting to a few. When we arrived, half of the team had already assembled, but they were still waiting on the rest. Relief flowed smooth and sweet as honey. At least we wouldn't start off the assignment on Longshot's bad side. Not that I thought he was as touchy as Silk. He didn't seem to possess much sense of his own importance.

Stalker strode up a few minutes later, and to my surprise, Fade waved in greeting. The blond boy paused, brows drawn in obvious puzzlement. And then he maneuvered around a cluster of men to join us. If Stalker thought I was better than our fellows, then they didn't rate with him at all. I shouldn't have smiled at the implicit insult, but in truth, I didn't think highly of our comrades, either. If they'd been Hunters at heart, they would've stepped forward of their own free will. Yet they didn't deserve to die for their timidity.

Fade shook his head at the both of us, though I doubted the guards had noticed the silent interplay. "We have to work with them."

"There might be hope for some," I said softly. "Brats can be trained."

Both boys took a second look and Stalker laughed. "Old brats."

A few minutes later, the rest of the men turned up, sullen and unhappy. Longshot spoke for a few minutes about his expectations, outlining his plans, which were logical and well conceived. There would occasionally be town furloughs, after the first week, where two guards rotated in and out. That, he said, should cut down on soldiers deserting their posts.

"It's gonna be tough," he went on, "but we stick it out or the town starves. That's a fact. Them Muties have figured out how to hurt us, and we can't let that stand. It's been a long while since we had a proper war, but I'm afraid it may come to that."

The guards murmured, some worried, others speculative. We fell into formation, two by two, and marched through the dawn, our advance blessed by the rising sun. Maybe it was just the normal progression of the day, but as it grew brighter, I could almost believe that luster meant something special—that we would succeed—and the damage wouldn't be catastrophic.

Seventeen growers met us at the town entrance with wagons full of seeds. This time, they appeared cowed, none too eager to return to the fields. If anything went wrong, Salvation wouldn't have the supplies to plant a third time. And I tried not to contemplate that outcome. One of the planters distracted me by lifting a hand—and when I stepped closer—I recognized Tegan with her hair bound in tidy braids and wearing a length of cloth around her head to protect her from the sun.

I hurried over to her. "How does Doc feel about you volunteering to help with the harvest?"

"He required some persuasion with all the problems we've had this season, but they were short on willing hands, and I know what I'm doing."

"I'll watch your back," I promised.

Tegan nodded. "I know . . . or I wouldn't be here."

Longshot hollered for the guards to fall in so I waved as I went back to formation. There was no fanfare as the gates opened. None of the townsfolk came to wish us well as we went out to protect the fields. It was just as well; it would have made leaving harder for those who were, at best, reluctant.

"Stick close to the wagons," Longshot ordered. "I want guards posted on either side, and keep a sharp eye on the tree line."

"Yes, sir," I murmured, along with nineteen others.

I sniffed the morning air, seeking any sign that all wasn't as it should be. Only the scent of green grass broken underfoot reached me, chased with faint animal musk, and the sweetness of white flowers, unfurling in the distance. I found constant beauty in this new world; it had not yet become familiar to me, and I marveled that natives could find so little to enchant the eye.

Likewise, the birds assured me things were safe for now. Flashes of color fluttered in the green, aerial maze. This morning they chirped and whirred and churred their morning songs, undisturbed in distant boughs. Yet the peace was unnerving, for we had trod this path before, and we *knew* that danger lurked within the twisted tangle of branches. For a Huntress, waiting could be infinitely worse than fighting. I fingered my knives as we grew closer to the first field, ruined with runnels of Freak claws. Only dead plants remained, so dry and brown that it hurt to look at them. They'd represented the hope for the town's survival.

We'll do better this time. Longshot has a plan.

Shortly, he proved me correct in my assessment. He barked instructions to the growers riding in the wagons, telling them to get down and get to work. Tegan shouldered a bucket, which had a long strap attached, and her partner—an older man who seemed protective—carried jugs of water. She would put the seeds in the ground while the man covered and watered them.

I paid close attention to them as they worked the fields, but I had to watch all the growers. The rest of our cohort stood guard with me, watching in all directions. I could tell many of them were frightened by the way they clutched their weapons.

Frank Wilson, the guard I'd fought to earn my place, came over to stand with us. He looked about twenty, though he might be older, based on how people aged Topside. His brown hair needed cutting, and a beakish nose dominated his narrow face. To his credit, Frank wasn't rigid with dread like the rest. I didn't know if that meant he was brave or foolish. Some Hunters were both in equal measure, but Silk once told me that only an idiot feared nothing. Smart Hunters knew when situations were dangerous, and made the choice to risk their lives for the good of the enclave.

"Can't believe we'll be outside all summer," Frank said, shaking his head.

Stalker eyed him with dislike. "*We* spent the whole winter outside."

Technically, we spent it in a little house, but Frank seemed so impressed with our survival skills that I lacked the heart to disillusion him. Fade was watching the tree line, as Longshot had said, seeming to pay the exchange little mind. Just looking at him filled me with warmth, but I didn't let the feeling distract me.

"I heard about that," Frank said. "Did you really come from Gotham?"

If I had a new knife for every time we'd been asked that, I wouldn't be able to carry them all. I let Stalker field the question.

"It's true," he answered.

"What was it like? Were there horseless wagons and flying carriages?" Right then, Frank seemed younger than I'd initially thought.

"Of course," Stalker said, playing with him. "There were also fountains with all the cider you could drink and shining towers of pure silver."

Frank colored. "Sorry."

I took pity on him. "It's all in ruins."

Still, he wasn't discouraged, and I guessed he hoped to bond with us because everyone else on the squad was at least ten years older. Most of them had families of their own and stood in knots with their weapons loosely held while complaining bitterly about drawing this duty. Since Frank wasn't like that, maybe he did belong with us, more than with the others, anyway. I'd promised to show him some moves; maybe there would be time for that later.

Trying again to make conversation, Frank said, "Who could've imagine the Muties being smart enough to hit our food supply?"

He reminded me of Twist, who nobody had liked down below. Twist had been a small, weak male in the enclave, who served as the headman's second in command. Though he'd lacked a certain charisma, he'd also turned out to be our greatest ally, so I didn't think it wise to alienate Frank. We might need him.

"They're different," I said thoughtfully. "There might be two types, the mindless kind, and these new ones, who seem to think and plan."

That was only speculation, of course. I remembered how Fade had said we needed to study them to figure out why they were changing. That didn't seem a likely avenue for answers, however. I imagined what Elder Bigwater would say, confronted with such a crazy, dangerous scheme.

Stalker shaded his eyes, gazing with silent frustration out toward the trees. "If that's true, then we're doomed."

That dried up the talk until we moved. The day went slowly, mostly standing at attention, surveying the landscape for danger signs. At noon, we ate a cold lunch of bread and dry meat. Hopefully meals would improve once we finished the initial planting and decided where to set the outpost. Tegan ate with us, her bad leg stretched out before her.

"Are you hurting?" I regarded her with a half-frown.

Her brown eyes darkened with outrage. "Did you ask anyone *else* that?"

"No, but—"

"Leave her alone," Stalker said, surprising me. "She's tough. She'll be fine."

I eyed him in astonishment, but he'd already turned away to tell Frank about how we'd gone a whole week without eating anything but fish. Sadly, the story was true; if I never saw a fish again, that would be just fine. Tegan watched him, her expression perplexed but grateful. I could tell she didn't understand Stalker at all.

"I know you mean well," she whispered as she rose, "but I don't need to be coddled. I know exactly what I can handle."

"Sorry. I won't do it again."

She nodded to show we were fine, and then she rejoined her partner to continue planting. By late afternoon, the growers finished. The seeds didn't need special care this early, but they did require someone to watch them and be sure Freaks didn't come in the night to rip them out of the ground. We returned to Salvation in near-silence, but as we approached the gates, a guard muttered:

"This is ridiculous. We haven't seen or heard a peep from the Muties today. We ought to be sleeping warm in our beds tonight."

"Odell Ellis, I recognize your voice," Longshot barked without turning. "If you wanna explain to Elder Bigwater what you're doing when you abandon your post, go right on inside with the growers. But if you do, I feel pert near sure that he's not gonna be amenable to you eating our food, come winter. But that's your call."

"I know my duty," Odell muttered.

"Then quit your bellyachin'." Longshot raised his voice, calling to the guards on the wall. "Open up quick, just long enough for the wagons. It's clear."

"Take care," Tegan called as she went. "I'm sure I'll see you soon."

In the falling light, I raised a hand in farewell and saw Stalker and Fade do the same on either side of me. All told, it only took a few minutes to get the civilians to safety. I felt more combat ready at once. Longshot signaled, and we moved out, back toward the fields. It had been a long day, where inaction grated heavy. By that point, I was a taut-drawn wire, waiting for pressure to make me snap.

But guard work wasn't all excitement and action. I'd known that coming in.

Longshot chose an excellent site on a low rise that permitted a sweeping view across the newly planted fields. The wind carried a loamy scent, that of fresh-turned earth. From this position, we'd see if anything went awry, and the incline offered an advantage to the riflemen. With any luck, they'd drop a vast number of incoming Freaks, and our close-combat crew would devastate the rest.

"In the morning, we'll fell some timber for a proper watchtower. For tonight, let's build a fire and a simple camp. Who knows how to make soup on the trail?"

Fade raised his hand. "We've done it more than once. Where's the pot?"

I fell in to help him, and Stalker built the fire. This was almost like old times, if I ignored Tegan's departure, and sixteen strange men grumbling about being forced to sleep on the hard ground when we'd clearly eliminated the Mutie threat.

I wasn't so sure.

Their behavior indicated they were capable of devious planning that, when taken in combination with their strength and terrifying numbers, presented a daunting challenge. Fortunately, Fade and I had survived worse. At least, here, we had men to fight with us; and Salvation remained nearby if the field situation became untenable.

Those thoughts occupied me as we prepared supper. Fade filled the pot half full of water from the canisters we'd brought from town and I sliced vegetables and then added dried meat.

Longshot offered various pouches of spices; I examined them with a sniff before deciding which ones to add to the soup.

One of the guards elbowed another and muttered, "So *that's* why we brought her. At least she can cook."

A third snorted. "Bet that's not all she's good for."

Fade froze. Before I could tell him to ignore it, he had his knife against the man's throat. "If I hear another word like that out of you, we'll be one man short before we see a single Freak."

"Stand down, son." Longshot put a cautioning hand on his shoulder, and after several deep breaths, Fade stepped back, his blade dropping to his side. "I'll handle it. She's your girl, I know, but these are *my* men."

The man he'd threatened showed equal measures of fear and fury, but Longshot gripped his arm, and dragged him to one side. Whatever he said, it was too low for me to hear, but when the man came back—Gary, I believed his name was—he couldn't meet my eyes as he tendered the apology. I just shrugged. There had been Hunters down below who were quick with a Breeder joke. If I let them get to me, then I was as soft as they said, and I didn't fear any human male. While they might be stronger, they wouldn't be smarter or faster.

"That goes for all of you. This girl fights as well as any man here, and better than some, so I won't hear any more of that. Is it clear?"

The rest mumbled an assent. Dinner was a muted meal, but gradually, the guards forgot the incident as their bellies warmed and they appreciated the sparkle of the bright stars overhead. With hot soup, a cozy bedroll, and a clear sky, things could definitely be worse.

After cleaning up, I sank down beside Fade and laced our

fingers together. "You can't threaten to kill everyone who bad-mouths me."

"Why not?" he muttered.

"Mostly? Because they'll start seeing me as your weak spot and they'll use me to get at you. It doesn't matter to me what they think of me. Only what you do."

He leaned in and whispered, "I wish I could kiss you."

"Save them up. I'll take them all at once when you can."

In reply, he brushed his hand over my hair. Shortly thereafter, Stalker and Frank joined us. The conversation grew more general, speculation on what the summer held and anticipation of how hard we'd have to work in the woods tomorrow.

Eventually, we rolled into our blankets as true night fell.

No nightmares came that night, but they would begin in reality soon enough.

Creep

The night passed in shifts, and there were enough guards that I wasn't chosen to stand watch. It would be my turn the following day. Leftover soup and stale bread made up our breakfast. During our travels, Fade and I had discovered, quite by accident, that soup left to cook indefinitely on the fire became thick and hearty, and the constant heat reduced the chance of spoilage.

Living rough as we were, it made sense to use the knowledge we'd gained traveling north. I ladled out the food, the jut of my chin daring anyone to make a comment about my gender and the reason I was serving. After the meal, Longshot drew lots to see which half of our group went to the woods to saw the timbers for the watchtower. Fade and I drew short straws, but Stalker and Frank did not. The other eight men were older, and I knew them only by reputation. None seemed happy with the situation, and I suspected they were remembering the number of Freaks that had poured out of the forest recently.

On some level, I shared their doubt and fear; it seemed impossible to expect so few to act on behalf of the whole town—and yet the majority of Salvation couldn't survive out here.

Offering the Freaks free food in the form of helpless females and brats served no purpose. So we had to make this work.

One of the guards fell in step with me on the way. He was a short, stocky man with shoulders that seemed broader than he was tall. Iron-gray hair marked him as at least as old as Longshot, but he wore his face clean-shaven. I wondered how long that would last out here.

"Hobbs," he said. We shook hands as we walked, as that was how one greeted another politely, Topside. "Jeremiah. But everyone calls me Hobbs."

"Deuce."

I didn't have a surname; there had been no need down below. There weren't enough of us for there to be a shortage of names, which came from our naming-day gifts. The Wordkeeper had told us from our earliest brat-hood that our names meant something special, and that whatever object our blood chose was sacred. That was probably more rubbish he'd made up, but I kept my card safe just in case. I'd shown it to Edmund during my first week here and he said it was a two of spades, an ancient playing card, liberally speckled with my blood. This object contained my essence, and they'd taught us in the enclave that something terrible would happen to us if we didn't safeguard it.

"I know who you are," he said. "I reckon everyone does."

Unsure of how to take his comment, I slid him a sidelong glance. "Oh?"

He offered a reassuring smile. "You have your detractors, miss, but I'm not one of them. We could use a little more bravery in Salvation."

"Thank you." I didn't know what else to say.

I wasn't used to elders being kind when they didn't want

something. Any moment, I expected him to order me to do something awful, for that had been my experience in the past. But he only walked in silence, eyes trained on the trees that grew closer with each footstep. Dread ratcheted up. I didn't like dividing our forces, but I understood the need for a lookout post. That would permit greater weapon range for the rifleman on watch and even better vantage for distant threats.

Providing we survived this task.

The idea was for us to cut a young tree, small enough that two of us could haul it back on the ropes wrapped around our shoulders, which would be knotted into a type of harness. I didn't know how to do that but the older guards did. What they lacked in combat prowess, they made up in other skills.

"Would you steady for me?" Hobbs asked. I must have looked blank because he explained, "Hold the tree while I saw it down."

"Oh. Of course."

I cast a glance at Fade, but another guard had already conscripted him. He nodded to show he was all right, and I hoped his back wasn't bothering him much. I'd packed some salve in my things, so if I got a chance later, I'd apply another coat, but I had to be careful how much attention I paid him. The tentative peace Longshot had imposed with his barked order for equal treatment wouldn't last long if the guards caught Fade and me acting like lovesick fools.

The forest rose to meet us, thorny brambles barring the way. With muffled curses, the men cut them back. I followed their lead, as they had greater physical strength. If Freaks attacked, I would leap to their defense, but it didn't make sense for me to clear brush when they were better at it. I'd done some sneaking in the woods with Stalker during our journey north, but we'd never created any paths. I certainly didn't know anything about cutting trees.

Within, the wood was shady and cool despite the morning brightness, green-cast shadows tinting our skin in sickly hues. Movement in the branches overhead reassured me. The birds protested our incursion with squawks and chastening chatter. I ignored their outrage and followed Hobbs to a likely tree—slim and supple, but not too heavy for us to manage.

"Put your hands here," he told me, "and hold tight."

I did as he ordered; this was something at which I excelled. For my whole life, I had done as the elders told me. Pity they didn't know much about the world. This was a mindless task, so mine wandered, stealing down little-examined memories. I remembered the exiles—those sent on the long walk—and I fought down the spike of pain. When it kept happening, I should have known they were sacrifices to needless devotion to custom, not true lawbreakers. So far, I didn't detect the same blind obedience in Salvation, but there was enough zealotry to make me nervous.

Hobbs drew his saw repeatedly across the tree. At first, I thought he'd invented my role because the trunk didn't seem to need steadying, but as he cut deeper, it listed, and I applied myself to keeping it still. He inclined his head to show his approval of my work. I heard only the normal animal noises in addition to the grind of metal on wood, so I was reassured that no Freaks lurked nearby.

They might be deeper in the forest, I thought. *If there are any left.*

So far, we hadn't seen signs of their presence. *They might have moved on, gone seeking easier prey.* As Longshot had mentioned, briefly, the night he rescued us, established trade routes ran between each town, and during the fall, wagons ran fairly often. In the cold months, they traveled only in an emergency. Longshot's presence, therefore, on that wintry night had been even more of a miracle than I'd initially realized. He had gone to trade for medicine, among other supplies, in Appleton, hoping to stave off an epidemic; he'd volunteered for the dangerous mission, just as he had this one, and I thought he was the best elder that I'd ever encountered. He'd told me he didn't have anyone waiting for him at home, so I figured that was why. Longshot believed it was better he take the risk than some family man.

At length, the trees fell and we lashed them into the harnesses. I took one rope and Hobbs took the other. It was harder than it looked, but the fields were still quiet when we returned. Some men had occupied themselves leveling the top of the hill in preparation for the construction. Others had laid out the supplies that would be needed, including hammer and nails.

It took many trips and half the day before we could start building. Longshot supervised the work, telling men who had little experience in such things how to put the tower together. By nightfall, we had a primitive structure in place, made of raw cut logs, and the first sentry went up to stand watch on the platform.

"Tomorrow," the outpost commander called, "we'll start collecting stones. I want fortifications around this encampment in the next two weeks."

After the evening meal, I sought Longshot. He was savoring a cup of herbal tea, which wafted a sweet, agreeable steam in the night air. Though it was warm during the day, it dropped off cool at night, and I wrapped my blanket around my shoulders as I sat down beside him. Maybe I should have waited for an invitation, I thought belatedly, but he wasn't the sort of elder who inspired terror. Instead, I felt only a profound and abiding respect. If he ordered me to cut off my foot and feed it to the Freaks, I would obey him, trusting that it would forestall a worse fate.

"Something on your mind?" he asked without looking at me.

"It's been quiet," I said instead of what I wanted to talk about.

"You're not gonna start whinin', are you?"

"No, it's smart to establish an outpost here. But I suspect the Freaks are biding their time or maybe rallying greater numbers."

"You and me both." He took a sip of his drink. "Now, why don't you come on out with whatever you need to say?"

"If we're overrun, these men need to know how to fight better, hand-to-hand." He nodded, so thus encouraged, I went on, "They wouldn't welcome lessons from me, but we should be training. You could do it . . . or Stalker and Fade. They're both excellent with their blades."

He allowed: "We do need discipline . . . and a regimen like that would cut down on the time and energy left for complaints. I'll see what I can do in the morning."

"Thanks." I pushed to my feet, content that these guards wouldn't always be so unskilled. That affected me because they were watching my back, and if they couldn't do it properly, then it increased my chance of an untimely death.

"You and Hobbs have second watch," he told me.

Disappointment curled through me, because I did wish it could be Fade, but I understood and respected the decision. With Hobbs, there was absolutely no chance either of us would get distracted and neglect our duty. Plus, he was practical and polite, not making a big stink about working with me. Hobbs had my respect.

Mealtime offered no surprises. Everyone was sick of the soup, but it was still edible. As we finished the pot, I realized someone had to come up with an alternative, but since Fade and I had already taken a turn cooking, it wasn't our problem again for another two weeks or so. By that time, the shoots should be coming up, proving our presence had been worthwhile.

I didn't mind eating the same thing over and over, though. Down below, we did so on a daily basis and called ourselves lucky to have meat . . . and on the road, we'd eaten rabbit and fish without much variation. So I had an advantage over those who were used to sheep and venison and the occasional roast bird; I hadn't been in Salvation long enough to forget that such bounty was a blessing, not a right.

Though I tried, desperately, to sleep, I couldn't, for fear I would miss my watch. It wasn't a reasonable worry, but it cast me back in time to the night before my first Huntress patrol with Fade. Tonight, my nerves held the same ragged edge, as if I were on the verge of something exciting and new. Rationally, I understood that wouldn't be the case. I'd stood watch before. So instead I listened to the guards on duty whispering; they didn't seem to care if they bothered the others.

Hobbs tapped me on the shoulder when our shift began. I scrambled out of my bedroll with a nod of thanks while the other two guards made their report in low tones. "Nothing moved, not even a jackrabbit."

"Good news," Hobbs said. "We'll take it from here."

I sat by the fire with Hobbs across from me; we stared in different directions, time passing like it had frozen solid. Hobbs and I didn't talk because the others were asleep. Most of them snored. Stalker lay nearby, almost as if watching over me, and he kept one hand on his knife. He was right, I suspected; I had more in common with him than Fade, but that was the problem. We were *too* much alike.

At last our shift ended. Hobbs gave the report—same as the one before, all quiet—and two new guards took over. Afterward,

I rolled up in my blanket, lying there while sleep eluded me. I'd just managed to drift off when something roused me. A sound, a smell? I drifted, half wakeful, eyes blurring the dark sky with their slow blinking. Movement nearby reassured me. It should be the guards on watch shifting positions to stay alert, but instead, I had the impression of a dark figure. Shining eyes flickered past, sunken in the ravaged face. It was a visage from nightmares, a Freak seen too close up, only if there had been one in camp, it would surely be dead . . . or we would be. I must be dreaming.

I sat up cautiously, expecting to find I was suffering from a lingering nightmare, but the camp was still. *Too* still. The two men who were supposed to stand third watch had fallen asleep. In the distance, running away, I saw that same tattered form, clad in rags. The stink was less than I expected from Freaks, just a trace of rot, but the fact that a Freak had slipped like a shadow into our camp? That wasn't what concerned me most.

No, big trouble came in the form of the flaming brand the creature carried.

"Wake up!" I shouted, kicking the guard who should have been our sentry.

He jolted away with a curse, and he came up swinging, but he was doltish and clumsy. I dodged.

"Take a look out there. What do you see?" I demanded.

He squinted into the distance. "Naught but a will o' the wisp, you stupid—" Fade's hand clamped on his throat, silencing him, and he didn't let go until the other man's face went purple. I tried to get him to stand down, but he had no tolerance for men messing with me or calling me names.

Seeing the situation going from bad to worse, I roused Longshot. He came awake fully alert and scanned the terrain behind me. "What's wrong?"

I summarized what had happened and he frowned at me. "You expect me to believe a single Freak sneaked up on us . . . and stole fire?"

His skepticism didn't insult me. If I hadn't seen it with my own eyes, I wouldn't credit the story either. With one hand, I indicated the guard I'd woken. "He saw the light receding in the distance, going away into the trees. Ask him."

The man hunched his shoulders. Belatedly, I realized it was the same one who had made the joke about what else I was good for, besides cooking. He hadn't done himself any favors by failing his duties on watch.

"It was just a will o' the wisp."

"Would you swear to that?" Longshot asked, shoving upright.

There was a long silence. "No."

"You're digging the latrine in the morning, Miles, you and your partner. That thing—if it was a Freak—could have cut all our throats as we slept."

It could have. It hadn't. Though it was still the middle of the night, I paced, worry eating me from the inside out. Who the devil knew what they'd do with that lit branch? Maybe it would go out. Maybe nothing bad would happen.

How I wished I believed that.

As their attacks had shown, they grew more dangerous all the time. Hunger no longer predicted their movements. These Freaks had enough to eat with all the game in the woods. Big game, like deer and moose, offered plenty of raw meat. I'd sampled both at Momma Oaks's table. For them, this was no longer about food.

It was something else. Something scarier.

Recon

For the next week—as we built fortifications and put up tents—the others treated me with a combination of anger and distrust. The bulk of the ill feeling came from Gary Miles, who felt I'd gotten him in trouble over nothing. Half the squad agreed with him, as we'd seen nothing the following nights. They thought I was a hysterical female who'd had a bad dream due to sleeping outdoors. I couldn't swear to what I'd witnessed, of course, but however unlikely, my version of events was more probable than what Miles claimed—that we'd seen some magical ball of light, believed to be spirits who came out at night to lure people to their doom.

More alarming, the Freaks had been ominously silent since that sighting. I turned the event over and over in my head, wondering if I'd gotten it wrong. During the daylight, it seemed so implausible. Freaks didn't sneak, but then, until recently, they hadn't posted warnings, and they hadn't used camouflage either. Their cunning made their behavior more difficult to predict—and it made them harder to fight.

No, I was right. It happened. The only question came in terms of their intentions . . . what they would do with the flame they'd stolen.

"This is duller than I expected," Stalker said, dropping down beside me, where I sat sharpening my blades. I was glad he seemed to have put the awkward personal stuff behind him. I wanted to be his friend.

"It's waiting," I answered. "Which is, by definition, boring."

"We should go looking for them. Root them out."

Stalker had suggested it before, and Longshot always rejected the notion. He'd say, "We have orders to guard these fields, and by the devil, that's what we'll do. I don't care if that forest has a Mutie in every tree. We'll leave them alone as long as they return the courtesy."

The men were getting antsy, driven by Stalker's impatience. There was only so much you could do while walking around patches of ground without losing your mind. The other guards didn't necessarily want to go after the Freaks, but they were tired of doing nothing. Longshot said we were lucky we hadn't been annihilated as we built the watchtower. In my opinion, that would've been too easy. The Freaks had something worse in mind, something to cripple us and destroy our will to keep watch over these fields. I couldn't imagine what it might be.

At least Longshot kept his promise and had Stalker and Fade teaching hand-to-hand. Frank showed potential; he had good reflexes and reach. But most men were old enough to resent being taught by boys half their age. That was pure pride, a mistake in our circumstances. They should grasp any advantage for the coming fight.

Stalker drew out his weapons and set to with the whetstone, looking pensive. "If Longshot can't officially send us, we should see for ourselves."

"Better to ask forgiveness than permission?" It was the only saying I recalled from my history lessons, but I couldn't recall who said it or why. I had an idea it was a famous female warrior, though, which made me like the quote more.

"Something like that. You in?"

I shouldn't. But if we hadn't been ordered not to go, then it wasn't exactly like insubordination, a charge Silk loved to harp on time and again. More information to arm ourselves sounded like a good idea. On the other hand, when we were still down below, Fade and I had gone to Nassau strictly for recon purposes, and that information hadn't helped us at all. If the situations paralleled, we'd be driven out of the summer patrol and maybe from Salvation entirely. Though I didn't believe Longshot was that sort of elder, I couldn't be certain.

"Let's ask Fade."

Stalker's lips curled into a sneer. "You won't make a move without him, huh? That's embarrassing."

"No," I said softly. "It just hurts because you wish it was you."

The truth could be brutal. He flinched, and then went back to his knives. I put mine down and circled the fire to sit by Fade, who had been watching our whispered conversation with a faint frown. Though he trusted me, he didn't like Stalker; it was astonishing he hadn't come over to interrupt.

"Everything all right?" he asked.

"More or less." I outlined the idea, watching his face to see his true reaction. He had good instincts and since I was conflicted, he could cast the tiebreaking vote.

"We should go," Fade said.

Surprised rolled through me. I'd expected him to err on the side of caution. There had to be a reason behind his choice, so I waited for him to continue.

"We'll scout tonight. We're not on the watch rotation, so it's our right to give up our sleep, yes?" I nodded, and he went on,

"It's been bothering me ever since you said a Freak crept inside our line. Did it take the wood out of the fire, or did it bring a branch with it?"

I understood why he asked, but I shook my head regretfully. "I wasn't fully awake until it ran away. I didn't see."

"So what's the verdict?" Stalker asked, joining us.

Fade inclined his head. "It's on."

I checked my knives, knowing they were pristine and ready for action. "Longshot will be mad if we stir the Freaks up and draw them back here."

"Then we make sure they don't spot us," Stalker said.

Fade added, "And *if* they do, they don't reach the outpost alive."

I asked myself, *What would you do if you sneaked into a camp of sleeping Freaks? Would you slit all their throats?* The answer that emerged made me wonder if I were more of a monster than the creature that stole our fire. *That doesn't necessarily establish that they're capable of mercy. Maybe it was just cunning enough to know that stealth was its only chance to survive the theft.*

For obvious reasons, it was terrifying to consider what Freaks could do with a burning brand. As far as I knew, they didn't cook. Mind racing, I considered other alternatives. It hadn't smelled as rank, so maybe it had been some deformed human, living as an outcast in the dangerous forest. I would love if that were true.

We'd find out shortly, one way or another.

After dark, the three of us crept out of camp without alerting the sentries. Though we were skilled, the guards' lack of attention to the area alarmed me; they *missed* our departure, and they weren't even asleep. Longshot needed to hear about this security lapse. Stalker shook his head in disgust as we circled behind the watchtower. By walking along the side of the hill and around, it was possible to use the sentry's blind spot up top. That weakness needed to be addressed in the morning.

But for tonight, it served our purposes.

Sitting around didn't suit me, so I was glad to see some action, even if our leader hadn't directed us to do this. *But he might have,* I reasoned, *if he knew how good the three of us were at moving unseen.* We were all at a disadvantage in the trees, however, as we'd trained on different natural terrain. Stalker was used to creeping through the ruins; both Fade and I had learned our skill underground. I was confident we could disguise our movements beneath normal night noises, though.

I took point, charting a clear path into the forest. The twist of limbs overhead blocked most of the moonlight, but I could see well enough. *This* was where I shone. I could find the places where the thicket was thin. In fact, here it looked as if feet had trod this path often enough to thin the ground cover. I bent and touched my fingers to the damp soil, as if it could answer what had come this way.

In my heart, I feared I knew.

Night birds sang to each other in the trees. Squirrels chattered. As we traveled, I'd learned the names of the creatures whose world I shared. Sometimes I ate them. I always admired them. There was far less life down below, where I had grown up.

From this lower vantage, I saw a way through the tangle of undergrowth. The bushes gave with a whisper of foliage on our skin. I hoped there was no scratchweed nearby. We'd learned the hard way that certain leaves growing near tall trees could inflict the most rotten rash. I didn't want to cover myself in mud again, and it was all that relieved the awful itching.

Too late for second thoughts. If we came out of this exploit only with irritated skin, that'd be like no consequences at all.

I pushed forward into a different world. We hadn't come this deep for timber, reasoning that young trees on the outside would be easier to cut and haul. Natural trepidation bubbled up—not at the darkness, but at being surrounded by so many trees. I found them faintly disquieting, things that lived and seemed to watch, but never moved. It was like being surrounded by a silent army that might, when you least expected, strike you down.

Kneeling, I examined the ground again; and once more, I found signs of frequent passage. I couldn't make out tracks, but the plants were trampled. Small animals like rabbits and squirrels wouldn't do this. I glanced at Stalker for confirmation, and he nodded. It went without saying that we'd stay quiet until we found what we were looking for . . . or until we judged the forest uninhabited.

For good or ill, I decided to follow where this led. I kept my steps slow and gradual, easing over obstacles like fallen branches and logs. It was too early in the year for dead leaves, a factor for which I was grateful, as the ground was soft, making for easier silent travel. We plunged deeper into the woods. I had been told only those hunting meat for the settlement came this deep, so that meant we were doing as we were on target, though we weren't stalking game. Instead, we were after information, which could offer as much value toward survival in some cases.

My ears perked first.

In the darkness, I heard a low grumble, not a growl, exactly, but like nothing I had ever heard before. At my look, Fade shook his head; he didn't recognize it either. We'd all heard Freaks scream as they died and their horrid shriek just before attacking, but none of us had ever witnessed them . . . *communicating* with each other.

It might not be that, of course. Maybe there were animals in here we'd never seen or imagined. But as we drew closer, I became positive that wasn't the case because the smell kicked in. The deeper we went, the more the woods stank of Freak—rotten meat, unclean flesh, the sickly sweet of a putrid wound. How could they stand each other? But I supposed one got used to anything. When I lived down below, I only noticed the unpleasant smell on bad days, but by contrast, the air Topside smelled of a hundred things—most of them beautiful and fresh as a morning rain.

I went down on my hands, coming in so that I crept along on the soft ground like a four-legged creature myself. Hopefully I would stir the bushes less. My heart thundered in my ears, like the smith banging his anvil. Behind me, I heard the boys' quick, anxious breathing. I wanted to tell them to be quiet, but if the Freaks couldn't hear the inhalations, they would hear my voice. So there was nothing for it, but to part the final barrier, and see what we were up against.

It was terrifying. It was a village, a hundred or more Freaks cohabitating in what seemed to be a cooperative manner. Impossible to tell from the movement, from the way they went about their business. They were *building*, these Freaks, and they had a campfire, like ours. So I'd been right, after all. One of them had come to steal our fire because they'd recognized its value. Perhaps they were no longer content to devour their prey fresh from the bloody kill, though some of them still had little compunction about doing so. One Freak brushed past, fearfully close to our hiding place in the bushes, gnawing on what looked like a human arm.

My stomach churned.

They'd constructed lean-tos out of leaves and branches, small structures, to be sure, but there was no mistaking their purpose. They roasted flesh of some kind over the flames, and the stench of charred meat mingled with their own unique stink, until the whole clearing glowed with an unwholesome miasma. And yet, they did chatter to one another from hideous, misshapen mouths. One touched another on the head in what I took to be a soothing manner, and the worst thing? There were small Freaks here. I had never seen their young, never given much thought to how they repopulated, but this proved they weren't created through biting or infection. They were legitimate, natural creatures of this world, just as we were, though how they had come to be was still a matter of some disagreement and conjecture.

Nausea simmered in my gut. I didn't want to see this. They had learned too much. They were becoming more like us, only they were too far from original humanity for me ever to see this ending well—for the mutants *or* us.

Drawing back, I pulled the boys with me. There was no way the three of us could mount an attack against so many. Not unless we wanted to die. My heart in my throat, I scuttled along the path, retreating for all I was worth. I hadn't expected to find such an impossibility. I had no context to explain it.

In silence, we retraced our steps until a stray Freak lurched out of the bushes. It was obviously wounded, clutching its bloody side, and I sank my daggers into its throat before it could snarl. The beast died quietly, which was what we needed. *We couldn't let it return to the others and warn them,* I thought. But the ruthless act troubled me. The one that had come into our camp could have killed so many of us, but it had chosen another course. *Why?* I wanted to believe it was all part of a plan to intimidate us, but I no longer felt sure of anything about these creatures.

Fade and Stalker helped me lower the body to the ground in

silence, then I signaled for us to move out. With them behind me, I ran until I was sure our voices wouldn't carry, either to the outpost or to the Freak village deep within the dark and spooky wood. At last I stopped, my hands trembling, knees weak.

Horrible. So horrible. Freaks had children; that meant breeding. My dinner threatened to come up.

"What the devil," Stalker said. He'd been learning the bad words, I gathered, from the other guards.

"They're never going to believe us." Fade rubbed a shaking hand across his eyes. "This is just like Nassau."

I turned, gazing back into the trees, feeling uncertain. "Longshot will. He knows we wouldn't lie. Though what he can do about it, I have no idea."

It was time to head back and face whatever consequences came from our unauthorized recon mission. I only hoped the warning came in time to do some good.

Revelations

I didn't have an opportunity to confess what we knew and how we'd learned it until the next afternoon. Sleep eluded me, and I suffered from its lack. My eyes burned, my head ached, and I found it difficult to eat. As the sun crept toward the horizon, Longshot stood apart from the men, watching them train.

Since I already knew what Stalker and Fade could teach me, I joined him. "I need to talk to you."

There was an air of weariness and isolation about him, as if this task weighed heavier than he could bear. Longshot glanced over his shoulder, his expression a mix of curiosity and resignation. "Why is it every time I hear your voice, girl, I know my life's about to get more complicated?"

His good-natured tone removed the sting from the words, however, and gave me the courage to continue. "I guess because you've gotten to know me."

He chuckled. "It seems like a tall order, doesn't it?"

I knew what he meant. Safeguarding the fields was an enormous responsibility, entrusted to so few of us. Our scarce numbers added another layer of tension to the task. "Are you mad they didn't send more help?"

Longshot shook his head. "Then I'd just have more men cryin' because they have to sleep on the ground. I'm not cut out for this."

"Seems like you're doing a good job." I'd never had an elder speak to me like I was his equal before—and I liked it . . . a lot.

He sighed. "I'm not a leader of men. I drive head wagon on the trade runs, and sometimes I make trips by myself. It's not the same."

"Then why did you volunteer for this?"

His serious gaze swept me from head to toe, suddenly somber. "Because you made me feel ashamed."

"Of what?" I held my breath, wondering why. I admired Longshot *so* much.

"The whole damn town."

Shock rendered me speechless for a while. "You think that highly of me?"

"You fishin' for compliments, girl?"

I wasn't even positive what that meant. "I don't think so."

"Anyway, that's not what you came over to talk about. I'm listening."

In as few words as possible, I explained our nocturnal findings. His reaction to my news defied my ability to interpret. He scrubbed a hand through his shaggy, gray hair, eyes on the sky above. It was a fair day, blue sky and bright sun. Not the sort of weather you expected for such grim tidings. By all rights, it should be pouring rain, booming thunder and lightning.

"I'll forget for a moment that you went beyond the scope of your own authority," he said curtly. "You're positive this was a settlement?"

I nodded. "A primitive one, but yes."

"You didn't rouse their attention?"

Remembering the Freak we'd killed, I shook my head. None

of the others had seen us. If they found his body, they couldn't know for sure what had happened, and with any luck, forest scavengers would get at him to make it even more uncertain.

"That much is good. But, thunderation, I have no idea what to do about this."

It seemed like a bad sign that Longshot would speak so freely in front of me. He was the elder, and he should display certainty to keep the men following him without question. Or maybe that was a trait encountered only down below. Topside leaders might be more honest about their lack of knowledge. If nothing else, it made him seem more human. That wasn't necessarily a comfort in times like these.

I ventured, "You said we could leave them alone, as long as they don't attack. Has that opinion changed, now that you know they're building nearby?"

"I'm not sure," he admitted. "Really, I just want to survive the growing season, bring in the harvest, and get behind those walls. When I'm traveling the trade routes, I don't stay in one place this long and it's making me jumpy."

"The men too. If they knew what we do—"

"They'd light torches and burn the forest down," he finished. "We need that wood, not to mention all the game they'd scare away. We can't tell them until I make up my mind how to handle it . . . and that means I need some thinking time. Will you tell your friends to keep quiet for now?"

"Of course. We already agreed we wouldn't say anything until we talked to you about it."

He touched two fingers to his forehead. "Appreciate it. As for the matter of you three roaming at night, don't do that again. Since you didn't get caught, I'm going to pretend it didn't happen."

I smiled at him, despite my general exhaustion. "So that's the rule? No witness, no crime?"

Longshot laughed. "You've got guts, girl."

Belatedly, I remembered to warn him about the ease with which we'd sneaked out of camp last night. A Freak following that same route could get in unseen. So I summarized the path we took and told him how distracted the guards were. "Anyway," I concluded, "it shouldn't have been that simple. Someone should've noticed and stopped us."

A deep breath escaped him, not quite a sigh, more of a huff of exasperation. "I try not to get agitated, but you'd reckon these morons might get better, the longer we're in the field, but they seem to imagine this is a family picnic."

"None of them are soldiers," I said quietly.

"True. But that's no excuse for simple incompetence. I'll have a word." Longshot made a shooing motion. "Get out of here. Go toughen up those muscles."

Obediently, I went back to the drills that increased my stamina and strength, and then I worked with Frank a little, keeping my promise. Once I finished, I sat down, waiting for Stalker and Fade to complete their classes. They each met my gaze and came over as soon as they could. Stalker sat to my left and Fade placed himself on my right. For the moment, the lingering tension between us had gone, banished by the dangerous situation.

"What did he say?" Fade asked.

I filled them in, and Stalker shook his head. "So he's going to do nothing?"

"Nothing right now," I corrected.

"I don't think those were all hunters," Fade said. "They might be the Freak equivalent of women and children."

I considered. "That would explain why they're leaving us alone."

In the past, Freaks had shown no signs of specialized behavior. They all attacked; they swarmed and ate and moved on to the next kill. In the tunnels, I had noticed different sizes, but I hadn't thought anything of it. It never occurred to me that the smallest ones could be Freak brats.

Stalker drew a pattern in the dirt, something abstract and complex. "I don't like leaving them so close. They might have sent for reinforcements."

I reminded him, "We don't have the numbers to take them on."

"If they're not fighters, we do," Stalker argued.

Fade seemed troubled. "But should we attack them unprovoked?"

"Damn right, we should. If we fail to strike now, we'll regret it." Stalker couldn't take any other stance; life had taught him to fight hard for his territory, and though he was learning other ways in Salvation, he still had wolfish tendencies. "And it wouldn't be unprovoked, anyway. Remember, they hit us when we were trying to plant the first time . . . and don't forget what they did to our dead."

"It's not our decision." And I felt grateful about that. "We pushed Longshot as far as we can regarding the recon mission. If we do anything else without his approval, he'll send us back to town."

The three of us shared a look of mutual horror at the idea of being stuck inside and forced to do chores. While living rough had its disadvantages—no proper baths for instance—at least out here, we had the possibility for excitement and that something we did might make a difference. Plus, it would be beyond shameful to be sent back as unsatisfactory when these other guards were still on duty. None of them fought half as well as us.

Shortly thereafter, a runner came from the settlement. The Salvation guard rummaged in his pack and produced two stunning, supple pairs of boots. "Edmund sent me with these for Fade and Stalker."

The boys took them with awed expressions, for this was some of my foster father's finest work. For my part, I was astonished he'd found someone willing to journey out to the outpost. I watched as they donned their new gear quickly and I beamed at the messenger in thanks.

"Tell Edmund I appreciate this," I said softly.

"Me too," Fade put in.

Stalker looked as if he didn't have words, but he finally muttered, "This is really something. Thank him for me."

The guard tipped his hat and headed back toward Salvation. Longshot sent a couple of men to see him halfway back to town and they reported no problems on their return. I could tell the rest of the guards envied our fine, elegant footwear; they should all be lucky enough to have Edmund care about them. He was a good man, and I felt proud to be his foster daughter.

Later, I patrolled with Hobbs, checking the outlying fields for damage. The rest of our squad kept in touch via hand signals Longshot had devised; they were simple, like need help, all clear, and immediate danger. We noticed signs of rabbit infestation, nibbles at the green shoots, but no hint that the Freaks had been here since we found the severed heads on poles. Hobbs was a trustworthy companion who kept his mind on his business and didn't waste time with inessential chatter.

"It's time to get the growers out here," Hobbs said. "They'll spread stuff to drive away pests, discourage weeds, and nourish the plants."

"If they gave us the supplies, we could do it. Lessen the risk."

Hobbs was already shaking his head. "The growers spend their whole lives studying the best ways to do things. If we try their methods and the crops fail, we'll be responsible for people starving."

Put that way, I decided I'd rather perform escort duty too. Maybe Tegan would come out with the growers to take care of the pests. I missed her and my foster parents more than I'd expected. I had put down roots in Salvation, though I didn't love all of the rules. One day, maybe I could do trade runs with Longshot, if I wasn't destined for a permanent role in the town guard. It was a dream worth keeping close.

As we returned to the outpost, I saw the site with new eyes and realized it was starting to look official; Longshot forced the men to work even when they weren't drilling. Consequently, a low stone wall surrounded the tents, set up around the watchtower with an area set aside for exercise and training. *Not bad*, I thought, *for such a hurried effort*. The men glanced up as I went past, but most had grown used to me. At least, they no longer muttered just out of my earshot or made rude gestures they knew I could see in my peripheral vision. Likely Fade's temper had something to do with their courtesy. He might be young, but he could slit them throat to thigh before they found their knives. It didn't bother me much; people—like the girls at school—usually disliked me for reasons more compelling than my gender.

Hobbs made our report to Longshot, who nodded thoughtfully. "I'll send a runner to town to get the growers out here to tend the crops."

"Glad it's not my job," I muttered.

Longshot flashed me a smile. "Me too. From what I can see, your skills tend toward killing things."

The boss called a briefing thereafter. "We're starting furloughs tomorrow, as promised. I'll draw lots to see which squads go first. Then you can vote amongst yourselves as to who goes first. You'll go off duty in pairs, understand?"

That sent a wave of excitement through the camp. Many men had families in town, and they weren't used to being away from them. As for me, I longed to see Tegan and the Oakses, but I could wait. To my surprise, our team came up in the second round. My crew appeared delighted with our good fortune; the other guards liked Hobbs and Frank well enough not to complain too loudly.

Just before dark, the last patrol returned, carrying an unexpected boon. They'd shot a deer, already field dressed and cut into manageable chunks of meat. It smelled delicious roasting on the fire, and everyone was glad to wait a little longer to avoid more hard tack and dry meat. I joined the food line near the end, and took my plate over to where Frank sat, devouring the juicy venison with obvious relish.

For a few moments, we ate in silence while I tried not to notice Stalker and Fade arguing on the other side of camp. Their faces bore twin scowls, and Fade had his hands curled into fists. Now and again, they glanced at me, which made me think they were fighting about me somehow, but they weren't speaking loud enough for anyone to overhear.

It isn't my business, I told myself. I wouldn't go over and intervene.

"What are you going to do in town?" Frank asked, distracting me.

"Take a bath."

He laughed like I was kidding. "I'm gonna eat all the cake I can hold."

Sweets were off the menu out here, so I could understand his craving. I listened with half an ear as he yammered on about how well his mother cooked. While I watched, the boys concluded their argument and Fade wheeled away to queue for some roast venison. The blond boy followed with a surly expression, chin up in a way that said he was spoiling for a fight.

Stalker hadn't been pleased with our plan of inaction in regard to the Freaks. I didn't blame him. The Huntress in me fought the urge to resolve the threat, but I respected Longshot's orders. Yet that village in the forest bothered me—not just because it meant Freaks were acting counter to my expectations.

"This seat taken?" The question came from the man I'd guessed least likely to seek my company, Gary Miles. We had tangled twice, first with his stupid joke about me, and then over his failure on watch. Consequently, he'd loathed me ever since. Miles had a rat-faced look with a long, pointed nose and a nonexistent chin. Graying hair fell in lank locks down to his shoulders, and he reeked like a bucket of vomit. None of us smelled great, granted, but he didn't even do spot washes.

I didn't want him to join us, but I couldn't conceive a way to refuse without being churlish. So I said, "Suit yourself."

"What are we talking about?" he asked, once he made himself comfortable. His smile showed brown-stained teeth, some broken and black at the roots. There was no way around it; the man made my skin crawl, almost as bad as the first time Fade and I came upon a Freak feeding in the dark.

"What we're going to do when we get our furloughs," Frank answered.

Miles tightened his mouth into a bitter white line, but the

look was gone before I could be sure of it, replaced with false friendliness. "Isn't it *lucky* you get to go so soon?"

"Longshot drew for it," I pointed out.

His amiability cracked. "And you've got him wrapped around your little finger, don't you, puss? There's no fool like an old fool. We all saw how you stood by him, exchanging soulful glances, while we busted our asses to learn fighting techniques that we'll never use."

Surely he wasn't implying I garnered special treatment by breeding with our commander? That was utterly disgusting— not because Longshot was old and horrible, but because he'd never do something so blatantly unjust and immoral. I eyed Miles with open dislike; he had a mind like the latrine he'd dug for punishment.

Evidently, Frank came to the same conclusion because he shook his head. "You're talking nonsense."

"It was her idea that we all get posted here, and now she struts around like she owns the place." He put a dirty hand on my thigh. "It's only fair she gives me a little consolation, ain't it?"

With my left hand, I whipped my knife from its sheath and I pricked him between the thighs. I knew exactly what I was doing when his face paled, throat working with sudden fear. Frank looked as if he feared to intervene—and well he should have. If he'd touched me, I might have castrated somebody.

"Leave me alone," I warned him. "It's out of respect for Longshot that I'm not killing you, but if you trouble me again, I *will*, and that's a promise."

When I eased back, he scrambled to his feet. "This isn't over."

"Yes, it is." I didn't do him the honor of watching him walk away. That would imply I thought he was worthy of my wariness.

"Why do you think he's so mad at you?" Frank asked.

"Some people just need somebody to blame." *But it was deeper than that for Miles,* I thought. He was likely one of those men who couldn't stand for a female to do anything besides cook his food and lie down for his pleasure. If he had a partner back in Salvation, she had my sympathies.

Fade put his hand on my shoulder, dropping down beside me. It was funny, because Frank immediately felt the need to be elsewhere. I supposed Fade had made it clear how he felt about me when he first defended me from Miles. His face tightened with chagrin that he hadn't been here to threaten the guy again.

"Don't worry about it," I said, absolving him. "I can handle myself."

"Miles is going to be a problem for you," he said.

I nodded. "I don't think it's going away. It would be best if Longshot replaced him, but that would send the message that giving me a hard time gets a man posted back to Salvation."

He set his hand on my thigh, consciously erasing the memory of Miles's greasy fingers on my leg. I didn't mind. Fade had the right to touch me. But he drew his hand back before anyone could remark on the familiarity and then come at me later with evil insinuations.

"Any ideas on how to discourage him?" he asked.

I had lots of them, all unpleasant. "I might have to kill him."

That made him smile. "Short of that."

"I prefer the killing," I muttered.

"Me too. But it might be bad for morale." He considered for a moment, and then slid me a sidelong glance. "We could deliver him as a gift to the Freak village."

"Tempting. What were you saying to Stalker earlier?"

He froze, dark eyes flickering guiltily to his plate. "You noticed that?"

"The whole camp did." I nudged him with a gentle elbow. "Come on, tell me."

"I might've mentioned that he needs to stop staring at you like a hungry wolf."

I slid Fade a sidelong look. "Isn't it enough that *I* gave you exclusive kissing rights? What does it matter how he looks at me?"

Color touched the tops of his sculpted cheekbones, and my fingers itched with the impulse to smooth his raven hair away from his forehead. "When you put it that way . . ." Fade leaned close to whisper, "I'm dying to be alone with you."

At his words, an ache sprang up—and I almost touched my lips in memory. I wished we'd stolen a moment the night before, but Stalker had been there, and I couldn't feel right about flinging our closeness in his face, especially when he craved that connection with me himself. Rejection didn't mean rubbing salt in the wound.

My body felt like it could light the whole outpost with anticipation. "We'll be in Salvation next week. Not on duty."

His answering smile said he couldn't wait.

Furlough

A week trickled by in relative quiet, though I sensed trouble brewing from Gary Miles. He had a small, bitter crew who watched me as I went on patrol. They never crossed any lines so I could report them to Longshot, but they made it clear we were enemies. Stupid. We didn't need trouble at the outpost; Salvation already had more than it could handle. To reassure myself, I touched the bloodstained card I kept in my pocket at all times. As long as it was intact, nothing truly dreadful could happen to me. That was enclave lore. Unfortunately, I didn't know if I believed it anymore.

If we put faith in anything down below, it was in the power of a naming token. My foster mother would say it held something of our souls . . . but that was a confusing thought. Stalker—and all of the folks in Salvation—lacked such an item, so did that mean they were soulless or just unprotected? Maybe it was nonsense, something the Wordkeepers thought up a long time ago.

The first team went on furlough without incident, two by two. Then our squad took a vote and decreed Fade and I should go together for the first holiday. At first it seemed too good to be true, and if I hadn't been so excited, I might've been embarrassed, as the vote led to ribbing from Frank and Hobbs as well as a sullen growl from Stalker. To my mind, it had been wise of Longshot to draw for each squad, and then let them decide who went on leave in what order. That move offered the sense of having some control over their lives. He might not think he was a natural leader of men, but from where I sat, he was doing a fine job.

Before we left, Longshot paid us our due. This was the first time I'd earned any tokens of my own, but as a guard, I received a small stipend in return for my work, as he'd promised earlier. These small bits of wood could be traded for goods and services in town. Holding them made me feel more powerful.

Fade and I set out for Salvation after the last of the first crew returned, carrying letters and treats from families in town. There was some risk in this because the Freaks might decide to pick us off, but we could move fast, and if necessary, sprint for the gates if threatened with a battle we couldn't win. He set a bruising clip, reminiscent of our run to Nassau.

"Do you think the Oakses will put me up again?" he asked as we ran.

I breathed through my nose, pacing myself so as not to become winded. "She said you're welcome anytime."

"Sometimes that's just what people say."

"Momma Oaks isn't like that. Neither is Edmund."

He nodded. "I didn't think so, but you know them better."

Branches and leaves crackled, the movement seeming to keep pace with us. Attention drawn, I focused on our surroundings. "Do you hear that?"

"Something's following us."

Both of us knew what it must be. The only question was how many . . . and would they strike before we reached safety? Even if the ones we'd spotted in the village weren't the *best* fighters, it didn't mean they couldn't attack. They might take the opportunity to target easy prey. If they hit us, it certainly revealed a particular, calculating intelligence. It meant they watched and gauged their assaults according to our behavior. Terrifying thought. Life had been difficult enough when they acted like mindless monsters.

Fade pressed into a flat sprint, and I flew beside him. He had the longer stride, but I was small and quick. I'd seldom had the chance to run like this down below. The sounds grew distant, as—whatever—chose not to leave the shelter of the forest. Instead, I sensed the weight of its hungry eyes, tracing our progress and promising itself, *next time.*

When we hit the gates, Fade called, "Open up, quickly. It's clear for now."

The guard took the time to scan the ground behind us, and then complied. We ducked through the narrow opening, and they slammed the heavy doors. The wood beam fell back into place; ever since the Freaks had tried to breach the entry, it appeared the guards used the reinforcement all the time. I didn't blame them.

Carefully cut grass and small meticulous gardens and flower beds made it seem like nothing bad could ever happen here. The buildings gleamed with fresh coats of whitewash; everything was under control. Since I'd been in the field, even the people looked cleaner and more wholesome. Girls walked in their long, pretty dresses, hems untouched by dust. Men removed their hats when ladies passed.

It felt like much longer since I'd been here, as if living with Edmund and Momma Oaks belonged to some other me; just as the one who lived down below was someone else, so many versions of the girl I glimpsed in the mirror. I felt grown, enough not to need to attend Mrs. James's stupid school, but maybe I wasn't the person I might become yet either. Perhaps that was the point; life, if you did it right, meant learning and changing. If you didn't, you died—or stopped growing—which amounted to more or less the same thing. So I would slide in and out of different roles until I discovered the one that fit me best.

As I studied it, I realized the town looked somewhat different. Fresh flowers adorned tables set up nearby, pretty white blossoms like the ones I had noticed on the way to the fields. Colored ribbons hung from businesses near the green, and music played, a sweet and cheerful tune. A number of men and women fiddled with their instruments, laughing with the ease of those who didn't worry about monsters eating them. I glanced at Fade, who shrugged. He didn't know what was going on either.

"Is there a party?" I asked a guard, remembering Justine's birthday.

"Kind of," he answered. "It's the Cherry Blossom festival. It's how we celebrate the arrival of spring every year."

"What does that mean?"

The man scratched his head. "Well, there's a dance tonight on the green. There will be food and drink. It's a chance for folks to show they're grateful that the cold weather is gone for a while."

"Sounds like fun," Fade said. "Thanks."

"What's a dance?" I didn't ask until the guard moved off, but Fade wouldn't mock me.

To my astonishment, he grabbed one of my hands and put his other on my waist. "Follow me." There, by the front gate, he spun me in a circle, his feet moving in time to the music.

When we stopped, I was breathless and laughing. "How did you know?"

"I used to dance with my mom."

That sounded like a good memory. For the first time, I wondered if my dam had been a kind girl and if she'd liked the boy who sired me. Occasionally, two Breeders grew close and petitioned for permission to create offspring together. Such cases were monitored closely to be sure there was no unnecessary contact after a successful pregnancy occurred. So there was a faint chance I had been born of affection. My existence might also have sprung from a breeding assigned by the elders. Fade's parents had chosen each other, I knew, and they'd produced an excellent son.

He was watching my face, trying to decide what I was thinking. Offering a half-smile, I gave him no clue. "Yes?"

"Would you dance with me tonight?"

"I'd love to. But if we're going to celebrate with the rest of the town," I decided aloud, "then we should go wash up."

"I'd like to see you in a dress again . . . and with your hair down."

Considering what we'd been through together, his words shouldn't have made me feel shy. Inexplicably, they did. Perhaps because he meant to spend the evening with Deuce the girl, not Deuce the Huntress, and I didn't know my feminine side very well. In fact, before Fade and his kisses, I'd have said there was little connection.

Abashed, I went in silence through the town, admiring the decorations on the green. I had no doubt it would be pretty when they finished. A couple of girls from school—Merry and Hannah— waved madly when they spotted Fade and me. I stopped long enough to be polite.

"Is it terrifying out there?" Hannah wanted to know.

"Sometimes."

We chatted for a time, then they needed to return to work. Fade and I walked on to the Oakses' place, which smelled of fresh baked bread through the open windows. My stomach growled.

Momma Oaks met us at the front door and grabbed me up in a rib-crushing embrace. Tears shone in her eyes, but since she was smiling, I figured she was happy. Like the first time we turned up, filthy, at her door, she hollered to Edmund to come and see, but this time he greeted me with a hug, and a wrinkle of his nose. Spot washing didn't do laundry or remedy all hygienic challenges.

"I'll see about filling the tubs," he murmured. "How're those boots working out for you?"

"They're perfect," I said truthfully. "I love them."

Fade copied the salute Longshot often used. "Mine as well, sir. They're fantastic. I've never had anything so nice."

Edmund's eyes crinkled into a smile. "That's fine. What about the other boy?"

"Stalker," I reminded him. "He said to pass along his gratitude as well. He'll probably come by on his furlough to thank you in person."

"Least I could do while you're fighting for Salvation."

Fade cleared his throat, drawing my attention, but he was focused on my foster father, his arms loose and nervous at his sides. "Sir, I need your permission to walk out with Deuce. My intentions are honorable."

What? Tegan had mentioned this to me in passing, but I wasn't even sure what "intentions" entailed.

Before I could get a word out, Edmund nodded. "It's good of you to ask. And granted." With that, my foster father headed for the kitchen to get started on our baths.

"How long can you stay?" Momma Oaks came into the room looking as if she'd happily keep us forever.

"Just until this time tomorrow. We get twenty-four hours' leave."

"Better than nothing," Edmund called, pumping water.

The older woman nodded. "True. And at least you won't miss the spring festival. It's my favorite time, and heaven knows we could use the cheer."

I agreed. It was important to keep people's spirits up during dark patches. Otherwise panic set in faster if the worst occurred. Not that I wanted to discuss that—or think about it—right now. Fade and I deserved to be lighthearted before we returned to endless dread.

"Come in here and help me, boy!"

With a bemused glance, Fade went into the kitchen. Momma Oaks hugged me again and then stood gazing at me at arm's length as if she couldn't believe I'd come back safely.

This time, anyway.

"Do you miss your children?" I asked.

"Only the one I lost. Rex comes to see us when he can." Her tone belied the easy words, reflecting the tension I'd noticed before.

Rex hadn't come for dinner even once in the months I'd fostered with the Oakses, but I didn't disrespect her by saying so. If I had a real mother like Momma Oaks, I'd treat her kindly and bring my family to eat her cooking every chance I got. But folks took for granted their blessings and often didn't appreciate them until it was too late to offer thanks.

"You had two boys?"

She nodded. "I always wanted a daughter, though." Smiling

at me, she added briskly, "And now I have one, so it's all to the good. What are you wearing tonight?"

"I thought maybe the blue dress, if you finished it?"

But I wasn't thinking about clothing. Instead, I turned over the idea that she considered me her own, her *real* daughter. Such a thing seemed impossible, but my throat thickened at the prospect. I'd never imagined a home like I found in Salvation, or parents of my own. I was also curious about that odd little interchange between Fade and Edmund.

She nodded. "It's clean and pressed, waiting in your closet."

"Thank you," I said quietly, and I didn't mean for the washing and ironing.

She knew. Her eyes grew suspiciously moist again, and she patted my shoulder. "It's my pleasure, Deuce. Believe me, it is."

Biting my lip, I considered my options, then I took the plunge. I repeated what Fade had said to Edmund. "So what does it mean?"

"He asked *that?*" Her hand flew to her heart in delight. "It means he's serious. When a boy goes to a girl's daddy, he's paying respect and promising he won't trifle with her. He's been raised right."

I puzzled over that revelation. "Which means no illicit breeding?"

"Lands, the way you talk." Her cheeks colored.

Fade came out of the kitchen then, freshly bathed and in clean clothes. My breath caught, but I only got to look at him briefly before Momma Oaks hustled me off for my turn. By accident or design, they kept us apart until after nightfall.

As she styled my hair, I asked, "What's Fade doing?"

Momma Oaks shrugged. "He told Edmund he had an errand to run."

Hm. Interesting.

As before, Momma Oaks pinned my hair up in rag twists, then when she took it down, she caught a cluster of curls at the crown of my head in a jeweled clip, so bouncy hair spilled down my back. Since the style wasn't as tall as it had been for Justine's party, I liked it better. I watched her work in the mirror, unsure of the girl in my reflection. I never cared how I looked; the only thing that mattered down below was keeping clean.

"This belonged to my mother," she said, unwrapping something from fine cloth that had started to yellow. In her palm, Momma Oaks held a silver chain, delicately forged and shining like a star. From it hung a little blue stone that bent the light. "I'd like you to wear it tonight. It'll be perfect with your dress."

I froze, afraid to reach for it. The only thing I had ever owned that belonged to my dam, I had traded for safe passage out of the tunnels down below. Even now, I wished I'd been able to keep that little metal case. It had a mirror inside and the sweet-smelling remnant of some powder long since crumbled away.

"It's too fine," I protested.

"You should have something pretty for your first official date with Fade."

Date. A new word. I suspected it had to do with sparking, and given what we planned to do that evening, it must relate to having fun. I didn't ask for clarification.

She fastened it around my neck without waiting for me to give in. It looked so lovely that I didn't have the heart to protest again. I'd never worn anything before that didn't serve some purpose, but this just hung around my neck looking sparkly. I loved it. I always had a weakness for glittery things, and since my exile, I owned nothing but my knives and clothes. Not that I owned this. I understood she was loaning it to me, not making a gift.

Momma Oaks left so I could finish getting ready, but she was beaming, so I knew I'd made her happy by not arguing. After I put on the blue dress, I stroked the soft fabric, admiring the fit. My foster mother did beautiful work, every bit as skilled as Edmund's boots. The gown came down to my ankles and the skirt belled out, but the bodice had no adornment, just a heart-shaped neck and graceful little sleeves that stopped just beneath my shoulders. Tonight, I showed my scars proudly.

I swept down the stairs to find Fade waiting for me at the bottom. His dark eyes widened, and for the first time since I'd known him, he was speechless. He stared up at me like I was everything he ever wanted. My heart skipped at the intensity of that expression, but it was a little scary, too, to have that much power. I took a step toward him, despite my uncertainty.

Edmund cleared his throat. "Pretty as a picture, isn't she?"

Fade only nodded. His hungry stare brought color to my cheeks, and I was too conscious of the warmth of his fingers when he touched me. Just on the arm, but my skin was bare, and it felt shocking, intimate, too daring in front of my foster parents. Nodding in answer to Momma Oaks's excited chatter and Edmund's more measured farewell, the two of us went out into the night, into fresh air and bright music.

"I want to drag you off and hide you away," he whispered.

"Why?"

"I always knew you were beautiful, but now everyone else will too. I won't be able to keep other boys away from you, and it'll make me crazy."

I laughed, thinking he was trying to make me feel less self-conscious about the dress and my hair, which tickled the back of my neck each time I moved. But he kept his hand on my arm, as if he thought someone would pop up to steal me away. Dazzling heat blazed between us, fiercer than the lamps hung around the green.

Not far from the dancers, he pulled me into the shadows and drew me up against him. "One kiss before I have to share you."

Hardly knowing myself, as Deuce the girl held sway tonight— and the Huntress watched with quiet embarrassment—I tipped my face up. His mouth touched mine, light as a breath, but brushed again and again, a tease, until I reached up and cupped his face in my hands. Then the kiss flared like lightning, deeper and more thorough than he'd ever dared before. When his tongue touched mine, I pulled back, shocked and breathless.

"Where did you *learn* that?"

"You'd only get mad if I told you."

I muttered beneath my breath. Probably, he was right. I didn't want to hear he'd kissed some girl down below. If there had been another female for him since we arrived in Salvation, I needed to cut off all her hair and beat her half to death. The strength of that impulse scared me, and I took a step back. Deuce the girl was every bit as vicious as the Huntress, it seemed.

He read my mood, even in the shadows, and he ran a hand under my artificial curls, fingers hot and tender against the nape of my neck. A shiver rolled through me. I felt helpless to resist him, incapable of knowing what was best for me. But this was Fade; he would never hurt me.

"It doesn't matter now," he whispered. "There's only you."

I didn't like the certainty that he had secrets, but then Fade didn't like the fact that Stalker watched me like a hungry wolf, either; so I couldn't hold it against him if he had felt like this before, if someone else had taught him about tasting a girl as if her mouth was full of honey.

"Do you want to dance?" I asked.

In reply, he took my hand and led me to the lamp-lit green, where other couples were already spinning. It took me a few moments to pick up the steps, but this wasn't too different from what we'd done at the feast down below; only here you did it with one partner instead of the whole community. I liked the intimacy of his hand on mine, our bodies moving in perfect rhythm, guided by the music and instincts that heated me all over. I didn't trust those impulses. Fade smiled at me as if he could read my thoughts. The night was cool on my bare arms, and his body warmed mine.

Eventually, we paused to nibble at the refreshments that had been laid out. Tegan joined us, looking bright and pretty in a pink dress. A boy stood next to her, older, I thought, but I couldn't remember meeting him. Politely, she performed the introductions. "Zachariah Bigwater, these are my friends Deuce and Fade."

Must be Justine's brother.

"You don't have two names?" he asked.

"Only need one," Fade said.

His manner wasn't short, exactly, but I sensed his impatience. This was *our* evening, and he didn't intend to spend it in conversation with the elder's heir. Zachariah must be a nice person if Tegan liked him, but I shared Fade's quiet urgency. Our time together was melting away. Tonight, I didn't even want to sleep.

"People call me Zach," he said then.

"It's nice to meet you," I offered, not really meaning it.

Tegan flashed me a knowing grin. "How do the fields look? I'm heading out tomorrow to do some upkeep."

"No major problems."

Beside me, Fade folded his arms in a hostile posture. I leaned against his side and gently dug my elbow in. While I didn't know Zach, Tegan was a friend, and I hadn't seen her for a while.

But Zach could read cues; he turned to Tegan. "Want to dance?"

The request revealed tact and sensitivity, as her leg might not hold up to a rollicking number, but the music had slowed. Relieved of the burden of courtesy when the other two moved off, Fade drew me against him, closer than the other couples. I didn't protest. Instead I leaned my head against his shoulder and let him guide my movements. That demanded trust I couldn't offer anyone else.

A scornful, speculative whisper pierced my dreamy reverie. "D'you think she's got knives strapped beneath those skirts?"

Someone snickered. "Probably."

I pretended not to hear, but Fade's fingers tightened on my waist. From the tension in his body, he was ready to fight on my behalf. Again. I put a hand on his cheek. "It doesn't matter."

"Maybe he likes girls who act like boys."

That time, it took all my strength to hold on to Fade. He wasn't dancing anymore, but merely standing while other couples whirled around us. His black, black eyes burned like dark stars, as coldly wrathful as I'd ever seen. If he got ahold of those idiots from school, they wouldn't walk for weeks. Moonlight silvered his features, lending him a fierce, unearthly beauty.

"Let's just go." I had an idea that it would cause trouble for Longshot if we got into a fight while on furlough.

"I think she looks pretty," Merry said. She was one of the girls who had been kind at Justine's party.

"Well enough," someone else admitted.

"I'm going to ask her to dance." Fade didn't like that either, but it was no reason to punch the boy in the face.

I didn't know his name until he came over. Terrence was shy and quiet, but he moved well enough. He kept plenty of space between us—and half the song passed before he spoke. "I hope Fade's not mad. I thought this might calm everybody down."

"It seems to be working." It was a good plan. The rest of our schoolmates had lost interest as soon as I proved willing to dance just like any other girl.

But afterward, it was like Terrence had opened the door, and once cracked, curiosity poured through. The one who had been cruel didn't ask, of course, but others did. I danced with five boys before Fade lost patience and reclaimed my hand. This was proper exercise, I thought, breathless from all the twirling.

"Told you," he muttered. "Now I won't get another moment alone with you."

"You could ask for one." My voice came out husky because if we slipped away, privacy would lead to more kissing. Shivers of anticipation curled through me.

"Want to go for a walk?"

I nodded, and his fingers threaded through mine in an unmistakable claim as he led me away from the green.

Endless

I followed Fade through town, expecting we'd wind up in the swing behind my house, but instead he led me in a direction that became more familiar with each step. In time, he stopped at the unfinished house where I'd trained with Stalker, before I realized those midnight visits gave him ideas.

"Shall we go inside?" I asked softly, wondering if he'd stumbled on this spot by coincidence or if he had a motive for bringing me here.

"Is there some reason we shouldn't?"

I shook my head.

Fade crept up to the window. "I'll go in first and unlatch the door for you."

When I'd come with Stalker, we both went in that way, but I wasn't dressed for climbing. So I nodded and pressed close to the frame, hoping nobody would spot me; I felt conspicuous in my blue dress. The wait quickened my heartbeat, making the minor misdeed more exciting. Soon, Fade pulled me into the cool, dark house. At once, I saw evidence of the errand he'd mentioned earlier and wondered if my foster father would approve.

Spread on the dusty floor was the blanket he'd carried from down below, and he had scrounged a candle for each corner of the cover. Smiling, he got out the device he'd inherited from his sire; in the tunnels, he clicked it when he was nervous, so it threw sparks in the dark. This time he held it longer . . . and the candles glowed into lovely, glimmering life.

"You were pretty sure you could get me here," I observed.

"Just good planning. Besides, *you* suggested we take some time to ourselves."

I eyed him warily, despite the romantic scene. "What do you think we're doing on that bedroll?"

"Sitting. It would be a shame if you got your dress dirty."

He had a point; if I came home grubby, Momma Oaks would demand to know what I'd been doing. "And the candles?"

"I want to see your face. Do you trust me?"

In answer I offered my hand, and he drew me down beside him. The cover was big enough for both of us as long as I sat close, and Fade showed no intention of letting me put any distance between us. He wound his arms about me and cuddled me to his chest. When he tugged me closer still, I settled between his legs, both nervous and excited. His warm breath stirred my curls, misted my neck, and I shivered.

"Cold?"

"No." In fact, I might have a fever. The chills got worse when he ran his palms up my bare arms.

"I can't believe you're here with me," he whispered in my ear.

"Where else would I be?"

"Here with him." Fade paused. "Again."

The good feelings died away, replaced with dread. I sat very still. "How do you know—"

"Because I *saw* you. It wasn't just my smart mouth that drove Jensen crazy, Deuce. Some nights I'd sneak out, wondering what the two of you were doing in here. And why it wasn't me."

A moment of shock held me motionless. This was the deep-seated doubt Fade had never been able to bring himself to voice. It had been eating at him for months, and he'd finally decided to confront me here. I might have feared his purpose, but I did trust him . . . and I had no dark secret to confess.

"He caught you?" I guessed.

I felt his jerky nod. "But I never broke. I never told him what I was doing. No matter what."

At that moment, I hurt so bad I thought my heart would crack in two. He'd kept my secret so I didn't get in trouble, even when he thought I was doing who knew what with a boy he hated. That loyalty terrified me, even as I exulted in it; I'd try to be worthy of such devotion.

"I would've understood if you told," I whispered. "I can take my own whippings."

He shifted, pulling me into his lap fully so he could see my face. "Whether you can isn't the point. I'll always have your back."

Even when we aren't talking, even when you doubt me. Oh, Fade. Some might argue that if he didn't track my movements at night, he wouldn't have been caught, and his punishment would've been less severe, but I suspected that Jensen was a mean man when he was in the corn liquor, and he'd have found another reason to hurt Fade.

"Why did you follow me?" I asked then.

He hunched his shoulders. "If Stalker tried something you didn't want and you needed help, I'd be here, just in case."

"To protect me?"

"Yes. Always." He was unshakable on that point, and it was sweet, except I could take care of myself.

I appreciated the intent even as I said, "I was fine."

"What does that mean? Did he touch you?"

Finally, I understood what else was going on. I might be slow, but given time, I put the pieces together. "You have no reason to be jealous, I promise. We talked . . . and trained. You're the only boy who gets close like this."

"Oh." A long, slow breath escaped him. "I feel so stupid."

I put my lips to his cheek and whispered, "Don't. I love you, Fade."

My time in Salvation had taught me the meaning of the word and not to be stingy with its use. I should tell Edmund and Momma Oaks, in fact, before I returned to the outpost. It was a different sort, of course, but each permutation made my heart better and stronger, so I could fight harder.

He took a quick, unsteady breath. "That's what I said to you in the wagon."

And then his lips found mine, hot as sunshine, sweet as clean water. He wrapped me up in his arms, so I was above him, perched on his thighs, and I kissed him like he'd shown me earlier with peekaboo teases of tongue. I was too shy to do much of that at first, but my hesitance seemed to make him hungrier. His arms tightened, and suddenly I understood how the puzzle pieces fit together. Shocked excitement washed my whole body, but I didn't scramble away. I trusted him, even when he fell back so I sprawled on top of him. His hands roamed, and mine did too, clumsy, strange, and irresistible. Then his palm closed on the curve of my breast, barely touched, pressed, through the silky fabric of my dress, and I felt like a sunrise.

Fade pulled me against him, hard, and then he rolled over, poised above me, and covered my face in quick, needy kisses. His breath hauled hard in his chest, a deep and desperate panting. I stroked lightly down his back, trying to comfort him, because I had some idea he was hurting. Certainly, I was, though I wasn't sure why.

"Enough of that," he tried to whisper, though it sounded like more of a growl. "I told Edmund my intentions were honorable." He dusted more kisses at my temples, rubbed his rough jaw against my cheek, and squeezed his eyes shut, trembling.

"Are you all right?" I touched his hair.

"I won't die," he muttered. But he didn't sound happy about the prospect of survival, and for some reason that made me laugh.

Fade bit my lower lip in retaliation. In time, my heartbeat slowed and the fever waned in my skin. Gradually, he calmed too and then he snuggled me against him, my head on his chest. A little awkward, I wrapped my arm across his waist. I'd never lain like this before, bodies close, arms and legs tangled. It had to be a good sign that he could bear to lie on his back; the physical damage must be healing.

"Where did you learn to kiss?" I asked quietly.

He tensed next to me but he answered. "There was a girl down below, a Breeder. She . . . liked to show me things."

That shocked me to my core. Other questions spun in my head, laden with doubt. "Did you—"

"No. There's no chance of any brats. We didn't breed."

"How did you feel about her?"

His shrug shifted my head on his chest. "I was lonely. Just . . . sometimes it was nice to be touched."

"You told me that Banner was your only friend."

"I wouldn't call this Breeder a friend, Deuce. There are people who like breaking the rules. They find it exciting."

"So she saw you as . . . a challenge?"

"I don't know. We didn't talk much when we were together . . . and it was only a couple of times. After Banner died, the other girl got scared we'd be caught. By that time, I had met you anyway."

For the first time, I understood why Fade could be jealous of Stalker when I had reassured him more than once there was no reason to be. There was no chance he'd ever see this girl again, and yet her existence burned in my head like a live coal, because there was somebody else who knew how Fade tasted, how he felt. She might even be dead, based on what Silk had told me about the enclave's fate in the fever dream, but that didn't dim my envy at all.

My silence worried him. Fade rolled onto his side, facing me, his dark brows drawn together. In the flickering light I read his concern. "I knew you'd be mad."

"It's not that."

"Then what?"

"I don't know." That was as honest as I could be. "There's nothing for me to fear, but hearing that makes me feel . . . sick, thinking of you with someone else."

"That's because I'm yours," he said softly. "Just like you're my girl."

This time, I didn't argue with him. I understood what he meant. This bond couldn't permit others inside; it required an exclusive devotion and commitment. He didn't mean complete ownership, as I had believed before. Instead it was more complex than that, born of nuance and emotional shading. We could have other friends, of course, but I grasped the significance of his desire for exclusive kissing rights. Since that wasn't my forte, I had to go on instinct and trust it wouldn't lead me astray.

At length, I curled against him. I liked it better when we lay face-to-face, arms about each other. This way I could watch him from close up, only without the furtive fear he'd rouse and catch me. Since it was a cool night but not cold, our bodies generated sufficient heat to keep us warm. I knew I should probably get home soon, as it must be getting late, but I couldn't bring myself to move.

"I wish this night could be endless," I whispered.

"Me too. So . . . you're not upset?"

I shook my head. "It happened down below, before . . . well, before *us*. If you tell me there's a girl in Salvation teaching you things—"

"No. There's no one, I promise."

We lay for a while, with him stroking my hair. Sleep crept toward me but I fought it. If this was the last night I had like this for a while, I intended to make the most of it. Fade looked drowsy too, his eyes heavy lidded.

To keep us awake, I asked, "What do you remember about your parents?"

He thought for a few moments, his fingers clenched around locks of my hair. "My mother made the best bread. She had a pretty accent, smelled like flowers . . . and she had dark hair. She sang when she worked . . . but I've lost the words." He hummed a haunting little tune, but I didn't recognize it. When he didn't go on, I realized he could recollect nothing more about his dam.

"Maybe someone here can tell you the name of the song and how it goes?"

"Maybe."

I cupped his cheek in my palm. "Tell me about your sire."

"What's the point?"

"I'd like to know more about you, but if talking about them hurts, forget I asked."

"Another time," he promised. "I don't want to be sad tonight."

Unfortunately, when the conversation lapsed, I drifted off in his arms, and it was just before first light when I woke. Momma Oaks, if she'd waited up, would cut my hair with a hand ax—an expression I'd learned from Longshot—which meant I was in big trouble and due for a scolding.

"Fade," I whispered. "We have to go."

With a groan, he rolled to his feet and we gathered the supplies. I took the melted candles while he grabbed the blanket. I went out the door and he latched it behind me, then slid out the window. In the uncertain dawn, we strolled hand in hand. There were no other citizens stirring yet. I worried about our reception at home, but when I slipped through the back door, the house was quiet. Relieved, I gave Fade a quick kiss as we put away his old bedroll.

"We should sleep a little more, if we can," he said, low. "I'll take the nook off the kitchen."

Nodding, I crept up the stairs and got in bed. With luck, they'd never know just how late I'd gotten home. It had been a long, emotionally exhausting night, and I was glad to rest in an actual bed. Sleep came fast despite my vague guilt.

Hours later, after Edmund had gone to work, I washed up, changed, and ate breakfast with Fade and Momma Oaks. She had a thousand questions about the dance, which I answered with his help. By tacit agreement, we didn't mention our arrival time. Eventually, she ran out of excited chatter and said, "I have to get to work . . . four dresses on order for Justine and Caroline Bigwater."

"Well, they have to look the part," I murmured.

Momma Oaks twisted her mouth like she had something to say, but basic kindness prevented her. I spared her by changing the subject. "We have a few hours yet. I need to stop at the store before I go back."

"Can I go with you?" Fade asked.

"Of course." I hoped he wouldn't ask about my alleged shopping in front of my foster mother.

At her waved dismissal, I kissed her cheek, put our dishes in the sink, and then left via the back door. It was a misty day, coming on to rain, and the light held a hesitant hue. He was good at reading my expression because he didn't open his mouth until we walked ten steps away from the house.

"What are you doing, Deuce?" His look was quiet and severe, as if he expected me to lock him out.

Instead I summarized what I knew about Momma Oaks and her problems with her son, Rex, then concluded, "I'm just going to talk to him, that's all."

Fade didn't argue with me. At the store, I bought a ball of twine with one of my precious tokens and then inquired as to the whereabouts of Rex Oaks. Since I was staying with his mother, the owner didn't question why I'd want to know. Salvation wasn't the kind of town to safeguard secrets or privacy, anyway.

"I take it we're visiting Rex," he said, as we left the shop.

I nodded. "Whatever's wrong, it hurts Momma Oaks, and I think somebody needs to tell him so."

"Is that your place?"

"I'm making it so."

Rex Oaks and his family lived in a cottage smaller than the one his parents had built; it sat close to the wall in the northwest corner, tucked to the side of the gate. It wasn't a prime location, and if families kept growing, they might have no choice but to finish the empty house Fade and I had cuddled in. But I wasn't worried about town planning. I strode boldly up the walk and rapped on the front door.

A pretty, blond woman answered. She looked ten years older

than me, small and slim, with high color in her cheeks. "Can I help you?"

"I'm here to see Rex."

"Can I tell him who's calling?"

"My name is Deuce." I held her gaze until she looked away first, and that told me what sort of woman she was.

It didn't surprise me when she stepped back, allowing us access. "Want to wait in the parlor? He's working in the garden."

Fade murmured, "That would be kind, ma'am."

After she seated us, she went to get her husband. I scanned the room and found it simple but nice. When Rex joined us, he was a big man, taller than Edmund, but I saw the resemblance in his features. He plunked down in a wooden chair, a frown knitting his heavy brows.

"Do I know you?"

"No," I said bluntly. "But you would if you ever visited your parents. I'm your foster sister."

His mouth worked. "Pardon me?"

"I have no idea why you argued and I don't much care. All I know is that you're hurting Edmund and Momma Oaks . . . and if you were any kind of man, you'd make peace before it's too late."

"You don't understand anything," he snapped.

I ignored his belligerence. "You're lucky to have a family who loves you. Don't throw them away. Stop breaking their hearts." Before he could muster the presence of mind to kick me out, I shoved to my feet. "Thanks for your time, sir."

Without waiting for a response, I strode to the door. Outside, Fade laughed. "His face . . . oh, Deuce. I hope you know what you're doing."

"Me too," I muttered.

Summer

The rain came on just before our furlough ended. That gave me hope that the fire the Freaks had stolen would be put out in the deluge, but I had no opportunity to worry as I dressed in my patrol clothes—tunic, trousers, and Edmund's fine boots. I braided my hair up in twin plaits, and tied them with some of the twine I'd bought at the store earlier.

It had been a good day—no word from Rex yet, but I expected him to stew for a while. Edmund came home for the noon meal, and he gave me a chess match. I still wasn't very good at the game, which meant he could beat me fast. Belatedly, I remembered I was still wearing the necklace she'd loaned me, so I returned it to Momma Oaks, who was working in the kitchen. In turn, she pressed a package into my hands.

"Take care out there," she whispered, hugging me.

Though I hadn't wanted to pry before, I had to know before I left. "What happened to your older son?"

Her lined face stilled, her eyes on some distant memory, but she did not try to avoid the question. Instead, she took my hand, and led me to the sofa in the sitting room. Upstairs, I heard Fade and Edmund moving about, but I hoped they wouldn't come down and interrupt.

"He became a guard," she said. "And I was proud of him."

It must have been difficult for her when I showed signs of following that same tradition. But I didn't think working the walls was too dangerous in Salvation. There must be more to the story, so I waited for her to go on.

"He was a good boy, Daniel." Her breath caught like it hurt to say his name. I almost told her to stop, but she went on despite the break in her voice. "One summer, not long ago, a young one slipped out with the growers when they went to tend the fields. She was a curious, lively child, ever asking questions about the world beyond the walls. It was night before anyone noticed she had gone missing."

"Did he lead the search for her?"

Her mouth firmed. "He was the only one who would go. The girl's father refused to venture out because Mutie presence had increased in the area. Her parents wrote her off as dead and wept for her loss. They wouldn't even try." Such cowardice was obviously distasteful to Momma Oaks—and I thought, in that moment, that she would come looking for me. I resolved never to put her in such danger.

"So he went out alone?" The scene came to me without my reaching for it. I saw a brave young man doing what none of the elders would, risking everything for a child that didn't even belong to him. I hadn't known him, but my eyes stung.

"In the dark. I stayed up all night with the lamps and candles burning."

Too clearly, I pictured the scene and her lonely vigil. I already knew how the story ended. "Did he find her?"

Momma Oaks drew in a deep breath and nodded. "When he staggered up to the gate, he had the girl in his arms, and he bled so that I don't know how he made it back from the forest."

"He died," I whispered.

"Of his wounds, yes. It took three days, but there was no saving him. He was covered in bites, clawed nearly to death."

I already knew the answer. "Not from an animal."

Hatred shone in her normally kind face. "No, it was them. The Muties. They'd attacked the girl, and Daniel saved her. Elder Bigwater gave a speech, honoring him for his heroism, but . . ." She shrugged. "It doesn't bring him back, does it?"

Now I wished I hadn't asked, because I understood how difficult it was for her to watch me go back out on patrol. It must seem like history repeating itself. For the first time, I realized how deeply my actions could affect others, even when I meant them in the best way.

"I'm sorry," I said softly. Not just for Daniel, but for what I was putting her through—making the loss brand-new and forcing her to worry all over again.

"Don't be. You're doing an important job. When I'm cooking supper this winter, I'll be proper grateful I'm sure." They were dismissive words, but they couldn't erase the shadows beneath her eyes or the lines beside her mouth.

Our farewells were quiet and subdued, for it would be some time before she saw either of us again. *If* she did. But she gave no sign of that uncertainty, her expression warm and serene as she waved good-bye from the front step.

"Did you hear?" I asked.

"It's a small house." That was my answer then.

"Do you think I should have stayed?"

Fade shook his head. "You can't live for other people. But I've never seen a man cry that way before."

His soft words rocked me. I imagined Edmund standing on

the landing upstairs, listening to their old loss, tears streaming down his weathered face. Caring too much could be dangerous; I saw that now. But the alternative was no better.

Fade led the way to where the growers had assembled. Tegan bounced and waved among them, but I didn't get a chance to talk to her. Outside, I heard Longshot's voice. The rest of the summer patrol had come to escort the planters to the fields; Fade and I would be traded for Stalker and Hobbs. After some discussion, the guards opened the gates, and we went out into the damp, gray day.

With rain trickling down their faces, it appeared that everyone wept, mourning Daniel's loss. Clearly I was feeling emotional because I had spent too long with Deuce the girl, who indulged her softer side more than was wise. I fell into formation around the growers, setting myself to their protection. The familiar weight of the knives strapped to my thighs made me feel like myself again. This was who I was, even if moonlight and music could make me feel like someone else, even if my foster mother's faith had shaken me to the core.

I didn't trust that softness. Not wholly. There seemed an insidious quality about it. If I became the girl in the mirror, I might lose my ability to protect myself, physically and emotionally. I *refused* to be that girl. Yet, I had two broken halves—and each quietly waged war against the other.

The procession to the fields went well. I kept a sharp eye out for trouble, but the weather was such that even Freaks chose to huddle within their lean-tos, opting to stay out of the wet. If true, that spoke volumes of their sense and our lack, but the growers had to tend the fields.

And it was our job to protect them.

* * *

The summer sped by, despite occasional inclement weather. I grew accustomed to my duties, and the men seemed to accept me. In the fields all around us, plants grew tall and green, well tended by the growers whose safety was our most sacred charge. They were nervous, more unwilling than ever to work outside the walls. I understood their fear. I talked to Tegan when possible, but she kept busy since there were so few growers. When she could, she brought me word from Edmund and Momma Oaks, never anything important, but it helped, reminded me why I was here.

"Incoming!" the sentry shouted, breaking my reverie.

The Freaks hit us in force. Since we'd drilled for this eventuality, nobody panicked. I slid my knives into my palms, bracing for the rush. Rifles barked, dropping the Freaks as they charged. These were big, brutish in comparison with the ones we'd seen in the village, and they outnumbered us by a fair margin.

Thanks to the sharpshooter on the tower, half of them fell in a bloody pile before they crossed the distance to the outpost. I held the line while other guards ran for the fields, bringing the growers in where we could protect them properly. Terror gripped me until I saw Tegan had gotten to safety. My heart drummed like thunder, and I realized how much I'd missed this rush. Fear had no place in a Huntress's heart. But I seldom felt it for myself; it was reserved for my loved ones.

Fifteen surviving Freaks charged the rise. Glancing to the sides, I found Hobbs and Frank standing beside me. Stalker and Fade met their enemies farther on, and I whirled into battle with a joy that told me I wasn't quite right. This beast had fewer lesions than the ones in the ruins, but it still stank of rot, and saliva dripped from its yellow fangs as it lunged.

Dodging the bite, I greeted it with a high arc of my right

blade. It took the slash along its forearm. Dark blood welled from the wound, but I couldn't rest until I dropped it. This fight went on longer than they usually did, as the Freak blocked and parried, and then raked at my face with its claws. It took my full reflexes to sidestep, narrowly missing a new scar, this time on my cheek. That set fury alight, as I liked my face unmarked, and I went at the thing with wild determination, my knives a silver blur in the afternoon sunshine. I stabbed three times in rapid succession, using the style Stalker had taught me. Too fast for any counter, it took the wounds and bled out, weakening, slowing, and then I took it with a final thrust to the heart.

All around me, Freaks fell. Rifles cracked, and guards fought with whatever weapons came to hand. When the battle ended at last, I bent over, resting my hands on my knees, catching my breath. The growers wept, but this time, none of them fled. They had seen what happened to those who lost their nerve.

We had lost two men—Ross Massey, who I didn't know at all—and Jeremiah Hobbs. Grief built into a silent scream in the back of my throat. He had been kind to me. Respectful. I knelt by his body, heedless of the blood, and touched his pale, red-spattered cheek. A claw had disemboweled him. I covered the damage as best I could and readied him to be returned to his family.

Like Daniel, I thought, remembering my foster mother's grief.

Tegan limped over to me and bent to rest a comforting hand on my arm. "I'm so sorry. He was a friend of yours, I take it?"

Fighting tears, I nodded and she drew me up into a hug. I stood for a few seconds with my head on her shoulder, and then I strode over to Longshot. "I'd like to escort the dead back to town, if I may."

A few others volunteered, and he granted permission, obviously distracted. "Take the growers as well. There's nothing more they can do today." To the rest, he called, "Drag the enemy corpses away from the outpost, and build a fire."

The men needed no further instructions. They knew they were burning dead Freaks both for hygienic reasons and to send a giant, smoky message. It remained to be seen whether it would instill fear or outrage. I had no ability to predict Freak behavior anymore. That troubled me, as did the stolen fire and the secret village, about which Longshot had done nothing. Putting those fears aside, I marched away beside the wagon, loaded with supplies and bodies.

Tegan walked beside me, making quiet conversation, and it steadied me. At the gate, she hugged me again. "I appreciate what you're doing out there, Deuce. So do the rest of the growers . . . and I'll see if we can make the rest of the town understand how important . . . and dangerous your job really is."

"It doesn't matter," I said. "It has to be done."

"I'll still try," she promised. It would probably make her feel better to do something besides clean Doc's surgical tools.

I nodded in thanks and headed out with the others. By the time we returned to the outpost, most of the mess had been cleared away. But the fire still smoldered, and the stink was horrendous. The night, however, remained quiet. Maybe we had taught them a lesson after all.

We had been on patrol for nearly two months when Longshot summoned me to discuss our recon findings. "I've decided it's best to leave them alone," he said without preamble. "Right now, we're maintainin' the status quo. They're not comin' at us in overwhelmin' numbers, and our assignment hasn't changed."

Longshot was a cautious leader, but not an incapable one. I

didn't disagree with his assessment, though Stalker would be furious at the wait-and-see tactics; he thought it would be best to put them all to the blade while they slept. *That would clear the region for good*, he said, *making it safe for the human inhabitants.*

"I'll tell the boys," I said.

"Do you think I'm right?" The question surprised me. No elder had ever asked my opinion with such sincerity, like my thoughts were valuable.

"I don't know," I admitted. "I suspect they're waiting for something, but who knows? It might be years before they strike. Or they might have changed to the point that they just want to be left alone to hunt moose and deer."

He said, more to himself than me, "I have an achy feeling in my bones."

I shivered. He wasn't the only one. And while it might be age catching up to Longshot, it didn't explain my mood at all.

That night, after supper, I beckoned to Stalker and Fade. They brought their plates over with expectant looks.

"What did he say?" Stalker demanded.

"That an attack would be unwise." He hadn't explained, but I understood why. "We don't have the manpower or resources to go on the offensive. We're better off holding here and completing our mission. Salvation needs the food for winter."

Stalker muttered a low curse. "I only volunteered because I thought I'd see some action. This is shameful."

"What is?" Fade asked. He sat close to me, and I wondered if he was conscious of trying to send a message.

"To have knowledge of your enemy and do nothing about it." The blond boy glanced at me. "You must agree. You're a Huntress, right? How can you stand this?"

It hit me then. I *wasn't* a Huntress. Not anymore. I had the scars, but not the office, for that way of life was gone. So I shook my head quietly. "I was once. Now I'm just me."

Whatever that meant. I had instincts, of course, that had become part of me. I enjoyed the lull no better than Stalker, but sometimes one had to wait in order to succeed in an assignment—and I dreaded failure more than inaction. Still, it gave me no peace picturing the Freaks in their village, so close in relative terms, and so untouchable in our ability to do anything about them.

Stalker shoved to his feet, fire in his pale eyes. "I hate this. It's worse than school."

On that point, I could not agree. At least here, I served a useful purpose. He wheeled away, pacing toward the far edge of the camp. Stalker fixed his gaze on the dark and distant trees. I could feel his yearning to break free. With a murmured "excuse me" to Fade, I followed the other boy and put my hand on his arm. The muscles were rigid beneath my fingers.

"Promise me you'll respect Longshot's wishes, and you won't go into the forest on your own," I said.

He laughed, showing too many teeth; wildness burned in him. "What value could my pledge hold for you? I'm not from your fine underground tribe. I have no honor, right? I am not special enough to earn your favor."

I had feared this moment would come. The fact that it had taken months instead of days spoke well of his self-control. But I hadn't understood how he interpreted my behavior until it was too late.

"You're not angry because Longshot won't mount an attack on the village. This is because I chose Fade."

"*Is* it?" he mocked.

I stared at him, waiting.

"Maybe. Help me understand, Deuce."

That wouldn't solve anything. The only answer I could give was one that wouldn't make him feel any better. I had known Fade longer, trusted him more. He had chosen to follow me into exile. Those actions, no other boy could ever match.

But I owed him some explanation. "We have history."

A history that didn't involve Fade kidnapping and tracking me through the ruins, but I left that part unsaid. Though I nursed no grudge because I, too, was a realist, Stalker would never be my first choice. It wasn't his fault where he had been born, or how he'd come up from brat-hood, but that didn't mean I wanted him as more than a friend.

"I see." His gaze flickered away from the forest. "Then I'll have to try harder."

He was persistent when he wanted something; I gave him that. But not like Gary Miles, at least. I didn't see why Stalker would be so set on winning me, except the challenge of my resistance. Or maybe it was more rudimentary, cast on a primitive level. He recognized me as a strong, suitable mate, capable of protecting myself.

"I still want your promise you'll keep your word. You've never lied to me."

Reluctantly, he nodded. "I won't go back unless we're ordered otherwise."

"That's good enough for me. Thank you."

I turned from him and went back to Fade. Stalker's gaze followed me, hungry and intent. That night, I dreamed of a boy with wolf eyes, waiting to devour me.

Taken

That awful day, I'd gone about my normal morning routine, cleaned my teeth, and spot washed in my tent. The others all had to share, but since I was the only female, I got one to myself. From time to time, I heard complaints about it, but everyone was too tired for it to be virulent. The summer had been tough on all of us, and nobody truly thought I didn't pull my weight.

When Fade failed to meet me for breakfast, I searched for him. I explored the outpost thoroughly and found no clue of where he might be. He'd taken no gear, not even his weapons— and then I knew something was terribly wrong. I slid into the tent he shared with Frank, wondering if the older boy had heard anything, but he was gone too. None of his things appeared to be missing, but as I knelt, I sniffed at their blankets. *Blood . . . and the unmistakable stench of rancid meat.*

The other guards hadn't believed me about the stolen fire. Not really. Our watchmen must still be falling asleep, and last night, they'd imagined we were safe because of our decisive victory. *Which is when the Freaks crept in and stole two of our men.* We hadn't received replacements for the ones we'd lost yet, either. Now there were only sixteen of us.

And *Fade* was gone.

Fade. My boy.

I bit down on my hand until my teeth drew blood to muffle the urge to cry. Physical pain helped me balance the emotional anguish. *Stay calm.* I had to think. Then I had the answer; Longshot would know what to do. I bolted from the tent and crossed the camp at a run. He was still eating his breakfast when I found him.

His gray caterpillar brows puffed up. "What's the matter?"

"We have to mount a search party. Fade and Frank were taken in the night."

"Whoa, girl, back it up. *Taken?*"

Impatient, I grabbed his hand and dragged him to their tent and invited him with an anxious gesture to examine the evidence for himself. He took his time, dragging the blankets out into the morning light to hold them up and turn them in his hands. Eventually he gave a heavy sigh.

"That's blood, all right, and a fair amount. Head wounds bleed a lot."

Knocking Fade out would have been the only way to remove him from camp without him fighting so hard he'd have woken everyone within a hundred yards. He must have been unconscious when they dragged him off. We'd find him, though. We'd get him back. I refused to consider any other option.

"Tell me who you can spare, and I'll set out now."

Longshot stared at me, head cocked in puzzlement. "Why? I understand you were close, but there's no call to waste resources retrieving their bodies."

The bald words drew a groan from me. I wrapped my arms around myself in defense against the horror. The truth hammered me down, inexorable as the sun that shone. Freaks didn't take prisoners. If they were gone, they *must* be dead.

Then I thought of Momma Oaks's son Daniel, braving the wilderness alone because he believed he could save that child. Shame heated my cheeks. If I didn't try, then I was no better than the rest of Salvation. I *wanted* to be better. I'd find Fade somehow; maybe faith alone could keep him safe until I saw him again.

I shook my head. "With respect, sir, I can't continue without making an effort to retrieve my lost comrades. I'll go with or without your permission, and if that means I can no longer serve in the summer patrol, so be it. If disobedience means I will be banished from Salvation . . ." I lifted my shoulders in a careless shrug.

No matter. I refused to stay in a place where they declined to rescue their loved ones. And if he didn't change his mind, then he wasn't the man I admired.

"Hold up," Longshot said, lifting his face skyward as if in supplication. I had the sense I was a trial to him. "I never said anything about exile. Going off half-cocked will get you killed. I appreciate your courage and loyalty, but what good is throwing away your own life?"

"It's worth nothing without courage," I said quietly.

He sighed. "I can't condone your mission, but here's the truth. I'm not willing to order you to stay. You'll sneak off first chance you get—and well do I know it. So here's my offer. Talk to the men. If anyone's willing to accompany you on this harebrained mission, you're welcome to take him. Wait long enough for me to get replacements from town, and then you're free to go."

Though I chafed at the delay, I wouldn't get a better deal. There was enough of the Huntress left in me, who believed in putting the good of the whole first, above her own feelings, that I realized I couldn't just take off with however many men wanted to go Freak hunting, leaving the outpost vulnerable. The Freaks might be hoping we'd do exactly that, giving them the chance to slaughter those remaining and destroy the crops, which were nearly ready to be harvested. I couldn't take the chance that this was a lure.

"Agreed," I bit out, and then went in search of Stalker.

It didn't take as much pleading as I expected to get him to agree. He'd tired of sitting around weeks ago. After that, I made the rounds, explaining the situation, and what I intended to do about it. I wasn't surprised when nobody volunteered. They shared Longshot's opinion that it was a waste of time—Fade and Frank were already lost. I'd imagined some might want vengeance for our fallen, but they weren't warriors at heart, even if they could shoot rifles from a wall.

Only two guards remained to be asked, Gary Miles and Odell Ellis. They were thick, always whispering about me when I went past. I hesitated over approaching them, given the bad blood between Miles and me, but if they could help find Fade, it would be wrong and cowardly of me to refuse to request their aid. Miles was up the watchtower, standing sentry, and I climbed to the platform.

Quickly, I summarized the situation. And then: "Will you help?"

He flashed me an alarming smile. "So you need me now, do you, puss? Will you make it worth my while?"

Sickness roiled in my belly. I wanted to stab him, but instead I forced a smile and sidestepped the question. "You'd be a hero if we succeed."

Miles tapped his cheek, thoughtful, and then called down to his pal, Ellis, "Have you heard about our chance to be heroes, Odell?"

"Sure have," his friend returned. "What do you think?"

"I'd love to spend some time tromping around the woods for a change."

I didn't trust their willingness to risk their lives, which meant they might be more trouble than they were worth out there, but it was too late for retraction. Stalker and I would be stuck with them. It occurred to me that I was going out to search for Fade and Frank with three angry males, none of whom had reason to wish me well.

Before he could do more than wink at me, I skinned back down the tower and went to find Longshot. "Ellis and Miles opted to come with Stalker and me."

A frown seamed his brows together, and he stroked his mustache as he did when he was troubled. "I don't like it. You watch your back out there. It'll kill Momma Oaks if anything happens to you."

That was a low blow, but I shrugged off the guilt. She'd survived the loss of her own son. Momma Oaks was as strong as the tree for which her family was named. She didn't deserve additional pain but I couldn't abandon Fade to spare her. He was mine, and I would get him back.

Somehow.

Even from the arms of death itself.

I doubted Ellis and Miles would prove helpful, but Stalker and I could take them. I was bringing them mostly because they'd make good Freak bait. As for their motives, I understood. They believed I'd make an easier target away from the outpost; they could get some revenge on me for humiliating them. Despite Longshot's worry, I wasn't stupid, and it wasn't going to happen.

"I'll rush it through," the elder said. "You'll be on your way by afternoon."

That wasn't nearly soon enough. While I waited, the trail went cold. He could be dead, as they all thought. I imagined Fade cooking over the fire they'd stolen from us, and I nearly died. Horror seared me like a live coal, burning endlessly in my heart. Unable to sit still, I returned to Fade and Frank's tent. Stalker was already there on his hands and knees.

I watched him for a moment, and then asked, "What are you doing?"

"Trying to see which way they went."

He had been good at tracking in the city, I remembered. It was how he'd earned his name. Out here, there were different signs to read, plants instead of dust and stone, but the fundamentals remained the same. Maybe he could discern something I'd missed. Hope tormented me.

"They dragged them that way," he said finally. "Out the back of the tent."

Squatting beside him, I saw the telltale broken blades of grass. People didn't walk as much back here as they did elsewhere, so the signs were easier to read for someone who knew what to look for.

"Can you tell how many Freaks?"

He shook his head. "Two or three, I'd guess, by the trample patterns. Just enough to move quietly and get the job done."

"Why would they take them? It makes no sense."

"Maybe to instill fear? They've learned they can't defeat us with a frontal assault. We have better weapons and training, so they do what's left, making us scared of the dark instead."

Though it was full light, a sunny day, a shiver stole through me. I had slept uneasily ever since the fire thief crept into our camp, but this was worse. I didn't know how I'd ever close my eyes again. When I had been banished from College, I thought I could experience no greater pain than watching my former friends stare at me with judgmental hatred.

I had been wrong. This hurt more.

Stalker covered my hand with his. "I know you're scared, but I'll find him for you if he can be found."

My jaw dropped. *Comfort?* I didn't expect that from him.

"Why would you—" I couldn't complete the question, couldn't accuse him of being secretly glad Fade had disappeared.

"If I ever win you," he said, anger bright in his pale eyes, "it will be because you want me more. *Not* because he's gone. I'm nobody's second best."

"I'm sorry," I said miserably.

He put aside his fury as if it were a pair of shoes grown too small. "It's all right. I understand."

He didn't touch me, other than his hand on mine, and I felt grateful. If he had, I would have lost control completely—wept or screamed or something worse—though I wasn't sure what. My head echoed with self-recrimination. I'd failed, utterly and completely. My tent wasn't that far. Why hadn't I heard something? The fact nobody else had offered cold comfort. It meant the Freaks were getting better at stealth, learning from the animals in the forest. They were already strong, fierce, and territorial. They didn't need to excel at quiet kills too.

When I calmed, he drew his hand away. "Let me finish scouting the area. You get our provisions packed."

That was good thinking. I'd prepare our supplies, so we'd be ready to leave when replacements arrived. Plus, keeping busy meant I couldn't imagine terrible, heartbreaking scenarios. I didn't need to think about Fade, dead, Fade bleeding out, his body covered in mortal wounds, never to kiss me again, never to touch me, never to hold or talk to me again. I couldn't picture his beauty cold and quiet for all time. Hands shaking, I rubbed my hands over my face, banishing the dark possibilities.

True to his word, Stalker gathered information while I packed our gear. It took longer than I expected because men complained about us taking anything. They thought it was a fool's errand, and that if I wanted to leave, it should be with my weapons and my clothes alone. I could survive in the woods on my own—or not. Ellis and Miles proved of some use in this endeavor. They took what they needed without asking, and glared the other guards into silence. Our uneasy truce lasted until the men arrived from Salvation. I had no great conviction they would continue to be obliging once we left Longshot's sight.

The new guards were a grim-faced lot, knowing they took the places of two who had died, and two more who went missing. The other four were simply unlucky, because Stalker and I were determined to search for our friends. Ellis and Miles were being replaced too. Still, the town must realize that this outpost was important. Come fall, the survivors could retreat behind the walls for another winter, and pretend no danger lurked in the wilderness.

Longshot stopped me on the edge of camp. He held Old Girl in the crook of his arm, anticipating trouble, or maybe he liked the reassurance of his weapon in difficult times. I felt the same about my daggers. Surreptitiously I touched them, making sure of their weight.

"Got everything you need?" he asked.

I nodded. "Thanks for not keeping me here. You could have."

"I've known you awhile, and I reckon there's no preventing you from doing what you think is right."

There was nothing I could say to that. At best, it meant I was principled; at worst, pointlessly stubborn. I'd never ask Longshot which he thought I was. Like most, I was a mix of good and bad, anger and protectiveness, kindness and pride. But right now, I had only strangled fear and the promise of revenge.

"It's time," I called to Stalker, Ellis, and Miles.

They fell in behind me, following the trail toward the Freak-infested wood.

Purpose

Stalker led the way with his keen eyes and as we walked, he scanned for more signs of passage. I took rear guard because I intended to keep Miles and Ellis where I could see them. They spoke to each other in low tones, occasionally laughing with malicious intent. It wouldn't be long before they tried whatever they had in mind and I had to be ready.

"Here," Stalker said. "They put down their burdens. See how the grass is flattened and the dirt is churned."

"How do you know a moose didn't lay down there?" Ellis asked.

"The drag marks further on. And there would be marks from the hooves."

When I bent, I saw them too, faint but unmistakable. Somebody's heels—either Frank or Fade—made those indents in the soil. I nodded my thanks, and we went on, into the forest proper. At any moment, I expected to stumble upon them, devouring their prizes. The shadows thrown by the trees seemed ominous, dedicated to keeping secrets.

"How did you learn all of this?" I asked.

Stalker shrugged. "I haven't been wasting my time in camp. I made friends with one of the hunters."

By which he meant one of the guards responsible for procuring fresh meat for the town. That was one key difference. Bringing back game had been part of our job description, along with clearing Freaks out of our territory and protecting Builders and Breeders. As they had more guards in Salvation than we'd had Hunters down below, their division of labor made sense.

"Are they heading toward the village?"

"What village?" Miles demanded.

Stalker shook his head faintly; he didn't think it was smart to tell them too much. So I seamed my mouth shut and let him motion them to silence. There would be less conflict if they thought he was in charge. While his youth made him unpalatable, at least he had the proper equipment in his pants.

Ellis and Miles whispered some more. I wished I hadn't brought them or that they didn't have rifles, but close up, those would prove of limited use. Most likely, I'd be faster than they expected. Men always underestimated me.

It grew more difficult for Stalker to read the trail signs the deeper we pushed into the forest. The ground was covered with damp leaves, obscuring all but the most obvious clues. For the first time, he hesitated. I told myself he was doing his best; he had promised he would, and I had no reason to think he took such words lightly. But every moment we delayed, Fade got farther away . . . and the danger of his situation increased. I refused to consider that it might already be too late, as everyone else already said. I wouldn't entertain the idea that my quest was hopeless.

"This way," Stalker said at last, but I could tell he wasn't sure.

To my relief, we turned away from the path that led to the village. Instead, it appeared these Freaks were circling around, though I didn't understand why. Maybe they hadn't been accepted into the settlement yet, and were hoping to use the men they'd taken as welcome gifts.

Stop it, I chided myself. *This isn't helping.*

Misery knotted into an iron ball just below my breastbone, tormenting me as we walked. Miles and Ellis hunched their shoulders and kept one hand on their rifles at all times. They were going to draw the whole village down on us the minute they fired off a round, but as long as I could run faster than either of them, I didn't care much. Only Fade mattered.

Only Fade.

Two or three Freaks, acting alone. Try as I might, I couldn't work out the sense of it. Fortunately, I didn't need to; I just needed to keep my wits about me and follow Stalker. Soon, there was no path, which made the trail easier to follow. Freaks pushing deep into the untamed wild left broken branches and churned dirt. Now and then, they had to put their burdens down. I didn't let myself wonder why there were no signs of a struggle. If Fade had come to, he'd have fought.

But it doesn't mean he's gone. It doesn't. There could be some reason. Maybe they keep knocking him out before he rouses fully.

Maybe he is dead, an awful voice suggested. *You're chasing a dream, unable to let go, because he wanted both sides of you—girl and Huntress.*

I shook my head, breathless with the pain.

A short while later, Stalker knelt. Despite the green-cast shadows falling on his scarred face, I read his reaction to whatever clue he'd found. Dread. Steeling my nerve, I crouched beside him and the smell reached me. More blood. I hadn't wanted to think about the stain on the blankets before now.

"How much is it?" I asked.

I might be able to tell for myself, if I looked closely, if I spilled the wet leaves through my fingers, and touched the moist earth. There was no way I would, especially if there was a chance it belonged to Fade; I wasn't brave enough in this moment. Stalker had to be my eyes.

"Not enough for a mortal wound." Of that, he sounded sure. Relief lightened the load on my chest. "But I don't think it's human. Here." He held a leaf to my nose.

Beyond the initial copper, there was an underlying aroma— sickly sweet decay, as if the sores that showed on their bodies went bone deep. Ellis and Miles came up beside us, sniffing with desultory interest. I thought privately that they both stunk too bad to smell anything else, but they both pretended to notice the difference.

"That's definitely Mutie blood," Miles said. "Hot damn. They must be injured. That'll make our job easier when we find 'em."

He sounded genuinely invested in the hunt. So maybe whatever he had planned for me, he intended to leave it until we killed the Freaks who took our men. If so, he was a better guard than I'd thought. I figured he and Ellis would jump me at the first opportunity, the minute I turned my back on them. Of course, I hadn't done that yet, so my theory hadn't been field-tested.

"Does that mean Frank and Fade are still alive?" Ellis asked.

Stalker shrugged. "Who knows? It might have been a predator, attacking the Freaks who were laden down and easier to hurt. But it could be Fade or Frank woke up and went after their captors. We won't know until we find them."

Until. I could have kissed him for that hopeful word. But that would only give Miles and Ellis ideas. Silently, I continued on our flank, eyes sharp for trouble.

Trouble lunged out of the undergrowth at us, and Miles shot

the creature instantly. The sharp report echoed through the woods, making me want to scream. Now anything in the immediate vicinity knew where to find us. The animal fell dead at our feet, but it had been wounded already; I'd recognize Freak-inflicted injuries anywhere. This might be what had attacked them. The thing had brown-spotted fur and pointed ears. It looked sleek, a capable predator.

"Idiot," Stalker bit out. "I could've killed it quietly."

Miles shrugged. "You weren't fast enough, boy. Remember that."

I wanted to stab him right then, but I had to wait until he attacked me. Then it would be self-defense. I was starting to look forward to the confrontation.

The animal twitched, death-throes tensing its muscles.

"What is it?" I asked, wondering if we could eat it. Not now, of course. I wouldn't put anything in my mouth that a Freak had touched. Not even fire could burn the meat clean enough.

Ellis stared at me with pure derision. "Bobcat. Not too much for a real hunter, but it might've had a go at the Muties, if they was weighted down. They've been known to go after deer."

Stalker seemed thoughtful. "So the Freaks are dragging Frank and Fade. The bobcat attacks. One or both is injured."

"We need to hurry," I said.

To my ears, every rustle, every whisper of the wind turned sinister. The whole village might have heard the rifle report; there could be a hundred Freaks crawling through the trees, ready to attack. Even the small ones I'd noticed, who bore an uncanny resemblance to brats, had sharp teeth and claws for rending. However skilled Stalker and I might be, we couldn't defeat a small army.

"Agreed." Stalker strode away from the animal corpse and the spilled Freak blood. He seemed confident that he knew which way to go now.

So I followed, hoping at any moment we would stumble on Frank and Fade—that they would have broken their bonds and overcome their captors. The light waned, and it didn't happen. Occasionally, I heard movement in the trees, and it took all my courage to keep moving. This wasn't like patrolling for Freaks down below, my home territory. I knew little about hiding in these alien trees.

But for Fade, I would continue despite my fear. I crushed it into a ball and pushed it down so far into my stomach that I couldn't feel it anymore. Nobody spoke, not even Ellis and Miles, who had finally caught the weight of this Freak-filled forest. It was a heavy, oppressive place. Overhead, the trees were hung with strings of bone that clattered in the wind. *Warnings,* I thought, *about pressing too deep, just like the severed heads they'd staked in our fields.*

Before, they had been a threat I had to eradicate for the safety of those weaker. No more. Now I hated them with a ferocity that heated my thoughts to boiling. They'd taken from me the one person I loved. Though the word was one I'd learned Topside, I grasped its meaning intuitively; it was a thing that could not be articulated or explained. It merely was, like the sunrise or a sheer and sudden drop to the giant water that had stolen my breath, where the land ended in the ruins. My love for Fade strengthened me, made me determined never to give up. I would follow him until the world stopped or until I found him. I believed love hadn't weakened me or left me soft; instead it made me powerful, determined beyond all belief.

Soon, we lost the light entirely. Leaving so late in the day, though we'd had little choice, slowed our progress and put us behind in the search. There was no way to follow the trail.

When Stalker said, "We have to make camp," I still wanted to hit him.

But he was right, and there could be no arguing, no matter how much I hated it. There was too much chance of missing a crucial clue and going off course. If we got turned around, marching at night, then Fade and Frank lost their lives. I told myself that if we couldn't continue, the Freaks might have to make camp too. Of course, they might be able to see in the dark. Perhaps they would run all night with their hostages, until they reached their final destination.

"No fire," Ellis said. "It's too risky."

I nodded. While he might be an idiot for befriending Gary Miles, he knew what he was doing in the wild. We were all silent and sullen as we ate our hard tack and dry meat, washing it down with tepid water. My mind circled with dire, unpleasant thoughts, most of which I couldn't speak out loud. If I did, then it was the same as giving up on Fade. I wouldn't do that to him.

When I went missing down below, Fade came back for me. He didn't panic. Any other partner would have shrugged and gone back to the enclave, reported me dead. New Hunters came up all the time, gained their names, and replaced the ones who were lost. Fade hadn't seen me as replaceable then. I wouldn't judge him so now.

"How're you holding up?" Stalker asked, sitting beside me.

He put himself between the other two males and me. If they tried anything during the night, he'd kill them, I had no doubt. Not for the first time, I wished he could be content with my friendship—and that I wasn't aware he wanted more. Despite his hurt and thwarted desire, Stalker was doing his level best to find Fade and Frank, not because they were his friends, but for me.

"Good enough." I paused, wondering if I should really talk to him about this. But he asked. "It's the uncertainty, you know?"

He nodded. "Sometimes the truth isn't as bad as you imagine."

Sometimes.

It was chilly tonight, but I wasn't ready to sleep yet, so I just wrapped up in my blanket, keeping my pack close. The canopy overhead prevented more than a hint of starlight from trickling down, and it gave things a murky, indistinct shape in the dark. I could hear the other two whispering again, though, and my skin crawled.

"Think we can trust them?" I pitched my voice so only Stalker could hear.

"Not even a little. They've got plans for you, dove." It was the first time he'd used the endearment since he came to warn me that I'd only wind up hurting Fade, because he wasn't my kind. Now I wondered if those words weren't prophetic. If Fade hadn't joined the summer patrol because of me, he wouldn't be missing. He'd done it to please me . . . and watch over me.

Oh, Fade, I'm sorry. I battled with the impulse to blame myself. *Best to focus on immediate problems, like the men sitting across from us.* I knew the fate they intended for me.

"Forced breeding?" My voice came out thin.

I'd never heard of such a thing until I came Topside. In the enclave, it wasn't an issue since brats came up knowing their roles. In Salvation, I didn't understand how Miles and Ellis expected to get away with it. Though I had an imperfect understanding of the society, the rules were clearly different than they had been in the gangs. Females were respected here, if not treated as equals.

"To start."

"What do you mean? Is there something worse?"

"Some people," Stalker said softly. "They're born broken. I knew some."

"But not you?" It wasn't until after I blurted the question that I realized it would hurt him.

His shoulders hunched, and his answer came on a sigh. "I fought a lot in the gang. I clawed my way to the top of the heap, but not because I enjoyed it. I did it because I could only make a difference if I held the power. I did what I had to and I don't apologize for it."

I'd never asked this before. "What was it like?"

"The gang?" He paused, considering. "Brutal. None of us lived long, and we took what we were strong enough to hold. I learned early on that I didn't want to be low in the pecking order. We focused on finding food and making more Wolves to fight the other gangs, hold our territory."

"Did you take hostages a lot?"

"You mean Tegan," he said.

I nodded. "Did you?"

"Three or four times, usually from other gangs, so they didn't fight. I didn't know what to make of Tegan. So defiant when she had no strength to back it up." He sighed. "It's strange . . . I did what I had to at the time, but now, when I look back at that, it's like I was someone else."

"You wouldn't do the same things now?"

He lifted a shoulder. "Does it matter?"

"It does to me."

"For what it's worth, no. I've learned so much. I realize now that one girl didn't matter. At the time, I thought I had to prove my power to keep the cubs in line. But I should've let her go. Not that it would've done her any good . . . another gang would've snatched her up and treated her worse."

Killed her, I thought. *Like the enclave would have.*

"That would've been the right thing to do," I agreed. "Just the same, maybe I shouldn't be, but I'm glad you kept her. If you hadn't, she might not have survived, and I wouldn't have her as my friend now."

Maybe it wouldn't matter to her, but he should apologize to Tegan. I didn't tell him so; that was between the two of them. I brought the conversation back to something else he'd said. "What do you know about the broken ones?"

"They live to hurt others." By his tone, he had some experience with that. It might even be what had driven him to fight his way to the top of the pack.

"You think Ellis and Miles are like that?"

I glimpsed the movement of his head enough to know he was nodding. "Miles more than Ellis, who follows out of weakness."

"So whatever they have in mind, I won't survive it." Somehow, it felt like a comfort to see my future mapped out. If I wasn't fast enough.

"It won't come to that." That struck me as a promise. "Get some sleep, Deuce. I'll stand first watch."

Damage

It wasn't quite dawn, faint light filtered by the leaves above. I lay in my blanket listening to the quiet wood. The silence had a waiting quality. No birds. No rustling of small animals. And from beyond our tiny camp, I heard movement.

Crunch. Crackle.

Something sniffed and gave a low growl. I'd never heard that from a Freak, but then, I had never encountered one hunting alone in a forest before. The ones down below fed in frenzied, starving packs. These creatures had very little in common with their weaker brethren.

An animal cried out—a hopeless wail in dying—and then it made no more noise at all. Wet sounds followed. I recognized the unmistakable sign of a Freak feeding on a fresh kill: the moist smacking and the groans of throaty pleasure. I squeezed my eyes shut. It didn't sound like many; they would surely be fighting over the meat if there were. How close was it?

I rolled over and found Stalker awake. The idiot Ellis had fallen asleep on his watch; he was probably the one who let the Freaks slip past and take Fade from his tent. I fought the urge to slit his throat. *You're not a monster. You're not. You have no proof.* Through sheer will I fought down the angry impulses. Miles hadn't roused either, but Stalker and I, by virtue of our upbring-ings, slept lightly and with one hand on our knives.

He made a few concise gestures, telling me he intended to circle and I should go the other way, so we could spring an am-bush. Taking a deep breath, I nodded, drew my daggers, and si-lently slid out of my bedroll. The soft ground made it easier than it would have been down below with gravel and broken glass. Without a glance back, I crept through the lacy green brush.

As I'd guessed, it was a lone Freak, and my heart nearly leapt from my chest before I ascertained its prey wasn't human. *Not Frank. Not Fade.* It had been a deer, I thought, but it was hard to be sure, considering how much of it the Freak had already de-voured. Glimmers of white bone showed through the chewed and ragged flesh. The blood welled up from the carcass, and the Freak lowered its head, lapping with its whole face. Red ran down its chin and neck, spattering its chest.

Before it scented me, I hit from the left and Stalker struck from the right. Our blades sank true, and it died instantly, fall-ing atop its kill. Reaction set in, then. I had been so afraid I'd find Fade. Here. Now. And I couldn't stand the damage.

Stalker put his hands on my shoulders—and for a moment, his pale eyes blazed with the power of what he felt for me. The reflected heat warmed me where I hadn't even known I was cold. Then his golden, spiky lashes swept down, veiling his thoughts. I shouldn't let this boy comfort me when I'd rejected him. Weak-ness made me selfish, but I didn't resist when he pulled me against him. I had a fleeting moment to wonder where he'd learned basic gentleness; when we first met him, he had been all attitude and snarling instinct.

He soothed me with slow strokes on my back. *As long as it's only this,* I told myself, *it's all right.* I shouldn't raise his hopes, but while my breathing steadied, I stood quiet. Then I stepped away with a murmur of thanks.

"Let's get back," he said without looking at me.

I'd hurt him. In that moment, I hated myself. I didn't deserve Fade or Stalker. They only wanted me because I was different, because I used my knives with expertise and I didn't ordinarily cling or look to them to solve my problems. Normal girls weren't like me. Mrs. James had made that abundantly clear during school . . . and I would never be able to go back down below where I felt like I fit. The enclaves were gone, and sorrow weighed on me like a bag of stones.

In camp, the other two were stirring. They were fixing breakfast when we arrived, just more cold camp fare. As he took a bite, Ellis made some joke about me sneaking off with Stalker, but his eyes held a covetous light.

Miles stared with an ugly, speculative look. "I thought you had a soft spot for the dark one. Aren't we risking life and limb for your pretty boy?"

"For Frank Wilson too." But they both knew I wouldn't have insisted on going after Frank. Not if he, alone, had been taken. With apologies to his sister, who had been friendly to me, I wouldn't wager my life for Frank. Miles turned away with a sneer, dismissing my halfhearted words.

Trouble stirred. These two wouldn't wait much longer. They didn't care about rescuing either of our men, and we were far enough into the woods for them to strike. Stalker and I ate in silence and then packed up. By tacit agreement we didn't mention the Freak we'd killed.

Miles found the trail through sheer luck. He stumbled into the undergrowth to empty his bladder. There, he found signs of a serious scuffle. It might have been the bobcat, but I didn't think so. The way the earth was churned made me think it had been Fade and Frank, fighting for their lives. *He wouldn't give up, either. He's trying to get back to me.* The thought offered the only brightness I could summon in this situation. I put aside the warmth that flooded me when Stalker wrapped his arms around me. Anyone would make me feel the same desperate gratitude, even Longshot, who was too old to be interested in breeding with a girl my age.

I hadn't slept well the night before, expecting at any minute for Freaks to attack; the one we'd found nearby only underscored the danger. That rifle shot echoed in my ears. It was unwise, certainly, to get rattled. More than ever, I needed to keep my wits about me. Otherwise, the odds of making it back to the outpost alive, let alone finding Fade, were slim.

Stalker followed Ellis to see what he could learn from the marks on the ground, and I went with them. It didn't reveal any particular truth to my eyes, but I waited with poorly concealed impatience for his verdict. If the Freaks were injured—first by the bobcat and now by Frank and Fade—they couldn't be moving too fast. We could catch up to them if we put on some speed.

He finally concluded his study. "Four or five participants in the fight. Two were incapacitated and hauled off. You can see where the footprints in the earth sink deeper. They headed this way."

"Lead on," Ellis said. "I'm more'n ready for some killin'."

Miles said nothing, still watching me with the look that made me feel dirty all the way down to the bone. I resisted the impulse to scrub my hands along my arms. He couldn't see my scars, but I touched them for reassurance. I wasn't an easy mark; if he tried, he would find me ready for a fight. With some effort,

I held his gaze until he broke eye contact and fell in behind Ellis, leaving me with rear guard again—the way I preferred it.

The day passed in silence and occasional pauses for hard tack and water. I chafed at the need for rest, but we had to be ready for a fight. That meant leaving ourselves something in reserve. With each step, my hope grew. I'd find Fade soon.

That afternoon, everything went wrong.

We stumbled out of the wood into a Freak hunting party, six strong, rested, and well fed. The tallest one screamed, and they ran at us with yellow teeth bared. The number wouldn't have been overwhelming, if Miles hadn't turned on me with his rifle, whipped his arm around my throat, nearly overpowering me with his stench, and then dragged me back toward the trees. I kicked and fought as much as I dared, determined not to leave Stalker to face the Freaks alone, equally determined not to let this filth hurt me.

"Keep it up," he snarled at me. "This gun's got a hair trigger, and I'll spatter your brain if you're not careful, puss. It doesn't have to be like that. I can be real nice to you if you let me."

In the distance, I heard the sounds of battle. Ellis's rifle went off twice, and then silence. Stalker called out to me, but his voice got softer, the farther we moved away. If Ellis managed to take out one or two, Stalker could finish the rest. I hoped. *Please be all right.* To make matters worse, Miles churned up the earth as he hauled me, so if any of those Freaks survived, they would have no trouble tracking us, just as we had been following Fade and Frank.

"I didn't think even a worm like you would betray his friends," I spat. "Ellis needed you in that fight. Instead you chose to turn on *me*."

He wedged the barrel of his gun more firmly against me. "It was perfect. For once you weren't even looking at me. My best chance to strike." His voice went dreamy. "I'm going to break you down, puss. I'll spend days on it. And then when you start liking it, start liking *me*, I'll cut out your pretty red heart. When I make it back to the outpost, I'm gonna be sad to report your loss . . . and that of your friends. But I'll get credit for trying, a bona fide hero."

Ha, I thought. *I'll tear your throat out with my teeth.* But it seemed best to feign fear, so I let a tremor run through my body and I didn't offer a reply. Instead, I made plans. Sooner or later, he had to put down his weapon. He couldn't rut on me with his rifle in one hand. At least, I didn't think so.

Gary Miles was *stupid*. He took my submission for granted, as if he'd won. I let him take my weapons from my thighs. His fingers lingered, making want me want to vomit. I fought the urge, though doubtless if I did lose my food, he would take it as a further sign of weakness. I didn't because I needed the energy. Once I killed him, I'd see if Stalker survived . . . and if so, then we'd go after Fade. If not, I would continue alone.

Silk's voice whispered, *You survived the Nassau run. You survived the long walk Topside. Gary Miles can't conquer you, Huntress.*

She was right. My love for Fade and my fierce anger would see me through. I might not be as strong as Gary Miles, but my brain was better. Quietly, I bowed my head, waiting for his instructions, and he liked it, from the scornful sound he made. Amused. Cocky. Oh, he'd regret it. He would.

"We might as well have some fun," he murmured.

And then he dropped his rifle. Miles stepped closer, probably intending to do something horrible. There was no reason for him to be cautious. He'd never taken my training seriously because I didn't drill with the men. I had fought Frank Wilson, but I didn't remember Miles being there. So he didn't know about my skill. He'd seen me fighting Freaks, of course, but they were nothing compared to the prowess of a human male.

To Miles, I was just a girl. Unarmed. Alone in the woods with a man who was bigger and more powerful. Right? Wrong. With a smile, I went for his eyes, gouging deep with my bare hands. Blinded, blood streaming, he roared and lashed out.

Too slow. I wasn't there. Dancing around behind him, I kicked his leg, popping his knee out of socket. He screamed in anguish and dropped, unable to bear weight, but I wasn't through. I took out his other leg at the ankle, aiming a blow with enough force to break the bone. The snap echoed, rousing a flutter of wings above us. With bleeding eyes, unable to run, he still punched the air, hoping to tell where I was by my movements. If he'd taken visual deprivation training, as I had, he might have a shot at connecting. I slammed a fist against his temple.

"How many girls have you hurt?" I demanded.

He gasped through the pain. "What's it to you?"

"Because I want to tell them personally, after you're dead."

"I'll *kill* you."

"I don't think so." There was no point in further conversation. Silk had taught me to end fights before they could turn on me.

With a twist of rage, I felt sure he'd never give up their names, though I was sure there had been others. The broken ones didn't stop hurting people; they fed on pain. So Miles had done it silently, in secret, and left his victims too ashamed to whisper of it. I wished I could comfort them somehow, but maybe his end would do that for me. Heart cold, I snagged my dagger and sank it into his heart. A cleaner death than he deserved.

I gazed down on his corpse, finding satisfaction in my fallen enemy. For this moment, the Huntress owned me. There was no softness in me and no mercy either. This day's work pleased me fiercely.

Then I wiped my blade clean on his filthy pant leg. *No respect for you, Miles. I'll treat you like a Freak.* When my fury subsided, I gathered his supplies and added them to mine. His rifle, I slung across my back. Though I wasn't as proficient with it as some, it offered reassuring weight where my club once rested. It wasn't tough to follow the path he'd left, dragging me as I struggled, so it shouldn't be long until I reached the battle site. Before I got there, however, Stalker staggered from between two trees, his hands red with blood.

I caught him with both arms. In top form, he could have taken all six of those Freaks without breaking a sweat, but we had been roughing it for months, and he hadn't slept any better than I had with Ellis and Miles lurking nearby. His breath came in great, ragged gulps, but I didn't hear the wet, sucking sound that presaged a chest wound. He leaned his scarred cheek against my hair.

"I was coming to save you," he said, his voice muffled.

That surprised a laugh out of me. "From *Miles*?"

Stalker managed a grin. "I should have known better."

"How bad are you hurt?" Without waiting for the answer, I checked him, raising his shirt to look. He'd taken several slashes, and the one just below his ribs was deep enough to trouble me. "We need to clean that, or infection might set in and carry you off."

"I think I'm insulted. I've had worse."

"Don't be a hero."

His mouth twisted. "I think we both know that's not me."

"I have no complaints," I said. "Let's get somewhere I can patch you up."

"There's a lake about ten minutes from forest's edge."

"Can you make it?"

Stalker lifted one shoulder, though the careless motion clearly cost him. "I don't see that I have a choice. We don't have enough water to waste on cleaning."

Since that was true, I didn't debate the matter with him. I merely offered my shoulder when it became clear he had other wounds he hadn't shown me. His right leg didn't straighten fully; I had no idea why.

I didn't ask what became of Ellis. When we pushed out of the forest for the second time, I found the grotesque remnants of their pitched battle. Blood hung heavy in the air, and I stepped over the man's corpse, leading Stalker toward the lake. This would delay our pursuit of Fade even more, but I couldn't rationalize letting one boy die over one who might not still even number among the living.

It was the hardest decision I ever made in my life.

Legion

So much water always amazed me.

Down below, we lived on a thin trickle and rationed it in case we ran out. Here lay an endless expanse of shining green, bounded by a field of gold on the far shore. The sun sloped down beyond the horizon, setting the sky on fire. I turned away, unable to bear so much brightness when I hid winter in my heart.

On the shore of this lake whose name I didn't know, I stripped Stalker half naked and examined his wounds. Blood crusted the worst of them, jagged tears from Freak claws. No bites, fortunately, which tended to fester. Not surprisingly, their mouths were filthy. I tore my spare shirt into strips, dipped half of them into the lake, and washed him. It would be better if we built a fire, so I could boil the water, but time was running out. Every moment we delayed, Fade and Frank got farther away. Makeshift medicine had to do.

Through my dubious care, he stood quiet, his eyes half closed, as if he found this pleasurable, even when I covered the injuries with salve. I knew firsthand how bad it stung. I didn't have much left; it had been made by a friend of Fade's, and soon it would be gone. Then I'd have only my daggers left from the enclave.

Using the remaining rags, I treated the injuries as best I could, knowing we had to keep the slashes clean.

"Show me your leg. Is it broken?"

He shook his head. "Just wrenched, I think. I went running like a fool, after Miles dragged you off. It'll be fine."

"You'd say that even if you had bone sticking through the skin."

His grin gained layers of attitude. "Probably."

Soon, I finished the rudimentary care our surroundings allowed, including a tight wrap around his knee. It felt odd to kneel before him, but he made no suggestive comments, or I might have hurt him. I made sure the bandage was secure and that he could bear some weight.

After rinsing my hands in the lake, I asked, "Can you go on?"

He tested by taking a step. Not quickly, but he could move. "It would help if you could find me a walking stick."

I wasn't eager to return to the forest, but I avoided the battlefield and found a likely deadwood branch on the ground at the tree line, long and sturdy enough for our purposes. Though I hated the feeling, I ran back to Stalker because he represented my only tie to safety. How crazy that it had come to this. I didn't like being alone, and silence could drive me crazy after the constant murmur down below.

"Will this do?"

He tested it. "Perfect, thanks. Time to see if I can pick up the trail."

If he couldn't, then this had been for nothing. I couldn't face that; I just couldn't. The ball of anguish knotted tighter inside my chest, stealing my breath. No, I'd find Fade.

Oh, Fade.

Stalker ignored my tense silence. He retraced his steps, pain in every movement. I didn't see how he could continue like this, but I said nothing as he scanned the forest's edge. Finally he clenched a fist and slammed it against his palm.

"Nothing. There's too much movement of other game in the grass. I could follow any one of six trails here, and I might find a herd of deer."

"What else can we do?"

He thought for a moment. "Let's walk the shore. If they were traveling hard, as we have been, I'm sure they were thirsty. Freaks drink, right?"

I had never seen one crouched at a river, but if they lived— and the small Freaks hinted at natural reproduction—then, yes, they needed water to survive. "And the ground will be damp enough there to show you more specific signs, like it did in the forest?"

"I hope so." The alternative went unspoken.

We traveled halfway around the lake before he found their tracks. Even I could clearly make out the spot where one man-size burden and a smaller bundle had been placed on the ground, and then three sets of clawed feet moved closer to the water. I stood staring down at the dark earth. The prints were wider than a human foot's, claws pricking the mud above the toes.

After we followed them a ways, Stalker said, "They're heading around the lake out onto the plains."

Away from the village? Unexpected.

It changed nothing, however. No matter what, I'd continue until the trail went cold, or I found Fade. There could be no other outcome. He had taken countless beatings for me, proven his love when he thought I'd chosen someone else. I trudged behind Stalker and wondered how he could stand the pain. I suspected he had the same steel as me, and that his quiet inner voice whispered things like, *You won't quit. You're a Wolf,* just as I bolstered myself with reminders that I had been a Huntress.

The light trickled from the day, dimming to black, and then the stars winked into sight. Once, I had thought they were torches that belonged to winged people who lived in a city high above, but Mrs. James had taught me otherwise. Sometimes truth pared away the magic. Darkness would soon prevent us from moving farther, but then—I drew up short. We didn't need the trail anymore.

I knew where they had taken him.

The Freak encampment surpassed anything I'd seen or imagined, a horde capable of conquering not only Salvation but *every* human settlement. It had to be a thousand strong; fires blazed into the night—doubtless stolen from our outpost—smoky signals announcing their presence without fear, for who would challenge them? Stalker grabbed my arm and pulled me down into the tall grass, though we were too far for them to smell or hear us.

Did that mean the village functioned as *their* outpost, keeping watch on us? I hadn't been able to figure out what purpose it served, but this thought sent a shiver through me because their behavior had become eerily similar to ours. I wondered now if these Freaks had been assigned the task of taking Fade and Frank in a coming-of-age rite; if they brought back human prey, then they could become adults or something, like earning a name in the enclave. There was no way for me to know for sure, of course; it wasn't like I could ask. But it made sense.

It was also possible that the village was unrelated to this horde. Just like there were different groups of humans, maybe there were other kinds of Freaks. For some reason, the monsters who stole my boy had avoided the forest settlement. Whatever the truth about the two factions, it didn't impact my goal.

"Fade's there," I breathed.

I felt it in my bones.

Impossible odds. With our skill, we'd had a chance against a small hunting party, but Miles's treachery delayed us too long, and they'd rejoined the horde. Keen night vision allowed me to glimpse their movement—so many Freaks. Quite apart from rescuing Fade, we had to get back and carry word. Preparations must be made.

"It's your call," Stalker whispered.

The seconds felt like hours and weighted with terrible uncertainty. But I could make the tough calls. I was pure steel.

"You can't go with me. Your leg won't hold at a run, and if something goes wrong . . . if I don't make it back, you have to carry word to Longshot."

His hands clenched into fists, and an agonized breath escaped him. "Don't ask me to leave you, dove. Ask me anything but that."

I touched his face, his scars, knowing this moment mattered. It might be our last. Stalker let me, as he *always* had, even when he said it would look like weakness. Something gave in my chest. "I don't know how long it'll take for me to find Fade. As long as it's safe, wait over there until just before dawn, and then head back. If it gets ugly before then, then go. Move fast and quiet. Above all else, warn Longshot what's coming. It might be our only chance."

I'd never seen him look so grim. Despair etched his features, pulling his red scars taut. "If you want me to do this, then you need to kiss me good-bye."

"Fair deal," I said.

He'd stolen a kiss once, but this was the first time I leaned in on my own. This felt different too, maybe because it was my choice. His mouth was soft and warm beneath mine, lingering; I sat back, startled, but he wasn't smiling. His expression told me he thought I wouldn't survive the plunge into the seething Freak multitude. I had to admit, the chances didn't look good. If I planned a frontal assault, I might as well stab myself in the chest and then lie down as breakfast.

That wasn't on the agenda tonight.

Quietly, I outlined my plan, and he nodded. "It's your only chance."

Now I had to gather the supplies and wait.

There was no moon, just the starlight, but darkness didn't frighten me. The horde did. Ruthlessly I fought down the fear and left my pack with Stalker. He was hidden in the tall grass near the lake, far enough away that the Freaks shouldn't detect him. If I couldn't get back before he left, I wouldn't need provisions anyway—and extra weight would make my passage louder as I crept inside enemy lines. To succeed, I had to move like a ghost, like fog.

Can't believe I'm doing this.

I'd returned to the forest's edge earlier to collect my gruesome accessories, and I shuddered at what I was about to do. But if Freaks hunted by scent—and they did—then I had to cover mine. I couldn't let a stray smell rouse them from their awful, flesh-devouring dreams. Closing my eyes, I took the entrails I had harvested from the Freaks and rubbed them all over my body and then added fetid blood.

Stalker watched me without expression. "I still want you, you know."

"Like this?" I laughed to pretend I thought he was joking. If it spared his pride, it was worth him judging me a bit dim. Then I sobered. "Good hunting." It was the highest compliment I could pay, acknowledging him as an equal, and he seemed to realize it. His smile came, quick as a cloud sweeping past the moon.

Without another word, I moved through the tall grass, slowly, so as not to draw attention. There might be sentries posted, or possibly some of the monsters were nocturnal. Either way, I had to risk it. This number of clustered Freaks smelled bad enough to make me nauseous. As I drew closer, I heard little sounds, like snoring, but more liquid in the throat, a wet gurgle, but it didn't make me think they were in pain, quite the opposite. It was contented, a rumble I'd never heard from the Freaks, and I'd heard all manner of their screams, keens, cries, and growls.

Please let them be resting.

They were. They slept in piles, like animals, and like them, they had natural weapons: fangs and claws for rending their prey. At the perimeter, I froze. My nerve failed me. And I almost turned. He couldn't possibly be alive in here. Not in this. At best, I'd find his corpse and die for nothing.

Better a dead Huntress, Silk said silently, *than a live coward.*

Squaring my shoulders, I agreed. I pushed forward at a measured pace, my movements small and silent. I sneaked past a knot of sleeping Freaks, my skin clammy with terror. Any minute they would rouse and snarl the alarm. Lunge at me with unreasoning hatred burning in their eyes, tearing me limb from limb.

I'll be overwhelmed.

And none of that mattered. I was committed; a plan in place

to ensure Salvation didn't suffer due to my loss. If I died here, it wouldn't be for nothing. It would be for Fade.

I swallowed hard, breathing lightly through my mouth. *He didn't want Stalker touching you, and look what you did.* I shook my head. Who I kissed was the least of anyone's worries. Emotions would get me killed, so I wadded them up and forced them away. I'd deal with it after I saved my boy.

Find him, Huntress.

Then I heard a noise that gave me hope. From somewhere within the camp came the sound of human weeping. I didn't think it was Fade, but who knew how he would react in these circumstances? I'd probably cry too. I felt grateful for the guidance as I maneuvered around the sleeping Freaks. I wondered if they felt the same terror when they crept into the outpost, fear of our rifles, fear of discovery. *Do Freaks fear death?* It seemed I should have asked myself that question before.

In time, and through pulse-pounding dread, I came all the way to the center of the massive horde. Crouched low, I stared with utter disbelief at the source of the weeping. Down below, dying brats sometimes sounded like this; the white-eyed brat Fade and I failed to save did as the guard hauled him away.

Human pens.

In Salvation, they kept small animals for milk, eggs, and occasionally meat. I was familiar with chickens and goats enough to understand the Freak purpose. Here, a rudimentary fence had been built, via stakes in the ground, similar to the ones they'd mounted the severed heads on, and those inside the enclosure had been hobbled to prevent them from escaping. Hysteria rose in me.

They want to domesticate us.

This must be a new development. If Longshot had seen—or

heard of—anything like this during his trade runs, he would've informed Elder Bigwater. People would be talking about this all over town. Since he hadn't, I could only conclude this was more emerging Freak behavior. Lucky me to get the first glimpse.

Regardless, I had a job to do. If Fade was anywhere, alive, he'd be in there. So I pressed closer, until I slipped inside. Most hostages lay insensible with horror or grief, apart from the woman who wept in quiet, choking sobs—and their captors were doubtless used to her noise; her pain covered my approach. I crept among the hostages, seeking Fade, and my heart fell a little further at each strange face.

They woke at my touch, moaning, recoiling when they smelled me. In the dark, they might think I was a Freak come for a midnight snack. I ignored their weak blows and scuttling movements in favor of cutting them loose. It was all I could do. Whether they chose to leave or stay, it was in their own hands.

"Be quiet," I whispered as I went.

Some immediately scrambled toward freedom. Others stared in dazed wonder, as if they'd dreamed my arrival. I never saw Frank. I looked for him; I did, thinking of how I'd face his sister in Salvation, but he wasn't anywhere in the pens.

Maybe they already ate him. Fade too.

No. I searched faster. At last I found my boy, beaten until I hardly knew him. His features were grotesquely swollen, eyes blackened, and lips split over his teeth. His scars identified him as I rolled him over, and I muffled his groan with a hand over his mouth. Fade fought me like an animal. Even in his battered state, he managed to throw me. I landed on my back, the wind knocked out of me.

Around us, the horde was stirring, roused by fleeing humans. If we delayed any longer, they'd have us.

"Fade, it's me. Deuce." Avoiding his flailing arms and legs, I slashed his bonds and rubbed his hands and feet quickly, desperately. "Can you run?"

Please say yes. I don't think I can carry you. I'd try, of course. And we'd both perish. I didn't want to die here. It might be a glorious death for a Huntress, seeing how many I could take before I was overwhelmed and eaten, but the girl in me would rather run into the dark, in the confusion, and live.

"Deuce . . . ?" He was making the connections too slow.

Snarls said more Freaks were waking up. Human screams filled the night air. I'd wanted to give them a shot at freedom, not use them to cover our escape. No time for remorse or regret. I couldn't have left them tied up here while I freed Fade. It was time to move or we weren't getting out of this alive. Our only hope was to be faster and bolder than those already fleeing through the horde.

"Run," I begged him. "Don't fight. Don't stop. Just follow me and *run*."

Flight

So many times, I shoved Fade ahead of me, dodged a lunging, snarling Freak, or leapt over the corpse of a person who hadn't been so lucky, and we ran. For our lives. Only the darkness and upheaval saved us.

And the others who died in our stead.

But surely some of them got away. Maybe they would find Salvation and receive a second chance, as we had. If not, at least they wouldn't die in the slave pens, butchered for their meat. Did the Freaks fatten them first? Revulsion shuddered through me, but I put it aside.

I covered the distance to the blind where Stalker waited in a much shorter time than it took me initially. Straggling monsters gave chase, but it was a starless night, I smelled like a Freak, and other prey confused their senses. We needed to put some distance between the horde and us. If they found us later, a few at a time, we could fight in retreat, as necessary.

"You did it," Stalker whispered by way of greeting.

Circling my hand in the air in a gesture that meant we'd talk later, I grabbed my gear. Stalker pushed upright; his knee had stiffened while he waited, and he muffled a sound of pain. Fade stood quiet, ominously so, but it wasn't smart to linger. I heard sounds of pursuit; it wouldn't take them long to figure out why my scent was confusing—and that other Freaks hadn't already captured us.

The boys followed me, and I set the pace according to our injuries. Fade's legs worked, but his ribs pained him, and Stalker limped even with the stick for support. As we moved, I listened to the distant growls and screams behind us. Normally I wouldn't travel at night, in case we got lost, but necessity trumped caution. I made it to the forest's edge before Stalker stumbled, his knee giving despite the wrapping.

Through gritted teeth, he admitted, "That's it for me."

Little as I liked it, we had to make camp. My eyes felt as though someone had rubbed hot coals in them, and exhaustion set into my muscles, leaving them sore. Even so, I was better off than the boys.

But Fade wouldn't let me touch him. When I stepped close to look at his bruises, he recoiled. It wasn't just a rejection; it was soul deep, vehement, reflexive.

"Don't," he rasped.

I hunched my shoulders. "Sorry."

This wasn't how I'd imagined it would go. *He's injured*, I told myself. *Head to toe. And you smell just like the Freaks that hurt him. Give him time. After he's rested and you get a bath, it'll be all right.* Fighting sadness, I backed off and handed him Miles's blanket; it stunk, but should be better than nothing. He took it without a word, and I wished I could read his face. But between the dark and the swelling, he might as well be a stranger.

Fade wrapped up, but he didn't lie down. Instead he propped himself against a tree. "First watch," he muttered.

Stalker said, "I'll take next. Wake me in three."

"That leaves me on third. Do you still have your dad's time-piece?" I asked.

In answer, he flashed his wrist, and the faintly glowing hands showed in the dark. I had one more question. "Do you want my knives?"

"Please," he said, his voice rusty with hurt.

Without fanfare, I handed them over. Then I offered my water skin, refilled at the lake. He drank deep and handed it back. He nodded at me in thanks, and then his eyes skittered away, like it pained him to see me. No more talking, then. I trusted the boys to wake me if trouble found us, not only because I was the most fit. After the day's terror and stress, I passed out as soon as I went horizontal.

I woke to a stabbing pain and rolled sideways from sheer instinct. When I opened my eyes, I saw Stalker with stick in hand, but Fade was handling the Freak that almost disembow-eled me. It had clawed me through the brush; fortunately, the thing was alone, and Fade fought as I'd never seen before, de-void of his usual elegance. His injuries probably accounted for some of that, as his movements were mechanical, like the toy men they sold at the mercantile. You wound them up and they moved their arms and legs, but there was nothing inside. He used my knives with calm, dead proficiency, and he killed. Effi-ciently. Silently. The Freak fell.

"We can't stay." Stalker's frustration showed in the low growl. Pushing his wrenched knee might cripple him, but we had to move.

One Freak corpse in the vicinity would draw others. Though Fade hadn't slept, he said not a word. He just shouldered Miles's belongings, handed me back my knives, which I strapped to my thighs, and moved off in the dark.

It's like he's here, I thought, *but not really.*

Reeling with weariness, I grabbed my things and followed Fade. At night, his eyesight wasn't as good as mine, but I'd speak up if he was heading off course. I had a general sense of where the outpost lay from here.

The remainder of the night, we walked without rest. By the dawn, I had to lend my shoulder in addition to the stick, or Stalker couldn't have continued. Yet he held his tongue, the same as Fade, and their stoicism wore until I wanted to scream. I wasn't used to this kind of weighty silence. It felt like everything had changed out there—in ways I couldn't comprehend yet.

By the angle of the sun, it was past noon when the watch-tower came into view. The sentry on duty fired in the air, letting the others know he saw us coming. Guards swarmed down the hill and, under Longshot's orders, formed up a litter of joined arms for Stalker. The fact that he didn't protest being carried back to camp told me he hurt fiercely. Fade followed, shaking his head at all offers of help.

In the light of day I could hardly bear to look at him. He'd suffered so much, and yet he stood determinedly upright, shoulders back, eyes fixed on nothing in particular. But before I could tend to Fade, I had to talk to Longshot.

The older man escorted us back to the outpost, shaking his head in wonderment. "You made it back. What happened out there?"

"I'll tell it once," Fade said quietly. "Not here. In private."

Well, as close as we could manage, anyway. At the outpost,

there were no walls to hide behind, except the ones in his night eyes.

As he led the way toward his tent, Longshot asked, "Where are the others?"

"Freaks got Ellis," I answered. "I killed Miles for attacking me."

The outpost commander sighed. "I wish I could say I'm surprised. He was a bad seed. Do you mind if I tell his family he died in battle? It might generate ill will toward you if the real story gets out."

"That's fine." Glancing at Fade, I wondered about Frank. I hadn't seen any sign of him in the horde. "And . . . I have more dire news."

Longshot thumbed his mustache. "When do you ever have anything else? Let's head inside, powwow some, and then get Fade patched up."

I didn't know what a powwow was, but I went with him. It was the first time I'd been invited to the leader's tent, and it was much like everyone else's except he had a camp stool and a few extra blankets for padding. I didn't begrudge him that comfort, seeing as he was so old and all. Fade sank down on the bedroll, so distant in manner and expression, that he might not have been there at all. I took my place beside him, leaving the more comfortable seat for Longshot. It should be easier for him to stand up from as well.

"What happened, son?"

"They took us," Fade said. "Frank and me. Partly, I think, to prove they could. To scare you with your missing men."

I watched him, my heart heavy with dread. He wouldn't look at me, maybe because I'd seen the pens.

"But that wasn't the only reason," Fade added.

Longshot prompted, "Go on."

"They came in the back of the tent, up the hill, I guess. Slipped out that way with their prizes too. I came to in the woods. They must've hit us. My head hurt like the devil, and it was still dark. They'd tied me like a deer ready to be field dressed."

Unable to bear the flat recitation, I reached for his hand, but he pulled back and laced his own fingers together. They didn't tremble. He wasn't . . . *anything*. He might have been talking about whether it would rain.

"They carried us for a while, I don't know how long. We got free once. Fought. But I was dizzy, and Frank was scared. They killed him first, and I watched how well they butcher a human with their claws. They had a sack to carry the meat that used to be Frank, once they deboned him."

Longshot sucked in a breath, his face pale beneath the weathered tan. Bile surged into my throat. I could imagine too clearly the scene. No wonder he'd shut down. He couldn't feel this, couldn't let it be real. *Oh, Fade.*

He went on, relentless in his desire to finish the story. "Eventually they bound me up, tighter than before, and went on. I suspected they had plans for me."

I cut in there. I had to. Invisible knives turned in my stomach, picturing what he'd suffered, *remembering* what I'd seen. "They took him to the horde."

Questions rose in Longshot's face, and quickly, I sketched a picture—the Freaks' number and the human pens. It was yet another step on the ladder in terms of sophistication, another way in which they were becoming more human. To them, I was sure it seemed no different from what we did to other animals.

"Domesticated long pig," the elder muttered. I raised my brow in confusion, but he only shook his head. "You're positive you didn't mistake the numbers because you were tired and frightened?"

He always asked confirmation on my reports, as if I got the information wrong. But that was tiredness talking. It wasn't that he didn't trust me; more that he didn't *want* to believe because every time the situation changed, it got worse. At least he wasn't refusing to hear what I had to say and threatening me with very bad things to keep my mouth shut.

"Did you take those injuries in the fight?" I asked Fade.

He studied me long moments, shifting in and out of shadow from the windswept tent fabric. The swelling made him look monstrous, and distorted his words, though he was still intelligible. So bad I wanted to touch him but he had pulled away from me twice. Some things just couldn't be fixed with a kiss . . . and I still reeked of the monsters that abducted him.

"No," he said finally. "That came later."

"Why?" Longshot demanded.

"You ever eaten dinner at the Oakses' house?" Fade wore a peculiar expression, this awful amusement, as if his world had broken wide-open, and he could laugh at everything now, even death itself.

"Sure," the older man said cautiously.

"Then you know how she pounds the meat to make sure it's tender."

There was really nothing I could say to that, nothing anybody could.

Longshot eased upright. "Our time is limited here. We can't stand against so many. So our only hope is to bring in the harvest and get behind the walls."

I didn't think the wooden barriers would hold against what we'd seen on the plains, but sometimes speaking out served no purpose. It only made people hate you. And I had no solution to the problem, no way to avoid the calamity.

I stood too. "How long before the crops are ready?"

"I have no idea, and it doesn't matter. We'll fetch what we can, while we can, and run for it. Tend to him, will you?" The elder left then, mumbling about finding a runner to carry a message to Salvation.

"Let's head over to your tent," I said, as gently as I could. "And get you cleaned up. I'll—"

"No." Just that, a flat rejection.

It made no sense; he'd let me tend him before when he didn't want Momma Oaks touching him.

"You don't want to go back to your tent?" Too late, I remembered the bloodstains on his blankets. Had anyone cleared up the mess? "All right, mine then. But you need to be treated, one way or another."

He rested his forehead in his hands, then, the only unmarred part of his face. "Please. I'll do it myself. Just leave me alone."

"Fade—"

"Leave me alone," he repeated, with no greater inflection, but I could tell he meant it.

Not wanting to make things worse, I did as he asked. Outside, the guards went about their business. They played cards, stood watch, sparred, and showed no sign they knew how great the danger. The elder had decided, then, to send the messenger without revealing anything. It was a smart, if ruthless, move. Once they got wind of the true situation, most of these men would run for the town walls without caring what happened to the crops—and they'd leave the growers to fend for themselves on the morrow and not venture out again.

I didn't feel like talking to anyone, and I was too tired to be of any use, so I got a pail of water from the common trough, and went into my tent. If Fade didn't want my help, then I desperately needed to be clean. I stripped off my filthy clothes and washed as best I could. The slash on my ribs stung, and it was puffy. I used my small sliver of soap to lather it twice and then I rinsed. It stung as I rubbed the salve in. With no way to wash my hair properly, I wet it down and slicked it back into a tail so its ratty state bothered me less.

There was no hurry to dress, as I wasn't on duty, but I couldn't be easy about standing in my skin with only a flimsy fabric barrier between the other guards and me. So I scrambled into my last set of clothing, ignoring the pull on the torn skin. I couldn't bandage it myself, but if I kept it clean, it should be fine. Though it wasn't too deep, it would give me another scar, proof of my strength.

That was what I used to think, anyway. What they taught me down below. But maybe that was wrong too, like everything else had been, and it was just a flaw.

After flipping my blanket to the relatively clean side, I lay down on it, but I couldn't sleep. I had too many unanswered questions, and I hurt for Fade until it felt like a scream stuck in my throat. Tears rose; they leaked out in silence and salted my cheeks. It was supposed to be all right now. I'd gotten him back.

Later, as it got dark, Stalker slipped inside. I had no energy to yell at him, and besides, there were no rules about chaperones here anyway. He had been in my bedroom window countless times. I was long past the fear that he would ever take anything from me that I didn't want him to have.

"Room for me?" he asked.

I nodded and slid over on the pallet. "How's your leg?"

"Hurts. But as long as I stay off it for a while, it'll heal." More accurately, he hoped it would. "Told you I'd find him for you."

"Thank you. I couldn't have done it without you."

No exaggeration. I lacked his skills, and his knowledge drove us to circle the lake, hoping there might be some trace. I never would have thought of that. I was a Huntress, not a stalker.

"That was the hardest thing I ever did." His icy eyes shone bright silver, like moonbeams on the water.

"The tracking?"

He shook his head. "Watching you go into danger without me."

I should ask him to leave. He'd checked on me, seen I was still breathing. We shouldn't sit together in the dark when Fade was alone and broken. But I was wounded too, and I didn't protest when Stalker put an arm around me.

Harvest

Longshot sent Fade and Stalker back to Salvation the next day.

Fade didn't glance in my direction, and his steps were leaden as he walked away. His distance stabbed me like a knife in the back. I didn't understand his behavior, but he'd suffered so much. In time, he would heal and be able to stand my touch again.

Things would be fine.

How I wished I believed that. Maybe some damage couldn't scar over; the wound just bled and bled until it drove you mad or you died of it.

Stalker paused long enough to whisper, "I'll see you soon." And he leaned in, but I turned my face, so his lips brushed my cheek.

The hurt flickered so fast that I almost missed it. Then he inclined his head, accepting nothing had changed between us despite everything he'd done in the forest. I hated this. It felt like nothing had been settled. Neither of the boys I cared about was happy, and I didn't want either of them to go, but it made sense; they were both too wounded to serve any purpose at the outpost.

Therefore, they needed to get to safety before our time ran out. Still, it increased my sense of isolation.

Tension infused the men. They'd heard whispers about why we had to hurry the harvest. In ones and twos, they beset me, asking for hints or confirmation. Distracted, worried about my friends, I found it easy to get rid of them. For old men, they were easily alarmed by a girl spinning a knife in the palm of her hand, a brat's trick. But maybe my expression related to their desire to be elsewhere too.

That morning, a cadre escorted the growers out with multiple wagons, empty and ready for the harvest. It would take all our combined efforts to do this quickly. This time, we couldn't just watch them work while standing guard. I took up a scythe for threshing the tall grain. I turned it in my hands, reflecting it would make a fair weapon too. *Let's hope it doesn't come to that.*

In the field, I found Tegan working as fast as she could. She looked pretty and pure in her yellow dress, dark hair shining in the sun. I hardly recognized her from the thin, bruised waif I'd brought from the ruins, near death and afraid of her own shadow. She looked healthy, now. I joined her with a sad look; she could tell something was wrong, but the head grower yelled at us to quit slacking, so I followed her lead with the plants.

Backbreaking labor followed. Tegan didn't make conversation; she understood the importance of our efforts here. If we failed, the settlement starved. All the while, I kept an eye fixed on the horizon, dreading the moment when it darkened with the onslaught of the horde. Without pausing for food, though I did swill water in the fields, I cut and cut, letting someone else gather the fallen grain and pile it in the wagon. Elsewhere, they pulled corn, dug potatoes, and whatever else the growers had planted. I didn't know all the names, but my sense of urgency spiked.

"Slow down," Tegan begged me. "You'll make yourself sick."

I just shook my head. We had little time left. I could feel it ticking away, as clearly as the hands on Fade's watch. He'd let me wear it down below, and as I lay watching him sleep, I'd felt that ticking in my skin. I sensed it now too.

"I'm gonna be so glad to see my wife," one of the guards said nearby.

"Been a long time," another agreed.

Chatting as they were, the men didn't seem to feel it. I worked faster. Feverish. This couldn't be done in a day. How I wished it could.

When the light went, the growers returned to Salvation with the laden wagons. I wasn't chosen for escort duty, and I prowled the camp like an angry spirit. Longshot stopped me on my second circuit, drawing me toward his private fire. Sometimes he let men join him as a mark of favor, if they'd distinguished themselves that day. I didn't think that was the case with me.

"You're gonna burn out," he said. "And you're making the others nervous. Do you want to go back and join your friends in town?"

"Would you ask that of one of *them*?" I demanded, jerking my head toward the guards clustered around the other fire.

"Nope," he admitted cheerfully. "But you ain't a grown man, either, for all you'd like to be."

I stared at him. "I don't want to be a man."

"You sure?"

"Positive. I know people think I'm strange in Salvation, but I'm not a bad example of a Huntress."

"Never said you were." Without asking if I wanted something, he fixed me a plate of beans and roasted meat. It was venison, I thought, left from the last hunt.

Though I felt too sick with anxiety to eat, I shoveled the food in anyway. My body would get weak if I didn't maintain it, and then I'd let one of my comrades down. Under the circumstances, we needed all the strength we could muster.

"How much longer?" I asked.

"Two days should wrap it up. The rest will rot in the fields, but it's not ready for us to bring it in."

"Will Salvation have enough food this winter?"

Longshot shrugged. "Might have to tighten our belts a notch or two, but nobody will starve, I reckon. And some could do with some slimming anyway."

"You've always been so nice to me," I said. "For precious little reason from what I can see. Why is that?"

He was silent for long moments, gazing out over the dark landscape. Then, unexpectedly, he smiled at me. "I brought you to Salvation. You're like my own."

What did that mean, exactly? Down below, I had no kin to claim me, just the good of the community. Topside, I had foster parents and Longshot too . . . whereas Fade had nobody. That seemed so unfair; he needed people to love him because he'd had that once and lost it. But maybe I could make up the difference. Perhaps my heart was strong enough to heal the damage. I clung to that hope, just as I had to the certainty he must be alive.

"Is that why you sent me to Momma Oaks? Because you knew she'd do more than tolerate me."

The elder inclined his head. "I hoped she'd love you, yep. Seemed like you could do with some."

That was when I knew—in his way, he loved me too. That was why he'd put up with my questions and visits to the wall, the nights he stood watch. Warmth bubbled up through the pain and uncertainty. It was hard to stay tense around Longshot, which was probably why he'd called me over. My muscles relaxed, both from his easy company, and the quiet warmth of the fire. Exhaling slowly, I closed my eyes and tried not to think about Fade. Or about Stalker, who had kissed me good-bye, but Fade seemed indifferent to that too. He no longer cared about anything—and maybe I fretted for no good reason. It might be normal for him to withdraw, considering what he went through.

Be patient, I told myself.

Before long, I excused myself and went to my bedroll. Sleep didn't come easy, and I roused at every night noise, expecting to find a Freak trying to drag me out of my tent. As they had Fade. If they'd intended to instill fear by their actions, then they'd succeeded. I didn't feel secure here anymore—not that there was safety anywhere. The whole world was a ruin, a place of sharp angles and pitiless lines that could cut you to the bone.

In the morning, I gulped water, hard tack and then sought Tegan in the field. She glowed a deep bronze where my skin burned from laboring in the bright sun, but there was no help for it. Momma Oaks would have some remedy when I got home. I wanted to see my foster mother with a desperation that bordered on unreasonable, but I felt like she could make everything better somehow, or at least explain to me why nothing made sense anymore.

I saved you, Fade. Why do you hate me?

Maybe that's why. Because you made him live with it.

Over lunch, Tegan cornered me. "I saw Stalker and Fade in town. What's going on? They look terrible . . . and so do you."

Knowing it was pointless to withhold the story, I led her away from the others. Then I summed up the events of the past days: Fade's absence, the rescue, and the horde. Her face paled beneath its pretty color, and she stared at me, eyes wide.

"That's . . ." Words failed her. "But it explains a lot. Stalker came to Doc's last night. He apologized. He also said he knew that didn't change anything, and I'm free to hate him forever, but . . . he's sorry."

"I'm glad," I murmured. "I'm sure it doesn't matter, but—"

"It does, actually. Hate is . . . it's a weight . . . and when he said those things, I felt it go." She paused. "I've considered what you said. I mean, what happened was terrible, but I understand that he didn't know better."

"I think bad things happened to him there too." Pain taught people how to inflict more of it.

Tegan nodded. "I wouldn't be surprised. What're you doing about Fade?"

"Give him time to miss me, I guess. It hurts when he pushes me away."

Before she could reply, the head grower shouted at us, and we went back to work. Two days passed in this fashion, full of mindless tasks and haunting thoughts, until at last we were ready to make the final journey back to town. The wagons sat heavy, and the mules brayed in protest. I would defend this caravan with my life, not just because Tegan was part of it.

When the sentry shouted as the wagons moved out, I knew. Oh, I knew.

And my heart died a little.

This, then, was what they had been waiting for. After they destroyed the planting once, we established the outpost, and they couldn't get close enough to do it again, due to our rifles. They spent the summer increasing their numbers—calling Freaks from far and near—and now they had a monstrous horde. In one fell charge, they would destroy our food source and starve us out, if they couldn't breach the walls. In such numbers, they probably could; they just hadn't figured out the mechanics of the task yet.

"They're charging," the sentry shouted. "Heaven have mercy on us, oh, have mercy." I didn't think he even knew what he was saying, or how much he was scaring the guards who lacked his vantage. "Look at them all, the land's dark with them."

"Shut it," Longshot bellowed.

The sentry complied.

I listened along with the rest of the men while the elder barked orders. "We're spread too thin, too few men for too many wagons. But I want you sons of Adam to fight like you never fought before. Drive 'em off. Protect these wagons at all costs. *Do you understand?*"

"Yes, sir!" came the terrified response.

I took my assigned position, knives at the ready. The best riflemen would trail behind, picking off as many as they could before the first wave hit us. Growers, who had been unlucky enough to be sent out on this last, fateful day, ran for the gates. My heart in my throat, I watched Tegan go. She wasn't fast, but the head grower was helping her. Gladness spiked through me. If they moved quick enough, then I didn't have to worry about protecting them too. It was some distance, but I hoped they didn't run into trouble, no random patrols lurking out of sight.

The crack of rifles made me spin, backing as we went. From behind us charged the first onslaught, and there were so many. *So many.* A chill spread over me. *We can't win this one. We can't.*

Not with that attitude. I trained you better. Part of me wanted to look for Silk, but the rational self knew she wasn't here. She was just an echo of my Huntress half, spurring me on when courage might fail me.

The drivers lashed the leads tethering the mules to the wagons, urging more speed. Freaks fell with bloody gullets, as Longshot had taught the guards to aim for the biggest part of their bodies. *No fancy shooting,* he'd said. *Just drop 'em.* Sometimes he reminded me of Silk; only he was a whole lot nicer.

I had Miles's rifle, so I drew it. This weapon would never be my favorite, but I did my share, firing again and again, then reloading with shaking hands. The recoil hurt. I fought on. Five, six, seven, I killed—and the other guards did likewise—but the horde appeared to be endless. Freaks spilled toward us in a hungry wave; the wagons trundled on toward the walls. If we held the monsters long enough, *if* we could—and if the growers weren't hit from the other side—then our people might make it.

Even if it costs us everything.

I was happy Longshot had sent Fade and Stalker to safety. Tegan had gone as well. Therefore, I had nobody in particular to worry about. Fear slipped away. Utterly calm, I centered myself. No pain. No distraction.

Just buy some time. Slow them down.

"I knew it would come to this," a guard said. He gazed skyward and then took his last shot.

Too soon, the vanguard reached us. I tossed down my rifle and drew my knives. Like death itself, I spun and slashed, whirling, dodging, blocking. Men fell around me, but I had been practicing for this moment from the first time I understood what a Freak was. Four of them attacked me, but they lacked my training. Their claws and teeth couldn't compensate entirely. Numbers would, in time.

But I'd take as many with me as I could.

Two died swiftly beneath my blades, their entrails spilling in a pile at their feet, slicking the ground. The other two learned caution, and feinted at me, snarling, growling. The Freaks lost a little ground, as they still weren't disciplined creatures—and some fell prey to the temptation to feed on the dead instead of fight. I noticed they weren't eating one another, as the others, the weaker ones, had done down below.

Two more came, and they encircled me. I blocked four strikes, but the fifth landed. I stabbed the slashing hand, and the Freak hauled back, screaming its pain. Its murky, almost-human eyes glared at me from within the monstrous face.

"Did you think I'd just let you eat me?" I demanded.

"Eat me," it growled.

I almost dropped my knives. Just a mindless echo. Not real speech. Right? Just in time, I recovered, stabbed the Freak through the neck. I took another with a spinning slash that Stalker had taught me. Another kill. Another. My arms were tiring, and I took two wounds in quick succession. Claws, not bites. Cleaner.

How much longer? I watched a man die in agony, screaming for his wife.

"The wagons are clear," a boy shouted from behind me, a valiant messenger from Salvation come to tell us we had been brave enough for long enough.

"Fall back!" Longshot called.

The feeding Freaks raised their heads from our fallen dead, yellow fangs dripping blood, and watched us break. Some gave chase. Longshot held his ground, covering our retreat with fierce determination. He clutched Old Girl like she was the only woman he'd ever loved, and fired. *Again. Again.* I looked back to see he still wasn't moving. Holding his ground as he fought for us.

"No!" I shouted. Turned. *"No!"*

"Go on, Deuce." Longshot touched his fingers to his brow in a final salute and then pumped his weapon. Another Freak died. He was backing up slowly, giving them reason to fear him. He could make it if he would just run.

Come on, don't do this. I need you alive.

I took two steps in the wrong direction, and I'd have gone back, if some guard hadn't grabbed me. He half lifted me and ran. I beat at him as the Freaks overwhelmed Longshot, the man who had saved my life, all those months ago. The outpost commander went down firing under their combined weight.

The guard dragged me, still screaming, toward Salvation, toward safety. Toward the guilt of surviving when Longshot had not. Finally, the watchman slapped me, openhanded, and glared. *"Don't* make his sacrifice worth nothing. He had a bad leg. He couldn't have made it . . . they'd have taken him from behind, and he didn't want to go out that way. Can't you understand that?"

I could. I did. The Huntress in me respected his choice, but the girl wept endlessly inside, mourning the man who died a hero. I recalled standing on the wall with him, seeing him rub his knee. With bitter knowledge, I shut the tears away. Sometimes I had to be all Huntress or there was no surviving the pain. Someday I might let the girl cry for him, but not today.

"Let me go," I demanded.

He took me at my word, and we ran together for the gates, open just enough for the survivors to slip inside. Of the twenty who had fought at the gate, four returned—the guard who grabbed me, two others . . . and me.

It seemed all too terribly familiar with the families waiting inside for word. Most broke down into sobs when they realized what a massacre it had been. Momma Oaks would be searching for me, frantic, her hand in Edmund's. I couldn't move. The area was a mess of wagons, mules, and weeping women and children. I scrubbed shaking hands over my face and sank down into a self-protective squat. My wounds didn't matter since I didn't care how badly I was hurt.

Longshot, I thought, and the name stabbed me. I hated him for being a hero.

Outside the walls, the Freaks feasted and prowled.

They weren't going away this time.

Stalemate

Tegan found me first. Beneath my despair, relief stirred; I was so glad she'd made it back since I'd suggested she volunteer to help with the planting. If anything had happened to her, I couldn't bear it. Eyes worried, she knelt in the dirt beside me, heedless of her skirt.

"Let's get you to Doc's office," she said.

I shrugged. It seemed like a lot of trouble to get up.

Then she took a closer look at me. "You're *bleeding*."

"Am I?" In more than one place, most likely. Because she seemed determined, I let her lever me up.

"Deuce!" Momma Oaks found us before we moved more than a few steps. Tegan fixed a stern look on her. "I'm taking her to my dad."

I wondered if she'd noticed what she said and how Doc Tuttle felt about it. But he'd fought hard for her life and her leg, so maybe he was happy to have gained a daughter. His wife probably was too. In Salvation I'd learned that family ties didn't always come from blood.

My foster mother went to hug me, and then stopped, hands on my shoulders. "Tegan's right. You need medical attention. Edmund!"

He came up behind me and gently lifted me into his arms. I wouldn't have guessed he had the strength, but in his shuffling way, he managed. My foster father delivered me to Doc Tuttle without mishap. On the way, my head went fuzzy, and my vision blurred around the edges.

"Another patient?" Doc Tuttle asked. "Damn those Muties. They're keeping me busier than I like. Tegan, honey, get the soap and water and my instrument tray." She murmured something that I didn't catch, and he answered, "Yes, you can assist."

I drifted off around the time Edmund laid me down on the exam table, and when next I woke, I lay in my own bed. Sitting up hurt more than I expected. Confused, I glanced beneath my nightgown and discovered four new scars, neatly stitched together. I'd been hurt worse than I realized.

As I debated whether I should get up, Momma Oaks bustled in with a tray. It smelled better than I deserved. She set it briskly across my lap.

"You gave me quite a scare."

I'd reminded her of Daniel. And I regretted it deeply.

"I'm sorry," I mumbled.

"Doc Tuttle says you'll be fine."

Fine, I thought, *was a relative term, but he couldn't sew up the wounds he couldn't see.* I picked at my food, nibbling to make her happy. Momma Oaks sat down in the chair beside my bed.

"How bad is it out there?"

She frowned. "Don't worry about it. You need to rest . . . and heal."

"Ignorance isn't conducive to rest."

Sighing faintly, she ran a tired hand through her hair. I wouldn't be surprised if she'd slept in that chair, determined not to budge until I woke up. Edmund peeked in on us while she debated which of us was more stubborn.

He took a step into the room. "I fixed your boots."

That was almost more than I could stand because I knew how he was. He had no taste for emotional business, so from Edmund, that was like a hug. I nodded at him through misty eyes.

"Thank you. I was pretty hard on them."

"It was my pleasure," he said softly, and then retreated downstairs.

"I suppose it can't hurt to tell you," she decided aloud. "But if you try to get up, I'll send to Doc Tuttle for another potion. You'll sleep two more days, then."

"It's been *two* days?" I couldn't imagine what must be going on, but then, it wasn't up to me to fix it. I'd played my part.

"Indeed. They've surrounded the town. So far, they're staying out of rifle range, and they seem to be watching."

"Planning," I said bitterly.

Momma Oaks's kind face tightened and turned grim. "Once, I'd have thought you were crazy for saying such a thing, but I believe you're right. They appear to be taking our measure and deciding how to get inside."

"But they can't?"

"No," she answered. "Of course not. Elder Bigwater is having guards shore up the walls, just in case. And they've doubled the watches. We're snug and secure in here, don't you worry."

Evidently she thought it was better not to upset me, but her eyes gave away what her firm words denied. She was scared to death and fighting to hide it. The dark circles beneath her eyes revealed sleepless nights, and her lower lip was rough where she had bitten it, not signs of a woman confident of our safety.

I pretended to believe her. "That's good."

"Eat now, and then rest. Promise me." She held my gaze until I mumbled the words she wanted to hear.

Then I asked, "What day is it?"

When Momma Oaks told me, I laughed, the sound bitter and mirthless. She had gotten up to join Edmund downstairs, but at my reaction, she returned, perching on the edge of my bed this time. "What's wrong?"

"It's my day." Her blank look prompted me to explain. "The day I was born. After fifteen of them, I earned my name. I've been Deuce for a whole year now."

"You mean it's your birthday?"

"Yes, that's what you call it here, I think."

Justine had a party, as I recalled. I had a body full of itchy stitches and a tray with herbal tea and weak soup. I poked at the toast.

"I had no idea. Let me make you a cake." She bent and kissed me on the forehead.

I couldn't remember a female doing that before, but . . . I liked it. Everything hurt less. To please her—and because I was getting cake—I drank some of the nasty tea. My lip curled.

"Is Fade here?"

I'd have to go looking for him if he wasn't. He had no safe foster home, unlike Stalker, Tegan, and me.

Her face softening, Momma Oaks nodded. "He's got the cupboard off the kitchen. Wouldn't hear of you staying there, even though he's hurt near as bad. You lost a fair amount of blood, my girl."

"I didn't even notice." Her mouth twisted in skepticism, and I tried to clarify. "When I'm fighting, when it's all perfect, it's like the whole world goes quiet. I can't hear or see anything but my next strike. I don't even feel—"

"Pain?" she guessed.

"Sometimes, I don't. I'm one with my blades. That's ideal for a Huntress."

"I don't care what you call it, but that's the reason you're in bed, and why you're going to drink that tea and not budge an inch until I call you down for cake."

"Thank you," I said.

Cake . . . and Fade. Despite the mess outside Salvation's walls and my grief over Longshot's sacrifice, a spark of bittersweet joy rose up. He'd be happy to see me, wouldn't he? *It's been two days.*

"I'll leave you water to wash," she told me in parting. "But don't you get up before I say so. And I'm fetching you some ointment for your poor burned skin."

Obediently, I drank the broth and the tea and then ate the dry toast. From downstairs, I heard Edmund talking and Momma Oaks responding as she banged around the kitchen. Nothing from Fade. But then, he hadn't been talking before he came back to Salvation. I was happy the Oakses had let him stay since he was injured and needed treatment.

It didn't take long before I was bored . . . and lonely. There was only one remedy. I crept out of bed, careful not to make the floor creak, and pulled the book that had seen me through such troubling times. *The Day Boy and the Night Girl* offered great comfort; I'd found this book when I first came Topside, and the story had real meaning to me, unlike most of what I read for school. With reverent fingers I traced the design on the cover and the letters. I could decipher the words on my own now. When I touched this, I felt closer to Fade. I heard his voice as he revealed the end of the story, the wagon jostling us ever closer to Salvation, and a new life.

To renew my faith, I read them aloud myself. I hated doing so in class because I was slow, slower than anyone but Stalker. Not elegant. Not emotional, like some, who could make the words sound like they came from real people. I couldn't.

But I read the words anyway.

"The king gave them the castle and lands of Watho, and there they lived and taught each other for many years that were not long. But hardly had one of them passed, before Nycteris had come to love the day best, because it was the clothing and crown of Photogen, and she saw that the day was greater than the night, and the sun more lordly than the moon; and Photogen had come to love the night best, because it was the mother and home of Nycteris."

That felt like a promise. Except Fade was a between-child. He'd spent time both above and below. In the most accurate terms, the book meant Stalker and me. He was the one with hair like sunlight and who had been raised where it was bright. I had always lived in the dark. Suddenly unsettled—the book had lost some of its magic—I slipped it back on the shelf.

Then I went back to bed, as even those few steps exhausted me. I must have dozed, despite my best intentions, for I roused to Momma Oaks calling, "The cake will be done soon. Get ready if you can manage."

"I can!"

It wasn't a dishonest claim, though it took longer than I expected, mostly because I washed my hair in the basin. I hadn't known a proper bath since the furlough, and I'd lost count of how many days that had been. I couldn't go downstairs to greet friends and family looking like this. In order to finish, I had to request more water, which brought Momma Oaks in, clucking.

"Oh, look at your wet head. You're going to catch your death of cold."

"I'm fine."

I eyed her, wishing she would help and not complain. She took the silent hint and fetched several pitchers. On her return, she set a pot of cream on the dresser. "This will reduce the redness and make your skin sting less. You've got quite a sunburn, in addition to those stitches."

"I'll take care of it before I come down," I assured her.

She paused at the door. "Rex and his wife came to dinner last week."

"Did they?"

"He said you called on him during your furlough."

"I thought I should meet him since he's my foster brother and all." I'd also yelled at him; I wondered how much she knew, what he'd told her.

"I'm glad you did. It was beyond time he came home. So . . . thank you, Deuce. You've been a blessing to our house."

Once Momma Oaks left, I concluded my makeshift bath in a hurry. My strength wasn't what it should be yet, and I sank down on the edge of the bed, waiting for the dizzy spell to pass. While I paused, I did up my hair in an intricate braid, prettier than the twin plaits I'd adopted for fighting, then I tied the bottom with a green ribbon. After that, I investigated the pot my foster mother had left for me. It smelled nice, but it was tacky to the touch. Because I'd promised, I used the sticky cream on my face and hands.

Once I felt a bit better, I went to my closet, but I didn't

choose the blue dress I'd worn to the festival. I might never put that on again. Too many memories came with the silky fabric, making me worry Fade and I would never be together again as we had been that night. Fighting my fear, I donned the green one that matched the ribbon in my hair. I checked my reflection, pronounced myself passable, and made my way downstairs.

There, I found a number of guests waiting for me: Edmund and Momma Oaks, Doc Tuttle, his wife, Tegan, Stalker, his foster father, Smith, and to my relief, Fade. The swelling around his eyes and jaw had gone down enough so I could make out his features again. His movements appeared tentative, as if his ribs pained him. And he didn't smile at me. He looked away. When they noticed me, everyone spoke at once, murmuring good wishes and congratulations. Dumbstruck, I realized what Momma Oaks had done—and at such short notice too. This was a party. For *me*. I blinked away sudden, girlish tears.

Edmund took my arm, escorting me to the dining table as if he were just being polite, but I think he saw I could use the support. My stitches pulled, and two of the wounds throbbed with a low heat. But I couldn't be induced to go back to bed under any circumstances.

"You're looking much better," Doc Tuttle said with a jovial smile. "Just in time for a special day, I hear. How old are you?"

"Sixteen," I answered.

The elders all made noises about how I was growing up, and I didn't even want to stab them. I didn't tell them I was grown, and had been for a year. I was distracted by something else entirely.

The pile of presents.

Most had been hastily wrapped, and they weren't pretty like the parcels at Justine's house. I didn't mind at all. Nobody expected me to bleed for these, unlike the gifts that accompanied my scars on naming day. These offerings were arrayed for my pleasure—and to show affection.

"Thank you," I said, again and again, as I opened them.

Nobody had ever given me things because they wanted to. I'd only ever traded one object for another. It mattered not at all what the packages contained; I was delighted with the contents. I received more hair ribbons, a whetstone for my daggers, a fine leather sheath that fit neatly around my thigh.

When I thanked Edmund for the scabbard, he colored and asked, "How did you know?"

"The high quality of the work," I answered, and my foster father was so pleased, he bent down to kiss my cheek.

Once I finished opening all my gifts, I ate cake, chatted, and drank cider. It was a beautiful party . . . and awful too. Because Fade acted like he wasn't there. I didn't know which present came from him, if anything did, and I feared approaching him after the way he'd begged me to leave him alone at the outpost. I'd die if he said that in front of everyone. So I watched him from the corner of my eyes, tracking his restless movements.

Tegan sat down beside me. "Stop it."

My gaze snapped back. "What?"

"You're watching him to death." Her tone made me think she had something else to say about Fade, but this wasn't the time to talk about it.

"Sorry." I looked everywhere else instead. "Can you come upstairs with me?"

She nodded. "For a little while. Later."

After the cake, we moved into the sitting room with chairs carried in as needed. Lamps were lit, and candles crackled wax in their saucers, here and there. It was a merry occasion, though disaster and death lurked outside the walls. The elders talked amongst themselves, Edmund and Smith holding a lively conversation about their various crafts. Momma Oaks chatted with Doc Tuttle and his wife.

Eventually, I crept upstairs with Tegan, and nobody seemed to notice. At least, they didn't call to ask what we were doing. The movements pulled my stitches and made the wounds burn. She helped me to the bed and sat down beside me.

"You know what happened," I said then. "I thought if I gave him time, that would help, but it's not getting better. Do you have any idea why—"

"When you got me away from the Wolves, the thing I liked best about you was that you didn't treat me like a bird with a broken wing. You gave me a weapon and expected me to fight."

"I don't understand what that has to do with Fade."

"But deep down, I felt . . . dirty. Like I wasn't as good or as strong as you."

"What?" I gasped.

She held up a hand to stem my shocked protest. "What happened to Fade, happened against his will. He couldn't stop it. So if I had to guess, I'd say he feels like I did. And there's no magic to heal him. The only cure is time."

"So what should I do?"

Tegan shrugged and shook her head. "I wish I had the answers, Deuce, but you know him better than me. Whether you should push or let him be."

As we went back downstairs, I hoped I made the right call. Stalker limped over to join Tegan and me, his stick carved into an elegant shape and buffed to a high shine. "You had us worried. Passing out is more Tegan's style."

She laughed and nudged him with one elbow. "I'd like to see

you do better with a hole in your thigh. Which somebody then poked with a burning knife."

Had they become friends after his apology? I was glad they'd made peace but I hardly recognized my world anymore. Fade was a ghost. Stalker and Tegan were joking around together. I shook my head, feeling confused, tired, and sore. The initial rush of excitement died, leaving me ready to retire, but I couldn't be rude.

Momma Oaks soon interpreted my weariness correctly. The party broke up with smiles and more congratulations. Funny. I was old enough now, officially, not to attend school with Mrs. James. She had been such a source of misery for me when I first arrived; I'd longed for this day.

Now I didn't care at all.

I murmured my good-nights, accepting kisses on the cheek from Tegan and Stalker. With a grin, he pressed his lips to the one she didn't. Then the guests filed out. I turned toward the stairs. It seemed like such a long way to my room.

Halfway, a warm hand settled in the small of my back, making sure I didn't lose my balance on the stairs. I didn't look, too afraid to hope it could be Fade, but the unmistakable tingles identified him. The quiet between us lingered all the way up, until we reached my bedroom door.

And then he spoke:

"Happy naming day, Deuce."

A smile built inside me. But before I could offer a reply, he went on, "Forget me. Stop staring at me with those begging eyes. I can't be what you need now."

And then he went away, all ice and air, and left me dying in the silence.

Legacy

Doc Tuttle came later in the week to remove my stitches. His hands were steady and capable as he snipped, making small talk to lessen my embarrassment at having his hands in places I would never let anyone but Fade touch. Mindful of the proprieties, Momma Oaks stood by, reassuring me with a hand on my hair.

I'd never had so many people who cared whether my flesh mended. They both exclaimed over the scars I had on shoulder and stomach, mementoes of battles won. The ones on my arms I had earned through personal valor—and they didn't admire them, either. The loss of status didn't bother me as much anymore. I'd established my worth this summer.

Momma Oaks sighed. "I hate seeing how you've been hurt."

"Everybody in Salvation should be this strong," Doc Tuttle complimented me. "No malingering now."

Once he left, I asked, "What does that mean?"

"Pretending to feel worse than you do to get out of work."

"I'd never." I was genuinely insulted and tired of being babied.

Things hadn't improved with Fade. He spent his days with Edmund, learning to work with leather. I didn't see him as a shoemaker, but he could tool armor if he kept up the craft, which meant we'd have Tegan for healing, Stalker for weapons, and Fade for gear. That left me feeling like I needed to do something other than fight.

I spent my time mending with Momma Oaks and mulling dark thoughts. I couldn't believe Stalker hadn't come to see me even once. Not that I wanted him to. I was glad he'd finally decided to leave me alone. I *was*. But it stung a little that both boys had abandoned me.

When I had healed enough, Elder Bigwater sent for me. My foster mother did her utmost to keep the grim news from reaching me, but it came in trickles, and on this particular day, a messenger arrived with word. It was the same boy who had come to advise us that the wagons were safe. I recognized him, then, as I'd met Zachariah Bigwater the night of the dance.

Justine's older brother was a town hero—with people clamoring for his time and attention—but he stayed to escort me to see his father. Zach resembled Justine a little but his hair was darker, more like the grain I'd cut in those bloody fields. His eyes shone the same remarkable blue, though. His features were stronger as well, but he didn't look much like his dad.

"You fought with my friend, Frank Wilson," he said as we walked.

"He was a good man."

Zach must be hurting.

The boy nodded. "We went to school together."

"Did you want to know something particular?" I asked gently.

Clearly he did or he wouldn't have broached the subject. If it were me, I'd want to know exactly what happened. The endless uncertainty would haunt me otherwise, my mind conjuring worse fates. Only it was impossible to imagine a man leaving this world in a more awful manner; Zach just didn't know that. His fears were probably comforting in comparison.

His steps slowed. "Did he die well?"

No, I thought. *Nobody did. They just died.*

Dishonesty was foreign to me, but the truth would only haunt Zach's dreams if I repeated Fade's tale of how Frank had been murdered and deboned. So I lied, though the heartening words stuck in my throat. "He fought until the very end. Fade said he never gave up."

Not even when they butchered him.

Zach hunched his shoulders as we approached the house. As I recalled, it was nice, large as one might expect, and freshly whitewashed. Mrs. Bigwater had an herb garden to the side and flowers out front that rioted in pink and orange. Out back, she probably had a vegetable patch. I knew there was a green yard on the other side, where Justine had held her party.

"I wanted to volunteer," he said then. "My mother wouldn't let me."

If he had, he probably wouldn't be standing here. So few of us made it back. The last stand lingered in my memory, burned into sharp relief, all ashes and salt. I couldn't smile at him, wishing for glory or to feel worthy of his friend's valiant death. I just couldn't. The truth was too sharp and stark.

"It's better you didn't," I rasped, surprised at the thickness in my throat.

Longshot.

"Did you kill a lot of Muties?"

So many. Too many. It no longer felt brave to me, only inevitable. "As many as I had to," I answered. "And your message came just in time . . . without it, none of us would have made it back." In my mind's eye, I saw again that wave, coming after the first. Another minute and we wouldn't have been able to outrun them. Strange to think I owed my life to Zach Bigwater. "So thank you."

"Well." He seemed uncomfortable, whether from his own emotions or my gratitude, I didn't know. "Let's not keep my father waiting."

I hadn't gone into the house last time, so I felt odd following him up the stairs. Within, it was finer than my home, more fancy things that had only a decorative purpose. There was a lot of glass, more than I'd ever seen in one place before. I didn't feel comfortable here, too easy to break something. Zach led me through the sitting room, and then we went farther, down a hall, and into a room on the left. It was nice enough, I supposed, with a desk, two chairs, and endless rows of bookshelves. *Fade would want to read all the titles.* His name knifed me with the echo of his distance, so I fled from the thought and focused on Elder Bigwater, who stood to greet me.

It was polite to offer one's hand, so I crossed the room and did so. He seemed surprised when I shook his.

"You're an unusual young woman," he said.

I glanced between him and Zach, wondering what I'd done wrong.

"Men shake," his son explained. "Girls usually curtsy."

Hm. Since I had no idea what that was, they wouldn't get one. People sometimes looked at me like I was defective for not knowing rules they took for granted. Fade probably felt this way when he arrived in our enclave and got chided for unfamiliarity with customs foreign to him.

I figured it was time we got down to business. "Maybe we could talk about why you wanted to see me?"

The elder tilted his head. "Of course. Zach?"

The young man lifted a hand to me in farewell and strode out, shutting the door behind him. With a quiet gesture, Elder Bigwater invited me to take a seat in the chair opposite his desk. I did so, wondering why I felt such trepidation. Was I in trouble? I hadn't been the most obedient Huntress this summer. Maybe Longshot included something about my conduct in the message he'd sent to town. But I didn't imagine so; if he had found it necessary to discipline me, he'd have done so himself, not fobbed the task off on Bigwater by courier. He had been that kind of man.

"Sir?" I prompted.

"First, I must tell you that Karl thought highly of you."

That was Longshot's given name, as I recalled.

"He did?" Such news was a balm to my sore spirit. Longshot had made it clear before he died, but it felt even better, hearing it. That meant Longshot had spoken well of me to someone else.

Bigwater nodded. "He wrote to me before the battle, apprising me of our circumstances. He said you had proven invaluable in the field, primarily as a scout. That you could move in and out of the enemy lines like nobody he'd ever seen."

"Stalker and Fade can too."

The elder smiled, and the look sat ill on his cadaverous, austere features. "He mentioned them as well. Don't fret, your friends won't be shorted any credit."

"I'm glad he was pleased with my work." There was so much more I wanted to say about Longshot, but *not* to Elder Bigwater.

"Yes, that's why I asked to see you."

Finally, I thought.

He went on, "You may not be aware, but Karl left you his worldly goods. If you have no further questions, I'll have Zachariah show you to the house, and you can decide what you want to do with it."

No questions? I had a hundred.

"I don't understand."

His look remained patient. "His home and the contents therein now belong to you, Deuce. It's not a large place since he was a widower with no mind to remarry after his wife died. They never had children. But it's all yours, now."

That couldn't be right. "Doesn't he have family?"

"Not anymore. The fever took many of us, fifteen years back. I nearly lost Zachariah."

"This doesn't make sense. Surely—"

"I understand your shock," he cut in. "But Karl made his wishes clear."

For the first time, he revealed his impatience by shuffling some papers on his desk. I took the hint. He had more important things to do than argue with me. The horde prowled outside the walls, and he had to reassure people that he could figure out how to save them. I didn't envy him that task.

"Can you answer one question for me?"

By his expression, he thought it was related to Longshot. "Of course."

"How bad is it out there, really?"

His amiable aspect slipped, revealing a man on the bitter edge of exhaustion. He pinched his fingers over the bridge of his nose as if smoothing away the ache. I'd misjudged him the day of the meeting; he wasn't a leader who used other people's ideas and did no real work of his own. His face was fair worn ragged from trying to figure out how to break the Freak siege.

"We're holding them at bay for now, but anytime they press, the guards run through the ammo faster than Smith can make it. That young friend of yours is helping, but we can't last forever." *Ah.* That explained why Stalker hadn't been to visit me. The band around my chest loosened a little. "Unless something changes, we'll run out of bullets sooner or later, and they'll charge the walls. Once that happens, I figure two days, before breach."

Unrelentingly grim this news, but it was about what I expected. I nodded. "Thanks for your honesty."

He continued, "You're not to share this information, but Karl gave me to understand you can keep a secret."

"I can. Let me know if there's anything I can do, if you want me on the walls. I'm not as good a shot as some, particularly during the day, but at night, I can hit a Freak at a hundred paces." I rose then and offered my hand again.

He shook it and then called for his son. "Zach!"

Who appeared with such speed that I suspected he had been waiting nearby. The doors were thick enough that I didn't imagine he'd heard much, if he had been attempting to listen.

"Show Deuce to Karl's place, please." Elder Bigwater smiled at me. "*Your* place, now, I suppose."

"Ready?" Zach asked.

Nodding, I stepped into the hall with him, only to find a woman lying in wait. She had the air of an angry Huntress, her mouth tight, and her arms folded as if to keep her from striking me. I drew back instinctively and Zach set his hand in the small of my back. Normally I'd snap at him for that, but danger hung heavy in the air.

"What's *she* doing here?" the woman demanded.

Zach stepped between us. "We're leaving, Mother."

So this was Mrs. Bigwater. She drew away from me and stalked into her husband's office. Her voice carried. "I can't believe you had her in the house, knowing how I feel. She's the reason we're suffering like this. The pride plagues will be next. You need to do something, but you refuse to listen to me. And to make matters worse, you permit her to associate with our *children*? I won't—"

"Sit down, Caroline."

Pulling me away from the office, Zach guided me out of the house. I went blindly, remembering the woman at the assembly who tried to rally the town against me. That had been the elder's wife, I realized. And it heralded bad things.

"I'm sorry about that," the boy said.

Boy. He was older than me, but he didn't seem so. He had an innocence that I'd lost, long ago. I felt sure his father hadn't shared the truth about Salvation's situation with him. Zach wouldn't have such clear eyes if he knew.

"Some people have a hard time accepting those who are different."

"You don't seem that different to me," he said.

That was because he judged from the surface; he looked at my hair tied neatly in a ribbon and my clean, well-pressed gray dress. Zachariah Bigwater couldn't imagine the things I'd seen.

But I saw no benefit in making him feel dumb. "Which way?"

"Over here."

He led me back through town toward the gates. I wasn't surprised Longshot lived nearby; it would prove convenient for his trade runs. Who would take on that job now? I'd hoped he would recommend me as his successor, but that was the least of my worries at the moment.

"This is it?" I asked, a few minutes later.

It was a small, plain house, not even as big as the Oakses', but it seemed snug and cozy. Part of me didn't want to go in and look at his things, now mine. Because that meant accepting his loss. The other half stepped up on the porch, reluctantly tantalized by the idea of a place of my own.

Zach nodded. "Here's the key. Would you like me to come in with you?"

This, I felt, was something I ought to do alone, so I shook my head. "I'm sure you have places to be. Thank you."

The boy lifted his hand in farewell and I went into Longshot's home for the first time. Inside, it smelled faintly of the herbs he used to keep his clothes fresh. I came into a sitting room at once, filled with wooden furniture that looked rough made, as if he'd built it himself, impatient with the need. Cushions softened the effect somewhat, and I knew his woman had sewn them. He might have promised his wife he'd do better for her in time, but she died, leaving him with the wish to keep the things they'd used together, or he might lose her entirely. Seeing his home taught me about Longshot—his grief and his loyalty.

The house had a simple design, kitchen to the left, bedroom behind the sitting room. And from the kitchen, a ladder led up. I climbed it. Above, I found a loft, all empty space with a finished floor and polished rafters. Longshot's home would be big enough for a man and his wife. The loft could hold a couple of children, but he never had the chance. Tears burned in my eyes. On the day he died, I'd thought, *Someday I might let the girl cry for him, but not today.*

It was someday.

I sank down onto the bare floor and let the sobs come.

Much later, I dried my face on my sleeve and went downstairs to look around. I found Longshot's presence concentrated in the bedroom with spare parts for Old Girl, rounds of ammunition, and a few dirty clothes he hadn't gotten around to laundering before we went out on patrol. I wished I understood why he'd chosen to give his place in the world to me.

Then I found the most significant legacy: his papers.

Thumbing through them, I realized they were maps of all the trade routes, names of settlements, facts about how many people lived there, and what they needed to barter. I clutched the documents to my chest, heart beating like a wild thing. This was power—it felt like the keys to the *whole world* to me. With growing awe, I read, lips moving as I shaped the letters into words: Appleton, Rosemere, Otterburn, Lorraine, Soldier's Pond, Winterville, and more. *He meant to leave me this.* Freedom. *Not a house.*

I recalled how we'd stood on the wall and talked about me going with him on his trade runs. Earlier, I'd wondered who would take over, and this was his answer, given as clearly as he could make it. I would be his true heir, and he'd given me all the information necessary to make that dream come true.

With careful hands, I slid the papers into a leather folder for safekeeping. Now that I had it, I didn't want anyone taking this information away from me. Maybe I would see if Tegan could help me write some copies, just in case. Once, I would've asked Fade, but he had made his feelings clear. Much as it pained me, I respected his need for distance. I wouldn't push him; I understood what Tegan meant by saying there was no magic that could fix him, just because I wanted him back the way he used to be. But he was worth waiting for.

As I glanced around, I realized I could help Fade even more.

Siege

"You were gone awhile," Momma Oaks said.

Her words constituted an invitation to share, so I told her what had happened. She listened with an attentive air, nodding in all the right places. Then she hugged me. "He was important to you."

She referred to Longshot, not either of the Bigwaters I'd spoken with today; though they were both decent men, one old and burdened, the other young and blissfully ignorant. Zach seemed innocent to me, childlike. He had no scars at all. But he was a brave soul, and Salvation needed as many of those as it could muster.

I considered how much the outpost commander had meant to me. "He was, more than I realized. I wish I'd told him so."

"I suspect he knew or he wouldn't have left his things to you."

Small consolation, but better than none. I doubted Longshot would've been comfortable with an emotional scene in any case. He had seemed like the sort of man who preferred those attachments going unspoken.

"Where's Fade?"

"Down at the shop with Edmund."

"Then I'll be back directly."

Her gaze followed me as I went back out the door, leather folder still in my hand. I also had the key tucked in my pocket. As I strode through the center of town, I became conscious of the stares. A few women gazed at me with open dislike, friends of Caroline Bigwater, most likely. Lifting my chin, I ignored them and continued on my quest, pushing open the door to the building hung with the COBBLER sign, where Edmund worked most days. The scent of leather livened the air, but unlike the tannery, it was a nice smell, once finished, smooth and buttery.

Edmund was working on a pair of shoes when I walked in. His face reflected surprise, quickly hidden. "Deuce! Good to see you."

I chatted with him for a few minutes so he wouldn't be hurt that I hadn't come to see him specifically. "What are those?"

"These will be a fine pair of slippers when I'm finished. Did Doc Tuttle check you out yet?"

"He removed my stitches too. I'm good as new."

Not quite. I hurt in ways I hadn't before—the pain not physical—and I worried about the town, which had become my home. Not that it was my place to be concerned. The elders would solve the problem. I just had to find some useful way to occupy my time, now that I didn't have to attend school, though I didn't look forward to advising Mrs. James of my decision. Everyone in Salvation worked—and I didn't want to apprentice to Momma Oaks and become a dressmaker. But I'd figure out a way to persuade people that I ought to be allowed to take over for Longshot, once the trade runs commenced . . . after they dealt with the Freaks outside the walls.

Not a small job.

Then Edmund proved he was more perceptive than he seemed. "Fade's in the back, cutting patterns."

"Do you mind . . . ?"

"Go on. He's welcome to take a break. Hard worker, that one . . . doesn't talk much, though."

He used to, I thought.

With an indistinct murmur, I brushed past Edmund into the work space at the back of the shop. Fade glanced up—and I could've sworn for an instant that he was happy to see me, but the look vanished so fast I thought I imagined it. He put down the tool he used on the leather and cocked his head in challenge.

"What are you doing here?" The unspoken meaning was clear: *I told you to leave me alone, to forget about me. I meant it.*

I ignored the pain, doggedly clinging to my mission, and flattened my palm on the counter. When I pulled my hand away, the key lay atop the half-trimmed leather. "I see that you're unhappy . . . you feel trapped. But I can help."

"What do you mean?"

"Longshot left me his house. I wouldn't like living alone, and I don't mind Edmund or Momma Oaks. So you can stay and take care of the place. It'll give you more peace . . . more privacy." I stared over his shoulder, wondering if he could tell how much this hurt me. "Nobody will bother you there."

You won't see me. You can lick your wounds and miss me until you come searching for me . . . because you're mine, and I'm yours. But I left that part unspoken.

His throat worked. "I . . . really appreciate this."

"Do you know where it is?" It was hard for me to be casual with Fade when I wanted so much to reach for him, to twine our fingers together and kiss his palms, and to tell him he was acting crazy.

He inclined his head. "Longshot had me over once."

I hadn't known that. But during those first few months in

town, I'd hardly seen Fade. Given how Mr. Jensen had treated him, it was no wonder he'd spent as little time at the livery as possible. I imagined him looking for a different place to be every night, and how I wished it had been with me.

"That's all, then." I turned, determined not to humiliate myself.

"Deuce . . ." For a moment, for a glorious, bright, hopeful moment, I thought he was going call me back. But he only added, "Thank you."

"Welcome," I muttered.

I managed a wave for Edmund, busy again. Little wonder he enjoyed resting at home when he spent his days hunched over a workbench. As I hurried out, rifle shots rang out, one after another. Instead of going home, I went to the wall to see for myself how bad it was. More than once, I'd sought Longshot when he was on duty to complain about my problems. I couldn't anymore. The guards might not let me come up, but the sentry recognized me—well, sort of.

"I know you," he said, frowning.

My cheeks heated; the dress must be throwing him. I'd known him at first glance. It was, in fact, the man who saved my life.

"I patrolled with you all summer," I reminded him.

"You look different dressed as a female." His brow cleared, the question answered to his satisfaction.

Despite my mood, I smiled, pointing at the ladder that led up to the platform. "May I?"

"I probably shouldn't, but after what you've already seen, it doesn't matter. Come on, then."

After I clambered up, I took position beside him, shading my eyes, because the sun hurt them a little. My skin was still peeling in places from the burn I took bringing in the harvest, but I had some color for the first time in my life. At last, I'd lost the total underground pallor and, secretly, I felt, part of myself too. I wasn't the same Deuce—and it was too soon to tell whether that was a good thing. I felt a little wiser, maybe, less inclined to believe whatever people told me.

It took me a minute to focus in the daylight, and what I saw horrified me to the core. The horde had arrived, encircling Salvation like a dark cloud. The Freaks stood just beyond rifle range as if weighing their options. Eventually—though they weren't lightning fast in the brain—it would occur to them that if they charged at once, we didn't have enough riflemen to kill them all. They'd reach the walls.

In that awful, seething mass, I also glimpsed glimmers of brightness—our stolen fire—and Salvation was made of wood. I closed my eyes, overwhelmed. It didn't matter how Fade felt, or where he lived. The town had a matter of days, and I'd seen no signs of an imminent solution, despite Elder Bigwater's good intentions. He was a man with limited resources and infinite trouble.

"It's bad." The guard hesitated. "I'm afraid I don't recall your name."

That made me feel better. I couldn't be wholly hated, like those staring women had made me feel, if someone I'd served with could forget me. That sense of relief intensified when I recalled this man had saved my life and slapped me for being a hysterical idiot. I should've been memorable to him, even notorious. It was comforting that I wasn't.

"Deuce."

"I'm Harry Carter."

I remembered the name being read on that fateful day

during the initial lottery and wondered how he felt about being one of the few survivors of the summer patrol, if it weighed on him like it did me, and if he felt like he wasn't worthy. But he was an older man, nearly of an age with Longshot, and I didn't feel comfortable asking him such things. Not without the same connection I'd shared with the outpost commander, at least.

"Thank you for my life, Harry Carter," I said gravely.

"You're from Gotham." It wasn't a question, though it led to one, and as I nodded, I braced for the inevitable. Nobody ever asked anything clever. But Harry surprised me with a thoughtful silence. And then: "I'm sorry your people got left."

That evacuation had been such a long time ago; I was surprised he'd give it a thought. That he did showed his kindness. "I guess they took everyone they could."

"Maybe," he murmured, lifting his rifle.

Another wave of Freaks charged the walls, and the guards fired desperately, dropping them, but more ran on, dodging, weaving, pushing closer. I touched my knives, hidden beneath my skirt, but they couldn't help from this distance.

A few stragglers got close enough to slam against the wood, but they didn't come bearing fire. Soon, though. Soon, they'd work it out. Harry leaned over and nailed one through the top of the head, a perfect vertical shot. Brains spattered against the walls, and I smelled its death, a stench fit to empty my stomach.

"You should go," Harry said.

Because I couldn't bear to stand there and not fight, I obeyed. I still had Miles's rifle, but I didn't want to cause trouble. Maybe, though, under the circumstances, the guards would take whatever help they could get. Momma Oaks could probably advise me. Alight with purpose, I ran home. I'd guard the walls and put my Huntress training to good use. Surely I'd get better using the rifle with practice, and standing on the wall offered endless targets. I'd aim for the fire-bearers too.

I burst in the front house, skirts flying, and startled Momma into dropping the dress she was hemming. "Are you hurt?"

"No, ma'am," I said. "I just need to get my rifle."

She stared as if I'd announced I intended to breed with Edmund. "What for?"

"They need me on the walls. Do you think anyone would mind?" To me, my gender seemed like a stupid reason to object if I could shoot—and I could. But for all I wanted to help, I didn't want to enrage the general populace, either.

Brow furrowed, she thought long and hard on it before finally shaking her head. "If you go quietly and don't draw attention, it should be all right."

Well, I didn't mean to run through town, shouting, *Look at me, I'm a girl in pants, watch me shoot this gun.* Leaving this obvious truth unspoken, I acknowledged her caution with a murmured "I'll be careful," as I ran past her up the stairs.

Before anything else, I put away the leather folio that contained Longshot's legacy. Then I changed clothes and searched for my rifle. Someone had stored it beneath my bed and unloaded it as well. I found the rounds in my dresser and loaded my weapon. Feeling better than I had since Longshot's death—as if I might prove useful—I scrambled into my soldier gear, plain brown pants and matching tunic. When I added Edmund's boots, I remembered how proud he'd been, how carefully he measured my feet and tailored them just for me. The leather was soft and worn from a summer of wear, and they fit perfectly. I took the ribbon from my hair and exchanged it for a simple tie.

Today, I felt like a Huntress.

Momma Oaks kissed my cheek as I went out to fight, and I was careful to avoid the main avenue, circling the perimeter instead. Nobody gave me a second look. They might've even thought I was a boy, recruited young. That suited me fine.

Harry Carter was still on duty when I climbed up, this time without waiting for permission. He didn't ask what I thought I was doing; I guessed he could tell by the rifle in my hand. And he looked so very tired. There weren't enough guards to man the wall all the way around, and those who did worked incredibly long shifts.

He spoke as I checked my gun. "They've dropped back for now, but they'll make another run. You'll get your shooting in."

As he'd predicted we didn't wait long. I raised my rifle and aimed for the torso as Longshot had taught me. One jerked and fell. *Mine.* Another kill. Nobody was ringing the bell anymore; there were just too many, and it would create an unbelievable racket. The guns and Freaks were bad enough. In quick succession, I shot five more, and then had to reload from Harry's ammo bucket. Miles's rifle was nice enough with a smooth, black barrel and a walnut stock, but I wished I had Longshot's—for sentimental reasons.

I had been fighting for a while when calamity struck. As disasters went, it was a small one, but tiny troubles had a way of swelling, like ticks grown fat with blood. At first I paid no attention to the voices behind me, focused on preventing the Freaks from completing their charge. Harry was a quiet companion, capable and composed.

But they just kept talking louder. I blocked them, shooting on, until the charge dropped. Freak bodies lay strewn all over the grass outside the walls, and the stink grew in proportion to each death. In the distance, I heard them growling and wailing, screeching of grief in their terrible, inhuman tongue.

Finally, I wheeled to inflict some verbal hurt on whoever was yelling at the base of the wall. I froze. Caroline Bigwater stood with a group of citizens, some women, some men, all bearing the same look—judgment. She had a book in her hands, the age of which I would compare with *The Day Boy and the Night Girl*; it looked about that old.

"You *see*." Her voice rang in a shrill mix of fear, anger, and loathing. "Just look at her, arrayed as a man. This is what comes of breaking covenant with heaven. In all our years, Salvation hasn't seen such misfortune since the pride plagues. Something has to be done, or we'll all pay the price."

A rumble rose up in agreement. I slid a sidelong look at Harry, wondering if he agreed. He put a gentle hand on my arm and whispered, "Stay here. I won't let them take you."

Take me? Where?

Caroline Bigwater opened her ancient book and read from it. "'Women must adorn themselves in modest apparel with shamefacedness and sobriety. Let the woman labor in silence and with all subjection. At all times must the females be wise in mind, clean in heart, kind; working in their houses, living under the authority of their husbands; so that no evil may befall us.'"

The woman glanced up, gauging their reaction to her words. More angry cries erupted, and their eyes gleamed as they stared up at me. I recognized that look from down below; it meant I dreaded the outcome of this confrontation. For me, it could not end well.

"Caroline's right," a woman shouted. "The troubles started right after she came!"

Mrs. Bigwater agreed, "So they did. And this is why: 'Woman

shall not don the weapons and armor of a warrior, neither shall a warrior put on a woman's raiment: for all that do so are abomination unto heaven. Plague shall descend upon your houses, so long as you suffer this atrocity to live.'"

They stared up at me in my man's clothing, a rifle in one hand, and the mood turned darker still. Suggestions spilled from one to the other as to how to atone and make Salvation clean again. I was afraid to move; I didn't recognize these people. Fear and loss had twisted and broken them.

"How can we make it right?" a man asked.

Caroline Bigwater smiled up at me, all saintly sweetness. "You don't want us all to die, do you, dear? You *know* what you must do."

Inevitable

"What on earth is going on here?" Elder Bigwater boomed. He didn't always employ his big voice but today he did to good effect.

The crowd started, guilty looks on most of their faces, but they didn't disperse. The woman faced her husband, serene in the backing of her fellow believers. They needed somebody to blame; I understood that. It didn't change how scared I was.

Mrs. Bigwater tried to explain, but he silenced her with a single sentence. "Your husband wants you to go home. Are you being womanly by disobeying?"

I didn't agree with the notion that women should follow orders given by men, but it showcased the discrepancy between her attack on me, and her own behavior. With an angry grumble, she took the core of her coterie when she stormed off. I didn't fool myself that this was over; only the immediate danger had passed.

"Come here, Deuce." The elder wore a kind expression, one I'd learned often masked bad intentions. But I couldn't stay on the wall forever, so I scrambled down the ladder with a nod at Harry.

Bigwater set a hand on my shoulder, guiding me away. I didn't like it, but I thought he meant to show support, making anyone think twice about messing with me. So I let the familiarity stand without elbowing him in the gut.

"I think I can solve this problem in a way that would satisfy both of us."

"How's that?" I asked, wary.

Like the guards, he looked weary in the waning afternoon light. His thin face had new lines, and his eyes sank even deeper in his head. "You already know how dire things are. We can't last."

He'd already made that clear enough, earlier in the day. "I'm aware."

"I need someone to go for help," Bigwater said quietly. "There are other settlements on the trade route—"

"I have Longshot's maps."

"Good. I believe he had this solution in mind when he left you the bequest, Deuce. Now that he's gone, you have the best chance at completing this mission. Nobody else has much experience in the wilderness, certainly not like you."

I turned the idea over in my mind, seeing eerie parallels to the suicide run the blind brat had undertaken from Nassau. There was no guarantee my experience would let me survive, but if I stayed, I'd die. That was a given. Either one of the zealots would find a way to sacrifice me, or the Freaks would break in, eventually. I didn't see a way out. At least by accepting this assignment I could choose my death as Longshot had done. Maybe he *wouldn't* want me to go; maybe Elder Bigwater only said that to make me fall in with his plans.

But it was working. I liked the idea of making Longshot proud. He'd saved me twice, so it was my turn to do something for him, even if he was past caring.

"All right," I said slowly. "Give me a chance to say my good-byes and explain things to my foster parents. Momma Oaks will take it hard."

Real sorrow touched his sunken eyes. "Because of Daniel."

"Yes, sir."

"I'll prepare supplies for the journey and have them wait-ing." He paused. "You're a brave girl and a credit to the town, no matter what my wife says."

"Thank you." It shouldn't matter what he thought, but it did. His approval meant I hadn't wasted my time here; I'd made a dif-ference. But there was one problem, as I saw it. "How will I get out?"

"Few know about this, Deuce, but when the town was founded, they dug an emergency exit. The tunnel runs from the cellar in my house out past the back wall. I have no idea what state it's in, since nobody has used it in fifty years. So you'll need to be careful as you go."

I offered a fleeting smile. "It's best if I leave tonight. Darkness will make it easier to avoid the Freaks."

"Then I will see you shortly."

He pressed my shoulder in parting, and I went home to Momma Oaks for what might be the last time.

"I heard about the scene with that awful Caroline Bigwater. I'm so sorry, child. Not all women are like that, I promise." She took a closer look at me, studying my stillness, and her face paled. "What's the matter?"

Quietly, I told her that I'd be leaving—and why. I could see she wanted to protest, *Why must it be you?* and I loved her for it. Momma Oaks would miss me. She'd remember me if I didn't come back. Bravely, she blinked away tears as she pulled me to her chest. I stood quiet because I feared how I might react—and how hard it would be to leave—if I broke down.

Pulling back, she said, "I suppose you need to pack."

"I do." I headed for the stairs.

"I was saving this as a surprise, but you need them now. While you were gone, I sewed you some new patrol outfits. They should do nicely for the road."

That did it. I threw myself at her and hugged her around neck. I wept a little against her shoulder. In that moment, I was only a girl, not a Huntress, and I did not want to leave my mother. The steel would return, I had no doubt, but not just yet.

She didn't try to hush me. Momma whispered nonsense against my hair and told me it would be all right. This kind of lie, where both of us knew the truth, choked me up, and I loved her for that too. At last, I stepped away, brushed at my eyes, and went up the stairs.

Packing didn't take long. She helped me, folding my new clothes into small, neat squares that would likely be rumpled before I left the house. We both knew the point was for her to do *something*, so she didn't cry. *Thank you,* I thought, *for not making this impossible.* I tucked Longshot's leather folder into my things, for I would need maps for the journey.

"Edmund will be home for dinner soon. Will you stay that long?"

"Of course." It wasn't fully dark anyway.

To my surprise, Rex showed up with his wife, whose name I hadn't learned when I stopped to chastise him. Ruth was a gentle person, nervous around Edmund and Momma Oaks, but I was happy to see her making an effort. My foster parents would need their son more than ever after I left. Maybe I had done the right thing with my meddling.

The meal was quiet, and Edmund's mouth drooped at the corners as he ate. Momma Oaks tried to keep up a conversation, and Ruth carried more than her share. Now and again, Rex volunteered a comment, but he seemed aware it was a sad occasion, even if he hadn't heard the news.

Then he proved he had. "I want to thank you," he said quietly. "I had forgotten what's important . . . and it's not my pride."

"I was rude," I murmured.

Rex shrugged. "I had it coming."

I ate the rest of my meal with determined cheer. Afterward, I was in the kitchen, washing up with Ruth, when I asked, "What was the matter, anyway?"

She stared at the plate in her hands. "A combination of things . . . normally, I wouldn't tell you, as you're a stranger, but you're family too."

"Thank you." I was touched.

Ruth went on, "I was . . . with child when Rex married me. His folks thought that meant I wasn't a good girl, and then we lost the baby. A few people said it was punishment from heaven."

Those people needed a boot in the face. "I'm sorry."

"Then he argued with them because he loves me. He refused to work with his father anymore, and it just got worse over time, until they weren't talking at all."

Until I came along and demanded they make up.

Once we finished clearing up the dinner dishes, Rex and his wife bade me farewell. It was almost time for me to go, and Momma Oaks got misty again. Just before my departure, Edmund cautioned me to take care of my boots, and then hugged me awkwardly around the shoulders. His tired eyes said other things, like, *I'll miss you,* and *come back safely,* and *don't break your mother's heart.* For one glorious moment, I marveled at the fact that I had a family.

And then I left them.

Only three farewells remained. Nobody else mattered enough to me; Elder Bigwater could make an announcement if he so chose.

I went to Stalker first because he'd remained steadfast, no matter what, and so he deserved to hear the news before anyone else. Despite the hour, he was still working in the smithy, pouring molten metal into the molds. Those would become ammunition when the process was complete. His face shone with sweat, glossing his scars, but he seemed glad to see me—until he noticed the bag on my shoulder and the rifle in my hand.

"Going somewhere?" he asked.

So few words to sum up the situation, but I managed, and his eyes snapped with cold fury. "You came to tell me *good-bye?*"

"This is how it has to be."

Rage fueled his movements as he jerked off his leather apron. "No, it's not. Say 'Come with me, Stalker.'"

I stared, shocked. "Are you sure your leg is strong enough?"

The last time I saw him, he had been using a stick. I saw no evidence of it now, and he'd been putting in long hours at the forge. His arms were corded with muscles, but that didn't address the condition of his knee.

Apparently outraged by the question, he kissed me, hard, before I realized what he meant to do. His lips felt angry and famished at once. "Say it, Deuce."

"Come with me, Stalker."

Then he smiled and I took a step toward him, unwillingly drawn by his ferocious beauty. "I'll tell Smith and get my things."

"Meet me at the Bigwater house when you can."

My spirit felt lighter as I made my way to Doc Tuttle's place. I wanted a hug from Tegan and her good wishes. She was eating dinner with the doctor and his wife when I arrived; she jumped up and offered me a plate, which I declined.

"Could we talk in private for a moment?"

Her parents graciously excused the interruption, even more charitably ignored the fact that I was dressed for war, and we stepped outside.

"I'm leaving," I said, and then explained the circumstances.

"I hate that Caroline Bigwater," she snapped, her small fists clenched. "*Hate* her. You know she says the same thing about me helping Doc in the office?"

It didn't surprise me. "I hope she won't make trouble for you, once I'm gone."

Tegan grinned. "She won't."

"How can you be so sure?" I tilted my head, puzzled.

"Because I won't be here. You'll need a doctor on the road, and even Doc admits I'm almost as good as he is."

I didn't make the mistake of asking about her leg; she didn't limp as much as she had once. Plus, if she had been tough enough to handle the backbreaking work of the growing season and then the harvest, she could withstand this journey too. Tegan might be the strongest of us all.

She ran back into the house, addressing her next words to the Tuttles. "Help me pack my medical bag."

"Is someone sick?" Doc asked.

I let her do the talking, and then, he left the table to divide up his supplies, allotting her needle and thread, bandages, ointments, and sundry items I wouldn't know how to use. Clearly Tegan did.

"Are you *sure* about this?" I asked, wondering if she understood the danger.

"Absolutely. You saved me, more than once. It's my turn to repay the favor."

"But you love it here." I was surprised Tegan would venture out with me when she'd been searching for safety as long as I'd known her.

"It's my home," she said simply. "So, I'll do my part to protect it. And I owe you, too, so . . ." She shrugged. "I need to do this."

Humbled by her loyalty, I told her to meet me at the Bigwater house as soon as she was ready, and then I went on, feeling even better. I might not be a normal girl by Salvation standards, but I had good friends. No question. And there must be something worthwhile about me if they were willing to accompany me now.

That left only one person. *Fade.* Maybe given his own pain, he wouldn't care that I was going, but I owed him the courtesy of seeing him before I left.

As I'd expected, Longshot's house was dark. No candles. No lamp. But Fade must be there since he wouldn't remain in the shop after Edmund left. It took all my courage to climb to the porch and rap my knuckles against the door.

For long moments I waited, until at last I heard a rustle of movement from within. Fade answered the door, his face in shadow.

"Did you forget something?"

"Just this." When I kissed his cheek, his instinctive flinch shocked me. That was a revelation; my touch no longer brought him pleasure; maybe he associated *all* contact with physical pain, and I grieved for everything we'd lost. I thought he just needed some time . . . I hadn't realized his damage ran so deep.

Stalker whispered in my head, *He's soft in ways you and I aren't. Ultimately, you're going to break him.*

Maybe, I thought. *But I can save him too.*

It just wouldn't be today. My boy had suffered enough. I couldn't ask him to fight more on my behalf. He needed what little peace Salvation could provide in these difficult times.

"Good-bye, Fade."

I lacked the heart to tell the story again. Edmund would mention it, if Fade kept helping out in the shop. Lightly, I ran down the steps, away from him, toward the future, toward uncertainty and danger.

"I deserve that," he said softly.

His pained words stopped me, but I didn't turn. "What?"

"That you don't trust me enough to ask for my help." The words burned with raw anguish, as if he'd let me down somehow. "Or maybe you think I'm not strong enough to be of any use."

So he already knew. I didn't ask how. Secrets had a way of spreading, whispers carried on the wind.

"I don't think that," I answered honestly.

But you do.

"We're still partners, aren't we?" His voice carried a desperate hope.

The question hurt—that he even needed to ask. This was the second time he'd shut me out after taking a wound, as if I held nothing inside me to offer him, no ability to console or comfort, and it broke my heart into a thousand pieces. But it wasn't time to be angry; I couldn't focus on how his behavior made me feel. I had to recall that self-doubt sliced at him like hidden knives. So I put on a neutral expression as I faced him. Pity would destroy him.

"I never left," I said. "I didn't request your help because I was trying to do what was right for you. Obviously, having you there is *always* best for me."

"I don't want to stay here. I don't even want to be in my own skin. Can I come with you?" The ache in his question made me feel gentle.

"Fade, you said you can't be what I need, but you're everything I want. Even if you give up on yourself, *I* never will. I'll fight for you."

"You shouldn't say that," he whispered. "I'm not worth it."

"That's not true."

I wanted to throw myself into his arms, but I'd made him flinch from a kiss. I had to take this slow; it was enough he was talking to me again. As Tegan said, I couldn't make him believe how important, how valuable he was, no matter what the Freaks had done. He had to come to that conclusion himself, and I'd be waiting when he did. No matter how long it took.

In a moment of whimsy, I blew Fade a kiss, as I'd seen other girls do with their sweethearts, and his hand came up slowly to catch it. Hope winged through me like a bird. I strode away, smiling, careful to avoid any zealots who might be lying in wait. A few minutes later, I arrived at the Bigwater home and found Zach watching for me in the front yard. He guided me through the house, so I gathered his father had taken the boy into his confidence. I didn't speak until we reached the cellar, a dry room with a dirt floor and baskets of vegetables.

Then I said, "I have three friends on the way, if you wouldn't mind meeting them out front."

"It's my pleasure." He hesitated, visibly torn. "I wish I could go with you. I hear Tegan's one of your companions . . . and I really like her."

I applauded his valor and his desire to prove himself to my friend, but he didn't have the skill or experience to serve as an asset. So I discouraged him politely. His face fell, but the easy way he accepted my refusal told me even more about his character. He wouldn't make it where we were going, and I didn't need to give Caroline another reason to hate me. Plus, Tegan had never mentioned him, and she might not be happy for Zach to tag along.

Elder Bigwater soon joined me, laden with the promised provisions. "I heard you've assembled a team for your mission. Most enterprising. I had to make a second trip to the mercantile."

I let him praise me, even though I hadn't asked anyone, except Stalker, and I wouldn't have in his case if he hadn't rattled me with that kiss. But it seemed better to let the elder believe the best about my motivational abilities.

To my relief, he didn't talk. In my view we had already said everything that mattered. I was doing what he'd asked. What more was there?

The others arrived before much longer, Stalker first, then Fade, and finally Tegan. It was night, the perfect time to slip out unseen. The Freaks would be sleeping, out of rifle range, and if we ran into any hunting patrols outside the tunnel, we could handle them. By morning, we should have put considerable distance behind us.

"I'll spare you any ceremony," Bigwater said, "as you already know our fate rests in your hands. So I'll merely wish you well."

"Good hunting," I corrected.

He gave me a puzzled look, but repeated the words nonetheless. "Good hunting, then, all of you." The elder stepped over to a rough wood shelf, currently full of canned fruit. "Help me move this, lads."

They accomplished the task in short order, revealing the

dark tunnel beyond. Cool air blew in and stirred the veil of cob-webs that clung to the opening. It smelled of earth and freedom. Odd I should think that, but the very darkness beckoned, reminded me of my life down below. That made it easy for me to step in.

Bigwater offered a lamp, but I shook my head. It might give us away as we emerged at the other end. Better to make our way without. In the field, we all knew how to fashion torches as needed.

I took the lead, because once my eyes adjusted, I could make out the rough dirt walls and the occasional timber, now half rotten from neglect, wedged in for support. It was a narrow shaft, much shorter than the ones I'd lived in down below, so I moved in a crouch, constantly scanning for trouble. In a space this size, combat would prove all but impossible. Fortunately, I encountered nothing scarier than rats and spiders, who scuttled as I pressed forward.

"This is awful," Tegan whispered. "We could die down here."

Stalker's careless answer drifted up to me: "We could die anywhere."

So true. Good people had been lost this summer. And more would perish if we failed to bring help. A deep empathy for that poor blind brat down below settled in my stomach; I hoped I fared better than he. Fade held his silence, but I wondered if he shared my thought.

Countless moments later, a chill breeze blew down. Loose dirt lent it a gritty flavor. I scrambled up the gentle incline, using my hands for purchase. Beyond, the unknown lay before us once more, and another impossible task. The four of us emerged from the earth and turned our steps west, toward the last hope for Salvation.

Author's Note

I have done my best to envision what an emerging society, founded on religious tenets, might be like after pandemics and worldwide catastrophe. The survivors who settled in Salvation have their roots in fundamentalist doctrine; they are the descendants of the Pennsylvania Amish, who migrated north after endless wars and the bio-plagues referenced in this novel. The society reflected here, however, is not intended to be a representation of any existing faith or culture. It is an anthropological extrapolation based on available data. Therefore, based on that historical proscription on technology, the citizens of Salvation eschew all old world artifacts. Instead, they prefer to craft things and to lead a simple life.

There are clues in the text as to where they are. If you Google the Aroostook War, it mentions the boundary between New Brunswick and Maine being disputed. Salvation is, in fact, located on the site of Fort Ingall, which is also hinted, when Edmund tells the story about how the town has been settled thrice. More information about the locale is available here: http://www .fortingall.ca/en/history. The lake, therefore, is Lake Temiscouata, though the names have been lost. The terrain will have changed, obviously, in two hundred years with limited human impact.

And yes, as you've likely figured out by now, the Freaks are not zombies. They're mutants. More information will be forthcoming on them in book three.

I hope you enjoyed your second glimpse of the apocalypse.

Acknowledgments

First off, I appreciate Laura Bradford for being 100% awesome all the time. She's like a fairy godmother with a wand or maybe Kevin Costner building my *Field of Dreams*. (If I write it, they will come?)

Next, I offer paeans of gratitude that I get to work with the amazing crew at Feiwel and Friends: Liz Szabla, Jean Feiwel, Anna Roberto, Ksenia Winnicki, Rich Deas, sales, marketing, publicity, and everyone who contributes to creating these beautiful books. Producing *Outpost* has been a pleasure and an honor. Copyedits are a joy when they're handled by an expert, and for that, I thank the incomparable Anne Heausler.

Mega thanks to my early readers: Jenn Bennett, Bree Bridges, and Karen Alderman, who helped make this book the best it could be. Thanks also to the PoP loop, who help me keep the crazy in the can. Hats off to my amazing proofreader, Fedora Chen.

Thanks to my family, who believe in me even when I don't. Just like Deuce and Fade.

Finally, thanks to my amazing readers, whose letters make me laugh and cry, and keep me writing. I am a woman alone with my keyboard without you.

Thank you for reading this FEIWEL AND FRIENDS book.
The Friends who made

OUTPOST

possible are:

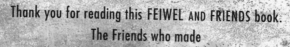

Jean Feiwel, PUBLISHER

Liz Szabla, EDITOR-IN-CHIEF

Rich Deas, CREATIVE DIRECTOR

Elizabeth Fithian, MARKETING DIRECTOR

Holly West, ASSISTANT TO THE PUBLISHER

Dave Barrett, MANAGING EDITOR

Lauren A. Burniac, ASSOCIATE EDITOR

Nicole Liebowitz Moulaison, PRODUCTION MANAGER

Ksenia Winnicki, PUBLISHING ASSOCIATE

Anna Roberto, EDITORIAL ASSISTANT

Find out more about our authors and artists and our future publishing at
macteenbooks.com.

OUR BOOKS ARE FRIENDS FOR LIFE